Praise for The Thin Black Line

"Realistic, vivid, dramatic, this is a story told by someone who knows what he's talking about. I offer a bow to this exciting debut and to the newest member of the thriller writing community. Make a note: in the years ahead Simon Gervais is a name you'll be seeing on many more book covers."
– Steve Berry, *New York Times* bestselling author

"When Simon Gervais writes about the world of high-stakes global security, he knows what he's talking about. His world-class security expertise shines through in *The Thin Black Line*, a high-speed, break-neck, turbo-charged thriller that takes readers behind the scenes of the war on terrorism."
– David Morrell, *New York Times* bestselling author of *The Protector*

"*The Thin Black Line* is a refreshingly smart and blisteringly original tale that's equal parts financial thriller and cat-and-mouse game with the survival of the United States economy hanging in the balance. Simon Gervais puts his own law enforcement background to solid use in hitting a home run his first time at the plate. A major debut that places him on the level of Nelson DeMille and Brad Thor."
  Jon Land, *USA Today* bestselling author of *Strong Darkness*

"Chilling, compelling, and cutting edge. Global security expert Simon Gervais gives us a husband-and-wife counter-terrorist team that must fight inner and outer demons – and find a way to survive both."
– Barry Lancet, author of *Japantown*

"Drawing from his military and tactical training, Gervais offers up a crisp, taut thriller that action fans can really sink their teeth into."
– Steven James, national bestselling author of *Checkmate*

"*The Thin Black Line* is a heart-pounding read! Simon Gervais weaves bona-fide tradecraft into a high-octane story that never lets up. This is one thriller you don't want to miss!"
– James R. Hannibal, author of the Nick Baron black ops thrillers

The Thin Black Line

The Thin Black Line

Simon Gervais

THE
STORY
PLANT

Studio Digital CT, LLC
P.O. Box 4331
Stamford, CT 06907

Copyright © 2015 by Simon Gervais
Cover design by Barbara Aronica-Buck

Story Plant Paperback ISBN: 978-1-61188-205-6
Fiction Studio Books E-book ISBN: 978-1-936558-59-9

Visit our website at www.TheStoryPlant.com

First Story Plant Printing: April 2015
Printed in the United States of America

0 9 8 7 6 5 4 3 2 1

To my brothers and sisters in uniform.
I know and understand the sacrifices you're making.
This book is for you.

PROLOGUE

Algiers, Algeria
Two years ago

B ack to the embassy, Eric," Ray Powell told his driver. "Let's make it quick."

"Sir."

As soon as his bodyguard settled himself in the passenger seat, Powell felt the big armored SUV move forward.

"Justin, do you know if the communication officer was able to fix the truck's secured satellite phone?" Powell asked his bodyguard.

"Don't think so, sir," Justin replied. "They told me they'd need the truck for at least ten hours in order to do the work."

"Goddammit! Why is it that the technology never works when we need it?"

"Sorry, sir," Eric said after a short pause.

I shouldn't have snapped at them like that. Keep your cool, Ray.

"Listen guys, I know it's not your fault. But could you see that it's done today?" Powell said seconds later.

"Will do, ambassador," Justin replied.

Powell knew that the six military police officers assigned to his detail were true professionals and recognized they were doing their best with the limited resources of the embassy. And if somebody understood how challenging it was to protect someone in hostile territory, it was Ray Powell. Prior to being named Canadian Ambassador to the Democratic Republic of Algeria, Powell had served over thirty years in his country's federal police force and had retired eighteen months ago as the officer in charge of the Prime Minister Protective Detail. For years, he'd traveled the world offering the PM the exact same service Eric and Justin were now providing him. Nevertheless,

Powell's nerves were now being tested like never before. If the intelligence he'd just received from the US ambassador was true—he had no reason to doubt its validity—it would be the last piece of the large puzzle he had worked on for months. A puzzle, if assembled correctly, that would lead directly to the Sheik. And since an hour ago, everything had become time sensitive.

Dreadfully time sensitive is more like it.

The Sheik. Nobody knew who he was. Until today, Powell even wondered if he truly existed. He had first taken an interest in the Sheik two years back, while still serving the PM. An intelligence report had mentioned the death of a Saudi prince whom the PM had hoped to meet during a future trip to the Middle East. Powell had followed through with an investigation and had discovered that the members of the terrorist group who'd claimed responsibility for the hit hadn't actually done it. The tapes of their brutal interrogations conducted by Saudi Arabia's Mabahith were forwarded to him. The first time he watched them, he'd tasted bile in his mouth, appalled at the violence used by the Saudi interrogators against their prisoners. The results were conclusive, though. They weren't the ones. The pure terror emanating from the men being interrogated couldn't be denied. Couldn't be faked. Powell had felt it simply by looking at the screen in front of him. The screams. The damned screams. The same sound a tortured soul would make just before it died. What kind of man commanded such authority over other human beings that they wouldn't say a word, except the ones they were told to say, against overwhelming physical pain? The only clues left by the dying members of the arrested terror cell were the two words they repeated over and over again: *the Sheik.*

Hoping to find something the others had missed, Powell had spent hours in front of the computer watching the merciless interrogators do their work. Apart from the visions of the terrorists' mutilated bodies that were still haunting him, he had come out as empty-handed as the other ones.

Then for weeks nothing else. No more mention of the Sheik. It was like he had disappeared. But every time Powell was about to close the file, something happened. A known jeweler who specialized in blood diamonds found dead in Zurich, a Palestinian leader secretly negotiating a ceasefire with the Israelis assassinated in Cairo, a North Korean general executed in a Thailand brothel. And more recently, the death of an Islamist clergy. Powell sensed the momentum building. Something was in the wind. Of that he was sure. The proof was in the evidence he was holding in his briefcase. It was spectacular, maybe dangerous.

Definitely dangerous.

The more he thought about it, the more confident he became that he was holding the key to a problem that didn't yet exist. So far the Sheik had never directly attacked a Western government or one of its institutions. It was time to take him out.

Now.

Powell doubted the Sheik would stay at the same location for a long period of time. If the rumors about the Sheik were true, he had eyes and ears all over Africa and the Middle East. And noises on the street indicated he was about to make a bold move. That was why he had to communicate to his boss what he'd discovered during his meeting with a longtime friend at the American embassy.

I still can't believe this. No wonder my friend is afraid. I would be too if the Sheik had direct access to POTUS—the President of the United States. I wouldn't know whom to trust around me.

Once the minister learned about it, Powell hoped it would be enough to convince him to go to the PM and ask to place a JTF-2 strike team on alert, the Canadian Tier 1 special operations unit, to apprehend the Sheik before it was too late.

Powell bent forward in his seat. "Would you mind contacting the military attaché, Justin? Tell him I'll need to speak to the foreign affairs minister once I'm back at the embassy. Ask him to make the necessary arrangements."

"Yes, sir. No problem. Should I mention the subject matter?"

Powell thought about it for a second. The minister was famously difficult to get on the phone. "Yes. Tell him it's about the Sheik."

That should get his attention.

Powell shook his head. The Sheik. So close. Here, in Algiers! Why? What was so important in Algiers? Why had he left so many bread-crumbs behind him after being so careful for so long?

I'm missing something. But what?

From the backseat of the SUV, Powell caught himself scanning the rooftops, looking for anything out of the ordinary. *If I had known what the meeting would be about, I would have asked my friend to come to the Canadian embassy, not the other way around.*

"Traffic's getting bad, sir," Eric said.

"Can you see what's causing the delay?"

Eric and Justin both turned and twisted in their seats, trying to get an angle on the source of the traffic jam.

"Negative, sir," Eric said after a while. "We'll take an alternate route once we reach the next intersection."

With a sigh, Powell sank back in his leather seat and cranked up the air conditioning. With the digital display indicating an outside temperature of over 105 degrees Fahrenheit, he unbuttoned the top of his shirt and loosened his tie. He was well aware that the armored SUV he was riding in needed to move for the air conditioning to work properly and cool the stuffy air trapped inside. Powell felt perspiration forming on his forehead already. It wouldn't take long before his shirt became damp with sweat, sticking to his skin. Algiers's chronic traffic problem wasn't helping.

Powell reached behind his seat and grabbed three Gatorades from the cooler. He passed two of them up front before half-emptying his in one long swig.

"Hydrate guys. Hydrate."

"Thanks much, sir," Justin said.

"No worries," Powell replied absently, his mind already planning what he'd say to the minister.

—

Less than a mile away, standing on the highest balcony of a nondescript apartment building, the Sheik, standing tall with a satellite phone pressed between his cheek and shoulder, watched the black SUV turn left in a futile attempt to escape the traffic jam he'd orchestrated.

"Let the game begin, my dear friend," he said to his interlocutor from the United States.

"It's our time now. Good luck," was the reply before communication was terminated.

"Only a few more minutes," the Sheik mumbled to himself, binoculars in hand.

After more than a decade spent inserting his peons and setting his traps, he was ready to start playing. And Ray Powell was the spark that would start it all.

—

"I reached the attaché, sir," Justin said. "He'll be waiting for you in your office. He already spoke to the minister's assistant."

"Good," Powell replied. For his upcoming conversation with the minister, he'd written two pages of notes to help him with his arguments in favor of a preemptive strike on the Sheik's location.

Suspected location, Ray. Nothing's been confirmed, yet. It may well be rubbish. All of it.

"Ah, for God's sake!" Eric said, bringing the SUV to a stop. He hit the horn twice.

Powell looked up from his notes to see two cars blocking the road ahead of them. "What's going on?"

"I finally managed to get us off the main road, but these two clunkers just pulled up in front of us, and now they've stopped for no apparent reason."

Powell started scanning the rooftops again. "Something's not right." Over the years, he'd learned to trust his instincts. "Let's get out of here."

"Roger that, sir," Eric said.

"Back up, Eric. Back up," Justin ordered a split second later. "One armed man. Our front, twenty meters. He's sprinting across the street, left to right."

Shit.

Powell felt the heavy SUV accelerating in reverse. Looking behind him, he couldn't help notice that no other cars had followed them off the main road.

Weird. Or lucky? It doesn't matter. We have room.

When the SUV reached a speed of about sixty kilometers an hour, Powell saw Eric let go of the gas pedal. Still holding on to the steering wheel in at seven and five, he brought his left hand to his right hand in a rapid movement, effectively transferring the momentum of the SUV, before bringing it back to the seven o'clock position. He then used his right hand to slam the transmission back into drive as soon as the nose of the SUV came about.

Good J-turn, Eric. Now let's get out of here.

The SUV accelerated quickly and was out of the danger zone in no time. Powell saw Justin reach in front of him for the MP5. He knew his detail carried with them in a specially designed backpack. Once the MP5 was out of its bag, Justin grabbed the radio.

"XCA-31, this is Beaver 1 detail, Bingo, Bingo, Bingo. We're presently at the corner of—RPG!"

Powell didn't actually see the warhead. All he saw before Eric punched the gas and broke right was a plume of white smoke. The HEAT—High Explosive Antitank—round hit the pavement less than one meter to the left of the SUV. The explosion propelled Powell hard against his seat belt at the same time the SUV rammed a parked vehicle at full speed. The SUV seemed to crush the smaller vehicle under its weight but embedded itself into the outside wall of a neighborhood supermarket.

"He's reloading!" Justin yelled. "I see the shooter. Back up! Now!"

But the SUV wouldn't move. Eric's airbag had deployed, and he couldn't reach the gear stick. Powell, still scanning the surrounding area, saw movement behind them. "Two guys approaching from the rear."

"Fuck this," Justin said, opening his door and walking to the side of the truck.

Powell glimpsed at Justin firing his MP5 at the two men he'd just mentioned. One of them fell while the other one returned fire. Rounds hit the back window, cracking it.

AK-47. Shit. Things are getting worse.

"Hand me your weapon," Powell said to Eric.

"I can't move the damned gear stick," Eric replied, now free of his airbag.

More rounds hit the truck, adding cracks to two other windows.

"Just hand me your fucking weapon!"

"Negative, sir. You stay in the vehicle. Don't move!" Eric said, exiting the relative safety of the armored SUV.

Where do you think I'll go? We're surrounded, for Christ's sake!

Eric hadn't made five steps out of the vehicle when Powell saw him crumble to the ground.

More rounds. More cracks.

—

Omar Al-Nashwan fired two rounds at the man who'd exited at the driver's door. Al-Nashwan could have killed him as soon as he opened the door, but he had to make sure it wasn't the ambassador. The Sheik's orders were clear. Ray Powell was to be brought to him alive. As the man fell, Al-Nashwan took an extra second to aim his third shot, then squeezed the trigger gently. The bullet entered the side of the man's brain, killing him.

"Two, this is One, sitrep," he ordered his man in Arabic via their communication system.

"One, this is Three. Two's down," Mohammad Alavi replied in the same language. "The shooter is using the vehicle as cover, and I'm pinned down on the other side of the street. I didn't see the ambassador come out. He's probably cowering inside the armored SUV."

"Not for long, Three. Not for long," Al-Nashwan replied. The thick file the Sheik had prepared on Powell had said the ambassador wasn't the type of man who'd be afraid of a gunfight. "He'll come out soon enough. Be ready."

—

Seeing the pool of blood under Eric's corpse becoming larger by the second, Powell knew he had to move. He had tried to see where the shots had come from but hadn't been successful at doing so.

I need to make contact with the embassy. He reached inside his suit pocket for his cell phone when Justin opened the door.

"Follow me, sir. One bad guy's down. There's at least one more across the street, hidden behind the cement wall next to the red car. See it?"

"I see the car, yes," Powell said, running behind his bodyguard.

They stopped behind an old Toyota fifty meters away. Justin unsnapped his holster and handed his pistol to Powell.

"Fifteen in the mag plus one in the pipe."

"Roger that," Powell said. He risked a peek through the Toyota's windows. One of the armed men he had seen earlier dashed across the street. Powell fired twice but couldn't say if he'd hit the man or not. "He's behind the engine block of our SUV."

"Cover me, sir. I'll try to hotwire the car," Justin said before using the butt of his MP5 to break the window.

Powell kept his pistol toward the SUV, hoping to hear the old Toyota's engine start. Instead, he heard gurgling sounds that sent shivers down his spine. Powell turned toward the noise only to see his bodyguard on his knees clutching his neck with his two hands. Behind him, holding a silenced AK-47, stood an Arabic-looking man with blue eyes.

"Drop your pistol, Ambassador," the man said.

Ray looked at his pistol, then at the MP5 lying next to his dying bodyguard.

"Don't even think about it, Ambassador. You'll be dead long before you can squeeze that trigger."

Powell swallowed hard. He'd been played.

Suddenly, he understood why the Sheik was in Algiers.

He's here because of me! He must have learned about my meeting, somehow.

The Sheik had been a step in front of him the whole time. He had lured him into a corner. Powell was aware he was to be taken alive.

They would have killed him already if murdering him had been their objective. But Powell had seen too many diplomats get their heads cut off. He wouldn't be taken alive. He'd go down his way. Fighting.

As Powell brought his pistol up toward the man, his mind flashed back to the softness of his wife's skin and the fishing trip in Maine he'd always wanted to take with his son. But this is as far as his thoughts went, for the man with the blue eyes had been right; there was no time to pull the trigger before something sharp cut through his flesh with tremendous force. Then blackness enveloped him.

PART 1

CHAPTER 1

Macdonald-Cartier International Airport
Ottawa, Ontario

Asad Wafid entered the airport and cursed the brisk spring air. Rubbing his hands together in an attempt to warm them up, he hurried to the Air Canada reservation counter, where a return ticket for his flight to Washington, DC, was waiting for him. It didn't matter that he'd lived here for five long years; he couldn't get used to the cold. The winter months, which never seemed to end, were once again on their way to swallow the first few weeks of spring. But the terrible weather was just a small impediment compared to actually living among the inconsiderate women who didn't mind exposing their flesh in public. Even worst were their fathers and husbands; they were the ones unable to control them. That behavior would have never been allowed in his household back in Pakistan.

I would have taught them proper respect.

Obedience.

Total obedience.

Wafid wondered for a moment if he would have accepted the mission knowing what he knew now about the infidels populating this Godforsaken country.

Yes, I would. The Sheik chose me.

To be selected by the Sheik had been a surprise. Or was it? Deep down, Wafid had always known he was unique. His years with Pakistan's Inter-Service Intelligence had been worthwhile, after all. The two weeks he'd spent in jail for beating to death a subordinate who had refused to comply with a direct order had certainly helped him to get noticed by the Sheik. *He must have seen something special in me, or else he never would have brokered the deal for my release.*

"May I help you, sir?" the lady at the counter asked, breaking his reverie.

"Yes, of course. I'm here to pick up my ticket to Washington, DC. My name is Ziad Saab."

"Can I see your passport?"

Wafid handed it to her. A forged one.

Getting into Canada had been easy for Wafid and his crew. People from Iran, Libya, Pakistan, and even Afghanistan could claim refugee status and get new identities on the black market within weeks. If they never showed up at their immigration hearings, their names would simply be placed alongside those of the thousands of other illegal immigrants that entered Canada each year, never to be seen or heard from again. In this way, Wafid's entire network had been operating under the radar for years. And God willing, today would be the day they would finally collect the benefits of their hard work.

"Any luggage to check in, Mr. Saab?"

"No, thank you. I only have my carry-on," Wafid said pointing to the black suitcase next to him.

"You're all set then," the counter lady said, handing Wafid his ticket. "Enjoy your flight."

Wafid smiled, forcing himself to be pleasant before walking away. *Does she really think sporting a scarf around her neck makes her attractive?*

A subtle *bing* emanating from his phone indicated he had a message waiting.

Wafid looked at his screen and read the communication: *We're in. No problem.*

Good, he thought. *We're only missing two.*

Wafid looked at his watch, and for the thousandth time that morning, his mind wandered to his brothers in faith: Muhammad Hassan and Masri Fadl. Where were they? He had worked for months to ensure that nothing would go wrong on this day, but his plan would fall apart without those two peons.

If they didn't arrive soon, he would kill them himself before they had a chance to be sent to paradise as heroes. He picked up his phone and dialed Fadl's number.

—

Muhammad Hassan and Masri Fadl arrived at the airport thirty minutes late. Nervous and shaking, Hassan had taken a wrong turn en route and had gotten stuck in traffic trying to find his way back to the airport. They parked their car in the long-term parking lot and hurried inside the terminal.

As they passed through the automatic doors, Fadl's cell phone started to vibrate. He answered it, and, after listening for a minute, he hung up without saying a word.

"That was Wafid. We must go through the last security checkpoint on the right and ask for a private search, Hassan. Believers are manning that security lane. That's where our brothers went through, and they were able to pass all their equipment without any problems."

Hassan nodded stiffly. He was still shaking and didn't trust his own voice.

"Now, we do as we planned, and we go our separate ways," continued Fadl. "We'll see each other in paradise, my brother. *Allah Akbar!*"

"Allah is with us today, my brother," Hassan finally managed. "May all blessings be upon him and his Prophet." He nodded once in farewell to his longtime friend, then headed left while Fadl went right. He began to go over the plan one final time in his head.

Over four months of preparation had been needed to make sure that this day would work perfectly. Setting it up had actually been quite simple once the proper airport security officials had been bribed. Wafid had already accomplished the hardest of the tasks—facilitating their entry into the secure side of the airport. In fact, Wafid had recruited the employees that were now manning the security lane that Hassan was waiting to enter. Of course, the low-paid security agents had absolutely no idea that the money they received was coming from the Sheik's terror network; they thought they were closing their eyes to no more than illegal drugs.

Now all Hassan and Fadl had to do was take possession of the aircraft with the help of Wafid and his crew. By the time the bribed security guards at Ottawa International Airport learned that they'd let six terrorists armed with automatic weapons and grenades go through their checkpoint, it would be much too late.

CHAPTER 2

Macdonald-Cartier International Airport

To: Inspector Robert McFiella OIC/RCMP APOFU
From: Inspector Myles Gregory OIC INSET Ottawa

Robert,

We just got a report from Ben Cohen of Air Canada Security that four Middle Eastern passengers purchased last-minute tickets for Air Canada Flight 7662 Ottawa–Washington, DC. They were booked separately but by the same travel agency. Their names were run through our databases, but nothing came up.

Knowing that you have two air marshals onboard this flight, we checked the rest of the passenger list for anything suspicious and found that two Saudi nationals are also on the flight, and they only have one-way tickets. Both are in Canada under student visas that will expire in two days. Their names are Muhammad Hassan and Masri Fadl. Technically, they're still in Canada legally, but I contacted our INSET team in Toronto to follow them on arrival for the next forty-eight hours to see if they will depart Canada or not.

To help your officers identify them, I've attached the passport pictures of Hassan and Fadl, as well as their seat assignments for Flight 7662.

Myles

The note was short but to the point. The threat level for their flight to Washington, DC, had been upgraded to "High." As a member of the federal air marshal program of the Royal Canadian Mounted Police, Sergeant Mike Powell was used to this kind of message.

More often than not, the passengers mentioned in these notes had triggered an early warning detector embedded within the airline reservation software. Whether they had paid for their tickets with cash, had purchased one-way fares, or had done a multitude of other things the computers were looking for, it didn't matter to Mike. He would treat this piece of information seriously. He always did.

As he stood in the main terminal of Ottawa International Airport, his eyes were in constant motion. The long hallways were packed with passengers, as everybody was either going back home or visiting family for the Easter weekend. On his left he'd noticed an army captain with a black backpack sipping a cup of chain-restaurant coffee. To his right, a nice family with three young children was eating their breakfast burritos while chatting about their upcoming trip. The excited laughs of the children brought a rare smile to Mike's lips as he remembered his daughter, Melissa, doing the same thing three weeks ago prior to their flight to Mexico.

Before putting his secured Blackberry away, Mike read the message once again.

After affixing the pictures of Hassan and Fadl in his mind, Mike replaced his phone in his pocket.

While most of messages were somewhat similar to this one, this particular communication was the first with such a textbook scenario. Mike didn't like the idea of an attack in his own backward but couldn't help enjoying the adrenaline rush such thoughts provided.

It would be a lie to pretend he didn't wish to kill a terrorist or two. Since his father's kidnapping exactly two years ago today, he'd craved revenge. Not only for himself, but also for all the pain the loss had caused his mother. It was one thing to lose a loved one in battle; it was another to have someone you love taken away from you and knowing this person was being tortured.

A wave of nausea passed through Mike as he remembered the terrible day he learned his father was still alive.

His mother, usually so composed, had called him early in the morning, yelling for him to come over. When he'd opened the front door of her luxurious downtown condo, his mother had been holding a knife to her throat.

"Mom?"

"I can't take it anymore, Mike," his mother had said. The hand holding the butcher knife was shaking. Her whole body was shaking.

"What's going on, Mom?" he said a lump in his throat.

"Why don't they fucking kill him? Why don't they kill him, for God's sake!" his mother screamed before collapsing on the hardwood floor. Mike ran to her and picked her up off the floor. Tears were flowing down her cheeks. "I can't sleep anymore, Michael," she murmured in his ear. "The only thing I dream of are the pictures."

"What pictures, Mom?"

"Your father's."

The first picture, or proof of life, had come two weeks after his father's abduction. Then another followed suit every second Friday. The Sheik had sent them directly to the home of Mike's mother in Ottawa. A note attached to each picture commanded that it was only for her, not to be shared with anyone else unless she wanted her husband to suffer an atrocious death.

At first, he hadn't understood why she was crying. Proof of life was a good thing, right? It meant that his father was alive. But when his eyes gripped the cruelty of the pictures, even Mike had to hold on to the table. His father's features were barely recognizable. His face, unwashed, was so swollen that his left eye couldn't possibly open. Another picture showed a severed finger, his father's wedding ring still in place. The only thing that had kept him from loosing his mind was the knowledge that he needed to stay strong for his mother. Later that day, Mike's mother, Celina, accepted his invitation to move in with him and his family. Mike was still angry with himself for not asking his mother to live with them sooner. Celina's health was better now, but Mike highly doubted that anything less than the Sheik's head would make her happy.

—

Seated near Gate 17, in a manner that allowed him to observe most of the passengers who would shortly be boarding his flight, Mike glanced at his partner, Staff Sergeant Paul Robichaud, who was sitting close to the Air Canada ticket desk.

Robichaud was a twenty-three-year veteran of the Royal Canadian Mounted Police and former member of the Emergency Response Unit of the Integrated National Security Enforcement Team, or INSET, the semi-covert unit of the RCMP tasked with acquiring and analyzing intelligence regarding terrorist threats. He was more than just Mike's partner. He was his mentor.

As Robichaud had said several times before, he had seen a younger version of himself in Mike the moment they'd met at the high-pressure INSET selection training four years ago. Mike, with Robichaud's support, had been recommended to the INSET unit after only five years of service with the RCMP. His previous service spent as an infantry officer within the elite Canadian Special Operations Regiment had helped. Plus, the experience he'd earned leading combat operations in Afghanistan had given him an edge that none of the other candidates possessed. On average, less than fifty percent made it through the training, but Mike had excelled in all quadrants and had even broken all the shooting scores—including the ones held by Robichaud.

As Mike's gaze rove among the passengers, his Blackberry started to vibrate. After entering his twelve-digit password, he opened his most recent e-mail:

> To Mike and Paul: Please be advised I sent Agent Zima Bernbaum to back you up. She's our new liaison officer from the Canadian Security Intelligence Service. Her instructions are to remain covert and to act as an extra pair of eyes. You've never met her, so I've attached her photograph.

Mike gasped when he saw the picture. *I know her!* His wife, Lisa, had met her in Toronto while taking jujitsu classes. They'd quickly become best friends and salsa dancing buddies. Mike, who'd be working long hours, never had the chance to really know her except for the occasional dinner. He knew his wife had kept in touch with Zima after their move to Ottawa and had even spent a girls-only weekend getaway in Las Vegas a few years back. Mike vaguely remembered his wife telling him Zima had accepted a position as an auditor of cultural content at a museum.

Great cover for a CSIS agent, thought Mike. *I'm wondering what Lisa will say when I tell her Zima's CSIS.*

Mike stood up and slowly started to walk across the waiting area, scanning the section around Gate 17 to spot any of the six Arabic passengers. He saw no sign of them. He entered the men's restroom to check if anyone was hiding. Remaining anonymous, he strolled to the sinks and glanced at the stalls behind him in the mirror. He had let his black hair grow a little longer since he had left ERT. His hair was now in a controlled freestyle that required nothing but a little hair gel and a good shake in the morning. At five foot ten inches, Mike was not tall, but he carried his 190-pound frame easily. He was proud to say that at thirty-eight years old, he was in the best shape of his life.

He smoothed his navy herringbone suit and blue dress shirt from Savile Row. Mike looked the part of the rich executive he was using as a cover for today's flight. But if anyone were to look closely at him, they would see that amid his tanned skin and slightly crooked nose, his piercing green eyes did not miss anything. His movements were light but precise, and a contagious energy surrounded him.

Mike spied no sign of movement after thirty seconds. He purposely dropped his Montblanc pen on the tiled floor, and the sound echoed through the space. As he bent to pick it up, he quickly scanned every stall. Nobody. He was in the process of exiting the restroom when his Blackberry vibrated twice.

"Yes?"

"Mike, it's Paul here. Anything suspicious your way?"

"I just checked the restrooms. They're not in there."

"They still haven't shown at the gate either."

"That's strange," said Mike. "Their flight boards in two minutes. What should we do?"

"I'll board first and get to my seat to get a good view of every single passenger getting on that plane. You board last. That way we won't miss them if they are, in fact, on this flight. And why don't you call Zima? Use her to cover more ground," instructed Robichaud.

"Sounds good," said Mike before ending the call. He refocused on the crowd milling about the gate as he dialed Zima's number. He wanted to know if she was in the area in case he and Robichaud needed assistance.

"Yes? This is Zima." Her voice was soft and gentle.

"Hey, Zima, it's Mike Powell."

"Hi, Mike. It seems like we'll be working together on this one."

"The museum knows you're here?" he asked, a big smile on his lips.

He heard Zima's laughter across the line. "C'mon, Mike, you know how these gigs work."

"Just pulling your leg, Zima. How are you?"

"Living the dream," she replied. "How's Lisa?"

"She's doing great. I'll see her later this afternoon. You should call her. I know she'd love to speak with you," Mike said before getting back to business. "Are you at the airport yet?"

"I'm here now," said Zima.

"At the airport?"

"That's correct, Sergeant. I'm watching you as we speak."

Mike twitched in surprise. He hadn't made her. He closely examined his surroundings but to no avail.

"I can't see you, Zima. Where are you?"

"You just looked at me, but you didn't see me," answered Zima, clearly enjoying herself.

Mike took another careful look. He was about to surrender when he noticed a flight attendant seated by herself next to the duty-free shop. She smiled at him.

"Clever," Mike said over the phone.

"Thank you, Sergeant."

"Were you briefed on the situation?"

"Yes. What can I do to help?"

"My partner will be boarding first—" started Mike before the gate's PA system interrupted him.

"Welcome to Air Canada Flight 7662, soon to be departing Ottawa for Washington. We will now preboard passengers traveling with young children, or any other passengers that may require more time or assistance. We invite our executive-class passengers to board at their leisure..."

"Oh, shit," muttered Mike.

"What's going on?" asked Zima.

"I think I know where some of our suspects are," Mike said and hung up.

Mike punched in Robichaud's number.

"What's up?" answered Robichaud.

"Is it possible that some of our friends have business class tickets?"

Robichaud let out a breath. "Damn, you're right. And, if that's the case, they might be sitting in Air Canada's executive lounge right now, sipping coffee and waiting for the last possible moment to board."

"Okay. Board the plane as planned. I'll go check the lounge. Call Zima to task her with monitoring the gate area and the terminal hall," Mike said.

"Sounds good. I'll send you and Zima a text message if I see one of them board," said Robichaud.

"Roger that," Mike replied already on the move.

The Maple Leaf Lounge was still a good three-minute walk from the gate, and Mike was doing his best to get there with enough time to visually check the lounge and make it back to the gate in time for departure.

—

Mike entered the executive lounge and showed his business-class ticket to the Air Canada employee at the reception desk. With a nod from the agent, he stepped into the lounge and scanned the area.

Twenty people were scattered at tables throughout, enjoying the buffet breakfast that had been laid out on the bar. Sleek computers lined the back wall, and a fireplace with cozy sofas and armchairs occupied the center of the space.

Mike could not locate the faces of Hassan or Fadl. On the other hand, he noted four Arabic males sitting in the farthermost corner of the lounge. One of them, completely bald, was talking into a cell phone.

When the call was finished, Mike saw them all stand up at the same time. He confirmed that none was Hassan or Fadl. *They are getting ready to leave,* thought Mike. He hung back, seeing no point in getting too close now. He would follow them at a distance and see if they were going to board the flight to Washington.

Mike exited the lounge ahead of the group and stopped at a nearby book kiosk, pretending to study the cover of a paperback. Soon the four men passed in front of him. He started following them once they were about thirty feet past his position.

Were they looking at someone in particular? Would any of them make a subtle gesture that would mean something to someone watching for it? Was anyone else watching them? These were all questions that Mike asked himself while they walked toward Gate 17.

Grabbing his Blackberry from his jacket pocket, Mike hit autodial.

"Yes?" answered Robichaud promptly.

"I'm following four possible matches. They were sitting together in the lounge."

"Copy that. Fadl and Hassan just boarded the plane separately. They each stowed a medium-size carry-on in their overhead compartments. They're doing everything they can not to look at each other, but I'm definitely picking up a weird feeling. I don't like this at all."

"Do you want to call it in, Paul?"

"Let's advise the captain to have the passengers rescreened. And I want it done by Canada customs this time, not by those rent-a-cops who usually man the lanes. I wouldn't trust half of them to find a rocket launcher on my grandma."

Mike chuckled. "Good idea. My little group is about a minute from the gate. All of them are wearing long coats, and they could be carrying weapons. I'll call the Ottawa police's airport division to provide some uniformed officers to back up the customs guys. I'll let Zima know what's going on as well."

"Understood," Robichaud said. "I'll talk to the captain. See you at the gate."

—

Mumbling that he had to go to the bathroom to the fat man seated next to him, Robichaud stood up and approached the flight attendant.

"My name is Paul Robichaud," he told her quietly. "I'm one of the air marshals aboard this fight, and I need to talk to the captain immediately."

"Oh, I...hmmm...okay. Just one moment please," said the young blonde flight attendant, picking up the intra-plane phone.

"Captain? It's Nadine," Robichaud heard the flight attendant say into the receiver. "I have an air marshal here who is requesting to speak to you. Ah, okay," she said before turning to Robichaud. "The captain is on the line."

Robichaud took the receiver and smiled his thanks to the flight attendant. "Captain? I'm Paul Robichaud from the RCMP Aircraft Protection Unit," he began, keeping his voice low. "I believe we may have a situation aboard this aircraft. I recommend that we rescreen every passenger aboard this flight."

"Is that really necessary? We're already on a tight schedule, and the airline will have to pay a hefty fee for departing late."

"I feel it's very necessary, Captain."

A sigh came over the line. "Okay, but I don't want any mayhem aboard my aircraft."

"My suggestion to you, sir, is that you make an announcement saying that there is a mechanical failure with the ventilation system and that a maintenance crew will have to come onboard to fix it. Tell the passengers to remove all their luggage from the overhead bins."

"All right," said the captain after a long pause. "I'll contact flight control, then I'll shut down the system. I hope you're sure about this." Then the line went dead.

Robichaud noticed how tense his jaw was as he hung up the phone. For the first time in his life, he prayed he was wrong.

—

As the four men approached the boarding gate, Mike realized they would probably be the last ones to board the airplane. With Zima already briefed by Robichaud, Mike had just completed the calls to Canada customs and the airport division of the Ottawa Police Services when he decided to close the gap. The four men had stopped at the gate and were now waiting to present their boarding passes and photo identification to the gate agent, who was presently on the phone.

"Oh, I'm sorry, gentlemen. You'll have to wait for a few moments before boarding," Mike heard the gate attendant say as she hung up the phone. "It seems like everyone will be deplaning shortly due to a mechanical problem with the ventilation system onboard the aircraft."

"Do you know how long we'll have to wait?" asked the bald man standing in front of the attendant.

"I have absolutely no idea, sir. Please have a seat, gentlemen, and I apologize for the delay."

—

With his back facing the flight deck door, Paul Robichaud positioned himself to better watch Fadl and Hassan. He'd just started to engage Nadine, the young flight attendant, in a casual conversation about her favorite local restaurant when all the lights in the cabin suddenly shut down and the whirring of the ventilation system stilled.

There is my signal, thought Robichaud, watching the two terror suspects in his peripheral vision. *They just looked at each other for the first time.*

"Ladies and gentlemen, this is your captain speaking," came the commandant's baritone voice over the intercom. "I'm sorry to inform you that we seem to have a problem with our ventilation system's electricity supply. I just contacted a maintenance crew, and they advised me that they have to come onboard to fix it. Unfortunately, that means that all passengers will have to deplane with all their personal belongings, including luggage stored in the overhead compartments. The flight attendants will direct you in deplaning. I apologize for the delay, and we thank you for your patience and understanding."

Following the captain's announcement, before anyone could even unbuckle his or her seat belt, Fadl stood up and pulled a micro Uzi submachine gun from the inside of his jacket. He aimed it toward the flight deck and started firing.

Damn it! thought Robichaud as he dove for cover. At only 9.84 inches long, the micro Uzi was the smallest version of the Uzi submachine gun available. Due to its short length, it lacked a forward grip and, hence, accuracy. But the micro Uzi could fire more than twelve hundred rounds per minute, allowing Fadl to unload his twenty-round magazine in less than the second it took for Robichaud to reach his own gun.

The first six of those twenty bullets hit the pretty blonde flight attendant in the back. A seventh entered Robichaud's right shoulder, and the remaining thirteen lost themselves in the ceiling of the aircraft. As Robichaud was thrown back by the impact, he saw Hassan stand up and take the pin out of an M67 fragmentation hand grenade while Fadl inserted a fresh clip into his Uzi.

The other passengers on the airplane began to scream and tried to take cover in any way possible. Unable to use his right arm, Robichaud used his left hand to cross-draw his pistol. But by the time he was ready to fire, Fadl was once again spraying the first-class cabin with 9mm Parabellum bullets. Robichaud, now on his knees using one of the front galley walls as partial concealment, was hit one more time in the chest as he fired his first shot. Consequently, his round went high, but his second shot, fired less than half a second later, hit its target between the eyes. Fadl collapsed on the elderly man cowering in the next seat.

Coughing up blood, Robichaud saw that Hassan was about to throw his grenade into the rear of the plane. With a one-handed left grip, he fired two more rounds into the back of Hassan's skull. In slow motion, Robichaud saw the grenade slip from the dead terrorist's hand and fall in between two seats before rolling toward a crying mother and her young son.

Fuck!

Knowing he was fatally wounded, Robichaud willed himself to get up but couldn't muster the force. The excruciating pain in his chest prevented him to yell a warning. Only a gurgle and a fresh spray of blood came out of his mouth. Using his good arm, he tried to alert the passengers of the impending disaster, but chaos and panic had overtaken them. Everybody was running toward the exit, oblivious to the grenade lying only a few meters away. With his eyes fixed on the grenade, Robichaud used all of his remaining strength to crawl toward it. But in doing so, he felt the passengers running over him, stomping him with their feet.

Robichaud died from his wounds less than one second before the M67 exploded.

CHAPTER 3

Ottawa Via Rail Train Station

Dr. Lisa Harrison Powell was cruising in her new Range Rover Sport through the Ottawa traffic. She checked her rearview mirror to find the reflection of her twenty-two-month-old daughter, Melissa, smiling at something out the window. *She's so sweet, this little one*, thought Lisa.

"Do you really have to drive that fast?" Celina Powell said from the front passenger seat.

"I'm driving at the speed limit, Celina," Lisa replied.

"The speed limit is the maximum speed allowed in perfect conditions, my dear. It doesn't mean that you have to always drive at the limit," Celina countered. "Think about your child."

Lisa took a deep breath and slightly relaxed her foot from the accelerator. Since Mike's mom had moved in with them a year ago, she was always careful not to be too confrontational with her mother-in-law. But it wasn't easy.

Not easy at all.

She wasn't angry at her husband for asking Celina to live with them. Truth be told, she thought it was nice of him to do so. But Celina had become a very opinioned lady who wasn't shy at letting you know how she would have done things differently. Lisa knew her mother-in-law hadn't always been like that. Her husband's kidnapping had changed everything. Something had snapped in Celina's head, and Lisa hoped she'd get better soon, because she was getting tired of being criticized day in and day out.

She was aware that Mike was worried about his mother, too—especially today, the second anniversary of his father's kidnapping. To be on the safe side, Mike had asked her to bring Celina along to pick up her parents at the train station. Her feeling was that her husband didn't trust his mother to be alone on this day.

"Don't worry, honey. I'll take good care of her," she had said to him at breakfast.

Lisa had met her husband thirteen years ago while they were both serving in the armed forces. At the time, Mike was a young but promising officer attached to the Infantry School in Gagetown, New Brunswick, and Lisa a newly graduated aerospace engineer posted to Canadian Forces headquarters in Ottawa. She had been sent on temporary duty to Gagetown to replace a colleague on leave. A friend living on base introduced her to Mike, and the two of them had clicked right away. Lisa had admired Mike's intensity. He seemed so passionate about everything he did, including taking care of her. They became inseparable for the rest of Lisa's stay until it was time for her to return to Ottawa. Surprising herself, and maybe feeling a bit adventurous, she canceled her flight home to spend a romantic getaway weekend in Halifax. The fact that they barely left the hotel room during those forty-eight hours still made them laugh.

Lisa shook her head as she remembered the years that followed. As much as she had liked building planes and piloting them, she had a change of heart, professionally that is. At the time, the military was offering its officers career changes. So at the same time Mike was sent to Afghanistan as a platoon leader with the newly formed Canadian Special Operations Regiment, or CSOR, she started medical school. She had always felt that helping save people's lives was more in line with who she really was. After being selected to attend medical school, the Canadian Armed Forces had sent her away to study at the renowned Uniformed Services University of the Health Sciences in Bethesda, Maryland. She never looked back. She studied hard and achieved top marks. Even though she was extremely busy with school and the interminable rounds at the hospital, the absence of Mike by her side was weighing on her more than ever. It was not so much the distance that was concerning Lisa, but that Mike's numerous missions abroad were considered high risk. At first, the worries were present but bearable. But one evening, Lisa received a phone call from Mike's commanding officer in Afghanistan. He informed her that Mike was unaccounted for. She learned only two days later that he had returned safely—he had lost any way of communicating during his disappearance. From that moment on, she started to have panic attacks and anxiety.

After her graduation from USU, she was posted to the Canadian Forces Health Services Center at Montfort Hospital in Ottawa. Her dedication and exceptional work ethics saw her in no time promoted to the rank of major and transferred to Toronto as the commanding officer of the local Health Services Center. Luckily, with Mike back from Afghanistan, her panic and anxiety attacks somewhat subsided.

At first, she refused to talk about her problems with Mike. But the day she finally did, after a severe anxiety attack that had forced her to park on the highway's emergency lane, Mike had been very supportive and apologetic. Less than a year later, Mike had quit the army and was sworn in as a RCMP officer assigned to Toronto. From then on, life had been much more enjoyable.

Reflecting on these tough times, when she and Mike were far apart, Lisa realized that these hurdles had actually made their love grow stronger until they were finally reunited for good and got married on a beautiful summer afternoon in Ottawa.

"What's wrong, Lisa? Why are you crying?" Celina asked.

"What? Am I?" Lisa brought her hand up to her face and felt the moisture of a tear on her cheek. "I was just remembering how Mike and I met...and thinking of our wedding day."

"Oh, I sure remember that perfect day! Ray and I never expected anything less grandiose from you two," Celina said, her voice breaking with emotion at the mention of her husband.

"I'm sorry," Lisa said, reaching for a Kleenex. But Celina was quicker and handed one to her.

"Here, honey. Take this one," she said. "And I think I'll get one, too."

"Thanks." Lisa looked at the older woman. Celina's tears were flowing freely, sabotaging her makeup. She placed a comforting hand on her mother-in-law's arm. Celina squeezed Lisa's hand with her own.

"And just the thought that Ray never met his granddaughter Melissa," Celina said, sobbing. "And Chloe, he'll never see Chloe either."

Lisa didn't know what to say. She knew how in love her in-laws had been. Just by thinking for a second that Mike would have been the one kidnaped, she felt the excruciating pain Celina must be feeling.

She looked down at her stomach. She was eight-and-a-half-months pregnant with their second child, another baby girl, whom they planned to name Chloe. Tonight, Mike was supposed to let her know if he'd be able to take a few months off work to stay with their newborn. He had already taken a two-month paternity leave to stay at home with her and Melissa two years ago. Lisa recalled how proud her husband had looked when he first held his baby girl in his arms in the delivery room. Lisa had experienced firsthand how sweet a person Mike could be. He had been so gentle and tender with their newborn that she had decided on the spot that everything would be all right as long as they were together.

"Shouldn't we hurry a bit more? The train is due in a few minutes," Celina said, her finger tapping at the nonexistent watch on her wrist.

Lisa smoothly accelerated back to the speed limit.

—

Arriving at the train station, Lisa was surprised to see that the parking lot was already full.

"I'll let you go in with Melissa if you don't mind, Celina," Lisa said looking at her daughter, who was starting to fuss in her seat. "I might have to circle the parking lot a couple of times."

"I don't mind. It will be good for both of us after this long ride."

Lisa watched as Celina took the stroller from the SUV's trunk and arranged Melissa inside it before kissing her on the forehead. Celina waived at her and started to walk toward the terminal.

Lisa looked at her watch, trying to remember what time her husband was due back from work that afternoon. Was it four o'clock or four thirty? *Better call him, just to be sure*, she decided.

Lisa reached inside her brown Luis Vuitton handbag and felt around for her cell phone. *So much stuff in this thing.* Eventually, her fingers found the smartphone, and she extricated it.

"Yes?" Mike answered after the first ring. His voice sounded strained.

"What's going on?" Lisa asked, instantly concerned.

"Everything's fine, baby, but I've got to go. I'll call you back, okay? I love you." Suddenly the line went dead.

Disconcerted by how brief the conversation was, Lisa wondered what was going on. But her thought was cut short when her SUV shook slightly. The Montreal train was just entering the station.

—

Yaser Yussuf and Malik Fareed knew that they would never hear from Asad Wafid again. Wafid had called Fareed that morning and said only four words: "It is sunny today."

Those words had been the ones Yussuf and Fareed had been waiting for. Their only regret was that they wouldn't be able to celebrate the economic destruction of one of the Great Satan's closest allies.

Kneeling down in the direction of Mecca, they prayed that Allah would guide their hands so they could kill as many infidels as possible. After their prayers, Yussuf and Fareed helped each other put on their explosive vests. They had fabricated the improvised explosive devices themselves.

They'd both been top recruits at the Sheik's training camp in Iran, where they had learned how to build explosive vests from their teacher, Mohammad Alavi, one of the world's most accomplished bomb builders. Following Alavi's custom design, they had constructed their vests not for destroying infrastructure but for killing people.

Each explosive vest was packed with four pounds of C-4 explosives and more than a thousand two-inch nails. After detonation, nobody within a hundred-foot radius would have any chance at escaping unscathed.

"Now we just have to wait, my brother," said Yussuf, adjusting the trench coat over his bulky vest. The weight felt pleasant on his shoulders. Soon they would be in paradise.

—

After looping three times around the parking lot, Lisa managed to find a parking spot at its far end. She hurried out of the Range Rover and fast-walked to the terminal's main entrance. Once inside, she scanned the electronic board next to the escalators, confirming that the Montreal train had just arrived at the same time as the one from Toronto.

No wonder the parking lot was full, she thought, looking around. At least a hundred and fifty people had gathered in the train station to wait for friends and loved ones. She made her way toward Gate 1 of the arrivals area, where passengers from the Montreal train would disembark. That's where she found Celina, seated next to Melissa's stroller.

"Took you long enough," her mother-in-law said. "Did you park across the river?"

"Don't worry," answered Lisa, keeping a pleasant tone in spite of Celina's sarcasm. "I'll call you a cab if the five-minute walk proves to be too much for you."

Without waiting for a reply, Lisa approached Melissa's stroller.

"Are you excited to see your grandparents, sweetie?" she cooed softly, poking her head around to look inside the stroller. Her daughter had fallen asleep and was drooling slightly.

—

Yaser Yussuf unlocked the door of the cleaning room. He assessed once more Malik Fareed's dark expression and saw the same raw determination that he himself felt.

"The train is coming, brother. This is the moment we have been waiting for," he said, his voice charged with emotion. "Don't forget to wait until after most of the passengers have disembarked but before they have the chance to leave the station. You go to Gate 1, and I will be at Gate 5. May Allah be with you, all praise be to him."

Fareed bowed his head. *"Allah Akbar."*

They embraced one last time and exited the large cleaning room that had been Yussuf's workstation for the last few years. They headed in separate directions without a backward glance.

—

From the waiting area, Lisa spotted the first-class car and watched for the familiar faces to appear. She felt a smile pull at her lips. The first-class upgrade had been her and Mike's little surprise for her parents. If asked, they would both deny that they had played any part in it.

Lisa soon caught sight of her father emerging from the car. Her mom followed a few steps behind. Once they were both on the platform, they started walking hand in hand toward the station. Lisa raised her arm and waved at her parents, beckoning them over.

"You look beautiful, my darling," said a smiling Andrew Harrison as he entered the large waiting area. He held his daughter tightly in his arms. "Now let me get a look at this belly!"

"Good morning, Dad," said Lisa, returning her father's kiss and taking a playful swing at his arm.

"Wow!" exclaimed Francesca Harrison, picking up little Melissa and her arms. "She's really grown since the last time I saw her."

"Don't wake her up, Mom!" said Lisa too late. Her daughter was all smiles at the sight of her grandmother.

"Gran-ma, Gran-ma!"

"Grand-ma missed you too, honey! You'll see, we'll have lots of fun together," Francesca said before continuing with the voice of a conspirator. "And I brought a lot of candies."

"Candies! Candies!"

"Shh," said Francesca, a finger on her lip. "Not a word to your mother."

As Celina exchanged greetings and kisses with her parents, Lisa couldn't help but wonder, *She looks genuinely happy to see them...For some reason, she's impossible only with me.*

Big deal. I can take it.

"While you guys wait for your luggage, I'll bring the SUV curbside," Lisa said.

"Thanks, baby," her father replied. "You want me to go with you?"

"I'm fine, Dad. Help Mom with her things, will you? Is she still packing like she used to?" she asked, thinking about the heavy suitcases her mother would bring for a two-night stay.

Her father nodded but not before he had looked in his wife's direction.

He's afraid of saying it out loud!

"Okay, then. I'll be in front in ten minutes."

Walking toward the exit, Lisa noticed two males emerging from a utility closet. The duo muttered something to each other before heading in opposite directions.

Weird. Why all that heavy clothing?

A strange feeling was gnawing at her gut. She just couldn't put her finger on what it was exactly.

—

Thirty seconds later, Lisa crossed the loading lane and was heading toward their SUV when suddenly she heard a thunderous explosion. She felt the ground shudder beneath her, and the concussion blast from her rear sent her pitching to the ground, scraping her hands and knees.

For a few moments, she could think only of the pain. Then a horrifying revelation dawned on her. "Oh, my God! Melissa!" she yelled, scrambling to her feet and running back toward the station.

A taxicab hit her at approximately thirty-five kilometers per hour. The driver, who had been distracted by the explosion, had no time to press the brake pedal after he realized that a pregnant woman had dashed out in front of him.

Lisa felt a huge force hit her right leg and had the sensation of being lifted into the air. Then her head collided with the taxi's windshield and everything went black.

—

Inside the train station, the explosions from four pounds of plastic C-4 attached to Yussuf's and Fareed's vests caused thousands of tightly packed nails to travel faster than three hundred kilometers an hour. Everyone, including Francesca Harrison and Celina Powell, within a forty-foot radius of each terrorist died instantly from the shock wave created by the force of the explosions. Their bodies, completely distorted, were hurled like rag dolls left and right.

All the glass windows shattered, cutting and blinding even more people. Ultimately, what caused the most damage were the nails. The passengers close to the detonations absorbed the shock waves. The nails, however, continued their trajectories until they impacted something solid enough to stop them. Unfortunately, the open-space concept of the Ottawa train station didn't help the situation.

Twenty-two-month-old Melissa never felt the two-inch steel nail penetrate her throat. Her little body collapsed in a tiny heap. Her grandfather had three nails hit him. The first and second lodged themselves in his right leg just above his kneecap. The third and fatal one entered his abdomen, which caused him to fall on his side still aware of the mayhem being unleashed around him. The pain became unbearable when he saw the lifeless body of his granddaughter a few feet away. He crawled toward her, leaving a trail of blood behind him. Lisa Powell's dad died five minutes later, holding his granddaughter in his arms.

CHAPTER 4

Macdonald-Cartier International Airport

Mike was a few meters behind the four suspected terrorists when he heard the familiar sound of an automatic weapon firing in the distance. He whipped his head toward the noise and decided it was coming from the direction of the tarmac. The Ottawa police officers who had just arrived on scene looked at each other in disbelief.

Then time seemed to shudder to a stop.

As if the clatter of gunfire was the cue they'd been waiting for, the four suspected terrorists pulled out AMD-65 submachine guns they had concealed under their heavy clothing and opened fire on the startled police officers. Several of them tried to reach for their guns but were cut down before their hands touched their holsters. Rounds upon rounds were lodged in the officers' chest cavities, for their bulletproof vests weren't designed to stop the 7.62mm rounds.

As Mike was reaching for his 9mm Smith & Wesson pistol, he heard a muffled explosion coming from the airplane. *Shit.* Dropping to one knee to make him as small a target as possible, Mike tried to aim his pistol at the nearest shooter. But with all the scared and panicked passengers running to and fro struggling to find cover, he could not get a clear shot.

Cursing, Mike looked around, trying to find something he could use as cover. He spotted a concrete pylon five meters to his left and went for it.

What the fuck? This isn't Afghanistan! Mike thought, clenching his teeth.

—

Asad Wafid had the pleasure of seeing the five police officers he fired at go down as he emptied thirty rounds into them. He expertly released the magazine and replaced it with a fresh one. He was proud of Hassan and Fadl. They had initiated contact the moment they thought they were compromised. *Well done!*

Focusing his attention on the unarmed Canada customs officers who were trying to hide behind the Air Canada ticket counter, he grabbed an M67 grenade from the left pocket of his overcoat and took out the pin. He calmly counted to three, then lobbed the grenade behind the ticket counter. It exploded two seconds later. Wafid was rewarded with strangled screams. When several wounded officers crawled out from behind the counter, another grenade thrown by one of his brothers in faith finished them off.

Wafid felt a sense of accomplishment. No more screams came from behind the desk.

—

Zima Bernbaum's heart had jumped when she'd heard the crackling of gunfire. She quickly deduced that terrorists were fighting over control of the aircraft with Paul Robichaud. Before she could provide backup for Robichaud, the four men Mike had been following had suddenly opened fire on the crowd.

After reaching for her pistol inside her purse, she slipped off her high-heel shoes and took cover behind the metal recycling bin on her left. It wouldn't stop a bullet, but it did provide concealment behind which she could assess the situation. She looked for Mike, but he had disappeared the moment the bullets had started flying. She pointed her firearm toward one of the terrorists, but a terrified young father and his tall son darted in front of her, pushed away from an attacker's line of fire by a courageous army captain, effectively blocking her shot. Just as a spray of bullets cut down the military officer, Zima felt a tremendous punch to her stomach.

—

After safely reaching the concrete pylon, Mike scanned the area around him. Some people were still madly dashing for safety, but most were smart enough to have found some kind of cover. Just then a fusillade of bullets chiseled the concrete just inches from his face, forcing him to remain immobile.

Damn! That was close.

After the firing in his direction had subsided, Mike counted to five. Then, taking a deep breath, he poked his head out from behind the pylon just long enough to see one of the gunmen throw a grenade behind the Air Canada counter.

Another couple of rounds hit the pylon, forcing Mike to take cover and spattering pieces of concrete into his face and shoulders. The grenade exploded, followed shortly after by a second blast.

Damn it! cursed Mike. *Where the fuck is the backup? Where's Zima?* He had lost visual contact with her. With Robichaud having his hands full on the airplane and all the police officers down, Mike knew he was the only one who could stop this bloodbath. He was outnumbered and outgunned; but still, he had to do something or the body count would keep rising. Perspiration was quickly forming on his forehead, and his pulse was hammering off the charts.

I can't believe this is actually happening. Shit! Shit! Shit!

A little voice inside his head reminded him that next time, he should maybe be a little more careful about what he wished for...

Mike looked around him.

Chaos.

Think, Mike! he commanded himself as he concentrated on controlling his breathing. His first target should be the gunman who kept firing at his position. Kneeling down so he wouldn't appear to be in the same position he had been when he'd taken that quick look moments ago, Mike adjusted his stance. Making sure to remain under the cover of the pylon as much as possible, he extended his arm, took quick aim at the terrorist, who was busy reloading his weapon, and fired two rounds within half a second. He hit his target's center mass.

Goddammit! From his covered position, he saw that even though the gunman staggered a few steps backward, he didn't go down. *They're wearing body armor!*

Aiming higher, Mike fired two more rounds. This time his target went down with two bullet holes in the forehead.

That's for you, Dad.

Mike inched his neck out farther from behind the cement pier and saw the first passengers come pouring out of the aircraft and into the waiting area. With so many people rushing behind them, they couldn't turn back once they entered Gate 17 and realized what carnage was awaiting them there.

Mike caught sight of one of the three remaining gunmen pointing his AMD-65 in the general direction of the oncoming passengers. Mike raised his weapon and emptied two rounds into the terrorist's armor-clad chest. He adjusted his aim and pulled the trigger again. His third bullet entered the base of his target's skull and exited through his mouth. A gush of blood sprayed the wall to the right of the Jetway.

—

Twenty-seven-year-old police constable Matthew Lipton from the airport division of the Ottawa Police Service was writhing on his back, bleeding from a bullet wound to the left shoulder. Turning his head to his right, he saw his fiancée and fellow officer Melia McFerlane lying in a pool of her own blood. Her eyes were still open in surprise. She looked like she could still be alive except for the neat bullet hole in the middle of her forehead.

Looking in the direction of the threat, Lipton realized that two men were firing randomly at the people around them. With his left shoulder hurting like a bitch, he used his right hand to draw his firearm. He sat up and fixed his gun sight on the closest terrorist, but he couldn't shoot. His hand had started to shake uncontrollably.

—

Asad Wafid became suddenly aware that someone was returning deadly fire. Two of his men were dead, each cut down by an expert marksman. He threw himself on his stomach and started scanning the area around him. Where were they? How many?

Yet he discovered only the thirty or so passengers who were lying on their stomachs in the Jetway leading to the aircraft, hoping that nobody would see them.

"Ibrahim, throw a grenade in the Jetway!" he shouted in Arabic to his only surviving brother in faith.

Within seconds, Wafid's oldest friend, Ibrahim, had removed the pin of his grenade and was poised to launch it into the tunnel.

—

Zima opened her eyes and gasped. *I've been shot! Oh, my God, I've been shot!* Her hands moved toward her abdomen. No blood. The thin Kevlar vest she'd ultimately decided to wear under the flight attendant attire had stopped the bullet. Because she was still breathing, she knew the bullet must have been either a ricochet or its velocity must have been slowed down before it hit her somehow.

Where's my pistol? Where the fuck is my pistol?

Pushing against the acute pain of being shot by an AMD-65, she got to her knees and saw that it was abandoned next to the garbage can she'd used for concealment. A hole was clearly visible through the can, and she deduced that her life had been saved by its metal barrel. A quick look toward the threat and she realized two of the gunmen had been put down.

Mike?

Before she had the time to search for him, she saw one of the two surviving terrorists readying himself to throw a grenade. On instinct she pulled the trigger.

—

Just as his friend's arm was at the apex of its throw, Wafid saw a spurt of blood shoot from Ibrahim's wrist amid a spray of bullets. *That came from another angle*, he realized. *There are at least two of them. Where did they come from?*

The cooking grenade tumbled out of the terrorist's mangled hand and dropped to the carpet in front of them. As Wafid watched in horror, Ibrahim picked it up with his uninjured hand and threw it hastily in the direction of the Jetway. He missed, and the grenade exploded between two rows of nearby seats, causing more noise than real damage.

—

Zima! Mike realized.

Zima had joined the fight, and she'd given him an opportunity to change his position. Mike didn't know if the two remaining terrorists had seen him or not, but he'd learned long ago that whenever shooting was involved, continuing to move was the best option.

Mike scuttled rapidly toward his next hiding place, keeping his pistol pointed toward the threats until he safely reached the adjoining pylon.

Once concealed, Mike inserted a fresh magazine into his firearm. He got his breathing under control, then stretched his neck out from behind the pylon to scan the area.

"Holy shit," he said under his breath. He saw that one of the police officers had survived the massacre and was sitting with his back against a duty-free shop's window. He was badly injured and was presently struggling to point his pistol toward the remaining tangos.

Hang in there, buddy.

—

While yelling at the top of his lungs, Ibrahim used his left arm to fire wildly in the direction of one of the infidel shooters. He had seen who had fired at him—a woman! A filthy woman! She would pay dearly for her sins. But when he heard the empty click, he knew he'd depleted his magazine, and he saw his foe step out from behind the pylon she'd been using as cover. He had time to look into her cold eyes before she fired two rounds into his neck, right under his chin.

—

Mike had acquired a new target and was about to pull the trigger when the man collapsed. A spray of blood coming out of the terrorist's neck confirmed he'd been mortally wounded. They had one more bad guy to stop.

"Where are you?" muttered Mike.

—

Wafid felt the warm spatter of his friend's blood mist his face.

Crouching behind a row of seats, Wafid saw that a businessman carrying a pistol had stepped away from a concrete pylon. Not by much, but enough for a marksman like him to hit his target. He fired a three-round burst in the white shooter's direction, sending the businessman crashing hard to the ground on his shoulder. Wafid delivered a spray of bullets in the fallen man's vicinity, but he had miraculously rolled out of the line of fire and recovered into a crouching position. *Who the hell is this guy?* Wafid wondered. The last thing Wafid saw was the barrel of the businessman's gun.

—

Mike fired two quick rounds in the bald-headed terrorist's direction, hitting him both times in the face and killing him instantly. *Where the fuck had he come from?* With all the bodies lying on the floor, he had seen the last terrorist too late. The hole in his shattered clavicle was the proof of his misstep.

Breathing was difficult, but he had to keep going. Paul might need him. His bloody shirt was sticking to his back, and the pain in his shoulder was growing by the second. He was rapidly losing focus, and he feared he would soon black out. From the corner of his eye, he saw Zima standing tall and advancing toward the downed terrorists, yelling at everyone not to move.

Mike painfully got up and did the same.

—

Lipton knew he was dying, but worse yet, he knew he had failed. He had failed in avenging his fiancée's death. He had failed to protect the dozens of innocent victims who were now dead all around him. If he could take out one of those terrorist bastards before he lost consciousness for good, he had to try.

Forcing himself to open his eyes, Lipton saw a man with a gun advancing toward him, yelling something he could not understand. He wasn't wearing a uniform; he had to be one of the killers. This was his chance. Lipton brought his gun up and pulled the trigger of his Glock 22, firing a single .40-caliber bullet at Sergeant Mike Powell.

Seeing his blurry target collapse, Lipton's last thought before dying was that he had finally managed to do something right.

CHAPTER 5

Ottawa Via Rail Train Station

A violent headache woke her up. Lisa willed her eyes to open, but they wouldn't. Her belly was aflame, and she could feel fluids escaping between her legs.

She moaned. Loudly. Painfully.

Melissa! Where's Melissa?

Lisa felt two powerful hands grab her from under the armpits as two others held her by the ankles.

No! Wait!

"She's the one?" she heard someone say.

"Yes, that's her. Careful now, she's lost a lot of blood," someone replied as her back was gently put down against something soft.

A stretcher? Her thought was confirmed an instant later when she sensed herself moving backward before being lifted again.

"Close the doors," the voice ordered.

"Shouldn't we wait for another patient? We have room for two."

Yes! We have to wait for Melissa!

"There's no time, not if we want to save the baby."

The baby. Chloe!

Still incapable of opening her eyes, Lisa tried to touch her belly. Her arms wouldn't budge.

She groaned.

"She's trying to say something!" the voice said.

"Miss, you've been in a terrible accident. Do you know where you are?"

Lisa struggled to speak, but her mouth was too dry. She was too weak. She wanted to tell them to stop, to wait for her daughter, for her parents.

They're inside the terminal!

"Everything will be fine, miss," the voice continued. "We're on our way to the hospital. They'll take good care of you."

Lisa heard the ambulance's siren as they left the train station.

"You were lucky to have been outside, miss, 'cause inside the terminal, it's real carnage."

Carnage?

A single tear rolled down Lisa's cheek as she thought about the daughter she was leaving behind.

CHAPTER 6

Canadian Forces Health Services
Montfort Hospital, Ottawa

L ying in her hospital bed, Lisa woke with start. Heart pounding in her ears, she tried to scream. But she was unable to utter a sound. She was paralyzed by fear.

The explosion. The screams. The fire. The taxi. It was all coming back. She had been in and out of consciousness when the paramedics tried to save Chloe. They did everything they could, but in the end, it wasn't enough.

Melissa!

"Lisa, you're okay?"

She slowly turned her head toward the voice. When her eyes were able to focus, she recognized Major Daniel Caldwell, an emergency military doctor with whom she'd previously worked, standing in the far corner of the room talking to a uniformed police officer.

"Melissa?" Lisa managed to mumble. "Is...Is she okay?"

Major Caldwell quickly dismissed the officer. He then approached her. She could see his eyes were puffy, like he hadn't sleep for days.

"Lisa," he started, "I don't know what to say."

His watery eyes told her everything she needed to know.

Oh, my God, no! Please, no! Not my Melissa.

Burying her head in her hands, she started to cry.

This can't be happening. It just can't. Not to me! Not to us!

Major Caldwell sat next to her. He gave her a comforting hug.

"I'm sorry," he simply said. "If there's anything I can do—"

"Michael," she interrupted him. *Does he know?* "I want to speak to Michael," she added in between sobs.

Dr. Caldwell's face froze. He looked away.

"Daniel, look at me," she said, her voice pleading, cracking. She grabbed the physician's arm before continuing. "I want to speak with my husband, please."

"I...I'm not sure..." Dr. Caldwell started.

"What are you...What are you not sure about, Daniel?"

"It's your husband, Lisa. He was shot and killed earlier today," he said with a tremor.

"What? Where? How?" Lisa's mind was racing. *No!* "That's impossible, I spoke to him on the phone."

"I don't know, Lisa. The officer just told me a minute ago. There was another terror attack at the airport." Major Caldwell was shaking his head. "God, I'm so sorry."

Lisa couldn't swallow. Her head was spinning.

I've lost everything. Everything.

"Leave, Daniel," she murmured. "Leave me."

"I don't think it's a good idea," he replied.

"Leave me!" she yelled. "Leave me alone!"

Major Caldwell sheepishly walked to the door, looked at Lisa one more time, then closed it behind him as he left the room.

Why was I saved? Why me? Why not Melissa? Why not Chloe? I don't deserve to live. I don't want to live.

That was it. She knew what she had to do. Lisa unplugged the IV from her left hand and removed the electrode patches she was wearing on her chest. Immediately an alarm rang, but Lisa shut it off. Gathering her strength, she pushed her legs to the side of the bed and forced herself up. The movement required less of an effort that she would have thought.

I can walk. I've lost Melissa and Chloe. My husband's dead, but I can walk...Except for the bump on my forehead, I'm not even hurt. This is so fucked up!

With a few steps she reached the bathroom. Without hesitation, she punched the mirror. A dozen pieces fell in the sink. She selected the biggest one and placed it on her left wrist, applying just enough pressure to draw blood. Her eyes caught her reflection in the few remaining pieces of mirror left intact on the wall. She saw a broken woman. A broken mother. A shattered human being who had lost what she had cherished the most.

My family.

Suddenly rage took over Lisa's body, and she screamed at the top of her lungs. "My God, why did you do this to me? Why? Answer me!"

She crumbled to the floor of the bathroom, out of breath. She closed her eyes. She was going to finish it.

There's nothing left for me here.

She pressed the glass deeper into her flesh, feeling it cutting through her skin as warm tears glided down her cheeks.

But something made her stop. Someone. *Melissa.*

She could see her daughter crying, begging her to stay alive. To live the life she'd never be able to live.

And that was all it took. Lisa dropped the broken mirror on the floor and started to cry louder and louder, her sobs trailing off into a prolonged high-pitched wail of pain and anger.

She stayed there until a voice startled her.

"I'm no grief expert, Major Powell. But maybe I can help."

She hadn't seen or heard the man standing next to the bathroom door enter. She turned her head so she could see him.

"Who are you?"

CHAPTER 7

Canadian Forces Health Services
Montfort Hospital, Ottawa

My name's Jonathan Sanchez, Lisa."

Sanchez looked at her. She was seated on the floor of the bathroom with her back against the sink's cabinet, wearing only a white hospital gown. Pieces of mirror were in the sink and on the floor, some of them covered in blood. It didn't take a genius to know what she had tried to do.

"Leave me," she said, her voice trembling. "I don't need you."

Poor girl. She thinks she has lost her whole family. Well, she nearly did.

"I'm afraid I can't do that, Lisa," Sanchez said carefully sitting down on the floor against the bed. *Damn knee.* He placed his cane on top of the bed. "Michael's alive."

Her eyes were affixed on him. "What did you say?"

"I'm not lying," he offered.

She cocked her head. With a grating voice she said, "I was told by somebody I trust that my husband was dead. Why would he lie? What kind of sick game are you playing?"

"He told you the truth as he knew it, Lisa," Sanchez replied. "I know otherwise."

"Okay, then. Bring me to him," she said trying to get up.

Sanchez watched her struggle to stand up. He did the same, his left knee protesting the sudden movement by sending a burst of pain through the rest of his body.

Fetching his cane with his left hand, he offered Lisa his right one, but she pushed it away.

"I'm fine," she said.

"We'll need to take care of that cut first," Sanchez said, pointing to the slash on her wrist. "They'll never release you from the hospital like that."

"Just tell me where he is."

"For now, you'll have to trust me. I'll bring you to your husband. He's not here. He was injured; that much is true. But he survived, I assure you."

"Where is he?" she insisted, her voice getting louder.

Sanchez raised his palms.

"I don't know his exact whereabouts. As of now," he quickly added. "But I'll get a call in the next hour or so. Then I'll know."

"Who are you?"

Sanchez gave her a disarming smile but said with a hint of steel in his voice, "I told you already. I'm Jonathan Sanchez. I work for an organization headed by a man named Charles Mapother. And we're offering you a way to get back to the ones who wronged your family."

Lisa didn't reply right away.

She's curious now. She wants to know more.

"That doesn't tell me anything, Mr. Sanchez. I don't know who Mapother is or the reason why you know my husband."

"We served together," Sanchez replied.

"Special Forces?" she asked sitting in her bed while holding her left arm up.

"Something like that," he said. "Charles Mapother runs a small outfit where people like me try to prevent things like this tragedy from happening."

Lisa pointed to the drawer next to the bed with her chin. "You failed miserably this time. Pass me the emergency kit, will you?"

"Sure." But instead of handing it to her, he opened it himself and inventoried what was inside.

"I can do this," Lisa said.

"I know you can, Dr. Powell. But I know a thing or two about stab wounds and the like. Stay still," he added while gently grabbing her arm.

"Special Forces, you said? You look the part," Lisa said. "You know him well?"

Sanchez knew what was coming next. A few questions a friend of Mike would know the answers to. "I won't lie to you, Lisa. I don't know him *that* well," he stated while disinfecting the wound. "But we fought together, and for what it's worth, he talked a lot about you while we were in Kosovo."

"Kosovo? Mike has never been to Kosovo," Lisa said.

She doesn't know. He kept the horrors of the Kosovo mission from her. He didn't want her to worry. Good man, Michael.

"Well, that's something you'll need to talk about with him, I guess," he replied. "But Mike saved my ass back there. So I owe him."

"Is that why you're here? Because you owe him?" she asked.

"There's a bit of that, it's true. But there's more. Much more."

"Like what? Why don't you elaborate? Ouch!" she said as Sanchez sutured her cut.

"Rumors are that the Sheik might be behind all this."

"The Sheik? He's the one who kidnapped Mike's father. Did you know that?"

Everybody knows that. The poor guy's pictures have been circulating for a while now.

"We know all about it, Lisa," Sanchez answered. "Come with us, and I promise you a chance to take your revenge against that son of a bitch."

"What's in it for you, Mr. Sanchez?"

"Call me Jonathan, please."

"Doesn't change my question, *Jonathan.* What do you get out of it?"

"Somebody who'll do anything in her power to track the bastard down."

Sanchez hoped that Lisa was picturing herself over the Sheik's dead body.

"Here, it's done now," he said, applying the last of the antibiotic cream. "There's something I want to show you."

From the breast pocket of his jacket, Sanchez removed a battered photograph. He glanced at it before handing it to her.

"That's Mike and me," Sanchez explained. "We had just landed at Pristina Airport."

Lisa examined the picture, then turned it over.

"You recognize his handwriting?"

Lisa raised her head toward him. Behind her tears, Sanchez could see the hope he'd just given her.

"Yes, I do," she whispered. She wiped her tears away with the sleeves of her gown. "Let me get dressed. Then we'll go."

CHAPTER 8

The Sheik's Private Yacht
The Mediterranean Sea

The reports weren't satisfactory. The Sheik severed the connection and slammed his encrypted satellite phone on his desk. Seconds later, the San Pellegrino bottle from his right hand flew across the luxurious yacht's master cabin. It hit a glass sculpture before deviating into an oil painting. The bottle shattered on impact and sliced through the expensive art piece a longtime associate had given him more than a decade ago for his fiftieth birthday. With his eyes opened wide, the Sheik lifted the desk and shoved it upside down, causing the fresh-water aquarium standing on top of it to drop to the floor. He looked at the small tropical fish, now flopping and gasping for air amid pieces of broken glass, and wondered how long they had before dying of asphyxiation.

"They did what they could, Sheik Al-Assad," said Omar Al-Nashwan, his most trusted soldier. His voice was steady, and he didn't seem troubled by the Sheik's outburst. "They didn't die as cowards but as martyrs."

"And that's all we could really hope for," added the Sheik's personal physician and representative, Dr. Ahmed Khaled. He was seated next to Al-Nashwan on a large leather sofa tucked away against one of the walls.

In all fairness to his men, the Sheik had to agree they'd done well. Granted, his ultimate objective hadn't been fulfilled, but enough damage had been done to trigger negative economic reactions in North America, and in Europe, too, he hoped. The stock markets across the globe were already plummeting, and authorities had started issuing recommendations against unnecessary movements within Canada's capital city.

"You're right, Ahmed," replied the Sheik, pacing the large master cabin he used as office space when he wasn't sleeping. "One way or another, our next operation should push them over the edge."

"I know it will, Sheik," concurred Al-Nashwan. "The plan we put in place is flawless, but lots of work remains to ensure its smooth execution."

The Sheik stopped to look at Al-Nashwan's intense blue eyes. As always, Al-Nashwan didn't look away like all the others did. In all the years they've known each other, he didn't remember hearing his right-hand man give a false assessment or say something he didn't mean.

"What about our dear friend Ambassador Powell?"

"As per your instructions, we moved him to one of our safe houses in Syria," replied Al-Nashwan, shifting in his seat.

The Sheik raised his eyebrows. "Go on, my friend. Speak your mind," he said.

"Is there really a point in keeping him alive now that we know he didn't speak to anyone regarding my father?"

"In a few months from now, they'll come after us," replied the Sheik. "Let there be no doubt about this, my friends. The Americans will come with everything they have. Won't you agree that Ambassador Powell will be a nice diversion? They won't be able to resist focusing resources to find him, to liberate him. For two years, they've been losing face. We'll give them a big fat chance to redeem themselves."

"I understand," said Al-Nashwan. "Nevertheless, the risks of discovery are higher now that Allied forces are in Syria to fight our friends from ISIS—the Islamic State in Iraq and Syria."

The Sheik sighed. *Omar's right. Maybe it is time to say goodbye to Ambassador Ray Powell.*

"A valid point, Omar," the Sheik finally said. "Let me think about it."

"Of course," Al-Nashwan said, bowing his head.

Turning toward Dr. Khaled, the Sheik changed the subject. "I want you to meet with Major Jackson, our African ally, within the next month or so. Make sure he understands the time frame must be respected."

"With the money you offered him, it shouldn't be an issue," Dr. Khaled replied.

"For his sake, I hope so," concluded the Sheik. "What about Faruq, Omar?"

"After examination, I have no doubt that his call could have been intercepted, Sheik Al-Assad. It's impossible to say for sure, but we all know of our enemies' monitoring capabilities, don't we?"

The Sheik nodded. The National Security Agency and its allies were everywhere.

He had invested heavily to make his communication network as secure as it could be, but he had no illusions; he had to tread carefully and not allow anyone to communicate outside the dedicated secure network.

"He's waiting on the upper deck, in case you wanted to speak with him," continued Al-Nashwan. "He's not aware that we know about his use of an unsecured cell phone."

"Very well, Omar. I'll speak to him."

A smile appeared on Dr. Khaled's face, but one look from Al-Nashwan was enough to wipe it off. "There's nothing entertaining about this, Ahmed. This call could have compromised us," said the Sheik's enforcer standing up.

Dr. Khaled raised his hands in mock surrender. "Of course, Omar. Whatever you say."

Less than a minute later, three subtle knocks could be heard against the cabin's door.

"Come in, please," said the Sheik, stepping over some broken pieces of glass on the floor.

The door hesitantly opened, as if the man who was about to enter was doing so against his will.

"Faruq, don't be shy," said the Sheik to the newcomer. "Please join us."

Reluctantly, the man approached the Sheik with Al-Nashwan following just a few steps behind. Looking at Dr. Khaled, who was still seated on the sofa, the Sheik explained, "Faruq was our man on shore. He did an excellent job keeping the ship supplied according to my instructions. Isn't that so, Faruq?"

The man swallowed hard and nodded.

"However," continued the Sheik, "although it was clearly explained to him that the use of his phone was to call only the preapproved numbers already programmed, yesterday Faruq broke one of the rules when he decided to use his cell phone to call an unauthorized number."

"But my sister's sick, Sheik Al-Assad. She'll most probably die within a few days, well before I have the chance to see her one last time," pleaded Faruq.

"Your sister's sick? I'm so sorry to hear that," answered the Sheik, his tone instantly changing into one of pure compassion. "How could I have known? Really, how could I have known, Faruq? You should have told me."

Faruq looked up, seemingly surprised by the Sheik's reaction. "And the call didn't even last a full minute," he offered with a smile.

"But of course," the Sheik said. "I know it didn't".

He opened his arms, as to invite Faruq to close in. Obviously relieved, Faruq approached, but as soon as he was within reach, Sheik Al-Assad delivered a powerful strike to his throat with the tips of his fingers. The effect was instantaneous. Faruq's hands shot up to his neck as his windpipe collapsed. A few seconds later, he was on his knees, unable to breathe, his eyes in the Sheik's direction. The Sheik returned his gaze and smirked. With his left foot, he pushed Faruq to the ground next to the multicolored fish and applied pressure on Faruq's throat with his right. The Sheik's gaze moved from the dying man to the fish. Like Faruq, they were all gasping for air, well aware they were living their last moments on Earth.

"You failed me, Faruq. You failed me, and the rest of your brothers," the Sheik said, pressing his foot harder against Faruq's throat.

Thirty seconds later, Faruq's eyes rolled over and his feet stopped moving altogether.

"Throw him overboard, Omar," the Sheik ordered. "Once it's done, advise the crew we're returning to shore. As you've said it so well yourself, there's lots to do."

Al-Nashwan didn't answer. "Did you hear me, Omar? I said throw him overboard." When his right-hand man slowly raised his eyes from his secured smartphone's screen, the Sheik saw something rare: amusement.

"What's so funny, Omar?"

"My apologies, Sheik Al-Assad," Al-Nashwan replied, handing his smartphone to the Sheik. "I think you should read this."

The text the Sheik was reading was from the Al Jazeera media network. As he read through it, he understood why Al-Nashwan was amused. *I can't believe it myself. Could they be wrong?*

The Sheik passed the device to Dr. Khaled. "Read this, my friend." Then he turned to Al-Nashwan. "Show this to the ambassador, Omar. Take a few pictures, and send them to his family."

"With pleasure, Sheik Al-Assad."

"On second thought," the Sheik added, "send me a copy as well. I'm curious to see how the ambassador will react to his son's death."

PART 2

CHAPTER 9

The Oval Office
Washington, DC

The three sharp knocks at the door startled President Robert Muller. He glanced at his watch and realized that a full hour had passed since he'd started reading the UN's economic report on West Africa.

The Secret Service agent outside the Oval Office opened the door to let Director of National Intelligence Richard Phillips enter. President Muller had known Phillips for decades and was thankful for his loyalty. DNI Phillips liked to operate in the shadows and rarely did the president make a decision before first consulting with him.

"What's going on, Richard?" asked the president. He was always nervous when his friend visited him unannounced, as it often meant bad news was on the way.

"Don't worry, Robert," said Phillips, unbuttoning his suit jacket and sitting in one of the two armchairs in front of the president. "I have nothing to report."

President Muller relaxed slightly. "That's good."

"Not really." Phillips said.

His words caused Muller to cock his head. "What do you mean?"

"I spoke with Donald Poole this morning regarding last month's bombings in Ottawa."

"Did the CIA figure out who orchestrated it?" the president asked. He had hoped that with all the extra resources he'd given the CIA director, US intelligence would be able to come up with something actionable.

Phillips shook his head. "Poole signed off on the report, but I strongly disagree with its conclusion."

Muller pinched his nose. He could feel a headache coming. "How so?" he asked.

"The CIA seems to think that the attacks were in retaliation to the successes the Canadian's CF-18s had in Syria," Phillips said.

"That makes sense," Muller said. "The Canadians have killed many high-value targets within the last few months. Why don't you agree with this line of reasoning?"

"Because it's flawed," Phillips replied. "I don't buy that ISIS could mount a coordinated attack on foreign soil, especially not in North America. They just don't have access to the logistics needed for this type of operation. Think about it, Robert. The Ottawa bombings took many months, even years, to plan out. It just doesn't make sense to—"

"Okay, Richard. I get it," interrupted Muller. "If you're right, then why does the CIA think ISIS is responsible?"

"Poole's doing everything he can, but even with the added resources you've given him, the CIA is still stretched beyond its limits. They prioritize what needs to be done and allocate the resources accordingly. We shouldn't forget the attacks happened in Canada, not in the United States."

The president stood from behind his desk and walked to one of the big bay windows offering him an elegant view of the Rose Garden. "What's your take on it?"

"If I had to guess, I would say the bombings were carried out by sleeper cells inserted years ago."

"So that rules out ISIS?"

"Yes, it does. Their hands are full, for now at least," Phillips said. "We both know that to activate a deep-cover asset, someone very high up in the terrorist food chain must give the go-ahead."

"Meaning?"

"I don't think it would be far-fetched to suggest that the Sheik gave the order."

The Sheik. He had appeared out of nowhere a couple years ago when he had claimed responsibility over the well-executed kidnapping of Canadian ambassador Ray Powell in Algiers. Since then, the Sheik had been a thorn in the side of all the Western intelligence agencies. He'd continuously nagged them with pictures of Powell, often taken in brutal conditions. Muller had offered all his help to the Canadian prime minister, but the Sheik had so far eluded them. Was it time to turn the heat up?

Muller walked back to his desk and poured himself a glass of water. The headache was starting to throb, and he hoped a couple of Advils would relieve the continuous pounding.

"Why do you think it's him?" Muller asked.

"I think the attacks were meant to punish the Canadian government. For the last two years, our neighbors have been a lot more cautious about whom they were letting inside their borders. It's much more difficult to gain access to Canada now than it was three years ago. My guess is the Sheik felt that if the Canadian government wouldn't maintain its passive role as a safe haven for his men, then it would no longer enjoy the benefit of being off-limits."

"And they gave us their full support in our fight against ISIS," the president added.

"That's also true."

"That's an interesting theory, Richard," the president said.

"That's the problem, isn't it? It's only a theory," shrugged Phillips.

Muller wasn't fooled. "I know you, Richard. You have something in mind to prove you're right, don't you?"

Phillips smiled. "What about Charles Mapother?"

—

Oval Office
Two years ago

The president's three guests were not the richest men in the United States, but their combined wealth was over fourteen billion dollars. Even though it never hurt to spend a small fortune on the man who occupies the Oval Office, that wasn't the reason why they'd been able to secure a last-minute meeting with him.

They'd all been part of the Harvard Chess Club back in their college days and had remained close friends since then.

This unique gathering was informal; there was no pecking order as to who was seated where in the Oval Office. President Muller was across from the fireplace, and his three friends were stretched out on the two white couches on either side. No records would be kept, and the Secret Service presidential security detail had been asked to turn off the recording and video feeds.

"Robert, you need to let us try," said Andrew Fitzgerald, a tall, lanky man who had made his wealth in private banking. "Give us two years, and we promise that you'll see concrete results. And frankly, we have nothing to lose."

President Muller tossed the fifteen-page executive summary onto the coffee table. The cover page, with the words *IMSI: International Market Stabilization Institute* stared back at him. "Drew, I can't go along with this plan, and you know it. It's unethical. Plus, this country can't afford another intelligence agency."

Muller, the former governor of California, had been elected president ten months before. His confident leadership and no-nonsense manner had placed him in the media spotlight. He was seen as a man of the people.

"It won't cost the taxpayers a thing," said Steve Shamrock, CEO of Oil Denatek, one of the larger publicly traded oil and gas companies in the United States. "We will personally finance the whole shebang."

The president paused as he digested what Shamrock had said. "Do you know how much an agency like that would cost to operate? And how would you access the intelligence needed to accomplish such missions?" the president demanded, gesturing toward the executive summary on the table.

"I assure you we have the funds lined up," the third man said. He was the smallest, most out of shape of the four friends, and his thinning blond hair was kept a bit too long.

President Muller had been wondering when his diminutive friend would start talking. Simon Coyne of New York's Coyne, Robinson, and Sedaka law firm was the wealthiest of the group. His family owned the equivalent of two square blocks of prime real estate in Manhattan and a number of national hotel chains.

"We've already budgeted three hundred million for the initial start-up costs, with an additional four hundred million available for the first two years," Coyne explained.

"My God!" Muller exclaimed. He was not easily awed. "That's impressive!"

"Of course, if the results are positive, supplementary funds will be readily available after the initial twenty-four months," continued Coyne. "As for how we'll get the intelligence needed to succeed in our missions, we need your help."

The president became more cautious. "What type of help? There is only so much I can do by myself without asking Congress."

"We all know that you have limited latitude to operate. But we're confident that with these directions," Coyne said as he took out a five-page document from his leather briefcase and delivered it into the president's waiting hand, "you'll be able to give us the intelligence we need without exposing us to the public."

President Muller scanned the document once, then read it a second and third time before slowly placing it on the table beside the other summary. He looked up to see three sets of eyes awaiting his reaction.

"So let me get this straight," the president said, his hollow voice ringing through the room. "You gentlemen are proposing that we enable an organization that would enforce America's economic interests without being accountable?"

"Yes, sir. That's exactly what we're proposing," confirmed Fitzgerald.

There was a long pause before the president spoke again. "If—and that's a long-shot 'if'—I were to entertain this idea, who do you possibly propose would head this...this International Market Stabilization Institute?"

"There's only one man who could lead IMSI," Coyne replied.

"And that is?" prompted President Muller.

"Charles Mapother."

The president paused, hesitation creeping into his voice. "Where have I heard that name before?"

"He's the FBI's lost lamb," Fitzgerald prompted.

"Or black sheep, as some might call it," threw in Shamrock.

"Thirty years ago, he was the most promising young agent on the FBI's roster," Coyne explained. "But his biggest mistake was to start making waves. He was very vocal about how the Bureau's policies might be fine for murderers and con men but would be impotent against terrorists. Considering that terror cells hadn't really set their sights on us yet, nobody up the chain wanted to hear what he had to say. He hit the glass ceiling at the FBI, so to speak, and he left before he turned thirty."

"Where'd he move to?" the president asked, curious despite himself.

"Nobody's sure," answered Shamrock. "He was independently wealthy—his father hit it big in shipping containers—but rumor had it that he kept working for us; more specifically for the CIA as a private entity. Apparently, he was hired most often to extract information from troublesome elements in organizations like the Islamic Brotherhood."

"*Extract information*?" the president repeated. "You mean torture?"

"Among other things, but yes, Mapother is known to be ruthless," Shamrock confirmed. "He's also smart as hell, has an incredible network of contacts who owe him a favor, and always manages to get the best people on his team. He's our man."

A heavy stillness filled the room for a long moment.

"This organization couldn't run without some kind of oversight, gentlemen."

His three friends looked at one another. None seemed happy about his proposal. Steve Shamrock was the only one daring a reply. "We can't agree on these terms, Robert. We all know how inefficient and bureaucratic an organization's governmental oversight is. IMSI would need to be controlled by its investors," he said.

"And by that you mean you three?" the president asked incredulously. "You can't be serious."

Shamrock nodded, but Coyne raised his hand. "You don't need to raise your hand to speak, Simon," President Muller said. "You know that."

"What about an oversight committee of one?" Coyne asked.

"We never spoke about this," Shamrock argued furiously. "IMSI needs to be control—"

The president interrupted him by raising his hand. "What do you mean, Simon?"

"What if the only oversight committee needed was you?"

"I'd be happy with that," Andrew Fitzgerald said without pause. "That would work."

President Muller looked in Shamrock's direction. His friend was shaking his head. "I can't support this. I need to know where my millions are going."

"Do you?" Coyne asked. "I implicitly trust Robert."

"We can actually do this without you, Steve," added Fitzgerald. "It's not what I want, and I'm sure Simon will agree with me on this, but there's a greater good to achieve here."

"I couldn't agree more, Andrew," confirmed Coyne.

Shamrock's expression couldn't hide that he hadn't expected this. For a minute, President Muller thought he would see his friend walk out of the Oval Office. Instead, Muller saw determination in Shamrock's eyes. "Okay, then," he said. "If Robert agrees, I say we go ahead."

All eyes turned to the president.

"Gentlemen, I'll give a qualified yes."

—

Oval Office
Washington, DC

The man who stood in front of President Muller was over six feet tall and about sixty years old. He was dressed in a dark Armani suit and expensive loafers. His silver hair was carefully combed away from his face, exposing his high, wide forehead and strong jaw line. His Italian silk tie was perfectly centered, and his demeanor indicated that he was a man accustomed to being in charge.

"Richard Phillips told me you wanted to see me, Mr. President?"

"That's correct. I know it's unusual, but I wanted to let you know how much I appreciated what you and your agency have accomplished within the last eighteen months."

"Thank you, sir," replied his guest, more or less standing at attention. "What can I do for you?"

The president cleared his throat. "I'm very well aware that you've got carte blanche for your operations, Charles. However, if you would find the time to look into something for me, I'd appreciate it very much."

"DNI Phillips mentioned something about the Ottawa bombings."

President Muller gestured toward an inch-thick report on his desk. "The CIA thinks ISIS is behind the attacks. On the other hand, Richard is leaning in another direction. He believes the Sheik is responsible."

"What do you want from us exactly, Mr. President?" asked Charles Mapother.

"I want you to confirm that these attacks aren't in any way a prelude to an assault on our soil," said Muller. "I want to know who's behind it and how it was financed. If you find any evidence—and I really mean *any* evidence—that the United States might become a target, I want you to hunt down these animals and destroy them."

The president's eyes were focused and unwavering.

"I might have the perfect tools to do just that, Mr. President."

"And one more thing before you leave, Charles."

"Yes, Mr. President?"

Muller stood up from behind his desk and walked over to Mapother. He handed him the last picture of Ambassador Ray Powell that the Sheik had sent to the CIA. "Even though Powell's Canadian, we've lost a lot of credibility with our Middle Eastern allies over this. They know we've been helping the Canadians find him, with the results you know. The Sheik's playing us like fools."

"What do you want me to do, sir?"

"Find him, if you can. Bring him back to his family. They've suffered enough."

Mapother glanced at the picture.

"I'll see what we can do, Mr. President."

CHAPTER 10

Johns Hopkins Hospital
Baltimore, Maryland

Mike Powell woke up with a lurch. Immediately, a powerful ripping sensation seared through his body. He couldn't move, he couldn't open his eyes, and he could barely breathe. He felt trapped. He tried to talk, but no sound came out. His mouth was so dry.

"Don't panic. Relax and concentrate on your breathing," said a steady female voice. "My name is Christina, and I'm your nurse. I know how you feel. Right now you can't open your eyes, and your whole body feels like you ran fifteen marathons in a row. But don't worry—you're in good hands. Now I'm going to give you a light sedative that will put you back to sleep. Don't fight it. When you wake up, you'll be able to open your eyes and talk."

Thirty seconds later, Mike's eyes rolled back in their sockets, and his body relaxed again.

—

"Can anyone explain what just happened?" asked Dr. Fletcher Webb. In a conference room in the basement of Johns Hopkins Hospital, a group of medical experts was seated around a long table. "I thought this patient was supposed to be kept in a coma for another week."

"Plans have changed, Doctor," said a man who was standing at the back of the room, the only one who was not part of Dr. Webb's medical staff. Everybody turned to listen to what this stranger had to say. "We're moving ahead of schedule."

"The patient isn't ready," protested Dr. Webb.

"It's not for you to decide," the stranger replied icily. "Perhaps we should have this discussion in private, Doctor."

Not wanting to enter an argument he might very well lose, Dr. Webb dismissed his staff from the room. Charles Mapother was not someone you wanted to squabble with in public.

"I think that you're being overprotective of your patient," Mapother said once they were alone.

"Overprotective?" repeated the bewildered doctor. "Don't you remember that this man was shot twice less than three weeks ago? By all accounts he should have been killed."

"I didn't forget, Doctor," answered Mapother calmly. "And I'm sure you haven't forgotten that I've paid for his treatment. Yet we don't have the luxury of time. Our own specialists are saying that his body will heal much faster if he's conscious. Besides, it's time that we signed him out. We have plans for him, and they can't wait any longer."

Dr. Webb seemed to stumble for words. He wasn't used to being told what to do. "It might, but chances are that it won't. Listen, I can't approve this."

"I think you misunderstood me, Doctor. I don't make suggestions. I am telling you what to do. I expect him to be ready to receive visitors a week from now."

"B-but that's impossible."

"Make it happen, Doctor."

"But hospital authorities will never allow it. If the chief of medicine finds out—"

"I've already cleared it with Director Kern," said the silver-haired man. "It seems he likes the two million dollars in charitable donations I send this hospital every year."

Dr. Webb's mouth was agape.

The man continued, fixing his gaze on Dr. Webb, "You might be one of the best reconstructive surgeons in the country, Dr. Webb, but your job here is done."

—

Opening his eyes was the most difficult task Mike had ever accomplished. A massive headache made him wish he could go back to sleep, but he forced himself to take in his surroundings. The room was plunged in semidarkness. A few weak rays of sunlight were slipping through the closed drapes. Turning his head toward the window, Mike was surprised to see a man sitting in an armchair, watching him.

"Good morning, Mike," greeted the man with a jovial tone.

"Who...who are you?" he asked. His tongue felt like sandpaper.

"Let me get you some water," said the man, starting toward an en suite bathroom. He came back with a small Styrofoam cup filled with water and helped Mike take a sip.

Swallowing made Mike cough, and instantly his whole body was aflame. He nodded his thanks.

"I see you're still in some pain," said the man.

"Who are you?"

"I am a friend, Mike. A friend who took care of you when you needed help."

Mike realized that the man's intelligent eyes were deathly cold. Ruthless. He wouldn't want to make enemies with this man.

"Where's my wife? Where's Lisa? Where's Melissa?"

"Unfortunately, your wife isn't here right now. You've been in a coma for the last three weeks, Mike."

Three weeks? wondered Mike. *Lisa must have had the baby by now, and I missed it!*

"Once she recuperated from her own injuries, your wife spent nearly every waking hour here with you," continued the stranger. "We finally convinced her that she needed to take care of herself for a bit, while we took care of you. But she was contacted this morning. She is flying to Baltimore as we speak."

"From her own injuries? Why would she be flying to Baltimore? And who the hell are you?" Mike asked, his patience wearing thin. Nothing was making any sense to him.

"She's coming to Baltimore because that's where we are now, Mike. You're in the hospital. Do you know why you're here? Do you remember what happened?"

"I'm not sure," Mike admitted after a few moments.

"Do you remember anything about the terrorist attack at the airport?"

"The airport?"

Suddenly, it all came back.

Oh, my God, the airport. What about Paul?

He remembered Robichaud being inside the airplane when all hell had broken loose in the terminal. He remembered the blood and bodies of passengers all over the terminal. He remembered the wounded Ottawa police officer raising his gun and...

Mike tried to sit up in his bed, but the maneuver took more out of him than it should have, sending waves of pain over his entire body. As the blood rushed through his body, his face suddenly became very itchy.

"I wouldn't do that if I were you," the man said, seeing Mike's hand lift toward his face. "Your scars are still sensitive. I'll call Christina, the nurse. She's very good. She'll take care of any discomfort you might be feeling."

"What...what happened?"

"You were shot in the face, Mike. We almost lost you. Fortunately, your jawbone deflected the bullet away from your brain. But it did do a lot of damage. You've had to undergo a lot of surgeries...They had to reconstruct a lot of your palate and sinus cavities. But don't worry—the best surgeons this country ever produced treated you. Within a couple of months, you'll be completely healed."

Mike tried to imagine what the man was telling him. He just couldn't wrap his mind around it.

"Am I...am I disfigured?" Mike whispered.

"Take it easy, Mike. Considering that your face stopped a bullet, you look pretty good. But I'll bring you a mirror if you want."

The man got up from his chair and went back to the bathroom, this time returning with a small round mirror. He switched on the night-stand lamp beside the bed and held the mirror eighteen inches from Mike's face.

His green eyes and jet-black hair hadn't changed, but the surgeons had rebuilt some parts of his face. He still had a handsome, powerful look, but his features were all somewhat different, especially in the lower part of his face.

"But why am I at a hospital in *Baltimore* if I was shot in Ottawa? How did I get here? And how come my wife was injured?"

"Let's just say that this particular hospital could provide you with the kind of care you needed, Mike. As for your wife, I think it would be better if she explains everything to you herself."

Mike raised the mirror again and took another look.

Baltimore? What the hell?

His thoughts were interrupted by a set of footsteps entering the room. He looked up and placed the mirror next to him on the bed.

"Good morning," said the nurse, who must be Christina. She walked directly to the window and slowly opened the curtains. She approached the bed and placed a moist towel on the lower left side of his face. "How are you feeling?"

"All right, considering," he answered.

The nurse was a couple inches shy of six feet and looked athletic even though she was wearing loose blue scrubs. She wore her long brown hair up in a ponytail. Her movements were fluid and gentle as she brought the towel across his forehead.

"It's good to finally hear your voice. I feel like I've known you for a long time. But I have to admit that our discussions were a little one-sided, considering you were in an induced coma for three weeks," she said.

"An *induced* coma?" Mike repeated, confused. A million thoughts began to run through his mind.

"I've been wondering what the voice of my mysterious patient Mr. Walton sounded like," she continued as she set the washcloth on the bedside table. "And now I get to find out even sooner than expected. It's like Christmas came early."

"Walton? My name's not Walton. It's Powell," Mike corrected her, his mind still swimming.

A strange look came over Christina's face as she reached for the metal clipboard at the foot of his bed. After flipping through the papers of his chart, she gave Mike a concerned look.

"Why don't you get some rest, Mr. Walton? I'll come and check on you soon," the nurse said, returning the clipboard to its holder.

"It's Powell. My name's Powell! And why was I induced into a coma? What the hell is going on here?" he shouted, struggling once again to sit up.

The silver-haired man stood and placed his hands on Mike's shoulders, gently but firmly returning him to the mattress. "Calm down, Mike, just calm down."

"I won't calm down," Mike hissed. "I'll ask you this one last time. What the hell is going on here?"

The man sighed heavily, then turned to Christina. "Would you mind excusing us for a minute, please?"

The nurse nodded once and slipped out of the room.

"All right, Mike, I'll tell you." He cleared his throat and grasped Mike's arm to keep him calm. "You are no longer Mike Powell. Mike Powell was shot dead three weeks ago."

CHAPTER 11

Johns Hopkins Hospital
Baltimore, Maryland

Mike was stunned by the statement. How could he be alive if he was dead? Who was he?

"What the fuck are you talking about?" Mike yelled, ripping his arm away from the stranger's grasp, causing the hand mirror to crash to the floor.

Suddenly, two men wearing identical business suits entered the room. They must have been standing just outside Mike's door. *Security guards?* he wondered. *What the hell?*

"Is everything all right in here?" the larger of the two guards asked, a tall black man with a bulge clearly visible through his jacket.

"Yes, everything is fine," the silver-haired man answered.

The guards nodded and exited the room, closing the door.

This was all getting to be too much for Mike. All these unanswered questions were beginning to make him feel light headed.

"Where's my wife?" asked Mike, his voice cracking. "And what the hell do you mean, I'm dead?"

"Listen, this will all make sense soon enough." The man stood up abruptly, smoothing his expensive suit jacket. "I'll return tomorrow, after you've had a chance to speak with her. Until then, try to take it easy, Mike."

He strode out of the room without another word.

—

Mike was awash in the terror at the airport. The explosion coming from the airplane. The confused look in the wounded police officer's eyes as he raised his gun...Mike lifted his hand to his sensitive face. *Friendly fire by another cop.*

The sound of an opening door brought him back to reality. Dr. Lisa Harrison Powell stepped into the room, and Mike had never been so happy to see anybody in his entire life. She was even more beautiful than he remembered. Her strawberry-blonde hair was pulled back in a simple ponytail, leaving him a clear view of her perfectly shaped oval face and striking blue eyes. A small cluster of freckles rode the bridge of her nose. She was dressed in a beige pair of linen pants and a white short-sleeve blouse. Mike could see right away that she was no longer pregnant.

"Oh, baby, I missed you so much!" exclaimed Lisa, kissing her husband gently on the mouth before he could speak. "I'm so sorry I wasn't here when you woke up. Dr. Webb told me you'd be in a coma for another week..."

"I'm just glad you're here now," Mike said, breathing in the scent of her hair. They held each other for a long time without saying a word.

"There is so much to tell you, honey," Lisa finally whispered into his ear. Mike felt his wife's warm tears run down his neck and embraced her a little harder, kissing her head softly.

"How are Melissa and the baby?" asked Mike.

Lisa slowly pulled back, and her eyes became overcast. He could see that she was fighting back more tears, but within moments, they came flooding down her face. "Oh, Mike...I'm so sorry...I'm so sorry," said Lisa between sobs.

A wave of dread passed over Mike's body and settled into the pit of his stomach. "What happened?"

"There is no way to tell you this without hurting you," Lisa said, shaking her head as though she was trying to dislodge some thoughts inside her mind.

"Baby, you're scaring me," Mike said. "Please tell me what this is all about."

Lisa took a deep breath and took her husband's hands in her own. "Honey," she began, "on the day you were injured, there was more than one terrorist attack. They didn't just hit the airport. They hit the train station, too," finished Lisa, trying to control her voice.

"The train station?" Mike asked, not liking where this was going.

"Yes. Where I was with Melissa and your mom, picking up my parents," managed Lisa in a whisper. "Over a hundred people died in that attack. Melissa was killed, too, Mike."

Utterly astonished, Mike opened his mouth but could not say anything. An unspeakable pain started to build inside his body, threatening to hurl him back into darkness. His breathing became erratic and shallow. "How?"

"Suicide bombers," she said quietly. "After the train came in, I left Melissa with my parents inside the train station to bring the car around, and then..." Her voice trailed off. "They died instantly, Mike—Melissa, your mom, and my parents. The bombs were packed with nails. They didn't stand a chance."

Shock overtook Mike's body. He felt like he was watching a tragedy that was happening to somebody else—to some other family. Entirely numb, Mike asked, "And the baby?"

"After I heard the explosion, I lost my head, Mike. I was hit by a taxi when I tried to run back into the train station. They took me to the hospital, but it was too late. Our baby was gone. Chloe was gone." Lisa's sobs wracked her body. "I'm so sorry, Mike. I'm so sorry..."

"Shush, baby, shush," Mike soothed, smoothing her hair even as his heart felt like it was being ripped from his chest cavity. "It wasn't your fault, baby. There wasn't anything you could have done."

Lisa, emotionally exhausted, collapsed on the bed while repeating over and over how sorry she was. For the next hour, she cried helplessly in her husband's arms. Mike stood fast, fighting to remain strong for the woman he so deeply loved. But he already knew that he would remember this hospital visit forever.

Everything, all that he held dear, had changed for him. *Nothing would ever be the same.*

—

Mike opened his eyes the next morning, feeling disoriented. He looked around blankly, only to realize he was still in his room at the hospital. So, it hadn't all been a terrible nightmare.

His wife, curled up against him under the white hospital bed sheet, was breathing deeply. He debated if he should wake her but decided against it. Now that he was awake, he was plunged into despair again. How could his life have changed so drastically? How could someone kill his two children, his in-laws, and his mother in some senseless act?

He knew that the empty space his family's deaths had left in his life would never be filled.

Feeling movement, Mike noticed that his wife was staring up at him.

"It's so good to have you back, honey," she told him. "When you were in a coma, I felt so alone..." She trailed off. Whatever dark thought she had made her sit up in the bed. "I think we should eat something. Are you hungry?"

"Not really," Mike answered. With the news he'd learned the day before, he wasn't sure he'd ever have an appetite again. "All I really want is some answers."

"I know, Mike. But you need your strength. I'll go downstairs and pick up a few things, and after we eat I'll tell you everything I know, okay? I'll be back shortly." Lisa kissed her husband on the forehead and left the room.

He knew that his wife was right about regaining his strength. The day before, he'd tried to walk to the bathroom by himself, but his legs had collapsed under him. Lisa had needed to support him the whole way. By the time he'd gotten back to the bed, he was exhausted.

Lisa returned fifteen minutes later with a freshly baked blueberry muffin, two cups of applesauce, and two small bowls of vanilla yogurt. The muffin was still warm and smelled good. Mike felt guilty when his stomach told him he was hungry.

As if she'd been reading his mind, Lisa said, "Your body will appreciate it, you know. You're not yet ready for a muffin, but the applesauce and yogurt should do the trick. I'm sure you're sick of having nothing but meds and mashed potatoes, or whatever else they put in all those tubes." Her lame attempt at a joke fell flat, for he could see the sadness in her eyes.

Mike rewarded her effort to make him feel better with a weak smile. He immediately regretted it, as his face burned with pain. "I wish we could go back in the past, but we can't; we never will," he said tenderly, trying to comfort her. "I don't know what plans God has in reserve for us or what the future will be like, but it's important that you know this—I love you, and I'm grateful I didn't lose you."

"I wonder how you can say that, Mike," Lisa replied, crossing her arms over her chest.

"What do you mean?" Mike was surprised by the curt retort.

"That you choose not to say it aloud is understandable, even admirable, I might add, but you and I both know that I'm responsible for our daughters' deaths," Lisa said glumly.

Mike was lost. He could see she was upset but couldn't understand her reasoning." Why are you saying that, Lisa? Surely you recognize you're not responsible for the death of Melissa and Chloe. By that token, I am responsible for the dozens of innocents killed at the airport. It doesn't work this way, baby."

Whatever evil mood had overtaken her erupted with his comment. "Don't ever compare people we didn't know with Melissa and Chloe, understood?" she shouted.

"I'm sorry, honey, I didn't mean to—" he said, trying to defuse the situation.

"Don't honey me, Mike," Lisa went on, still fierce. "I can sense it, you know?"

"Sense what?" asked Mike, confused.

"How you feel about me." His blank face in reply only inflamed her more. "How detached you seem to be from all of this. You didn't even shed a tear yet!"

"I want to be strong for you, Lisa," Mike said, reaching for her hands. "That's all."

"Nah, I don't think so." Lisa was shaking her head. She moved back, out of reach. "You want to know what I think?"

"I'm not sure I do," Mike said, knowing that the situation was spiraling out of control. He couldn't remember his wife losing her temper like this before. For a few seconds, Lisa's cold eyes locked with his.

"Whatever," she said finally.

They finished their meal in silence, with Mike trying to make sense of what had just happened. A part of him wanted to comfort his grieving wife. Yet another part deeply resented that she was taking her grief out on him. What had he done to deserve that?

—

"Okay, Lisa, why don't you start from the beginning," said Mike, who was now sitting in a wheelchair that Christina had brought. It felt good to be out of bed at last. They'd just finished the yogurt, and Lisa had regained control over her emotions. Her aggressive behavior had disappeared as suddenly as it had come on.

I'll have to talk about this to the doctor. Maybe he'll be able to help her in a way I can't.

"Let's see if there's another room we can use," Lisa said, heading toward the door.

"Why? What's wrong with this one?"

Lisa didn't answer him. She stepped out of the room and returned a few moments later. "You ready to go on a road trip?" was all she said.

She wheeled him to a small office in an eerily quiet wing of the hospital. One of the plainclothes security guards had accompanied them and taken up a post outside the door along with another suited man who had been waiting for them when they arrived.

"Lisa, please tell me what I've missed," begged Mike as soon as they'd closed the door behind them. "I feel like everybody knows what's going on but me."

Lisa nodded. "What do you want to know first?"

"For starters, what happened to Paul?" Mike asked.

Lisa shook her head. "Paul's gone, Mike. He died the day you were shot. I'm so sorry. He was shot twice but was still able to kill the two terrorists that were on the airplane."

"Hassan and Fadl?" Mike asked.

Lisa nodded. "He died a hero, Mike. He did what he was trained to do. He never quit."

"My God," Mike said. "What about Mary?"

"After Paul's funeral, she and the kids moved to her parents' place in Seattle," Lisa said.

How could it all have happened in a single day? He had lost his two children, his mother, his in-laws, and his best friend. He started shaking with barely controlled rage.

"And Zima?" he suddenly remembered. "She was there too, Lisa!"

"I know, Mike. I know."

"Is she okay?" he pressed on.

"Yes. She's fine. Shaken, but fine."

"She did well, Lisa. She fought hard and saved countless lives. Did you speak to her?"

"No, Mike. I didn't. Couldn't."

Mike looked perplexed. "Why not? You've known her for over ten years."

Lisa didn't reply. Her phone was vibrating. She reached into her pants pocket for her smartphone. "Dr. Lisa Walton speaking."

Mike looked at her strangely. *Dr. Lisa Walton?*

"Yes, sir. No problem at all. I'll let him know. We're in a clean room. The guard outside the door knows where we are." There was a pause. "Okay. See you soon," she said before returning the phone to her pocket.

"What's going on here, Lisa?" Mike asked, searching his wife's eyes for answers.

"I guess I owe you an explanation," said his wife. "That was Charles Mapother. He's the man that you spoke with when you woke up yesterday. He's leaving Washington now and should be here in twenty minutes. He wants to speak with you."

"He'll be here in twenty minutes? I thought DC was a good hour-and-a-half commute from Baltimore."

"Well, it is...if you drive. He's taking a helicopter."

Mike narrowed his eyes at his wife.

"Who is this guy, anyway? I asked him that yesterday and he avoided my question."

"He's the director of the International Market Stabilization Institute. He's my new boss, Mike."

CHAPTER 12

Royal Canadian Mounted Police Headquarters
Ottawa, Canada

Zima Bernbaum could only shake her head in disbelief. *How slow could these elevators really be?* Moving from the ground floor to the third floor could take the better part of two minutes. But today the delay was welcomed. Since the shooting at the airport, she had been ordered to stay home. Of course, she'd received a commendation letter from the CSIS director, and numerous agents from both CSIS and the RCMP had stopped by to congratulate her on a job well done. She had smiled at them and thanked them for their support, but inside, Zima was torn apart. Her instinct was to move forward and forget the whole incident. Yet at the same time, she badly wanted to stick around and participate in the investigation.

She welcomed the phone call she had received this morning. The RCMP commissioner wanted to see her. She hadn't allowed herself to speculate on the reasons of the call. She'd tied her hair in a bun, applied some makeup, and put on a pair of blue jeans with a red blouse. The drive from her downtown apartment to the RCMP headquarters had taken twenty minutes.

As the door of the elevator opened with a series of jerks, Zima saw the commissioner's aide waiting for her. He was dressed in a nicely cut gray suit, and she immediately noticed his shoes. They were black and had been polished to a high shine like her father's paratrooper jump boots.

"Good morning, Agent Bernbaum. How are you?" he said.

"I feel great. Thank you for asking," she replied.

"Excellent," said the assistant. "Follow me. Everyone is waiting for you."

—

The office of the RCMP commissioner was vast and luxurious. It had previously belonged to the director of the JDS Uniphase campus. Acquired in 2006, the nine-hundred-thousand-square-foot complex, which included seven buildings linked by an atrium, a three-hundred-seat auditorium, a gym, and a gourmet kitchen, had cost over six hundred million dollars. To be fair to the commissioner, he wasn't the one who had chosen his office. The Treasury Board had assigned it to him. When Zima entered the office, two men were waiting for her. She recognized both of them.

"Agent Bernbaum, it's a real pleasure to meet you," said Arthur Green, the Canadian energy minister.

"The pleasure is all mine, sir," Zima said, accepting a cup of black coffee from the RCMP commissioner.

"Please have a seat," continued the minister, sitting in one of the four armchairs set up around the coffee table.

"Thank you."

"I assume you're well rested, Zima?" asked the commissioner, taking a cautious sip of his steaming coffee.

"The last four weeks have been a blessing," Zima replied, reaching for the sugar. "Nothing beats waking up late and watching television all day."

Green and the commissioner looked at each other.

They are wondering if I'm yanking their chains or not. Am I?

"Well," the commissioner said, "I'm pleased to hear that."

Zima poured a cloud of milk in her cup and used a silver spoon to add more sugar. "I'm ready to go back to work though."

Green smiled and leaned back in his armchair.

"We were hoping you would feel that way," said the commissioner. "Would you be interested in continuing to work with the RCMP for a few more months?"

Zima knew that if the commissioner was asking, he had already cleared it with the CSIS director. Furthermore, the energy minister's presence indicated she was about to be tasked with something significant.

"I serve at your pleasure, sir," said Zima. "As long as CSIS gave its consent, I'll stay for as long as you need me."

"Excellent," Green said, standing up. "I had a feeling you'd say that." He grabbed a folder he'd been keeping in a brown legal-size briefcase and gave it to Zima. "This package contains all the information you'll need to prepare for your next assignment. I want you to read it thoroughly and to forward any requests or questions you might have directly to the commissioner."

Zima could feel her excitement growing.

This is why I joined the CSIS. But also why I have to lie to my family, my friends, and everyone I care about. And probably why I'm still single...

She opened the file and quickly scanned the first few pages.

"I'm going to France?" she said, trying to keep her enthusiasm in check.

C'mon, Zima. Stay professional, she ordered herself. *They'll think twice about sending you if they see how excited you are.*

"Yes," said Green. "I'll let the commissioner give you a brief overview of what will happen."

The RCMP commissioner placed his empty cup on the table. He then leaned in toward Zima. "What we're about to discuss doesn't leave this room. Understood?"

Zima nodded.

"Everything is in connection with last month's bombings," stated the commissioner. "That's why we chose you, Zima. You understand?"

Zima's enthusiasm tempered immediately. "Yes, of course."

What is there to understand? The only thing I know is that I've lost two friends. But I didn't really lose them, did I? They were stolen from me. Murdered!

"The investigators assigned to these two cases have come across some evidence showing that the terrorists behind the attacks had outside help," the commissioner continued.

"That was to be expected," Zima said.

"Yes. But we never thought it would come from an allied country," Green interjected.

"We're not sure about that yet, sir," the commissioner said, turning toward the minister. "That's why Zima's here."

Zima was intrigued. *An allied country?* "You think France was involved in the bombings?"

"Not France per se, but maybe someone at the highest level of their national police force," continued the commissioner.

Zima was shocked. It was difficult to believe that someone who had reached the upper echelon of the country's police force would commit such an act of treason. "How did the investigators come up with this information?"

"They found a cell phone on Asad Wafid. We believe he was the man in charge of the sleeper cell," the commissioner explained. He walked to his desk, grabbed an eight-by-ten picture of Wafid, and showed it to Zima.

Zima remembered the face well. He was the guy who'd injured Mike Powell. "I believe that as well. When the investigators interviewed me following the shooting, I mentioned the same thing to them."

The commissioner sat back in his chair and poured himself a fresh cup of coffee. "The information we were able to retrieve from his cell phone was fascinating, to say the least."

"What did it consist of?" Zima asked.

"It contained encrypted data that, once cracked and analyzed, provided us with the specific coordinates of the Irving Oil Refinery."

"The one in Saint John, New Brunswick?" Zima was mystified. *What does that have to do with anything?*

"That's correct," the energy minister answered. "It produces over three hundred thousand barrels a day. Needless to say, Canada would suffer a disastrous long-term economic impact if it were to be shut down. The effects would be even more catastrophic than the minicrash we experienced worldwide following the bombings. "

"What's the connection to France?"

"That's where it gets tricky, Zima," said the commissioner. "The French gendarmerie's second-in-command is a general named Richard Claudel. Among other duties, he oversees the physical security of all energy-producing facilities, be it oil and gas or nuclear. He's well liked among the troops and seems to be above reproach. However, his name came up in a note found in another encrypted file on Wafid's phone."

"Could it be another Richard Claudel?" Zima asked.

"I doubt it," the minister said. "I should add that I've met General Claudel a few times in the last few months, mostly during oil and gas conferences, and I didn't like him. He seemed too nosy about very specific details regarding the Irving Oil Refinery. Following protocols in place, I spoke to the commissioner about my doubts toward Claudel."

"So when I read the investigators' report, I called the minister, and we put two and two together."

That's big, thought Zima. "So you want me to spy on Claudel and find out if he's dirty?"

The commissioner nodded. "Exactly. Your mission will be to collect as much information on General Claudel as possible. He travels a lot, but I believe that with the help of the support network CSIS already has in place, you'll be able to gather all the evidence needed for us to evaluate his allegiances."

A few minutes later, with her marching orders in hand, Zima shook both men's hands and exited the commissioner's office. His aide was waiting for her in the hallway. He escorted her to the elevator, where he pressed the *down* button.

"Here," he said, giving her a piece of paper on which a phone number was written. "It's the commissioner's direct line."

She put the paper in her left jeans pocket. "Thanks."

I'm back into the action, just like that, she thought. *I couldn't have hoped for a better project. Or a more dangerous one.*

CHAPTER 13

Johns Hopkins Hospital
Baltimore, Maryland

The man Mike recognized from the day before made his entrance. Dressed in a black Brooks Brothers suit, a crisp white shirt, and a two-tone red tie, he looked like a stereotypical Zurich banker. His deeply tanned skin was in sharp contrast to his full head of silver hair, stylishly combed back.

"Charles," Lisa said, smiling.

"Hello, Dr. Walton. How have you been?"

"He doesn't know about the new last name yet. I didn't have time to cover everything with him," Lisa said, looking at her husband.

"That's not a problem, Doctor. I know you two had lots to talk about. But let's get on with it now, shall we?"

Mapother approached Mike and extended his hand. His grip was strong and sincere. "Good morning, Mike. It's nice to see you sitting up and looking well. I'm Charles Mapother."

Mike stared at him, saying nothing.

"And they swept this room?" Mapother asked Lisa.

"Yes. A team came in before we got here, and it was clean. The regular sweeps of Mike's room haven't turned anything up either, but I thought it would be best if we held this little get-together in a soundproof room. We're actually in one of the psychiatric examination rooms."

"Good thinking," Mapother answered, sitting down in the chair facing Mike.

For the first time, Mike noticed the acoustic baffles on the ceiling. *They're probably in the walls too,* Mike thought. *Somebody better tell me what the hell is going on here soon.*

Mapother unbuttoned his suit jacket and crossed his legs. "I'm sorry I couldn't answer your questions yesterday, Mike. I thought it would be best to wait until your wife arrived."

Mike looked at Lisa, and she nodded.

Mapother reached for the briefcase he had placed next to his chair and positioned his thumb over an optical reader located next to the briefcase's handle. The scanner, satisfied that the incoming fingerprint matched the one in its memory, sent an electromagnetic signal to the two internal briefcase locks. Following a barely audible click, the briefcase opened, and Mapother removed a newspaper. He handed the well-thumbed issue to Mike.

"You should start by reading the article on page three. It will make you more receptive for what's coming next."

Hating the feeling of being the only one in the room who didn't know what was going on, Mike snatched the newspaper. He looked at the date, then opened the newspaper to the advised page. His eye was immediately caught by the eighteen-point headline about him, and he started reading.

> Sergeant Mike Powell of the Royal Canadian Mounted Police succumbed to multiple injuries yesterday at The Ottawa Hospital. Sgt. Powell, the Mountie who single-handedly killed three of the terrorists involved in the attack to the Ottawa International Airport, was fatally wounded during the ensuing firefight.

> In one of the National Capital Region's saddest stories in memory, Powell's pregnant wife, Dr. Lisa Harrison Powell, and their twenty-two-month-old daughter were killed at the Ottawa Via Rail train station the same morning when two suicide bombers detonated their explosive vests. The attack at the train station also claimed the lives of...

Mike raised his tearing eyes and searched Lisa's face. Her smile, encouraging and compassionate, reminded him he wasn't the only one feeling the pain. They thought she was dead, too? How could this be? He scanned down to the end of the article.

> At the request of the family, there will be no service or visitation. Donations in memory of Sgt. and Dr. Powell can be made to the Children's Hospital of Eastern Ontario Foundation...

Mike slowly closed the newspaper and handed it back to Mapother. *So that's what he meant yesterday when he said I had died.*

"All right, you've got me curious, Mapother. And you were right to wait until my wife arrived to show me this. Otherwise, I might have thought you were a fraud—and to be blunt, I'm still not convinced that you aren't."

Mapother smiled. "I assure you I'm not. Isn't that so, Dr. Walton?"

"Why do you keep calling my wife Walton?"

"Walton is my new name, Mike," Lisa answered. "From now on, you'll have to learn to call me Lisa Walton. Same goes for me—I'll learn to call you Mike Walton. And, to set the record straight, Charles isn't a fraud."

That's why the nurse called me Mr. Walton, Mike realized. The change was already in effect. "Why the name changes?" Mike asked. He wasn't angry; he was just trying to understand.

"I'll get to that soon enough," Mapother promised.

"Okay. Please continue," Mike said. What else could he say?

"After 9/11, the president decided to invade Afghanistan because that was where al-Qa'ida was hiding," Mapother said. "Our armed forces destroyed their training camps, smashed the Taliban's army, and put a new government in place. Did that stop al-Qa'ida? Did it slow the growth of homegrown terrorists? Or the creation of ISIS, for that matter?"

Mike wasn't sure if Mapother was asking rhetorical questions or not. He decided to answer anyway. "It put a dent in their ranks, that's for sure. But it certainly didn't stop them and probably sped up the process of radicalizing young Muslims at home."

Mapother nodded. "You see, Mike, the US military is the most powerful armed force in the world. It's great at protecting our interests abroad in a sort of wide strokes approach, but it doesn't have surgical-precision capabilities."

Seeing that Mike was about to interject, Mapother held up his hand and pushed on. "Of course, there are some highly skilled units, like the Army Special Forces, the Navy SEAL teams, and the Marine Force Recon, and don't get me wrong—they all do an excellent job. But they're still operating under the umbrella of the US Armed Forces. They have to obey the rules, and they're held accountable for their actions because American taxpayers pay for it all."

"But the SEALs did take out Bin Laden, and they did a pretty good job at it," Mike cut in.

"Yes, but what if I told you they'd known where he was for nearly fourteen months before the actual raid took place?"

Mike didn't know what to think. Mapother continued, "They couldn't get political approval to act on it. In the meantime, civilians all over the world lost their lives in terror attacks that he planned from his hideout in Pakistan. Same logic goes for the CIA, the NSA, the FBI, and all the other agencies. Congress and the Senate oversight committees are restricting their capabilities so much that they can't do the job."

"And in your opinion, Mapother, what exactly needs to be done?" Mike asked sarcastically.

Mapother didn't take the bait. "Well, off the top of my head, I'd say stopping a twenty-million-dollar cash transaction about to go down in Zurich between a Soviet banker and the chief financial officer of Hamas in, oh, I don't know"—Mapother looked down at his expensive Swiss watch—"forty minutes."

Mike raised his eyebrows. Was this for real, or was Mapother being dramatic?

Mapother continued, "Let's just say that we know half the money is going to be used to finance Hamas' combat operations in Gaza, but we have absolutely no idea what the additional ten million is for. What would you do?"

Mike thought for a moment before answering. "Well, it depends on what type of resources I had available. But I guess I'd try to stop the transaction."

"As you know, cash transactions are extremely hard to stop via official channels," answered Mapother calmly.

Mike could tell that the older man was enjoying every moment of this. "We certainly can't start *unofficially* bombing Switzerland."

"We certainly can't," Mapother said with a chuckle. "What if I told you that IMSI is a real eighteen-month-old company doing real foreign-market analysis for nine of the biggest corporations in the United States? You can find the company and its New York headquarters telephone number in the Yellow Pages," he said, "although we're not able to take on any new clients at the moment."

"Too busy with a little side project in Switzerland, perhaps?" Mike asked as the meaning of Mapother's words dawned on him.

This time it was Lisa who answered. "That's right, Mike. That project will bring terror to the terrorists. And we need your help. *I* need your help."

CHAPTER 14

Sierra Leone, Africa

The predominantly Muslim Pujehun District, one of the twelve administrative divisions of Sierra Leone, borders the Atlantic Ocean to the southwest and Liberia to the southeast. Prior to the civil war that raged in Sierra Leone from 1991 to 2002, the Pujehun District had huge potential for the two hundred and thirty thousand people who lived within its borders. Mining, agriculture, and fisheries had promised job opportunities and steady incomes, but the civil war had ruined it all.

The war, initiated by the Revolutionary United Front with the help of the National Patriotic Front of Liberia, killed tens of thousands of civilians and created more than two million refugees—all for the primary objective of controlling the diamond mines.[3] The RUF was merciless and didn't hesitate to hack off the arms and legs of villagers to make sure that they wouldn't join opposing forces. Recruitment of child soldiers was also common practice in the villages. Even though United Nations forces finally defeated the RUF, many senior RUF officers went unpunished and found great fortune in the diamond mines.

One of these ex-officers, Major Jackson Taylor, was seated in a wooden chair facing one of his team leaders. His men had just returned from an operation in Conakry, the capital city of Guinea.

"Have you personally checked all the explosives?" asked Taylor

"Yes. All of them."

"Good. That means if they failed to detonate, I'll be blaming you," Taylor said, poking his finger at the man's chest.

The team leader swallowed hard but nodded nonetheless.

"Give me the cell phone," Taylor told him. The man placed an old Motorola in Taylor's waiting hand. "You're dismissed," Taylor barked and watched his subordinate leave the hut without looking back.

Taylor examined the cell phone and glanced at the Sheik's representative, Dr. Ahmed Khaled.

"If my men did their job correctly, the Conakry Grand Mosque will crumble."

Dr. Khaled laughed out loud. "So, that means if the mosque doesn't collapse, I'll be blaming you?"

Taylor didn't respond directly. "Why does the Sheik want to bring down the Conakry Grand Mosque?"

Khaled's grin died away. "Who are you to challenge his will? You'll do as you're told."

Taylor briefly wondered if he should break the doctor's neck. *It would be so easy,* Taylor thought. He was tired of Khaled's condescending tone. While the Saudi Arabian doctor was short and fat with a long, unkempt black beard, Taylor was huge, strong, and in his physical prime. The scar from his chin to the middle of his forehead, courtesy of a British U.N. soldier's knife, reminded everyone how ruthless he was. Taylor didn't give much thought to the scar except to reminisce about the revenge he'd doled out for it. After he had wrestled the knife away from the British paratrooper, he'd turned it against its owner and plunged it deeply into the Brit's abdomen. But instead of ending the paratrooper's agonizing suffering with a merciful slash to the throat, Taylor had let him suffer for nearly two days until he died of thirst and blood loss.

Thinking about all the agony the Brit had endured before being allowed to die calmed Taylor down. He smiled at Khaled. "Of course, Doctor. I'll do whatever the Sheik requires of me."

Khaled appeared satisfied with the answer. "What about the other undertaking we talked about last week?"

"It will take a few months to mount the operation...and it will be expensive," said Taylor.

"We know it will be expensive, but we're confident that three million dollars will suffice. As for the time line, the Sheik wants this done before the end of August."

Taylor didn't like to be told what to do. He didn't like rules. But he loved money, and the job the Sheik was proposing promised lots of it—half a million American dollars, to be exact.

—

Taylor's first contact with the Sheik's organization had taken place in 2001 while he was fighting the British for control of a diamond mine.

He'd been desperate to buy weapons powerful enough to resist the well-equipped British Army. Machine guns, grenades, and antipersonnel mines were easily obtained, but what he'd really wanted were some surface-to-air missiles so he could take down the British helicopters. They had massacred his troops with their 20mm cannons and miniguns mounted on external pylons.

He didn't care much about his troops, mostly children between the ages of eight to fifteen, but he didn't want to lose the mine. His adjutant officer—the tall, lean, devout Mohammad Alavi, who always prayed the required five times a day—had mentioned that he might be able to tap someone who could help Taylor make his wish come true. If he could have a short leave from his training duties, Alavi had said, he'd try to make contact with this source on the major's behalf.

To Taylor's surprise, Alavi didn't desert but returned to the training camp a week later. Accompanying him was a young but tall and ruthless-looking man who never gave out his real name. The newcomer looked like he was of Arabic origin, but his piercing blue eyes and light skin tone indicated that one of his parents might have been Caucasian. The man said that he represented the Sheik, an insurgent who was sympathetic to the major's cause. He was willing to help and wanted nothing in return—except maybe a favor in the years to come. Taylor, knowing that the British would attack again soon, accepted the offer.

Even though Alavi had left the country with the Sheik's emissary, the organization that the mysterious man worked for had kept its part of the deal and sent, less than a week later, five Russian 9K32 Strela-2s—a man-portable, shoulder-fired, surface-to-air missile made to destroy low-flying, fixed, and rotary-winged aircraft. As a most appreciated bonus, the Sheik's representative had also dispatched a ten-man detachment to operate the missiles under Taylor's orders.

Years later, with the fortune he had made through the legal and illegal trading of diamonds, Taylor had built a five-hundred-man-strong rebel force that he used for his own personal protection against rival warlords. In the eastern provinces of Sierra Leone, Taylor's organization was a force to be reckoned with—especially since he'd continually strengthened his association with the Sheik, who'd himself become more influential.

The association had been fruitful for the terrorist group as well. Following the extensive pressure the US put on international banks to declare any suspicious transactions, terrorist organizations all over had found themselves strapped for cash. Mohammad Alavi, cousin of the Sheik's health adviser, Dr. Ahmed Khaled, had passed along an idea that was the solution they had been looking for. He suggested that they could use the illegal diamond trade to finance their activities. He explained that through contacts he had maintained, he had kept an eye on an ex-RUF officer who still owed a debt to the organization—a Major Jackson Taylor.

The business plan was simple. The Sheik's terror network would buy Major Taylor's diamonds with cash at a quarter of their market value, then sell them on the black market for half or three-quarters of their value, depending on market conditions. The Sheik had been thrilled with this idea and had sent Dr. Khaled and Mohammad Alavi to discuss the feasibility of the plan with Taylor.

—

"The end of August will be fine," Taylor finally said, wiping perspiration from his forehead with a white linen cloth. Even though they were shaded from the sun, the temperature inside the hut was close to 110 degrees.

"Good. The Sheik will be pleased," answered Dr. Khaled, baring his yellow teeth. "This blow will annihilate France's tourism industry for a very long time."

The sound of a helicopter approaching could be heard across the valley.

"My ride home is here, I gather," said the Sheik's doctor and emissary. He was about to get up but suddenly remembered something else he wanted to say. He settled his large frame back in the wooden chair, which creaked loudly under his weight. "There is another matter we need to discuss, Major."

"I thought everything was clear," countered Taylor, getting up to watch the helicopter approaching the landing pad. The brown Russian-built MI-8 helicopter with United Nations markings was now in its final approach. Its massive bulk teetered precariously in the air.

The noise created by the twin-turbo shaft engines was so overwhelming that Dr. Khaled had to wait for it to subside before continuing. "Yes, most of it," he said carefully. "I only wish to add that by the Sheik's generosity, he'll kindly send you his most trusted lieutenant to help you accomplish your task."

That did not sit well with Taylor at all. "I appreciate the Sheik's kindness, but I don't need anyone watching over my shoulder. Haven't I already proven myself on numerous occasions?" he said, his short temper rising.

"Of course you have, my good friend. Of course you have. Who told you he was here to supervise you? The Sheik has great confidence in your abilities, hence all the responsibilities he's entrusted you with. His lieutenant will be here to assist you as you please."

This qualification placated the major. "What's his name? Have I ever worked with him?"

"You've never worked directly with him before, but you have met him once, a few years ago," said Dr. Khaled with a devilish smile. "He used to be our contact in Africa while he was still serving his country's army."

Taylor frowned, trying to jog his memory.

"His name is Omar Al-Nashwan, and he's now the Sheik's right-hand man."

Major Jackson Taylor, merciless ex-RUF officer, torturer of children, and killer of men, took an involuntary step back. For the first time in his life, Taylor was genuinely afraid. Khaled approached him and placed a hand on Taylor's shoulder.

"Don't worry," he continued, "as long as you follow the Sheik's guidelines, everything will be fine."

Taylor had heard the stories of how cruel and fearless Al-Nashwan was. "I understand," he said, beaten.

"On a more joyful note," said Khaled, "why don't you give me the cell phone your man brought back from Conakry?"

Taylor cocked his head. He couldn't understand the logic behind obliterating Africa's fourth largest mosque—not that he was a believer; he couldn't care less about religion. He just didn't want to end up on the wrong side of some Muslim fanatics. Khaled, sensing Taylor's hesitation, exhaled loudly before explaining.

"Taylor, with the destruction of the Conakry mosque and a few well-placed pieces of disinformation blaming Christian extremists, Muslims all over West Africa will be lining up to join us. Now give me the phone and the number."

Taylor did. Dr. Khaled composed the number activating the explosive charges his men had strategically placed inside the mosque. Once he was done dialing, the Sheik's representative pressed the *send* button.

Anyone inside Taylor's camp expecting to hear the tremendous explosion, plus the screams coming from the injured and dying, that shook the entire city of Conakry, would have been disappointed. Conakry was located two hundred kilometers away.

"It shouldn't take long to see if you were successful, Major," said Khaled.

"You have someone in Conakry?" asked Taylor, surprised anyone would be crazy enough to stay close by.

"We have many people dedicated to the Sheik, Major. You should know that by now," answered Khaled, reaching for the cell phone vibrating in his pocket. He opened the phone and looked at the display. The numbers told him all he needed to know.

"Congratulations, Major. The Sheik will be pleased."

CHAPTER 15

Brooklyn, New York

W hat do you think about this one, honey?" Lisa asked her husband about the Brooklyn penthouse they had just visited.

"I kind of like it," Mike answered. "More than the other four, to be honest. Great location, better views, and bigger shower. What's not to like?"

"It's much nicer than the apartment we're in now. That's for sure."

"It isn't difficult to beat, Lisa."

Lisa reached for his hands and squeezed. "It's also much more expensive," she said while pressing down the button to call the elevator. She heard Mike sigh.

"Yeah, I figure."

"But we'll save on gym membership fees," she added entering the elevator. "Let's buy it."

"Just like that?"

"Why not, Mike? We can afford it. You've said so yourself, the location's perfect."

"All right."

Lisa's eyes opened wide. *What? He said yes? I expected I'd have to fight much harder to get him to acquiesce.*

"Really?" she said, tears welling up in her eyes.

My God! Stop crying, Lisa! Get ahold of yourself.

"Yes, honey. Really," her husband replied.

Lisa felt his arms around her. It had been two weeks since his release from the hospital. It was nice to have him back. The scent of his aftershave found its way to her nostrils and filled her head with sweet memories. For a moment she allowed herself to savor the comfort her husband's strength provided, knowing all too well the dark clouds were coming. They always did. They didn't give her any respite. Ever.

"You're okay, Lisa?" Mike inquired.

"Don't fight the memories, Lisa, good or bad," her psychologist had said. "Let them come to you. Embrace them. If you push them away, they'll come back as nightmares."

Allowing her tears to run freely, she looked at her husband, his face mere inches from hers. His eyes were dry.

As usual.

What did I expect? The psychologist had explained that it shouldn't upset her if her husband didn't cry. Everybody has to deal with loss in his or her own way. None was better than the other. But Lisa couldn't care less what the psychologist said.

It bothers me! He always looks at me with the same stony stare. As if I was the one not dealing with it properly!

"No. I'm not okay, Mike," she said escaping from his arms and exiting the elevator. "I miss them."

"I do too, honey," Mike replied. He stepped out of the elevator and hastened his pace to catch Lisa, who was already midway through the expansive lobby.

She stopped to face him. "Who would know?"

She saw the pain her words caused him. For a fraction of a second, she had seen through his mask. *Why do I get so much satisfaction out of it?*

"You aren't being fair, Lisa," Mike said, placing two hands on top of her shoulders. "I'd give anything to see Melissa again, to hold her in my arms and tell her how much I love her, and how lucky I am to have her in my life."

"What about Chloe, Mike? What about her?" Lisa said, jabbing her finger into his chest. "You already forgot about the little girl I carried for nine months? Is that so?"

Mike caught her hand and placed it on his heart.

"I'll never forget Melissa. And I'll never forget Chloe either, Lisa," Mike whispered. She could feel the warmth of his breath as he spoke in her ear. "As long as my heart's beating, I'll remember."

She tried to push away, but he was holding her tight against him. His right hand was gently stroking her neck. "I'm sorry if I said or did something I shouldn't have. I didn't mean to upset you. I love you, Lisa Harrison Powell."

"You can't call me that anymore," she hissed. *How dare he brake protocol!*

"That's why I whispered it in your ear, honey. Nobody's listening."

She was about to reply when her cell phone rang. Mike let her go, and she plunged her hand in her coat pocket to retrieve her phone. The display indicated the call was from IMSI.

"It's the office. I'll be a minute," she said. She waited until she was out of earshot and out of the lobby before taking the call.

"This is Lisa Walton," she said.

"It's Charles Mapother, Lisa. There's something I need to show you. Can you come to the office?"

Lisa looked at her watch.

"I can be there in half an hour."

"Fine. See you then," Mapother said before she heard him sever the connection.

What's so important on a Saturday? That was a rhetorical question. She knew that world events didn't stop because it was the weekend. What would she say to Mike?

I don't need to say anything. He's a big boy.

She didn't like where their relationship was going. She had been lost without him while he was recovering at the hospital. But something had changed. She didn't recognize the loving husband and father he had been prior to that tragic day anymore.

Or am I the one who changed? Maybe we both did.

These were questions best answered later. Now she had to go to IMSI headquarters, her boss wanted to show her something.

—

Mike watched the love of his life climb into a taxi.

Why is she acting this way? That's not her. Is it because of her job at IMSI?

Since his release from the hospital, he had moved in with her in the apartment she rented close to IMSI headquarters. It wasn't much, but it was enough. He had started to exercise again, and his strength was slowly coming back. He hadn't spoken to Mapother since their last meeting at the hospital, and Lisa categorically refused to discuss anything related to her work with IMSI. He'd asked her to tell Mapother he wanted to talk with him, but he never called Mike.

It crossed his mind that she might not be relaying his messages. Why wouldn't Mapother want to speak with him? He's the one who approached us. He would speak to Lisa again tonight about this.

He didn't know much about IMSI—yet. With the info he had gathered, he couldn't understand what Lisa was doing for them.

She's a physician, for God's sake! Not an operator.

"Mr. Walton?"

Mike turned toward the lobby entrance where a man wearing a lavish suit was standing. "Yes?"

"I'm Timothy Rothwell, the real estate agent," the man said. He approached Mike, and the two men shook hands.

"Nice to meet you, Mr. Walton."

"Likewise."

"Will your wife be joining us for the visit?" Rothwell said with a salesman's smile.

How can someone have teeth so damn white?

"We already visited the penthouse, Mr. Rothwell. You were supposed to be here at noon."

The smile vanished. *Afraid of losing your commission, aren't you?*

"I was busy with another client."

"You should have called," Mike replied as he started walking toward the exit. "Be on time next time." Mike heard the agent hurrying after him.

"But who let you in?"

"The owner's agent was there. He showed us around."

The agent caught up with him. "He should have waited for me."

"No, Tim. You should have been on time," Mike said pushing through the revolving door.

"I have other properties to show you, Mr. Walton. Much better suited for you than this one, I assure you," Rothwell said, hustling down the stairs leading to the sidewalk.

"That won't be necessary, Tim," Mike replied. "We're buying this one."

The smile reappeared.

"Through the owner's agent, of course," concluded Mike before hailing a taxi.

CHAPTER 16

IMSI Headquarters
New York

Charles Mapother's door was open. Lisa knocked twice nonetheless.

"I'm here, sir," she said, stepping in.

Mapother raised his eyes from whatever he was reading. "Thanks for coming," he said. "Far from me to want to take you away from your husband on a Saturday, Lisa," he started, "but this couldn't wait."

He grabbed a brown envelope from his desk and signaled her to approach. "This is for you," Mapother said. "You better sit down."

Lisa's heart started to pound in her chest. *What now?* Since she joined IMSI, she'd been dealing mostly with Mapother. She'd met a few others, but not many. He'd tasked her to plan a lecture on emergency medicine. When she'd asked him who the audience would be, he told her to prepare something similar to what she would do for soldiers deploying in a combat zone. Another day or two and she'd be done with her first assignment. She wondered what he would have her do next. When Jonathan Sanchez had brought her in for the first time, Mapother had sworn she would play an important part in the counter-strike against the people responsible for the Ottawa bombings.

Is this it? In this envelope?

She sat down in one of the two armchairs facing Mapother's desk. She opened the envelope and peeked inside. *A photograph?* She pinched the picture between her thumb and index finger and took it out.

She gasped. *Oh, my God! Is this for real?*

Mapother might have been reading her mind. "Our specialist confirmed its authenticity. If you look carefully, you'll see for yourself."

Lisa scrutinized the picture and accepted the magnifying glass Mapother pushed her way. A cold chill crept up her spine as her eyes met those of a terrified Ambassador Ray Powell. Mike's dad was tied naked to a cross, his body bloodied from a multitude of cuts on his torso. He appeared to be crying, but Lisa couldn't be sure because his features were distorted. Next to him, a man was standing holding a newspaper. Only his piercing blue eyes were visible because a balaclava covered the rest of his face. Lisa focused on the newspaper.

"Do you see it?" asked Mapother.

Lisa slumped back in her chair. "Yes, I saw the date. That's the same newspaper edition you showed Mike at the hospital, isn't it?"

"It is."

"That's why he looks so sad. I wasn't sure if he was crying out of pain or out of sadness."

"Or out of anger," added Mapother. "They told him about the death of the rest of his family."

This time it wasn't grief that overtook Lisa's mind and body; it was rage. She could feel her blood boiling, ready to erupt. She wanted to kill them all! These goddamn cowards who enjoyed killing little girls. She wouldn't rest until they were all dead.

"Can I show this picture to my husband?" she asked once she had regained control of her emotions.

"If you think he's ready."

Lisa nodded. "What are we gonna do about this situation? We need to find him!"

"I like how you used *we*, Lisa," Mapother said. "Do you feel you're part of the team?"

Lisa wasn't sure. Was preparing an emergency medicine lecture helping to take down the bastards who killed her daughters? "Not totally, yet," she said. "I want to do more."

"You will, Lisa. I promise. All in due time."

Lisa decided Mapother was being honest. He's the one who'd recruited her, right? Maybe he did have a more important role for her to play. She had her own personal life to put back in order. Her relationship with Mike was deteriorating. That was a fact.

If he could only open up and stop acting like an automaton. Is it too much to ask?

Mapother's voice brought her back to reality. "You heard me, Lisa?"

"Yes, of course I did."

"Something's bothering you?" Mapother asked.

The man is clever. He knows something isn't right with me. But this is not the place or the moment to talk about my personal problems.

"The photo is, Charles," she replied with her finger pointing at the picture on Mapother's desk. "Ray is a good man. He doesn't deserve this."

"I've never met the man," Mapother said, "but I heard he's very good at what he does."

"Yeah, he is," Lisa said, thinking about what a jovial human being Mike's father was. Always smiling, congratulating others for their accomplishments while diminishing his own. She continued, "It didn't matter if we were at a backyard barbecue or at a black-tie dinner. Ray, for as long as I can remember, was always the center of attention. People wanted to be close to him, to be associated with him in any way they could. He was just that kind of person."

"He still is," Mapother said.

"But for how long?"

CHAPTER 17

Brooklyn, New York

The steady rhythm of his running shoes impacting the gravel path brought a satisfied smile to Mike's sweaty face.

The penthouse had been a good purchase. It's close to the running paths, and there are enough trees around to forget I'm only ten minutes away from Manhattan.

He'd been out of the hospital for four weeks and in the new condo for ten days. To please the seller, who had accepted a job in Los Angeles, they had closed the deal rapidly. In return for a fast transaction, the seller had agreed to leave all the furniture behind. That had made Lisa very happy because everything was new and modern. Mike wondered if anyone had ever sat on the sofa. Without many personal possessions, it took only a few hours for him and Lisa to feel right at home.

As he pushed his legs to go faster, Mike realized how good he felt. Truth be told, he never thought that he could get back into shape so rapidly. His previous strength was gradually returning, and every week he was able to train with heavier weights. The results were impressive, and the doctors following his progress were astonished.

Mike was now reaching the halfway mark of his four-mile route. He was surprised by how quickly New York had come to feel like home to him. Born in Florida while his father was serving as a liaison officer for the RCMP, Mike had enjoyed the many benefits of dual citizenship and had traveled extensively in the United States for business and pleasure. He loved the anonymity that a big American city provided. And, he reasoned darkly, since he didn't have any blood relatives left, with the exception of his kidnapped father, anywhere on earth could feel like home.

As he rounded the northern end of Cadman Plaza Park, he checked his watch and was pleased to see that he had run the first three kilometers in less than thirteen minutes.

He went down on all fours to do his regular routine of midrun push-ups.

As he completed his seventieth, he heard a voice over him. "I'm glad to see that your fitness level is returning to normal."

Mike angled his head and saw Charles Mapother not five feet away from him, sitting on a park bench. He was dressed in a black Under Armour running outfit and white running shoes.

"Good morning, Charles," said Mike, hopping to his feet. "How did you know where to find me? I guess I'm pretty predictable, huh?"

That made Mapother smile. "Would it be all right if I joined you for the remainder of your circuit?"

"Sure," answered Mike. In fact, he'd been wondering for the last few weeks when the director of IMSI would make contact with him again.

"But you'll have to slow down to allow an old dog like me to keep up."

Mike made a mock groan as they started along the gravel path. As they ran, Mike noticed it was the older man who was doing most of the talking, yet he wasn't breathing hard at all. Seventeen minutes later, when they arrived in front of Mike's condominium, Mapother had still barely broken a sweat.

"Not bad for an old dog," Mike joked.

Mapother smiled modestly and looked off to the horizon. "So Mike, did you think about my offer?"

There it is.

"I did."

"Have you decided whether or not you want to work with us?"

Good question, Mike thought as he stretched out his limbs. He had talked a lot with his wife about the events that had robbed them of their children and parents two months ago. Each conversation had only fortified their desire for justice. And IMSI was one way to fulfill that desire.

Especially after what they did to my father.

Lisa was already working at IMSI headquarters doing "administrative duties," but she never discussed them with her husband. Not that he wasn't curious, but each time he asked, his wife would gently smile and tell him that she couldn't betray Mapother's confidentiality.

Of course Mike respected that—but still, he wondered about what she was doing every day when she left their new Brooklyn penthouse.

"It's certainly tempting, Charles. You played your cards well," Mike said. "How could I say no after viewing the despicable picture of my father you showed Lisa and me?"

"I really want you on our team, Mike."

"But don't you think it would be better if I knew exactly what I would be signing up for before giving you my answer?"

"I guess you're right," Mapother said after a moment of reflection.

"Why don't you join us for lunch? I'll grill some chicken breasts and sausages," Mike offered.

Mapother looked at his watch. "I can do that. Around noon?"

"Sounds good to me. Do you need a ride back?"

"No, thank you. My car will be here shortly."

As if on cue, a black late-model Jaguar XJ with heavily tinted windows pulled up next to them.

"See you later," Mapother said before getting in the backseat.

—

Mike spent an hour on the Internet reading the numerous newspapers he followed daily. The news was once again depressing. There was a minor bombing in Rome. Berlin's subway had ground to a halt because of rail sabotage. In Paris, two Islamic gunmen had opened fire on a group of tourists. Every day terrorists were making the front pages. People were scared. That much was evident. Businesses working with small profit margins were closing their doors. Even here, in New York, Mike had seen many business owners barricading their windows. And they weren't the only ones doing so. To Mike's surprise, he had also observed a few Starbucks stores with their doors locked during his morning run. *God knows the economy is going to shit when a staple like Starbucks closes shop.*

Frustrated, he got up from the kitchen table and headed toward the bedrooms. Lisa had turned one of the three bedrooms into a large office and another into a home gym. Even though they hadn't talked about it specifically, the meaning of this particular setup was pretty clear to him. There wouldn't be another child. At least not while they were living in this penthouse.

When Mike entered the gym room, he found Lisa running hard on the treadmill. Mike approached her from behind and looked at the LCD display on the machine.

Five kilometers in twenty minutes?

Lisa, still unaware that her husband was right behind her, pressed the accelerator key until she reached a speed of eighteen kilometers per hour.

That's faster than most ERT guys can run, thought Mike, impressed.

Finally, after two minutes, his wife pressed the decelerator arrow and settled in for a slow jog.

"Lisa?"

"Hey!" she answered between hard breaths. She pressed the *stop* key, and the treadmill slowly came to a halt.

"I didn't know you were that fast," he said, circling her small waist with his arms. "I'm glad I scooped you up when I did all those years ago, or else I'd never have been able to catch you." He picked her up in his arms, and she squealed, playfully punching him in the shoulder.

"Let me down!" she yelled, but Mike knew she loved every moment of it. It felt good to hold her in his arms. His wife had remained distant, even cold, with him since the tragedy. After giving her a peck on the cheek, he gently placed her feet back on the ground in front of the big floor-to-ceiling window overlooking the East River.

"By the way, did you know that I met Charles Mapother on my way back from my run?" he asked her.

Lisa turned around and looked at her husband. The playfulness had left her eyes. "Why would I know that?"

"Come on, Lisa. You've been working for him for a while now. How else would he know that I was ready to talk to him about IMSI?"

He never saw it coming. It was so sudden. She slapped him on the cheek so hard he took an involuntary step back. *What the hell?*

"Don't you trust me anymore? You think I'm keeping tabs on you?" she asked with barely controlled rage. She closed the distance between them, her fists closed.

Mike was at loss. He'd been walking on eggshells since he'd left the hospital. Following their psychologist's suggestion, he'd consulted a book that said someone's personality could change drastically after the loss of a child. No one reacted the same way following a profound personal tragedy. He understood that. But he never thought his wife would strike him.

Mike took a few steps back and raised his hands in surrender. "Let's talk about this, Lisa. Let's all calm down for a second," he offered with a weak smile that looked more like a sneer his cheek hurt so much.

"You want me to calm down?" she hissed. "You're the one who thinks I'm spying on you."

"I'm sorry. That wasn't my intention," Mike apologized. A little voice in his head was telling him that the best way to defuse the situation was to look remorseful.

"Bullshit! You don't trust me because I wasn't able to protect your children. Do you really think I don't know what's going on in your head, Mike?"

"If you really knew, you wouldn't talk to me like that," Mike muttered.

She responded hysterically to the tone of his voice. "Every time you look at me, I feel like a failure. Every time I look at you, I feel like a failure. Do you know what I mean? Do you really think I'm worthless?"

Mike fought to keep the tears he felt coming in check. He whispered, "No. You're the most precious person in my life, Lisa."

For a few seconds, Mike thought Lisa was about to become herself again. That thought didn't last long.

"Liar," was all she said before stalking out of the room. A few seconds later he heard the door of the penthouse slam.

Then the phone rang.

Like a robot, Mike walked to it and grabbed the receiver.

"Yes?"

"Mike, it's Charles Mapother. I'll be there in fifteen minutes, and I'm bringing someone along. You better have enough chicken and sausages to feed two hungry men."

Mike didn't respond. His mind was replaying over and over what had just happened with his wife.

"Mike? Are you still there?" Mapother asked. "I said I'm bringing someone over."

"Sorry, Charles. I have to step out. I'll call you when I get back."

—

After hanging up the phone, Mike ran to the door. There was no way he was going to give up on his marriage or let Lisa walk out of the building this way. He needed her, and he knew she needed him.

Are you sure about this, Mike? Or is it wishful thinking?

Refusing to let self-doubt slow him down, Mike willed the elevator to go faster. He was confident Lisa was in their interior parking garage. For as long as he remembered, Lisa had liked to drive when she needed a moment for herself. She'd done so more and more recently but had always come back to him. This time was different; there was a nagging feeling in his gut telling him he needed to stop Lisa from leaving.

As soon as the elevator doors opened, Mike hurried out of the vestibule. He jogged toward the two parking spots where their vehicles were located. Expecting one of them to be gone, Mike was surprised to see both SUVs at their usual places. Allowing himself to relax a little, Mike started walking while formulating what he wanted to say to his wife. As he approached the vehicle, Mike realized that the engine was running. Through the darkened windshield, he could see Lisa's silhouette slumped over the steering wheel.

Oh my God, no! Lisa! Mike's heart sank.

He ran to the driver's door and tried to open it.

Locked! Hang on, baby. Hang on!

For a second, he thought he saw Lisa move. Using his elbow, Mike hit the driver-side window, shattering it into a thousand pieces. Ignoring the pain caused by an embedded shard of glass, he was moving his hand inside the vehicle to unlock the door when he saw Lisa's head turning toward him.

"Mike! For God's sake, what are you doing?"

Mike, caught by surprise, couldn't utter a word. From her puffy eyes, tears were streaming down her cheeks. She was shaking her head at him.

"What are you doing?" she repeated.

"I thought..." he hesitated.

"What?"

"I thought you needed assistance, Lisa. I thought you needed me."

She wiped her tears with her forearm. "I came down here to think, Mike."

"I just...It's just that when I saw you with your head on the steering wheel and the engine running, you know?"

A look of disappointment washed over Lisa's face, "You thought I had killed myself?" Her voice was only a whisper.

Mike shrugged in apology. "I don't know what to think anymore, Lisa."

"You know me better than that, Mike. I'd never do such a thing. You and I might not grieve the same way, but I'm a fighter, too."

A sudden wave of nausea prevented Mike from answering. Lightheaded, he weakly walked to the rear of the vehicle, where he collapsed on his knees. Breathing hard, he heard Lisa's hurried footsteps behind him.

"Are you okay?" she asked, a hand on his shoulder.

Mike looked into his wife's eyes and saw she was genuinely worried. "I'm so sorry, honey, so sorry," he started before completely losing it. *How could I ever doubt my wife this way?* An overwhelming sadness took control over his will, and he began to cry. Memories of his daughter Melissa and his mother came rushing back to him, opening the valves he had fought so hard to keep shut. His father, tied to a cross, yelling his name over and over and images of his pregnant wife, laughing and beaming with joy cascaded in his mind. He was emotionally spiraling out of control, and he couldn't say if the guttural cry he was hearing was his or not. Despair had finally taken over.

—

Seeing her husband on his hands and knees, crying like she'd never seen him cry before, made Lisa feel powerless. And confused.

Maybe he does feel something after all? She kneeled down next to him and held him in her arms, saying nothing, hoping her presence next to him would be enough to make him understand he wasn't alone.

What happened to us? What happened to me? Lisa wondered, looking around her. *We're on our knees, in a fucking garage, crying our hearts out. That wasn't part of the plan. Shit!*

Deep down, she knew she was the one who'd pushed him over the edge. All the fights she'd picked with him, her hair-trigger temper, her rages—all had taken their toll on him she now realized.

With tears welling up in her eyes, she placed her lips to his ear and whispered, "I love you, Mike. I'm here for you as you were for me during all these months. I've let you down, I've let *us* down, but I'm back now, and I want to be close to you again. Will you let me?"

For a few seconds, Mike only appeared to cry even harder. But then, he opened his eyes and placed his right hand on top of Lisa's. "You didn't let us down, Lisa. We both drifted apart. We've been drifting for a while now. I couldn't seem to find the right words to comfort you. You were in a dark place, my love. A very, very dark place."

Removing her hand from under her husband's, she gently used both to force him to look at her. "I know, and I'm sorry," she said softly, feeling her throat tighten around each word. "For a while, I kind of felt like you didn't deserve me, Mike."

"But why?" her husband asked.

With the tip of her fingers, she wiped away the tears from his cheeks and tenderly kissed the place where they had been. "Because I had the impression that I was the one doing the suffering for both of us."

"Oh, Lisa, I'm sorry, I—"

"I know, Mike. I know now that you've been suffering too. You just never opened up to me like you're doing now...I felt so alone, but now I feel I'm the one who doesn't deserve you. I shouldn't have doubted you, my love."

"Don't say that," Mike replied in a broken voice. "I think we understand that we might not grieve the same way. And that's okay. The important thing is that we support each other, no matter what."

Lisa looked into the kind eyes of the man in front of her. She felt his warmth, and for the first time in a long while, she let her guard down and kissed him tenderly on his lips. A moment later, she heard him groan. "What's wrong?"

"Your hand," he replied.

She followed his stare. Her right hand was holding his left arm just over the elbow where a shard of glass was sticking out. "You're injured? Oh my. You did this when you broke the window." She stood up and helped her husband to his feet. "Let's go back to the condo. I'll fix you up."

—

Mike was seated on a chair facing the large bathroom's mirror. He had removed his shirt and was wearing only a pair of blue designer jeans with his brown sandals. His wife, kneeling next to him, was applying a bandage across his left bicep and triceps. She had easily removed the shard of glass that had embedded itself in his arm. To close the wound, she had sutured eight stitches.

Mike felt his wife's presence with an electric intensity. His heart, beating beyond a normal pace, was telling him he would always love this woman. Feelings that had faded since the tragedy were coming back with a vengeance.

"All right, you're good to go," Lisa said, finishing up the dressing. "We'll change it tomorrow."

Mike stretched his arm and flexed his bicep.

"Not a good idea," his wife warned him. "You should take it easy for a couple of days."

"Will do, Doc," Mike replied, smiling at his wife. "Thank you."

Lisa smiled back before adding, "Mapother did ask me a few questions about your health."

"Oh, really? What did you say?"

Lisa grinned. "That I wasn't sure yet. That I'd let him know as soon as I found out."

"I see," Mike said, teasing. He approached his wife and pressed his body against hers. "And how are you planning to find out?"

Lisa, still dressed in her Under Armour running gear, wrapped her arms around him. Her form-fitting shirt accentuated the curves Mike had always found irresistible. "Would you believe that women have a very acute sense of when their lovers are back in shape?" his wife whispered in his ear while slowly unbuttoning his jeans to reveal the rest of his muscular body.

Mike responded to her invitation by pressing his lips into the crook of her neck. Her skin, soft as silk, tasted delicately salty. Sensing Lisa's pulse accelerating, he pressed his body harder against hers. He looked at her beautiful face as he carefully traced the contour of her lips, then kissed her passionately, loving the slow sensuous dance of her tongue finding his as he reached for hers. Their kiss became more urgent, more demanding, which led them to the floor.

For the first time since the disastrous fatal day, they made love with total abandon, sometimes laughing, sometimes crying, but confident they'd never grow apart again.

CHAPTER 18

Brooklyn, New York

Four short knocks on the door jolted him out of sleep. Looking at the empty space next to him, he remembered hearing Lisa slipping out of bed. On her pillow, she had left a note written on a small piece of paper. Picking it up, Mike read:

> I didn't want to wake you. Charles Mapother called and said that because you hadn't called back, he'd be here at 1:00 p.m. He wanted me to remind you he'd be bringing someone over. I'm off to get a few things for the BBQ. Oh, and I told him you're back in shape!

Mike beamed, thinking about the magical moment he had shared with his wife. They both knew that something had changed. Their lives wouldn't be the same. But they would never be alone.

Hearing another series of knocks, Mike got out of his bed and picked up the pair of blue jeans Lisa had so eagerly removed an hour ago. To hide the bandage on his left arm, he grabbed a black long-sleeve shirt from his dresser before hurrying to the front door. Looking through the peephole, he saw Mapother standing in front of his door with another man he immediately recognized.

Jonathan Sanchez? It can't be! How long has it been? At least a decade, maybe more. The guy still looks like he's in his twenties.

Sanchez was shorter than Mike by two or three inches, but his weight was at least ten pounds more—all muscle. Though his name suggested a Hispanic heritage, with his blond hair and green eyes, Sanchez looked like an all-American boy in his white shirt and blue jeans.

Realizing he'd been standing at his peephole, Mike hurriedly opened the door to let the two men in.

"Good to see you again, Mike," said Mapother, who was about to shake hands with him when Mike and Sanchez embraced like brothers.

"How have you been, old friend?" said Mike.

"What happened to your ugly mug?"

"If you're with him, you know what happened," Mike said pointing to Mapother.

Sanchez took a step back. "Yeah, I know. One hell of a job you did there, brother."

Mike nodded his thanks. It felt good to see his friend again. Besides his wife, Sanchez was the only one still connected to his previous life.

"Sorry about your losses, though," Sanchez said.

"Me too," replied Mike grateful his friend didn't dwell on the subject.

But Jonathan wouldn't do that. He's as awkward as I am in these situations. And he's lost friends in combat before; he knows it isn't necessary to speak much.

Mapother changed the topic. "I was aware you guys knew each other. I was told you've served together. But that's all I know. Would you care to enlighten me?"

Mike and Sanchez exchanged glances.

"You want to tell him?" said Mike.

"I'll let you do it, Mike. You're the officer, after all."

Mike shook his head. "Go ahead, Joe, you've always been the better storyteller."

"Ok, then. It was in Kosovo, May 1999," Sanchez started. "Mike was there with a tiny contingent of Canadian Special Forces. Their mission was to assist us with acquiring targets of opportunity for NATO's warplanes."

"Weren't you with Delta at the time?" Mapother asked.

"I was. Mike and I worked together for weeks conducting reconnaissance patrols to pinpoint the exact locations of our targets."

"Wasn't that part of Operation Picnic?"

"That's right, Charles," Mike replied. "Picnic's objectives were to identify Serbian units' supply lines, SAM and AAA sites, while remaining undetected."

"Our team consisted of Mike, who was our CO; myself as the senior NCO; and eight other guys—two Canadians and six Americans," Sanchez continued. "Our operational task, which lasted six weeks, was to collect photographic evidence of Serbian war crimes."

"And," Mike continued, pointing to Sanchez, "he was the man who took the pictures of the mass graves that were later used in special judicial courts."

"Don't be so modest, Mike," Sanchez said. He looked at Charles Mapother before continuing. "Mike and his team are the ones who enabled us to send the intelligence we collected."

"What do you mean?"

"We were ambushed on our way to the extraction point. Two guys went down in the first few seconds, and I took a bullet in the knee," Sanchez said, lifting his cane. "Before we knew it, we were pinned down by overwhelming enemy fire."

"What happened?" Mapother inquired.

"Mike, who'd stayed behind to secure the site with the two other crazy Canucks from JTF-2, managed to outflank and kill enough of them to ensure our retreat."

"There's no mention of that in your military file," Mapother said, his eyes on Mike.

"Charles, you know how it is," Mike said, shrugging. "A lot of things don't make the files."

Suddenly aware that his guests were still standing in the entryway, Mike invited them in and offered them something to drink.

"I think a celebratory beer would be in order," Sanchez said.

"Charles? Anything?" Mike asked, already in the kitchen.

"Bottled water, if you have some," he replied.

A few seconds later, Mike approached them and handed Sanchez and Mapother two ice-cold Heinekens.

"I asked for a bottle of water, Mike, not a beer."

"Sorry, Charles. I only heard the word *bottle*," Mike answered as he sat down. "Would you like me to get up from my very comfortable chair, walk back to the kitchen, throw away an untouched beer, and grab you a warm bottle of water instead?"

"No, thanks. This will do," Mapother said, chuckling.

Mike and Sanchez clanked their bottles together, and each took a long pull of his drink.

"Listen, Mike," Sanchez said, placing his beer on the coffee table next to him. "There's something you need to know."

"That sounds official, Joe," Mike said. "Does it have something to do with the reason why you're here?"

"More or less, my friend."

"All right. I'm all ears."

"I'm the one who approached Lisa while she was at the hospital."

Mike cocked his head. "About what?"

"I asked Jonathan to go see your wife at the hospital, Mike," Mapother explained. "I wanted him to convince her to come and see me—"

"So *you* could persuade her to join your organization," finished Mike. He took another long pull of his beer. "I have no problem with that, Charles."

"You understand why I had to do this?"

"That's not difficult to understand," Mike replied. "I'm the one you wanted, and you knew the only way I'd say yes was to already have Lisa onboard."

Mapother acquiesced. "After everything that befell your family, I knew you'd stick with Lisa no matter what."

"You don't know her very well if you think she would have fought me over taking on whoever was behind the death of the rest of our family," Mike said, thinking about how fierce his wife had become.

"You're right, Mike. I wasn't sure how she would react," agreed Mapother, studying his beer's label. "But your father's still alive."

"I don't know for how long," Mike replied. "The government has been trying to locate him since his kidnapping. They don't have much to show for it."

"I know," Mapother said. "Keep the faith."

"Yeah," Mike mumbled. "Easier said then done."

The three men finished their beer in silence with Mapother typing something on his smartphone. He was the one who broke the silence. "Where's Lisa, by the way?"

"She's probably at the grocery store shopping for the barbecue," Mike said. "She should be back shortly. Why?"

Mapother looked at his phone. "We'll have to take a rain check on the barbecue, I'm afraid. I just received a message from the office. I need to get back, and I want you guys to join me. There's a lot we have to talk about."

"All right," Mike said. "Let me call Lisa. She'll join us there."

—

A black Yukon Hybrid was parked in front of Mike's condo tower. The driver—a tall, broad-shouldered black man wearing a tailored gray suit—walked around the huge vehicle to greet them. Mike remembered him as one of the two guards at the hospital.

"Good day, Mr. Walton. I'm Samuel Turner, the director's driver."
He extended his hand, and Mike shook it.

"Pleased to meet you, Sam. Call me Mike."

"Actually," Mapother cut in, "Sam is a lot more than a chauffeur.
He's my personal bodyguard, and he used to be with the FBI Hostage
Rescue Team."

Turner smiled modestly, then opened the back door for the three
men, who all climbed into the big SUV.

"Welcome to my second office," Mapother said once Turner had
closed the door behind them.

As the Yukon pulled smoothly into traffic, Mike took in his surroundings. The Yukon's rear compartment had been highly modified.
Instead of the regular second- and third-row bench seats, four leather
captain's chairs faced each other. In the center was a communications
console with two laptops on an extendable platform. Two twelve-inch
LCD screens played two different news channels.

"Control, Mobile One. We're heading to location Charlie. ETA fifteen minutes," said Turner over the SUV's communication system.

Mike looked at Mapother with raised eyebrows.

As if reading his thoughts, the IMSI director explained. "Control
is IMSI's communications center. They're on watch twenty-four hours
a day, three hundred and sixty-five days a year. They monitor all our
assets across the globe, including me. In fact, they like to know where
I am all the time."

"Where's your office located? Exactly, I mean," he asked Mapother.

"The Brooklyn Navy Yard," Sanchez said before Mapother had a
chance to reply.

They passed under the Brooklyn Bridge and made several turns
onto secondary streets before approaching a fenced area. A double
gate opened upon their approach. He hadn't seen Turner push any buttons on the front console; it most likely was activated from a remote
location. The chain-link fence was ten feet high, with barbed wire looping around its top. Beyond the gate, dozens of concrete wall panels had
been aligned on each side of the road, forcing the Yukon to follow one
preapproved route that led to a central checkpoint. The configuration
reminded Mike of several army bases he had visited.

Mapother confirmed what Mike was thinking. "Our cover is as solid
as it gets, but we can never be too careful. And for every security measure that you can see, there are another two that you can't."

They arrived at a large guard hut with a nine-foot concrete-and-
steel fence behind it. A man dressed in a nondescript security guard's

uniform walked over to the Yukon's driver-side window. Two other uniformed men, one of them with a German shepherd, circled around the Yukon.

Turner opened the window and handed his ID card to the guard. "The director is in the back with Mr. Walton and Mr. Sanchez."

"Unlock the door so we can take a look," ordered the guard.

Probably former military police, Mike thought. Suspicious eyes, square jaws, wide shoulders, and crew cuts always gave them away.

Mike heard the automatic locks pop open. The guard opened the rear door of the Yukon and stuck his head in.

"Director," the guard said simply before closing the door.

After giving the ID back to the driver, the guard went inside the hut. Moments later, the heavy steel gate slowly rose.

"Welcome to the compound, Mike," Mapother said.

Just beyond the wall was a medium-size gray concrete building that looked more like a storage facility than an intelligence headquarters. He could see no windows. An iron ladder led to the roof of the square-shaped building, where numerous antennas of different sizes were visible.

Their vehicle took a slight right, then headed downhill to an entrance marked by a large, solid garage door. "There is no other entrance but this one," Mapother said. "It opens automatically from the control room when, and only when, they receive the green light from our security people."

After the garage door opened, the Yukon continued making its way inside an underground garage. Thirty or so vehicles of all sizes were parked inside. Turner stopped the Yukon close to the only door that Mike could see. Mike opened his door and stepped out of the SUV. As he approached the steel main door, he realized that it had no handle or knob.

"You need a pass and a seven-digit code," Sanchez said, pointing to a little black electronic keypad installed on the wall. "If you're missing one or the other, you can't gain access unless you're escorted by a member of the security team."

"Got it."

"We'll set you up with everything you'll need first thing in the morning," Mapother said. "But right now let's go to the control room."

Mapother swiped his card and punched in a code. The door opened with a soft click to reveal a long hallway with white marble flooring and walls. Mapother led the way, followed by Sanchez. As he passed through the cool marble hallway, he looked for motion detectors and video cameras. Just because he didn't see any didn't mean that they weren't there.

As they proceeded down the hall, they passed many abutting hallways, each lined with a series of black doors. Mike noticed once again a lack of knobs or handles on these doors, just keypads.

Perceiving Mike's interest, Sanchez said, "Depending on each person's security clearance, they can enter certain areas while others are off-limits. Everything is monitored from a central computer, and all entries and exits are recorded."

"So we know exactly who comes in and when," Mapother added. He turned toward Mike to make his point. "All IMSI employees have been vetted by both the highest security clearance available as well as by me personally. I know every one of them. But you can never be absolutely sure of anyone, can you?"

At the end of the hallway loomed a double door made of darkly tinted glass panels. Mike and Sanchez followed behind, listening to Mapother as he continued. "Every employee knows the stakes here. Let me tell you this, Mike—we're playing a game of chess in the dark. A game of chess in the dark against a very dangerous enemy that seems to have an unlimited supply of pawns."

The control room was like nothing Mike had ever seen before. The wall opposite the door was covered entirely with flat screens projecting the latest closed-caption news from the United States and around the world. Four rows of desks were topped with state-of-the-art computers that Mike hadn't even seen on the market yet. Behind each computer screen was someone either speaking into a headset or typing on a keyboard, about twenty in all. Men and women were represented equally, and by their appearance Mike guessed that they had served in the military or law enforcement.

On the wall to Mike's right hung LCD monitors showing global maps on different scales. Over a blown up map of Zurich, Switzerland, Mike could see a large blue dot moving around.

"The blue dot is our asset," Mapother pointed out.

Mapother led them into an enclosed area at the rear of the room, overlooking the floor. "This is the bubble," he explained. "A perfectly soundproof area. And this," he added, pointing to an attractive black-haired woman in her thirties, "is Anna Caprini, my eyes and ears when I'm not here."

Anna ended the call she had just been on. "Hello, Jonathan," she said pleasantly. Sanchez reached for her hand and kissed it lightly.

"Always a true pleasure to see you," he said while Mapother rolled his eyes.

"And you must be Mike," Anna managed to say, still blushing. "Great to meet you."

The next moment she switched into business mode, focusing all her attention on Mapother. "Sir, we are receiving news from Support Four."

Mapother explained for the two newcomers. "Two gunmen entered and opened fire on students attending the Sunburst Elementary School and the North Toole County High School, both located in Sunburst, Montana. IMSI has an asset presently questioning the fanatic behind this operation. Does the name *Dr. Ahmed Khaled* ring a bell?"

"Yeah, he's the Sheik's personal physician," Sanchez answered.

"He's also handling the finances of the Sheik's terror network, if we're to believe the latest reports," Mike added.

"Let me correct you both, gentlemen," Mapother said. He had just finished reading the short transcript sent to him on his phone. "He used to be the Sheik's personal physician and financier. *Used to be* being the keywords."

"Meaning?" Sanchez pushed.

"Our asset just killed Dr. Ahmed Khaled."

Mike was dumbfounded. IMSI had killed Khaled? *What type of organization am I about to join?*

"Why not take him prisoner instead?" Sanchez asked.

Mapother turned to Anna for an explanation. "They say that our asset has successfully extracted himself from the hot zone. He was in the middle of interrogating Khaled when a member of Support Four advised him six of Khaled's associates had entered the lobby of the hotel they were in."

"Had to go," said Sanchez.

"Sure did," Mapother agreed. "Anna, I want you to work with Jonathan in collaboration with Support Four to ensure that our asset has a clean exit out of the country."

"Will do, sir."

"And let me know when the asset is ready for a debrief," concluded Mapother.

"Understood," Sanchez and Anna replied at the same time.

"In the meantime, I'll be in my office with these two," he said, pointing at Mike and Lisa, who had just entered the bubble.

CHAPTER 19

IMSI headquarters
New York

Mike and Lisa followed Mapother back out into the marble hallway. They didn't go far, though. The director's office was right beside the control room. After Mapother had swept his card and entered his code, he pushed the door open, and they followed him inside his office.

Although it was not large, Mapother's place of work felt comfortable. The walls were painted light gray, and the furniture was expensive. Along one wall was a one-way mirror showing the control room.

"Please, have a seat," invited Mapother.

Each sat in a chair facing Mapother's desk and waited for the director of the IMSI to start talking.

"I'm convinced that our best weapons against terror are the terrorists themselves," Mapother said provocatively.

Mike took the bait. "What do you mean?"

"I think that the best way we can stop Islamic terrorism from spreading is to encourage infighting among different factions and let them destroy themselves. Terrorists by nature are suspicious of one another. It doesn't take much to use their own paranoia against them. That's one of the ways IMSI comes in."

Mike was intrigued. "How exactly do you do that?"

"Sometimes we add money into an account that should be empty. Sometimes we withdraw money from an account that should have been full, always making sure that the balances are leaked to the appropriate paranoid persons. We might send a few e-mails indicating a possible breach of security within their ranks."

"So they waste time figuring out who is behind the leak or how come their financial sheets aren't balancing instead of planning future attacks," Mike finished.

"You got it."

Mike smiled as a feeling of inner calm washed over him. He hadn't felt such hope in a long while. He looked at his wife. She was smiling too.

"All right, Charles, what will be our part in all this?"

"I'm glad you asked," said Mapother. "That's the reason I wanted to speak with you two."

The IMSI director took a sip of water before continuing. "I'm sure you realize that we can't win using only delay tactics and forcing them to kill each other. At some point, we need to get our hands dirty. That's when you two will come into play."

"Details, please," Mike probed. *Does he realize Lisa isn't an operator?*

"IMSI has specially trained operators positioned strategically around the world. Their job is to kill the targets assigned to them without leaving any traces."

"How do you select these operators?" Lisa asked.

"They all have different backgrounds. However, most of them used to be in the military under the Special Operations Command. Right now we have a retired Delta, a former Ranger, two ex-Special Forces soldiers, and a bunch of former Navy SEALs—"

"Where do I fit in, Charles?" Lisa cut in, clearly exasperated. "I'm good at a lot of things, but I don't have the background Mike or these guys have."

"I agree," Mapother replied, raising his hands in mock surrender. "Let me finish, please."

"Of course. I'm sorry."

"These assets, or operators if you prefer, that we currently use work solo. They do have a support team to help them with the logistics, but when it's time to move in, they do so alone. So," continued Mapother, "understanding that Lisa's expertise isn't the same as a trained operator, I've decided that you guys will be IMSI's first two-man team. Or I should say, husband and wife team."

What? He must be kidding. Lisa will never go for this.

"You can't be serious, Charles," Mike said, looking at Lisa for support. He didn't find any. *Is she grinning?*

"I love it, Charles," Lisa said, confirming Mike's fear. "I think it's a great idea."

"I knew you would, Lisa," Mapother replied. "I told you I had something in store for you, didn't I?"

This isn't happening! Are they crazy? "No!" Mike said, standing up. "Are you out of your mind, Lisa?" He turned to Mapother. "And what about you, Mapother? You can't ask her to do this. And you know it!"

"I can, and I did," Mapother replied. "Please sit down."

Mapother waited until he did so before continuing. "I'm not an idiot, Mike. I've been in this game much longer than you. I would never send her in the field without proper training."

"Are you doubting my abilities to adapt, Mike?" Lisa asked. "I might not be able to hit a melon at twenty-five meters with a pistol, but I can fly an airplane and treat bullet wounds. Can you say the same?"

Fuck! I'm losing this. "No," he admitted. "But this is an entirely different ball game, honey—"

"I know this, Mike," Lisa said, her voice cracking. "A game I've been dragged into when my family was stolen from me." With an intensity Mike didn't expect, she said, "And I'll be damned if I stay on the side lines while you go hunting the bastards who did this to us."

Mike sighed loudly. *It could be worse*, he told himself. At least if she worked with him, he'd be able to protect her.

"Let's say we proceed," Mike finally said. "How are the assets given their targets?"

"IMSI can get involved in two ways," Mapother answered visibly pleased that Mike had somewhat agreed to move forward. "First, when the analysts from the control room find something actionable, they will come up with an operational plan. Among other things, it measures the odds of success and the impact it will cause to the targeted individual or organization. Once it's finalized, they come to me for approval. If I give them the green light, they will initiate aggressive measures. Occasionally, we get lucky. When you shake the tree hard enough, sometimes something falls out. When that happens, we send assets to intercept them."

"Intercept?" Lisa asked.

"More often than not, their order will be to terminate the target. However, from time to time, we will set up surveillance and hope that it will lead us to a bigger fish. You're still with me?"

"Yeah, we get it," Lisa replied.

Mike looked at his wife. "This is news to you, too? I thought you'd been briefed on these by the look of it."

Lisa shook her head. "Let's put it this way, Mike...I've been administratively involved."

"I see."

"So let me continue then," Mapother said. "Where was I? Oh yes, the second way IMSI will get involved is if a terrorist attack occurs close to an asset's location. All the news channels that we're monitoring in the control room allow us to know what's going on around the world. If our asset isn't involved in another operation, we'll request that he discreetly investigate the scene and see what he can sniff out."

"IMSI got a few successes today," said Mike, thinking about the death of the Sheik's personal physician.

"I'm proud of what we've accomplished. But the war is far from over."

"We want the Sheik," said Lisa with surprising authority.

Mapother looked at Lisa. "That's the ultimate objective, yes. But he's elusive, hard to track. And we haven't been able to turn anyone within his organization. If he was an easy target, your father-in-law would have been freed a long time ago."

The Sheik, Mike thought. *Not only did he kidnap my father, he's the sick man behind the attacks that killed the members of our families and the reason why my wife and I are suffering so much. He's why I'm willing to go to hell to avenge all the wrong he's done.*

So far Mike really liked what he was hearing about IMSI. When he'd been with the ERT, he and the rest of the guys had wet dreams thinking about an organization like this. The team had wanted to do a lot more takedowns on known terrorists, but unfortunately, any procedures were strictly forbidden unless authorized by RCMP lawyers. Mike agreed that law enforcement and intelligence agencies could not be let loose indiscriminately, but at some point, common sense had to govern which decisions were made. He and his team had stopped counting the times when they had missed a target simply because it had taken too long to get the green light.

"What's our next step?" he asked.

"Mike, I recognize the fact that you went through a multitude of selection and assessment phases during your military and law enforcement careers. What happened at the Ottawa Airport testifies to how well you were trained and how committed you are to achieving your objective no matter what. Lisa, you're an engineer, a multiengine pilot, a martial arts expert, and great physician but—"

"But what?" Lisa cut in.

"Yeah, there's always a *but*," Mike added.

"But some things you don't know yet," pointed out Mapother. "Skills that you'll have to perform flawlessly to survive in the world you're about to enter. You must accomplish your missions without leaving a footprint."

"You don't think we're qualified enough?" Mike asked.

"Consider the last decade of your lives as the selection process for what you're about to start," the silver-haired man replied. "Are you up for it?" he added before Mike or Lisa could muster a reply.

Mike glanced at his wife. She had her eyes fixed on him, begging him to say yes. Finally, he had a purpose in life again. He had a family to avenge. He would put all of his energy, training, and passion behind this single objective—to inflict as much pain and destruction within the ranks of the people responsible for the death of those he loved. *And, best of all, I'll do it with my wife by my side.*

"Am I up for it? More than ever," he told Mapother.

"Me too," Lisa said.

"Great. You're leaving in four days."

CHAPTER 20

Ottawa, Canada

The flight from La Guardia was uneventful, but Mike had gotten a painful headache that forced him to stop at the airport's drugstore. He purchased some Advil and a bottle of water and swallowed three of the little brown pills.

"That should help a little," he said to Lisa, who was waiting for him outside the drugstore.

"You're ready?" she asked smiling.

"Are you?"

She nodded. "Let's go, then," he said.

Mike was pleased to notice that all the damage the airport had sustained during the attacks had been repaired. But the atmosphere was different. Police officers roamed everywhere, and passengers were randomly selected for further screenings. He had recently read an article about how airline occupancy levels had reached a new all-time low since the additional security measures had been put in place, but he doubted that the reason was the security.

Customs was a breeze, and Mike and Lisa quickly exited the terminal. Gray clouds were hanging low, and the temperature was much cooler than in New York. He congratulated himself for thinking to bring a heavier coat.

They jumped in a cab and gave the francophone driver an address in Aylmer, Québec. The man smiled broadly, as it meant a big fare for him.

The cab headed north, toward the home where Melissa was born. Mike felt his throat tighten with emotion at the memory of his daughter, his mother, his unborn child, and his eyes started to fill with tears. The grief he was carrying weighed on him without any letup. He felt Lisa's hand in his own and gently squeezed it. She was looking away, but he knew she must have been feeling the same way he did. She had been hurt too, but they were together now. They no longer had to live a life of sorrow and misery without each other's support. Their shared desire to go after the people responsible for their families' massacre was the fuel they craved to walk the thin black line they were about to encounter. He had no delusions about what Mapother wanted him to be.

Do I really want to become an assassin?

That question kept popping into his head like a blinking streetlight. His heart and soul were fighting each other over it. His heart, where his daughter Melissa and the rest of his family resided, was telling him that he needed to really think about the reasons behind his desire for vengeance. On the other hand, his soul was pushing for retribution for the lives that were taken away from him. Not a day went by when he could close his eyes without reliving the airport's bloodshed.

Do I really want to become an assassin?

Is that what he truly wished for himself? Or for Lisa? Instead of being part of the solution, wouldn't he simply be joining the endless circle of violence and despair? He'd sworn to uphold justice and to defend the innocent. How could he even think of turning himself into an executioner? That wasn't right. That couldn't be right!

Or could it?

He had one more person to consult with before making up his mind for good. Because once on this path, there will be no coming back.

—

"*Monsieur, nous sommes arrives,*" said the driver.

"*Merci. Attendez-nous ici, s'il vous plaît,*" he replied, handing over ninety dollars. The driver thanked him for the generous tip and agreed to wait.

"So we're here," Lisa said.

Mike inhaled deeply. "Yes."

He had come to this sacred place only once before. Though he felt guilty about staying away, he didn't have the inner strength to make the trip more often. Visiting his daughters' graves always made him feel so terribly sad.

Charles Mapother had purchased ten plots to make sure that the whole family could be buried together. Mike led the way and slowly walked the path he knew would lead them to their daughters' graves. By the time they reached them, tears were running freely down his cheeks. He didn't try to wipe them away. He knelt down next to Melissa's resting place, and he spoke directly to her. Lisa stood behind him, her hands on his shoulders bringing him warmth and comfort.

"I know you're in a better place now, baby girl. You're probably having fun with your young sister, so I won't disturb you for very long. Daddy's just a little lost right now. I've...well, I've reached a crossroads. I don't know what to do. I thought I knew, but now that I'm kneeling here in front of your grave with your mother next to me, I really don't. I'm afraid that if I follow the path that has been offered to me, I might fall off the cliff."

Mike took a few deep breaths. The cool air felt good in his lungs.

"I'll leave you alone with her, my love," his wife whispered in his ear. "I love you, Michael Powell. Whatever you decide to do, I'll stand by you. But I'm ready. I'm sure." He felt her kiss on his cheek and heard her walked away.

Michael Powell. She's telling me that whatever I choose to do, she'll do it with me. Mike exhaled loudly and closed his eyes. *This is exactly what I needed to hear from her.*

"You're mother is such a great woman, darling," Mike said. "She's strong. Stronger than me, perhaps. But there's so much rage inside me, and I don't know what to do with it. I try so hard to keep it all in. I'm sure that you see my every move from where you're playing. I don't want to disappoint you, Melissa. I'm so afraid of letting you down—so afraid of doing things you wouldn't approve of."

Mike leaned forward and rested his two hands and his forehead on Melissa's cold tombstone.

"But what if, because of my inaction, some other little girl's life gets taken away by these monsters?" he whispered hoarsely. "I don't think I'd be able to live with myself. You know Daddy's good at stopping bad people, don't you? I've done it my whole life, and so did your grandpa. I know I'm asking a lot from you, baby, but would you help Daddy and Mommy remain on the road that has been mapped out for us? Will you help us? Please?"

For half an hour Mike waited, immobile, for some sort of answer. But one never came.

What did I expect?

Finally, Mike raised his head and looked around him. The place was entirely deserted with the exception of Lisa, who stood next to her parents' graves. He got to his feet and joined Lisa to pay his respects to his mother and his in-laws. They then spent some time at Chloe's, spilling tears for the daughter they'd never even held. Before they left the cemetery, Mike kissed the ground under which Melissa lay.

"I love you, baby girl. Please help us stay the course."

As Mike and Lisa walked away, a strong wind rushed by them, and the clouds parted. For a few seconds the sun shone down on them, and Mike could feel its warmth. In his heart, he knew Melissa had just winked at them.

PART 3

CHAPTER 21

Gendarmeric Nationale Headquarters
XVI District, Paris

Normally, Marise Martin, aide to the administrative assistant to the director general of the French gendarmerie, would have never gained access to the secure server. But today was no ordinary day. Anne-Marie Charticr, the young but efficient administrative assistant, had left in a hurry when she'd received news that her husband, a police officer, had been grievously wounded in a traffic accident. With the consent of the director general himself, she'd asked Marise to cover for her for the rest of the week. In order for Marise to carry out her new duties, Anne-Marie had given out her own password.

Marise was pleased. She had already provided the password to her CSIS handler, allowing them remote access to the secure server of the French gendarmerie. Zima Bernbaum—aka Marise Martin—was too busy to wonder about the consequences if she was caught. She hoped the RCMP and CSIS analysts working in concert on the case would find something soon. On the other hand, she had to admit she was enjoying working undercover. The constant danger made her feel alive. Never more so than last night's excursion inside General Richard Claudel's private residence.

—

Everybody in the intelligence-gathering business knew that acquiring useful information was a lengthy process. Nonetheless, after only a few weeks of being in place inside the Gendarmerie headquarters, the RCMP commissioner had called her on her secured CSIS-issued cell phone.

"Yes?" answered Zima, who was reading a paperback in the living room of her one-bedroom apartment.

"It's me, Zima," said the commissioner.

"One minute, please," requested Zima, climbing out of her futon. She didn't think her apartment was bugged, but she didn't want to take any chances. She grabbed her keys from the table of her modest vestibule and exited the apartment. Once she was outside, she made a right on Avenue Victor Hugo, heading toward the closest Starbucks, a block away.

"Sorry for the delay, commissioner. One can't be careful enough."

"Have you found anything, Zima?" asked the RCMP chief, not wasting any time.

"No. I haven't been in position long enough. Except for making photocopies and answering the phone, I'm not doing much and haven't come in contact with any confidential documents," she replied.

"I have a special task for you." [4]

Something in his tone made her stop. "I'm listening."

"General Richard Claudel won't be home tonight. I want you to search his residence."

"Are you serious?" asked Zima. When the commissioner didn't answer, she remarked, "I guess you are."

"We've received reliable intel that something big is coming up," said the commissioner. "Maybe as early as within a couple of days. My point is, we need someone to look into Claudel's personal belongings."

She wasn't crazy about the idea. "If I get caught, we lose everything." *And my mother, who thinks I work in a museum, will sue your ass!*

"I know the risks, Zima. But if something happens and it becomes known we had a lead on Claudel and didn't act on it, heads will roll."

Your head will roll, thought Zima, despite knowing the RCMP commissioner was right. They had to investigate the lead they had. Was breaking in the general's home the best way to do it? Considering the matter, she overcame her initial reluctance. She didn't see any other alternatives. The clock was ticking.

"I'll need special equipment," said Zima, entering the Starbucks.

"Already taken care of. You'll find all you need in the trunk of your car."

These guys are slick. "That's convenient."

"CSIS support personnel accessed your car earlier today," explained the commissioner. "If you need anything else, call me directly."

"Will do."

"You know what we're looking for, Zima. Find it before it's too late."

The RCMP needed proof. They wanted receipts, documents, bank account numbers, anything that could directly linked the French general to the Islamic terrorist group headed by the Sheik.

"How long do I have?" she asked.

"In theory, he's away until tomorrow morning, but you know as well as I do his schedule changes a lot."

"So we aren't sure when he's coming back?"

"Nobody said this gig would be easy," the commissioner said. "In any case, Xavier and Étienne will be close by."

Xavier Leblanc and Étienne Perrin were two CSIS operatives working at the Canadian embassy in Paris.

"That's good to know," Zima said.

"I expect your report by tomorrow morning," the commissioner said.

After hanging up, Zima ordered a tall café latte. While she waited for her drink, she was already plotting her next move. Getting the bag of goodies out of the trunk of her car was the priority. In an ideal world, she could have conducted reconnaissance on the residence for a few days prior to breaking in. It would normally be protocol, but the commissioner had made it clear he expected her to go in tonight. She didn't like it one bit. So many things on so many levels could go wrong. Plus, she had no clear rules of engagement. She would have to play it by ear.

If I find something on Claudel, how will the RCMP play it? Take him down? Turn him, maybe? It doesn't matter; I'll have done my job. But this isn't entirely true, is it? If this bastard is in any way responsible for Lisa's and hers family deaths, I'll kill him myself.

By the time her drink was ready, she wasn't in the mood for coffee any longer. She took a sip of her latte and then proceeded to dump the full cup in the garbage. She then headed to her vehicle to grab the bag her colleagues had left for her. Luckily, her Fiat sedan wasn't too far from her apartment, because she had to employ all her willpower not to open the bag. Once she was safely inside her apartment Zima unzipped the black duffel bag.

She lay out a set of lock picks, a pair of leather gloves, a wireless earpiece, a small flashlight, a radio set to the earpiece frequency, a throwaway cell phone, a flash drive, and a diminutive but sharp knife.

She inserted the drive into her laptop and read the instructions Leblanc and Perrin had left for her. After reading all the material twice, she checked her watch. Although carrying out a full surveillance on the residence was out of the question, Zima figured that she would observe the general's house for a solid hour before breaking in. That wasn't much but it would have to do.

After changing into a pair of dark jeans and a long-sleeve Under Armour sweatshirt, Zima headed to the kitchen to get the hairnet she would wear under her black baseball cap. Making sure she had all her equipment secured in her backpack, she ate a protein bar and drank half liter of water before she left.

Two hours before, she'd been reading a book on her futon, and now she was ready to put her life on the line to obtain some intelligence that might help save others' lives. That was how she wanted to live.

Much more exciting than working in a museum...Sorry mom.

And she meant it. Raised a good catholic, Zima hated the lies she had to tell her family and friends in order to protect herself and her colleagues. Only a handful of people knew she was a spy. Her unpredictable work schedule had forced her to accept she would stay single for a long time. Broken promises and missed opportunities had make sure that all the guys she had ever fallen for had fled for their lives.

I can't blame them. I would have done the same thing if I'd been in their shoes. Besides these eight-to-four kind of guys aren't really my type.

Walking to her car, Zima appreciated the gloom of the night.

I have to admit it would be nice to walk hand-in-hand with someone with whom I could be honest, be myself for once. Good Lord! What am I thinking about? Enough, Zima! Concentrate on the task at hand.

Zima laughed out loud. *I definitely need more sex.*

There was no moon in the sky, and the low-hanging clouds provided her with the perfect cover. Her black clothes would melt into her surroundings. She used the phone she had found in the bag to call Xavier Leblanc.

"Marise?" Leblanc said after picking up.

"Yes, it is. You've been briefed, I take it?"

"Étienne and I are already in position."

"Anything I should know?" asked Zima, starting her car.

"There's a cat in the house. I saw it sitting inside next to the window."

"So there is no alarm system."

"We don't think so. His housekeeper exited the premises an hour ago. I kept my binoculars on her, and I'm positive she didn't set an alarm. She left the door open for more than two minutes while she carried her cleaning stuff out of the house."

Zima was relieved. One less hurdle.

"Étienne is on foot, and I'm mobile in the vehicle," continued Leblanc. "There's a lot of traffic in the neighborhood, so another car won't be noticed."

"I'm on my way. I should be there within the next half hour," said Zima.

General Claudel lived in a row house in Paris's fifth administrative district. It was the oldest neighborhood of Paris and very popular with tourists.

"May I make a suggestion?" asked Leblanc.

"Shoot."

"Park your car one street east of the target. It's a one-way street traveling north and will give you an escape route."

Stopped at a streetlight, Zima studied her car navigation system. Claudel's house was located on Saint-Hippolyte, a one-way street toward the east.

"Will do," said Zima. "Thanks."

She was lucky to find a parking space close to Claudel's on her first try, half a block north on Rue Pascal. She then spent the next thirty minutes walking aimlessly through the neighborhood. She passed in front of her target's residence only once, but it was enough. The general's residence was a two-story brown brick house that had had its exterior recently renovated. The sizable garage door was made of expensive wood, as were all the window shutters. She waited until she reached the next intersection before calling Leblanc.

"I'm ready to go in," said Zima.

"Put on your earpiece," Leblanc replied. "Make sure it's on the same frequency as your portable radio."

Zima quickly confirmed the frequency and inserted her earpiece in her right ear.

"Radio check."

"I hear you five by five," answered Zima through her wireless mic attached to her Under Armour sweatshirt. "Where's Étienne?"

"I'm enjoying a cup of coffee at the restaurant at the corner of Brocas and Saint-Hippolyte. I'm fifty meters away west of the target's residence, and I have eyes on the prize."

"Got it."

Zima walked around the block one last time before approaching the house from the east. By the time she reached the front door, her lock-picking kit was in her hand.

"You've got time, Zima. No pedestrians in sight, and I don't see anyone standing on the balconies across the street."

Lock picking wasn't as easy as the movies portrayed it. A burglar needed a lot of practice and outstanding dexterity. Zima had both. She slipped inside Claudel's house within two minutes.

Gently closing the door behind her, she stayed stock still for a minute, listening to any noise coming from inside the house. It was dark, and she decided not to turn on any lights. Instead, she reached into her backpack and retrieved her night vision goggles. She powered them on and immediately noticed another door leading to a midsize courtyard shared by the different owners living on Saint-Hippolyte Street. She knew the courtyard offered her an alternative getaway in case the front door became compromised for any reason.

"I'm in," Zima whispered. "Commencing search." The first thing she did was to locate the study and insert the flash drive into the general's computer. The instructions given to her indicated she didn't have to turn on the machine. The drive would automatically copy everything that was saved on the hard drive. The consensus reached at the highest level of CSIS was that the general must be keeping a hard copy of his most important financial transactions. Everybody did.

Where would a top general hide documents he wouldn't want anyone to find? Yet, she considered, they needed to be readily available. She looked into the air ducts, peeked behind the numerous paintings, and tested drawers for hidden bottoms. She rummaged through the bathrooms, bedrooms, and closets, making sure to leave them the way they were. Two cats followed her everywhere, but they didn't answer when she asked them where the general secret cache was. After two hours, she had retrieved the flash drive but hadn't found anything. She was beginning to doubt the general had anything hidden in his residence. She was about to go back to the study when Étienne Pellerin's voice came through her earpiece:

"Marise, someone just got out of a taxi. He's walking toward the house."

Shit. What now? Zima felt her heart beat faster than she ever remembered.

"You have less than five seconds, Zima. I'm moving in to intercept and back you up. Let me know."

Zima was picturing Pellerin walking toward the residence, a hand on his hip where his firearm was secured. Five seconds wasn't enough to reach the back door, she decided.

"Stay put," said Zima, hearing the front door opening. "I'll let you know if you need to come in." She hurried inside the walk-in pantry and powered off her NVG. The light switch to the pantry was outside, and she didn't want to be blinded in case Claudel turned the light on. She placed the NVG on the floor next to her backpack and thought about grabbing her knife. She opted against it, but knowing it was close by made her feel better. She didn't dare take another breath, afraid Claudel would hear her heart pounding against her chest. She swallowed hard.

She could hear the thud of footsteps approaching. Hard soles on hardwood. *Please don't enter the pantry, please don't enter the pantry*, prayed Zima. The footsteps stopped. A kitchen cabinet was being opened and a glass was taken out. Shuffling inside the fridge followed by the sound of liquid being poured into the glass. Then a phone rang.

"Hi, Richard," said the voice of the man standing in the kitchen. The voice had a thick Arabic accent.

Richard? Then who's the guy standing a few feet away from me? wondered Zima. She wished she could hear more than one side of the conversation.

"I'm at your place. I thought you were going to be here."

"Yes, of course. I understand. I'll feed the cats."

"Listen, Richard, I got some last-minute instructions for you from Peter Georges. I'll put them in the atlas if you don't mind."

"I miss you too. I'm looking forward to seeing you in Portugal. I hope we'll be able to spend a few nights together."

What the fuck is that all about? Last-minute instructions? This was getting interesting. That might very well be the break they were looking for. *"I'll put them in the atlas if you don't mind."* An atlas was usually quite big and easily noticeable among smaller books. She'd wait until the man departed, then search the study one more time. In the meantime, she had to contact Pellerin to let him know she was okay and to remind him not to intervene unless she called him for assistance. She didn't dare speak, though, while the man was still only feet away from her. She forced herself to remain calm and to control her breathing. Moments later, she heard the man walk away and allowed herself to relax. But as she was about to contact Pellerin, she heard the man's footsteps approaching once again. This time he was moving fast, without hesitation. *Shit! I've been made!* The pantry's bright light came on, blinding her. She grabbed her knife, ready to defend herself, but the door was pushed toward her, forcing her back against the metal shelves behind her. She was holding her knife with such strength her nails embedded themselves into the soft flesh of her palm. She was about to push the door with all her might against the intruder when she saw his arm reach for a can of cat food.

"Anyone hungry?" she heard the man say before closing the door behind him. Zima didn't breathe for what felt like a full minute. *Oh, my God, that was too close.* Her throat was so dry it hurt. She was sure she'd been seconds away from dying from a heart attack. She took a few deep breaths before trusting herself to speak.

"Étienne, this is Marise. All is well. Stay put," she whispered in her mic.

"Copy that, Marise. Xavier and I are ready to move in."

Patience was the key. She didn't know how long the stranger would remain in the house, and she had to wait it out. She needed to get her hand on this *atlas*.

Minutes went by before she heard anything again. She thought she heard someone climbing the stairs leading to the second floor, but she couldn't be sure. If it was in fact the case, the man must have removed his shoes. *Maybe he was ready to go to bed. Would he be sleeping here?*

"A light came on on the second floor," she heard Pellerin say.

"He's probably spending the night here," said Zima. Knowing her colleagues outside would wonder why she'd know that, she added, "I'll brief you guys later, but I think this is the general's lover."

After a moment, Xavier's voice came over: "We'll let you know when he turns off the light."

Through her mind's eye, Zima could see Claudel's friend brushing his teeth, using the toilet, and putting on his pajamas. After what seemed like an eternity, Xavier let her know the light had been turned off. From that moment, she waited an hour before contacting Pellerin and Leblanc.

"There's been no noise for the last hour or so," she said. "Have you seen anything?"

"Negative," Pellerin said.

"Me neither," Leblanc said.

"Okay. I'm mobile again," Zima said, coming out of the pantry, careful to close the door behind her without making it creak.

She walked to the study and immediately started to look for an atlas. General Claudel's study wasn't large, but the number of books in his built-in shelves was impressive. From novels to college research papers, there must have been at least three thousand manuscripts. Fortunately for her, Claudel was tidy and the books were neatly placed in alphabetical order on the shelves. She took her small flashlight out of her backpack and screwed on a red filter. She found four large books on the last shelf. They fit the profile she was looking for, so she took them out and placed them on the floor. She opened the first one and went through all the pages carefully. She looked for any pages that might have been inserted in between already existing pages, but nothing came out. She looked for words that had been circled or notes that had been added to the bottom of a page. Nothing. She did the same for the second and third atlases. There was only one atlas left, and she knew she was running out of time. Xavier Leblanc and Étienne Pellerin had been standing watch for hours now, and the longer they remained in the neighborhood, the better chance somebody would notice they didn't belong. She opened the cover of the last atlas and proceeded as she had for the other three. Nothing grabbed her attention until she reached the twentieth page. Skillfully cut inside the book was a space six inches long by seven inches wide with a depth of less than three inches. Six flash drives were located inside.

Zima swallowed hard. She had found the mother lode.

Now what? She wasn't equipped to copy the drives on the spot. They were probably secured, and any attempts to tamper with them without the right tools might cause a loss of data. On the other hand, she couldn't simply take them. They would be discovered missing as soon as the general returned. His visitor had left him a message telling him explicitly that he had a last-minute message.

She had no time to mull over her decision. On impulse she pocketed the six drives. They needed to know what was on them.

—

Zima was pleased with the work they'd accomplished the previous night. She'd exited Claudel's residence through the front door, and Pellerin had escorted her to her car. Leblanc had kept watch on the house for an extra hour. "Just to make sure," he had said.

She told Pellerin where she'd found the drives and had briefed him on the conversation she overheard between the man and the general.

"I wouldn't be surprised if they were lovers," Zima added with a smile.

"We'll find out soon enough who he is. Xavier took a few night shots with his camera when he climbed out of the taxi."

Zima hoped it wouldn't be too long before the analysts went through the drives and assessed the data she'd collected from Claudel's computer. She had a feeling something big was coming their way. They needed to be ready.

CHAPTER 22

Nice, France

He couldn't help it. He was sweating profusely, and his eyes stung from the salt. He kept sponging his forehead with the dirty rag Mohammad Alavi had found under the passenger's seat of the gray Opel van they were riding in. His confidence was fast eroding, and he suspected it was because he'd shaved his beard the same morning. He knew he had to cleanse himself before entering paradise, but he'd never thought it would make him feel less of a man. His virility had been his beard. Now that it was gone, so was his self-confidence.

"Everything will be fine, Rukanah," Mohammad Alavi said from the front passenger seat. "Allah will guide you, His hand will escort you, and you will be successful because of him."

Rukanah knew his cell commander was right. He was doing Allah's will. Soon he'd be entering the Promised Land with seventy-two virgins waiting for him. That thought gave him courage. He knew what he had to do. He had memorized the face of the man he had to kill. He would be triumphant.

"Two minutes," Alavi said to him. "Are you ready?"

"Yes, I'm ready."

Alavi studied him for a few moments. "How many stages do you have to accomplish?"

"There are three phases in the operation."

Alavi nodded. "Very well. Explain them to me."

Rukanah collected his thoughts before answering. "First step is to place the secondary device, preferably in a place where there is no obstruction."

"Second?" Alavi asked, showing him the picture of their target.

"I will kill this man," Rukanah said, his bleak eyes fixated on the photograph.

"Tell me how, Rukanah. How will you kill the Canadian energy minister?"

"I'll shoot him as many times as I can," he replied feeling his confidence growing.

"And third?"

Rukanah beamed from ear to ear. "Then I'll enter paradise."

—

As the gray Opel made a right from avenue Thiers into the Nice train station's loading lane, Rukanah noticed Alavi giving new instructions to the driver.

"What's going on?" he asked.

Alavi made eye contact with him through the rearview mirror.

"Nothing to worry about."

"Why are there so many people outside the train station?" asked Rukanah, undeterred.

This time Alavi turned fully around in his seat to look at him. "I think the press conference is being held outside."

Alavi was right. The press conference where Canadian energy minister Arthur Green and his French counterpart, Alain Fosset, were to reveal a new eco-friendly transportation initiative had been moved outdoors. The beautiful weather had played a major role in the decision, as it was thought the opportunity to take gorgeous pictures would play well with the numerous media in attendance.

The gray Opel slowly drove past the elevated podium where the two politicians were going to make their announcement. Rukanah took it all in and decided that by moving the press conference outside, Allah had shown his hand. Too bad he was going to miss the second explosion. He wished he could see the slaughter.

As the Opel van came to a stop, Alavi put on a baseball cap and exited the vehicle. He opened the sliding door and placed both his hands on Rakunah's shoulders.

"It's now your turn to do your part. Do not disappoint him," said Alavi. "We're counting on you to create the breach that will allow us to strike at the heart of Satan."

Rakunah felt the pressure but decided he wouldn't let Allah or Mohamad Alavi down. "Count on me. Allah has given me all the strength I need."

He took several deep breaths before climbing out of his seat and stole a last glance at the Opel as it departed. Standing on the sidewalk right in front of the main entrance of the train station, Rakunah willed himself not to look down at the heavy dark blue bag he was holding in his left hand. It contained the exact same things his black backpack held, minus the pistol Alavi had given him earlier in the day.

To say he was a good shot would have been false. Yet he'd been taught how to handle the pistol in a way that would allow him to hit his intended target. *But that's only in stage two*, he reminded himself. What he had to do now was to find the perfect location where he could hide the secondary explosive.

Looking at this watch, he realized the press conference was about to start. He had to get moving. He crossed the street and joined a group of people who were waiting for the next city bus. He scanned his surroundings, trying to locate the ideal spot.

There.

A garbage can.

That was ideal. Or maybe not. What if a homeless person decided to look inside? He would take the blue bag away. Worse, what if he opened it and found the explosives? Authorities might be alerted before Rakunah had the chance to detonate them. Too risky. He had to find another location.

What would Alavi do? Rakunah remembered Alavi was a strong believer that sometimes hiding in plain sight was the best option. What about the palm trees a little farther west? He walked to their location fifty meters away. The three palm trees towered over a small patch of grass at the end of the off-loading lane close to where the bus and regular lanes of traffic joined together.

Perfect.

Rakunah semi-concealed the bag under the flowers that had been planted around the palm trees' bases. He was just standing up when he heard the crowd gathered around the elevated platform, clapping. The French politician had taken his place behind the podium and was about to start the press conference. Still no sight of the Canadian energy minister. Rakunah could feel his heart rate climbing. Where was he? They were supposed to make a joint announcement. What was going on?

Rakunah walked toward the crowd, seeking an elevated position that had a better view. Suddenly, the crowd started clapping again, and Rakunah saw him. The Canadian energy minister. The man he was about to kill. Unconsciously, he started praying while at the same time bringing his backpack forward. He unzipped it just enough to allow his hand to envelop the grip of the loaded pistol. With his hand still in the backpack and his eyes glued on Arthur Green, who was now speaking into the microphone, Rakunah pushed his way through the mob of people surrounding the platform.

He was within ten meters of the minister when he felt movement behind him. Instinct made him turn around, and what he saw frightened him. Two men wearing identical business suits were about to reach him. Police. Bodyguards. Whatever. It didn't matter. He had to act now. He whipped the pistol out of the backpack and up toward the minister in one fluid movement. To his dismay, by the time he pulled the trigger, a third man dressed like the other two had stepped in front of Arthur Green. The first two bullets hit the man in the right leg, and he collapsed on the platform. The third round hit the minister in his chest. Then all went black as Rakunah was shot numerous times in the back.

—

Through a pair of binoculars, Mohammad Alavi had followed Rakunah's progress from the top of an apartment building two blocks away. All had gone according to plan until Rakunah had developed tunnel vision, focusing on the minister. What a fool. How many times had he repeated to his trainees not to look at their target for too long? Alavi had thought the game was over before it had even started. But once again, the stupidity of the French police had surprised him. Even though Rakunah had managed to broadcast that he was a would-be assassin, the French had been incapable of bringing him down before he had shot a bodyguard and Arthur Green.

Now it was Alavi's turn to crash the party. Holding down the number one on his cell phone, he activated the trigger mechanism of the bomb inside Rakunah's backpack. He had conceived it himself, using Goma-2 ECO high explosives. Employing the same methods favored by the Basque separatist organization ETA during the 1980s and 1990s, Alavi had packed twenty pounds of explosives and added three pounds of nails and screws around it as shrapnel.

The explosion was powerful enough that the apartment building shook under him. To let the debris settle, Alavi counted to ten before bringing the binoculars to his eyes. The sight was everything he had wished for. Death and devastation. And his work wasn't over. He had one more surprise for them.

—

Alavi opened the passenger door of the Opel van and instructed the driver to get under way. The driver immediately started the engine and engaged the transmission. Joining the nearest lane of traffic, the Opel was almost hit by a police car driving in the opposite direction.

Nevertheless, the atmosphere in the van was euphoric. The driver and the remaining bomber, Abbud Raashid, had heard the explosion and couldn't wait for Alavi to give them the details.

"Is he dead?" asked Raashid. "Was Rakunah successful?"

Alavi, who was trying to monitor the police frequency, was annoyed at Raashid but didn't dare show it. After all, Raashid was shortly going to join Rakunah in paradise. A few encouraging words could go a long way toward cementing his resolve.

"Yes, Rakunah did very well," said Alavi. "He's with Allah now, enjoying the fruits of his labor."

Alavi spent the next few minutes taking notes while he listened to his police scanner. He didn't speak French fluently, but he knew enough to understand what was going on. Numerous police and fire vehicles had arrived at the scene of the explosion. Alavi presumed the paramedics had done the same.

It was time.

He powered off his scanner and turned on the radio. He changed frequencies until he found a station covering the Nice train station attack. He then flipped open the same cell phone he had used earlier, but this time he pressed and held down the number two. Thirty seconds later, he heard the news anchor scream.

Allah was great.

CHAPTER 23

New York City

Sipping on a glass of California chardonnay, comfortably seated at a table in his favorite New York restaurant, Charles Mapother was contemplating what to do with Jonathan Sanchez. He had brought him to IMSI not only because of his high intellect and deduction power, but also because Sanchez was the best operator he'd ever known. The bullet that had shattered his left knee might have finished his career in the field, but Sanchez's operational planning skills were still the best. Delta had trained him well.

Still, not everything was perfect. Walking with a limp or not, Sanchez's good looks brought him a lot of attention from the female crowd. And that wasn't a good thing for his line of work. Just now, the head waitress had left her phone number on Sanchez's white linen tablecloth.

And I'm well aware of the flirting between him and Anna at the office.

Mapother needed to evaluate Sanchez's emotional state to decide if he was ready to be entrusted with more responsibilities at IMSI, especially to help Anna Caprini in her duties. Once Mike and Lisa finished their training, IMSI's total number of assets in the field would be eight, and that was more than one person could handle. Sanchez could be the perfect handler for IMSI's new husband-and-wife team. To help him finalize his decision, Mapother had invited Sanchez for lunch to discuss his readiness at length.

Their appetizers had just arrived when Mapother's phone started vibrating in his jacket pocket. He apologized to Sanchez before taking the call.

"Mapother speaking."

"Sir, we have a situation in France that warrants your full attention," Anna Caprini said.

"What is it?" Mapother asked.

"Arthur Green, the Canadian energy minister, has been assassinated in Nice."

Mapother closed his eyes and forced himself to take two deep breaths. He could feel Sanchez's gaze upon him.

"How?" he asked.

"A bomb exploded at the Nice train station, where he was giving a speech about a new transport initiative."

"Damn it!"

"I'm sending all the intel we've got to your mobile desktop, and I already advised Sam Turner to bring your ride around."

"Thank you, Anna," Mapother said ending the call.

"What is it?" Sanchez asked.

"The Canadian energy minister has been killed in an explosion at the Nice train station. I'm afraid we'll need to cut our lunch short and head back to HQ."

"Of course," Sanchez said. "What about Mike and Lisa—aren't they in Italy finishing up their training?"

His reminder made him smile. "You're right. They're stationed in Ventimiglia, less than five kilometers from the French border. They could be in Nice within two hours."

"Do you think they're ready?" Sanchez asked.

"They're as ready as they'll ever be," Mapother answered, reaching once again for his phone.

CHAPTER 24

Ventimiglia, Italy

Mike and Lisa Walton's eight weeks of training had been mentally and physically exhausting. The days started at six in the morning and never ended before ten at night. Language training in the morning for both of them was followed by an intensive hand-to-hand combat session for Mike in the afternoon while Lisa headed to the firing range to polish her shooting skills. Krav Maga fighting was new to Mike, but he had learned rapidly. Already being a black belt in Brazilian jujitsu had helped, but having an instructor to student ratio of two to one was the key to his quick learning.

Experts previously working for the CIA, the FBI, and the US Army, as well as professionals from private enterprises, were called in to lecture, teach, and train the two future IMSI operatives. While the experts weren't told the whole truth as to whom their two students really were or why they were receiving such in-depth training, they had their orders and were paid more than enough not to ask any questions.

Lisa and Mike were constantly challenged by their instructors, and they were never told how well they were doing or what benchmarks they were supposed to achieve.

The two had spent countless hours in briefings on the geopolitics of countries where they might get deployed. They learned local customs and traditions, as well as the different allegiances of the political parties. They were trained in on-the-ground tactics, including the art of disguise and how to cross international borders without being detected. They acquired knowledge on how to set up a covert operation using clandestine bank accounts, and how to forge basic documents. They had spent many afternoons trailing practice surveillance targets around many of the world's biggest cities, trying not to raise the suspicion of their targets or get caught by their trainers. They were taught what their support teams could do for them and how to work with them efficiently. Mike had never been more impressed by his wife. She digested information faster than anyone Mike had ever known. She was a natural.

The final phase of the training had been the most intense. Mike was taught a hundred different ways to kill a human being without any weapons, as well as how to extract information from an uncoopera-tive subject. He spent hours practicing how to use a newspaper and other "harmless" objects as defensive or aggressive weapons that would leave no evidence of foul play. In the meantime, Lisa received refreshers on autopsies and what a coroner would be looking for after a suspicious death.

Week after week their skills were developed. They were finally ready to be sent back to the states, having completed a final tactical practice mission in Italy. That assessment had not only convinced their trainers that they were ready, it had also proven to Mike that he had been right all along: for him and Lisa, there would be no turning back.

—

Mapother had given them a few days off to visit the French Riviera before they were scheduled to fly back home.

"Lisa, we don't have any plans for tomorrow, do we?" Mike asked. He and Lisa were seated on a terrace overseeing the Mediterranean.

"I was planning on sleeping in."

For the first time in two months, she thought.

"Are you kidding me? We're in Italy!"

"So?"

Her husband acted like she had caught some type of deadly dis-ease. "Look around you, honey," Mike said with his arms opened wide. "The sun's out, the view is gorgeous. There's so much to do."

Lisa couldn't help but laugh. She knew her husband only wanted her to have a good time. The last two months had been hard for both of them, and she was glad that Mike had been there with her to share the pain. It was one thing to defend your country by wearing a uniform like she had done for years; it was another to join an organization where you were expected to kill people preemptively.

Exceptionally so for a physician, thought Lisa. *But we're way past the tipping point. There's only one way to go now: forward.*

"What did you have in mind, Mike?"

"I was thinking, maybe we could rent a Ferrari and drive around the coast. What do you say?"

Lisa was about to respond positively when her phone rang. She looked at the number displayed and mouthed "Mapother" to her husband.

"Yes?"

"Lisa, this is Charles Mapother." Unconsciously, she sat up straighter in her chair. Mapother's tone of voice didn't convey that it was a routine call.

"What's going on, sir?"

"The Canadian energy minister has been assassinated at the Nice train station."

For a couple of seconds, Lisa didn't say anything, gauging what this meant. "I believe Mike and I could be there within the next hour or two," she finally said. "We're both fluent in French and know the area quite well. What do you want us to do?"

Mapother remained businesslike, but he seemed relieved by Lisa's reply. "I'm sending all the info we have on your smartphones. See what you can sniff out, and report back to me in five hours."

"Will do," Lisa said, ending the call.

"Where are we going?" asked Mike, standing up.

Lisa sensed that her husband was as excited as she was. They'd barely completed their training, and already Mapother was putting them to work.

"We're going to Nice. It's only about fifty kilometers away."

As they walked to their rental car, Lisa explained what Mapother had said and what was expected of them.

"I'll take the lead on this one, Lisa," Mike said once she finished. "I'm more—"

"Sounds good to me," interrupted Lisa as she settled behind the wheel. "Let's do this."

"Okay, then," Mike said while releasing and inspecting the ammunition magazine of his small Taurus pistol. "I know you wanted to sleep in tomorrow, but I guarantee you this will be much more exciting,"

Lisa nodded. *I have no doubt.*

CHAPTER 25

IMSI Headquarters
New York

His eyes were fixed on the LCD screen next to him, where images from the latest terrorist attack were flashing across the screen like some horrible Hollywood action trailer. Apparently, a second explosion at the central train station in Nice, France, had killed a CNN reporter and his cameraman as they were trying to help free victims caught under the debris left by the first suicide bomber.

Even though Sanchez knew he should be used to bloodbaths by now, he wasn't. They continued to turn his stomach upside down.

"They don't say if the French authorities have any suspects yet," he said to Mapother.

The IMSI director raised his eyes from his laptop. "I don't think they do, but Mike is watching the train station's security tapes as we speak. He'll call if he finds anything."

"Why isn't the tape with the French authorities?" Sanchez asked.

"Lisa told me that apparently they're still waiting on a warrant for the seizure of personal information," Mapother said in a sardonic voice. "So our team stepped in and made a copy for their own perusal."

"Are they by themselves?"

"No, Support Five is on location and Support Six has been called for backup. They should be there within the next two or three hours."

Moments later, a red light started to blink on Mapother's phone. He reached for the handset located on his desk. "What do you have?" he asked. He nodded a few times as he listened to the caller, then finally, "I'll send him the message myself. Good work."

After Mapother hung up, he typed steadily without saying anything for the next five minutes. When he was finished, he read his message over, then pressed the *send* button. Looking up at Sanchez, he started to explain, "We might have caught a lucky break. Using the train station's security tapes, Mike was able to find the vehicle that dropped off the suicide bomber. Unfortunately, he thinks that there might be more suicide attacks planned for today."

"Why does he think that?"

"He saw more than one person in the vehicle that dropped the bomber off. It was a minivan with tinted windows, but when the bomber opened the door to get out, at least one more potential terrorist could be seen inside the vehicle."

"Shit!" exclaimed Sanchez. "You think they're dropping off bombers at different locations across the city?"

"Probably. There's no way for us to be sure," Mapother answered. "Control is sending the minivan's description to the Nice police department as we speak—under the guise of an anonymous tip, of course."

"Have we got someone at the Nice International Airport?" Sanchez asked. "That would be the next likely target, I'd think."

"Great minds think alike, Jonathan. I just e-mailed that exact order. Mike and Lisa are going to stay curbside at Terminal One and keep their eyes open for the van and any possible terrorists."

"Could they identify the suicide bomber or anyone else from the tapes?"

"No, the angle was all wrong. We didn't even get a license plate number," said Mapother. "There's nothing more we can do about it right now. I'm afraid we're playing catch up once again."

—

Using Lisa as navigator, Mike managed to get from the train station to the Nice International Airport within twenty minutes. They arrived at the airport's Terminal One and scanned the area for any signs of suspicious individuals or the gray Opel minivan he'd seen in the surveillance video. There was no sign of either. He feared that they'd changed vehicles—or worse, that they'd arrived too late.

When IMSI's Support Five van arrived ten minutes after them, he asked them to keep an eye on Terminal One's arrival ramp so that Lisa could go for a short reconnaissance drive around the airport perimeter. They agreed that one of them had to check the parking lots—especially the indoor garage, where a van packed with explosives could stay inconspicuous for days. Or until it blew up.

"Let's split up, Lisa. I'll walk into the terminal while you look for the Opel."

"Understood. Be careful, Mike."

"Always." Before climbing out of the vehicle, Mike added quietly, "We're a team, Lisa. If you see anything, you let me know, and we'll work together."

"Don't worry, honey. I'll do just that."

Mike nodded but remained concerned. Lisa had excelled during all the training phases. She even managed to wow the seasoned operators who acted as her instructors. Unwavering mental strength and extreme confidence in her own capabilities had made her a first-rate engineer and top-notch physician. In spite of this, Mike had noticed during their training together with IMSI that Lisa—on occasion, and especially when operating alone without precise directives— would act without thinking through the consequences. With so much on the line today, Mike had wanted to reassure himself that his wife wouldn't act on impulse. He wasn't sure he had succeeded.

—

As Lisa surveyed the indoor parking lot, her mind wandered back to what she'd seen at the Nice train station, and she immediately felt sick to her stomach.

That was too close to home.

As a physician, she had stared death down plenty of times before. But what she'd just seen at the train station was beyond disturbing. The terrorists had let the emergency crews and media arrive on the scene before setting off a second bomb. What had been their intention? Was it simply a dirty trick aimed at killing even more people, or was this scheme far more sinister?

"Mike from Lisa, do you have anything at the main entrance?" she said into her mouthpiece.

"Nothing. You?"

"Nope. I'm going to clear the last parking lot, and then we should regroup."

"Copy that. Keep me posted."

"What about you, Support Five? Anything interesting?"

Support Five was the newest of IMSI's eight logistical teams. It had been decided that Support Five would be assigned to Mike and Lisa's operation area. Each of the eight teams answered to a field operative who was assigned to a certain geographic area. Inside their specific region, a support team's primary duty was to provide their operatives with whatever they needed to complete their assignments. It could be as simple as furnishing a weapon or as complex as accessing an airline's software to see who was on a flight list.

On this particular day, before all hell broke loose, Support Five had been in Menton, a little town on the Franco-Italian border, setting up a safe house. Once news of the first bombing broke, Mapother had directed them to Nice on standby. Support Six, the team from Tunis, was also en route.

"We have a visual on a late-model gray Opel," Support Five team leader Jasmine Carson replied. "It's parked right in front of the D-Two entrance of Terminal One, right behind our Volkswagen Transporter. Somebody's getting out...and now the van is pulling away."

"Copy that. Stay with the van, but not too close," Mike ordered. "I'll take care of the passenger. Mark him down as Tango One."

"Understood," answered Carson. "Take a look at your PDA. We just sent you the picture we took of Tango One."

"Thanks," Mike said. "Could we have eyes inside the terminal to help me out, please?"

"Roger that. We're working on it. Give us five minutes."

—

Mike was now well inside the terminal, looking for the man depicted on his PDA screen.

"Lisa, this is Mike."

"I'm listening," his wife replied.

"Come inside the terminal to give me a hand. We might end up taking this guy out."

"I'll park the car and join you," said Lisa.

With his mocha-colored skin and black hair, their suspect was obviously of Arab heritage. The photo taken by Support Five showed that Tango One was wearing a pair of tan trousers and a loose-fitting navy sports jacket. He didn't have any luggage except for a small brown suitcase.

As he was walking through the terminal looking for Tango One, Mike took his cellular from his pants pocket, pushed an autodial button, and held the telephone to his ear.

"Yes," came a crisp voice seven thousand kilometers away in Brooklyn, New York.

"This is Mike. Please be advised that Support Five is now following a suspicious vehicle that resembles the one that dropped off a bomber at Nice Gare Centrale."

"Very well. We'll advise the proper French authorities. Anything else?" asked Anna Caprini.

"I'm inside Terminal One at the Nice International Airport, and I'm looking for one of the vehicle's passengers. He's got a good two minutes' head start on me. Support Five is working on penetrating the airport's system to access the security camera inside the terminal. I need authorization to proceed with force if necessary."

"Stand by," said Anna before putting him on hold. A minute later, she was back on the line. "Mike?"

"I'm still here," he said, scanning his surroundings for any traces of Tango One.

"I've just spoken with Charles. You've been authorized to neutralize the threat at your discretion."

"Copy that. Anything else?"

"We're going to try to get a French DCRI intelligence team to take over Support Five's surveillance duties to free them up. Support Six should be on the scene shortly as well, and we should have IMSI's Eurocopter at the airport soon to give you a quick exit if you need it."

"Thanks, Anna."

After his call with IMSI headquarters, Mike contacted his wife to fill her in on the developments. "Lisa, we've been authorized to use force to stop Tango One."

"That's good news," Lisa replied, hurrying toward the terminal. "I'm on my way to your location."

"Why don't we split up? I'm already on the main floor," Mike said. "Go to the second floor; we'll cover more ground that way."

"Roger that. I'll be on the second floor."

Mike hoped that the Direction Générale de la Sécurité Intérieure, the now intelligence agency in charge of all counterterrorism action within France, would be able to relieve Support Five quickly. He might need his support squad's help inside the terminal.

Mike had to formulate a plan. He couldn't simply approach Tango One, pull out his Taurus Millennium 9mm pistol, and shoot him in the head. That would be too easy—and extremely counterproductive. IMSI's main directive was very clear. All use of lethal force by field operatives, especially outside the United States, was to be clean. Absolutely no traces could be left behind to jeopardize IMSI. In other words, under absolutely no circumstances could a field operative be caught, or even draw attention to himself.

Mike brought up the picture of Tango One on his PDA once more. *Where is this little bugger?* he wondered. Suddenly Mike noticed something in the photo that he had missed earlier. A black plastic tube was coming out of the suspect's left sleeve. Mike recognized what it was immediately, and his heart sank. Tango One was attached to an IED plunger switch. He needed to let Lisa know right away, but Jasmine Carson came on the air.

"Mike from Support Five leader," Mike heard through the secure wireless minireceiver lodged in his right ear.

"Support Five leader, go ahead."

"We have eyes in the terminal, and both techs are working facial recognition software. With a little bit of luck, we'll find Tango One soon."

"I honestly hope so. This guy is attached to a plunger switch."

"Shit."

"Concentrate on the cameras located outside the secured area. I don't think our tango has crossed security yet."

"Will do. We'll be back at the airport to supply backup as soon as we can."

"Please do so," said Mike. "Lisa, did you copy our last transmission?" Mike wanted to make sure his wife knew about the new threat.

"Got it," came in Lisa. "Tango One has a plunger."

"We'll have to use extreme caution when we approach him," said Mike.

"I've taken down one just like him in training, all by myself," Lisa said. "The key is to control the plunger before anything else. Then we kill him."

What the hell? I hope she isn't thinking about taking him down by herself.

"We take him down together, Lisa," Mike cautioned. "I don't care if you've done it in training or not. Understood?"

"For sure."

CHAPTER 26

Nice, France

Jasmine Carson had both hands on the steering wheel as she discreetly followed the gray Opel. They were traveling westbound on highway A8 toward Antibes. She made sure to keep at least half a dozen cars between the target and their VW Transporter, but even so, the Opel was quite easy to trail. It made no sudden speed or lane changes and kept within the speed limit. She was grateful the terrorists weren't running any kind of countersurveillance moves. Although she'd spent eight years as a senior FBI investigator specializing in mobile surveillance, she was keenly aware it would be hard to remain undetected driving a Transporter.

Control had advised her that the French intelligence agency DCRI would take over as soon as they were able to position agents in the area. That made Carson slightly nervous. She had no idea how IMSI communicated the intelligence that was gathered by its field personnel to external agencies like the DCRI. All she knew was that IMSI wasn't supposed to exist as an intelligence agency; yet they were almost always capable of transmitting vital information to the appropriate authorities.

But what if the French became curious about how the United States had become privy to such intelligence? What if the DCRI not only tracked the Opel, but also used countersurveillance to find out who was tailing it in the VW Transporter—and why? She didn't think that the French government would be too pleased to find the United States playing dirty, even if it was to save French citizens' lives.

—

"Mike from Support Five, come in," Mike heard in his earpiece.

"Go."

"My guys just told me that we have a possible for you. We'll run him through our recognition software as soon as we can get a clear look at his face, but he's dressed exactly like the man who exited the Opel."

"What's his current location?" Mike asked.

"He's in transit. Right now he's on the escalator leading to the second floor."

"Got it," Lisa replied. "I'll run the intercept and keep watch."

"I'm on my way," added Mike, picking up his pace. "Try to figure out what kind of plunger he's holding."

"Will do, Mike. I hope it's the type where the bomb detonates only when the trigger is *pressed*, and not when it's *released*."

If it was the latter, they were in deep trouble. Once a plunger was already pushed down, it was extremely difficult to stop the bomb from detonating. If the person exerting the pressure was killed, his thumb would release the plunger and the bomb would explode. The only safe way to neutralize that type of threat was to physically hold down the plunger, making sure that the bomber didn't let go of it. But to be successful with this technique, two agents were required: one to hold down the threat's thumb, and the other to kill him. They would have to work together in close precision.

But even if by some miracle we manage to neutralize the threat before it is too late, how the hell are we supposed to do it covertly? Mike wondered as he rushed toward the escalator. The incident would draw loads of media coverage, and the French press wouldn't miss the fact that unknown Americans were responsible.

A voice over his earpiece interrupted his thoughts. "Mike, Lisa, from Support Five. We just ran our suspect on the recognition software using the initial picture we took as he exited the car. It's a match."

"Great. I just arrived in the main hall. Any ideas where he is?" asked Mike.

"Second floor, in front of the pharmacy."

"I've got visual on Tango One," Lisa jumped in.

She sounds too excited. She needs to calm down.

"Give me a minute," Mike said. "I'll be there shortly."

"He keeps looking toward the security checkpoint. Maybe he's waiting for a shift change or the arrival of an accomplice who will let him go through," Lisa said.

"It could be," answered Mike. "Support Five, try to hack into the names of the security employees working that checkpoint, then run a check on them."

"Okay. I'll let you know as soon as I have something."

—

Dr. Lisa Walton was twenty feet behind her target, trying to get a visual on the briefcase he was holding and the type of plunger Tango One had in his hand.

Luckily, she couldn't see any wires running from the target to the briefcase, so she could rule out that her tango was carrying a second bomb. But her heart rate accelerated when she confirmed that the terrorist already had his left thumb on the plunger—he only had to release the pressure to blow them all up.

—

Abbud Raashid was sweating. His faith was strong, but he wasn't sure how long he could hold up. The morning's attacks on the Canadian energy minister at the Gare Centrale had given him a boost of confidence, but he could feel his determination weakening. He'd been told that he was part of a much larger plan, and that his sacrifice would greatly help the Sheik accomplish his mission.

Raashid glanced once more toward the security checkpoint. His instructions were to martyr himself amid a large crowd of tourists. He knew that the largest gatherings were usually close to the security checkpoints, as they were well known bottlenecks. Unfortunately, it was a slow day at Nice International Airport; no more than twenty people were waiting in line. He was worth more than twenty infidels!

He had trained for months at the side of great jihadis like explosives engineer Mohammad Alavi and tactical mastermind Omar Al-Nashwan. Raashid decided that he would wait until at least fifty people were lined up before going in.

The problem was, his left thumb was starting to feel numb. He thought that maybe he was putting too much pressure on the button, but he didn't dare ease up any. What a waste it would be if the bomb exploded while he was in a duty-free shop!

Trying to relax, Raashid took three deep breaths and exited the shop. He spotted a Häagen-Dazs store and made a split-second decision. He'd wait inside the store, as he would be less conspicuous in there.

—

All became clear to Lisa when she saw Tango One take three deep breaths. She could not let terrorists blow up another target.

There's no way I'll let him slaughter innocent people just to remain covert. There are kids there, for God's sake! Some of them not older than my Melissa.

"Support Five, this is Lisa. Tango One has already started the trigger mechanism. I'm taking immediate action. Advise the French police."

"Roger that. We have a visual on you."

"Lisa, I'll be there as soon as I can. Wait for me; we'll take him down together," Mike ordered.

Sorry, Mike. I've got to do this.

"I can't wait, Mike. He's gonna blow himself up any moment now. There are so many kids around—"

"Wait for me, goddamn it! Lisa!"

"Don't come closer. I'll be okay on my own."

Ignoring the order, Lisa grabbed her small Taurus pistol and expertly dismantled it while walking toward a garbage bin. At just over six inches long, the Taurus was easy to conceal, and she had no difficulties throwing it into the garbage without anyone noticing. *Time to play the role of a random Good Samaritan,* she thought. And to pull that off, she needed to be unarmed.

"Support Five, my firearm and identity cards are in the garbage bin next to the Häagen-Dazs store, and I'm about to throw my earpiece in too. I'm going in to neutralize Tango One."

"We'll take care of it, and we'll keep an eye on everything that happens. Good luck."

"Lisa, wait up!" she heard Mike plead.

"Can't do it, honey."

Lisa casually extracted her earpiece and dropped it into the bin. *Okay, I'm on my own now.* She moved toward the entrance of the ice cream shop. In the final seconds before the takedown, she analyzed all possible advantages she had over this adversary. Although she was shorter than her target by least four inches, she had the benefit of surprise. The suicide bomber looked to be in superb physical shape, but he was wearing dress shoes, meaning that Lisa could probably make him slip easily.

And that might be my only chance.

—

Two customers were already waiting to be served by the one employee on duty behind the ice cream counter. Abbud Raashid took his place in line behind a young woman holding her three-year-old son. The young boy looked at Raashid with a big smile, as his mom had finally said yes to two scoops of chocolate ice cream in a sugar cone. Raashid smiled back, thinking that it would be nice if he could kill the mother and her son—poster children for Great Satan's excess and gluttony.

He turned and stole another look at the security checkpoint and realized that the volume of travelers had picked up. Excellent.

As he was turning his head back toward the service counter, his peripheral vision caught the movement of a woman thundering toward him, and he automatically started to release the pressure his left thumb had on the button.

—

When she was a few feet away, Lisa saw her target smile.

No! He's gonna blow himself up!

She sprinted the last meters and was on the terrorist less than half a second later. Using all her strength, she tackled him from the front while clamping both her hands over the bomber's left hand, preventing him from detonating the explosive. Her target slid along the tiled floor upon impact, nearly falling over. Using her momentum, Lisa shoved her target into the wall with such force that the terrorist's back cratered the drywall. She followed her tackle with a vicious knee strike to the groin.

Tango One's knees buckled, and Lisa head-butted him twice on the nose, breaking it. Blood poured over them, and the terrorist nearly lost consciousness right there. But unfortunately for Lisa, this target was a trained fighter. As she felt her opponent push forward, Lisa let him use his momentum and shoved her attacker over her shoulder. The terrorist went flying over her back and crashed onto the tiled floor. Lisa, her hands still firmly clenched around Tango One's plunger hand, let herself fall on her target, her 130-pound frame easily crushing two of his antagonist's ribs. Lisa heard bones cracking and soon after saw bloody drool begin to flow from her target's mouth. His broken ribs must have punctured a lung.

Seeing that a dozen people were staring at her in horror, she said as calmly as she could, "I could use a little help. Call the police, and let them know that there's a bomb under this man."

Lisa groaned inwardly as the word *bomb* exerted its universal effect on the people around her. Everybody in the vicinity of the Häagen-Dazs shop ran for their lives, shouting as loud as they could that there was a bomb in the airport. Lisa turned back to look at her target. The terrorist wasn't dead yet.

—

Raashid was beyond feeling pain. He was overwhelmed with shame; he had not been able to carry out his mission. Removing his thumb from the pressure plunger had now become an impossible task. This infidel whore was simply too strong, or he was simply too weak. It didn't matter; he had never felt so alone and useless in his life. Raashid's only solace was that he might still be able to create a diversion at the airport and distract the French authorities from his brothers in faith in Antibes so that their attack planned for the following day might have an even greater chance of being successful.

With all his remaining strength, Raashid forced his right hand into the inside of his pant leg, where a sheathed knife was concealed.

The pressure of the whore's weight on his broken ribs was causing him excruciating pain, and he was nearly choking on his own blood, but Raashid didn't dare quit. In his last few moments of life, in an ultimate effort to at least martyr himself and kill the infidel who had stopped him, Raashid withdrew the Blackhawk Crucible from its sheath and slowly pushed the three-and-a-half-inch blade into his attacker's back.

—

Lisa knew that the suicide bomber was finished. The only thing she had to do now was wait for her target to die and then face the music when the French police showed up. She was planning what she would say to the police when she felt something sharp penetrate her back. Her whole body froze, and she registered immense pain as she was stabbed again, this time close to her neck.

No!

The surprise was so total that she nearly lost her grip on the terrorist's left hand—and on the plunger. As she looked into the bomber's eyes, she saw a devilish satisfaction in them.

Lisa was aware that the man beneath her was about to stab her a third time, and there was absolutely nothing she could do about it.

I'll die here alone. For nothing.

She was bracing herself for the next strike when she saw Mike step in to block it with his forearm. Mike immediately disarmed the bomber and slashed his throat before plunging the knife into the terrorist's left eye socket.

Lisa could feel her blood-soaked shirt sticking to her skin. She had no idea how badly she was injured, but at least the pain was bearable. Her worry was that if the authorities didn't show up soon, she might lose consciousness.

"Get out of here before the cops show up, Mike," she managed to say to her husband.

"I'm not leaving you," he replied.

She tried to look up at Mike but found herself nearly incapable of moving her neck and shoulders. She felt her breathing become shallow, and her body was starting to shake pretty badly. She didn't have much strength left. *I'm going into shock.*

With little time left before she passed out, she had no idea when the bomb squad would arrive. Something had to be done, and soon.

"We need to secure the trigger," she said to Mike. But her husband didn't move. She could feel his arms around her. "Mike! I need you to listen to me," she said louder. That seemed to bring him back.

"Yeah. On it." Mike got up and ran behind the cashier. Lisa could hear drawers being opened and closed. Mike was back a few seconds later.

"What I am going to do is secure your hands, his hand, and the plunger with this big roll of duct tape," Mike said. "And I'll make it tight to keep the pressure on."

Lisa nodded feebly. "I had to do it. He was going to—"

"I know, honey. I know," he said stroking her hair. "You did well, Lisa."

"I'm sorry," she said in a broken voice.

"Stop talking. Keep your strength up; you'll need it."[5]

CHAPTER 27

IMSI Headquarters
New York

W as Mike able to slip out of the airport?" Mapother asked.
"Yes, sir," Anna Caprini replied. "He's on his way to Tunis with the help of Support Six. Because there were no witnesses present to say otherwise, he played the role of a victim when the cops showed up. The authorities were so overwhelmed they let him go without too many questions. He gave them an address in Ventimiglia and one of our covert phone numbers."

"Turn him around then," Mapother ordered. "I want Support Six to link up with Support Five in Antibes."

"Yes, sir," Caprini responded. "What for?"

"I spoke with a friend of mine at the DGSE. His brother is Yves Bleriot, the officer in charge of the GIGN, that special operations unit of the French gendarmerie. The unit has been put on high alert, and depending on the intel DCRI collected, they'll assault the terrorists' stronghold or the van itself while it's still en route. I want Mike to join with the GIGN commander and brief him on what he saw on the ground."

"Understood, sir," Caprini replied.

"What about Lisa?" Sanchez inquired.

"Support Five says they were able to retrieve all evidence, including her firearm. If we're to believe her tracking device, she's at Saint-Roch Hospital in Nice," answered Caprini.

"We'll take care of her," said Mapother, touching Sanchez's arm. He exited the enclosed area and walked into the middle of the control room. "Great effort, everybody," said Mapother, trying to make eye contact with as many of his staff as he could. "We saved lots of lives today. Now our asset is probably at Saint-Roch Hospital in Nice. She needs a cover story that will hold for at least seventy-two hours. That is the maximum time I want her to spend in France. Any ideas?"

"Sir, what about creating a reason for her to be at the airport?" said a young man in his early twenties who was seated in the first row.

"Such as?"

"She could have had a flight that was leaving from Nice. It would be easy to justify—we simply have to create a record that shows her traveling frequently within France."

"That could work, but do so with an alias. I don't want her real name to appear anywhere," Mapother said. "What about her extraction?"

Another analyst jumped in. "Maybe we could send someone to act as a representative from her insurance company?"

"Okay," said Mapother, liking the idea. "Do it. Create a paper trail with a real contact number. Use Support Five to work out the details. As for our 'insurance agent,' I'll send Jonathan Sanchez to Nice. He will act as a doctor working for her private medical insurance company, and he will repatriate her as one of his patients. Any questions?"

There were none.

"All right, people. Our asset has only a short period of time before the French authorities start asking her questions. She's counting on us to bring her home. Let's not disappoint her."

Mapother walked back to the enclosed area and closed the glass door behind him.

"All right. Jonathan, you'll be going to Nice. I believe you'll need all your medical expertise and a healthy dose of deceit to pull this off. Support Five will assist you once you reach France."

"Understood."

"Wheels up in ninety minutes from Teterboro. You will be traveling with the Gulfstream. Anna will contact the pilots to let them know to expect you. You'll be provided with the details of your cover en route."

"Very well," Sanchez answered.

CHAPTER 28

Antibes, France

The streets of Antibes, typically filled with wealthy vacationers in search of a good time, were uncharacteristically empty due to the cooler-than-usual temperature and light drizzle falling on the cobblestone streets. That made the job of Bernard LeBreton of the DCRI a lot more complicated, for conducting surveillance was much easier when he could hide in a large crowd. But LeBreton had been in the countersurveillance business for the last twenty-five years, and he was confident that his team would be able to do whatever was asked of them, crowds or no crowds.

The way they had received their directives for that evening's job was quite irregular. The head of the DCRI had called LeBreton personally to request that his team drop everything it was working on in Cannes and travel the seven kilometers to Antibes right away. They were to monitor a gray Opel van that was in a parking lot beside the juncture where Général Maizière Boulevard changed into Amiral de Grasse Parkway. The director had indicated that two Arab males had exited the Opel and entered a house across the street.

At that point in the conversation, LeBreton could see no reason why the DCRI's director had called him personally. After all, his team was used to doing that type of job. The severity of the situation became clear soon enough; however, when the director added that LeBreton and his team were to stay on station until the arrival of two troops from GIGN, France's antiterrorism team.

From his position on the far side of the parking lot, LeBreton could clearly see the house that the suspects were said to have entered. But the curtains were closed, preventing him from seeing what was going on inside. LeBreton had three other DCRI men with him, and they were positioned in such a way that nobody could exit the house without being seen.

According to the mailboxes outside the front entrance, the white three-story house had been divided into three apartments. He sent one of his agents to verify all of the building's entries and exits. The agent returned within minutes, confirming that the suspects were on the first floor and that the ground-floor apartment had only one entry—the front. The agent also believed that he'd seen evidence of a fire escape route leading to the roof of the building, likely accessible from the third-floor apartment.

LeBreton noted that the suspects might have access to the upper apartments, so they shouldn't disregard other points of entry. Confident he could monitor all ins and outs of the building with his three men, LeBreton deployed his last man one block away with the order that he follow any suspect exiting the building.

LeBreton was just about to check in with the director of the DCRI when his agent posted at the rear of the building called him. "I've got movement at the rear. Someone is exiting the second-floor apartment. He's wearing a white shirt, blue jeans, white sneakers, and a white baseball cap. Okay, he's moving. He's walking northbound on de la Tourraque."

"Thanks, Regis. Pierre will take it from there," answered LeBreton. "You copied that, Pierre?" he asked into his mouthpiece.

"Absolutely," responded Pierre Levasseur, the agent he'd posted down the street. "I'll be on foot."

Just as LeBreton ended the call, his cell phone vibrated again. "LeBreton here."

"This is Commandant Yves Bleriot of GIGN. We've arrived in the area and are on Cours Massena reviewing our assault plan. We should be ready to storm the building in about ten minutes. Will you be in position to give us a situation report before we move in?"

They're going to storm the building? wondered LeBreton. He'd thought this was just a reconnaissance mission. "Affirmative," he finally said. "We have eyes on the house."

"Great. Don't be alarmed if you see a man wearing a pair of blue jeans, black boots, and a bulletproof vest over a black T-shirt within our group," Bleriot said, giving the description of Mike Walton. "He'll be armed, and he's a friendly. Please confirm?"

"I confirm. Man with blue jeans and black T-shirt is a friendly. I'll pass it along," replied Lebreton.

On his radio, he could hear Agent Levasseur announce that his target had approached Cours Massena, then crossed the street and turned around. It only took LeBreton a few seconds to understand that something was amiss.

"Commandant Bleriot!" yelled LeBreton into his cell phone.

The GIGN commander was taken aback by the sudden panicked voice.

"Break away from your position now!" yelled LeBreton.

Bleriot's intuition told him not to second-guess the DCRI agent, and he quickly ordered his men to move out and regroup at their secondary rendezvous point located nearby at the intersection of the Boulevard d'Aguillon and Rue Vauban. Only when all his men were accounted for did he return to LeBreton.

"What's going on?" he asked.

"I think we've been compromised."

"What do you mean 'compromised'?" the GIGN commander cut in.

"One of the suspected targets exited the house on foot. Unfortunately, he was headed in your direction. My man just informed me that he must have realized who you were, because he suddenly turned around. He's now walking back toward the house."

"Fuck. Is your man armed?"

"Of course he is."

"I know you're not in my chain of command, but your man has to stop the suspect from returning to the house or contacting whoever's inside. And I mean by any means necessary."

"You want me to kill him?"

"If you have to, yes," answered Bleriot. "Listen, we've received information that these are the terrorists responsible for the attack at the Nice Gare Centrale earlier today."

What the fuck? For the second time in as many minutes, LeBreton wondered why the hell he hadn't been properly briefed.

"If we're to have any hope of surprising them," continued Bleriot, "you need to take that suspect out *now*. If not, we might get an unwanted welcoming committee."

"Understood. I'll contact my man."

"Thank you. We're now en route to the house and will start our assault within the next three minutes."

—

Mohammad Alavi cut short his walk for takeout food. He knew right away that the big Suburbans and the men dressed in black tactical gear he'd seen near Cours Massena were ominous. Their tinted windows and high-powered antennas were enough to send chills down his spine. One of the men, dressed in a pair of blue jeans and a black T-shirt, had actually looked him over. *Probably GIGN*, he thought as he turned as casually as possible back toward the safe house.

Could Abbud Raashid have betrayed them? Or had his men been followed from the airport?

Trying not to draw attention to himself, Alavi refrained from picking up his cell phone to warn those inside the house. Maybe he should have ordered them to ditch the Opel after the first strike against the Canadian minister at the Gare Centrale. They had allowed their arrogance to expose them. But it was too late to worry about that now.

After Alavi changed directions, he caught sight of a man across the street who seemed to be watching him. Although he avoided looking in that direction, he was sure his tail raised his hand toward his face. *Probably talking into a radio*, Alavi deduced. He cursed loudly in Arabic.

Suddenly, from the corner of his eye, he caught sight of the Suburbans departing. Years spent fighting the Americans and training young terror recruits had given Alavi a keen edge. He was quick to dissect a given situation and put two and two together. The shock troops had been warned that they'd been spotted, and that revelation had caused them to hasten their attack.

The time for caution had passed. He had to warn the others. He took out his cell phone and started dialing.

—

"Pierre, come in," came LeBreton's voice over the two-way radio.

"Levasseur here, go ahead," said Pierre Levasseur as he watched his target stride back in the direction from which he'd come. Levasseur hadn't had time to conceal himself when the terror suspect he'd been following abruptly turned around. Instead he'd tried to act as natural as possible until the target had passed him.

"Has the target made any cell phone calls since he turned around?" asked LeBreton anxiously.

"Yeah," answered the junior agent. "He's making one right now."

"Shit! Okay, listen up," LeBreton said, launching into a stream of directives that caused Levasseur's heart to leap into his throat.

Now aware that the man he was following was one of the terrorists involved in the Gare Centrale bombing, Levasseur took his MAS G1 pistol out of his shoulder holster. He held the weapon, which was in fact a Beretta 92F built under a French license, close to his right leg as he continued trailing the terrorist.

—

In full daylight, the advantage would have been against him. But at this hour, with no more than a few streetlamps shining and only a handful of pedestrians on the street, Mohammad Alavi knew he had the upper hand. Although the agent following him was good, Alavi was better. He took a sharp turn and hid under a secluded doorway. Then he waited.

The loud revolutions of the GIGN Suburban's engines could be heard a few streets away as they raced to conduct their assault on the terrorists' house. Alavi couldn't help but smile at what he knew was going to happen next. His predictions were proved true when, a few seconds later, the cracking noise of an AK-47 broke through the otherwise silent darkness.

As if on cue, the agent who'd been following him passed just in front of Alavi's hiding place. His attention was focused on the machine-gun fire a few blocks away. The agent didn't even notice Alavi tucked away under the porch less than five feet to his left.

Alavi pumped blood into his hands as he readied himself for his attack.

—

Pierre Levasseur was not yet panicking, but a great sense of unease washed over him as he heard the sound of AK-47 fire. That wasn't right. He knew that the GIGN's FAMAS pistols didn't make that sound. Had the terrorist he'd been following successfully warned his friends of the impending assault? And where the fuck was he, by the way? He'd had him in his sights not even twenty seconds before. *Damn!*

Levasseur was starting to regret not taking his shot when he was twenty meters away. The truth was that he didn't think he'd be able to hit his target at that distance. What if he missed? What if the terrorist was armed and started returning fire? A gun battle in the streets wasn't what they needed right now, no matter what LeBreton said. No, he'd decided it was better to shoot him at close range, just to make sure.

Shit! He knew he should have used the firing range more frequently.

Levasseur *felt* more than saw movement to his left. He barely had time to turn his head, let alone point his gun, before somebody was on him like a tiger.

—

Alavi was lightning fast. He placed his hands on the agent's gun, pulling it toward him while forcing its barrel up and away from him. With his hands never leaving the weapon, Alavi swung his left leg around for momentum and simultaneously smashed his left elbow into the agent's chin. The agent fell flat on his back on the sidewalk, and a dazed look slackened his face. He had been disarmed in less than two seconds. Alavi looked down at him and smiled, then shot him twice in the head. The sound of the MAS G1 was muffled by the AK-47 fire of his friends.

CHAPTER 29

Antibes, Frances

A llah is great," exclaimed Ali Ghassan after speaking to his friend, the feared Mohammad Alavi, for the last time. He looked at the five men with whom he had eaten, slept, trained, and killed for the last few months. They all looked back at him expectantly.

"That was our brother Mohammad. We have been compromised, and he believes that an attack is imminent," he announced. "Our final stand will not be tomorrow in Cannes as planned, but here, right now, together."

His five brothers in faith exchanged uncertain glances. This wasn't at all according to their plan. The Sheik had chosen Cannes, not Antibes, for their martyrdom. Cannes had a higher tourist density, and the bomb would have been more effective there. Antibes was only supposed to be their staging area.

"We have already accomplished a lot, dear friends," Ghassan continued, motivating his men and assembling his AK as he spoke. "Allah smiled at us today when he allowed his great and faithful warrior Mohammad to escape. He will continue the fight for us. He will work with the Sheik to fulfill Allah's will. Now we must make him proud."

Ali Ghassan approached his friends and embraced them one after the other.

"Make sure that the device is activated, and be ready to use it as soon as their first man comes through the door. It will not create as much death and destruction as we had anticipated with our primary objective, but Allah will understand. How long will it take to make it ready?"

"Without Mohammad here? Maybe ten minutes," came the answer from Karim Irfan, their junior bomb technician.

Ghassan snorted. "Make it five. The rest of us will hold on as long as we can to give you time. Complete your contingency tasks that brother Alavi assigned you, then take your positions. Go to a good death, my brothers. *Allahu Akbar!*"

The six men raised their fists and yelled in chorus, "*Allahu Akbar!*"

After he'd helped install the others in their positions, Ali Ghassan took up watch at one of the second-floor windows. His trusted AK-47 was in his hands, and three rocket-propelled grenades lay at his feet. He hadn't been at the window for more than thirty seconds when he heard the GIGN truck engines barreling down the street. The attack was occurring just as Alavi had told him it would. He took aim at the GIGN convoy and, at a rate of six hundred rounds per minute, he emptied his first thirty-round magazine into the third Suburban.

—

Sitting in the passenger seat of the leading Suburban as they approached the terrorist refuge, Commandant Yves Bleriot was about to radio LeBreton when machine-gun fire suddenly opened up from above. Looking in his side view mirror, Bleriot saw the third Suburban in line swerve off course and crash into a building.

Merde! Any hope of a surprise attack was now officially blown.

His orders from the top of the gendarmerie chain of command had been clear. He had to go in and stop the threat. Enough French citizens had died that day. His brother, a high-ranking officer within the DGSE, had also advised him that an American would be joining them on the assault. Because his brother had insisted that nobody else at the gendarmerie was to learn an American was participating in the assault, Bleriot guessed the American was a member of the CIA. He turned around to look at the American and couldn't help but notice how calm and focused he seemed amid all the chaos. That was for the best, because his initial plan was blown all to hell and he needed to be as composed as the American. As the four remaining Suburbans jerked to a stop, Bleriot steeled himself to deliver the most difficult directive of his life.

The outlook didn't look good. He had no backup except for LeBreton's noncombat troops, wherever the hell they were. He had no snipers and nobody on the roof yet. He had nothing except for a small group of assaulters bookending the main door and an unknown number of terrorists firing down on him. Ordering his men to storm the building under fire could become a death warrant for all of them.

—

Karim Irfan was working as fast as he could. He'd never expected that he would have to arm the device alone under such stressful conditions.

He knew that the GIGN troops could breach their defenses any second now, and it added urgency to the mission. He had so much to do in so little time. He tried to calm himself by pretending that his mentor and teacher, Mohammad Alavi, was standing next to him, telling him exactly what to do. *Yes, this is just like at training camp,* Irfan said to himself, trying to believe it.

Training camp or not, he was determined to make his mentor proud of him.

—

Mike Walton followed Commandant Bleriot out of the lead Suburban and watched him wave his arm toward the safe house just as a rocket-propelled grenade landed in the street under the rear of the second Suburban. The explosion blew off the back end of the giant SUV, and Mike protected his head with his arms as he felt a heat wave go through him. When he reopened his eyes, he saw the GIGN commander lying on the ground next to him, a burning piece of metal embedded in his back. Mike knelt down and checked for a pulse. He was gone. Mike locked his MP5 into place and dragged Bleriot to safety while other members of the GIGN covered him. Calculating that the GIGN had already lost at least five men plus their commanding officer in the last thirty seconds, Mike joined the huddle of officers flanking the front door.

"We need to move in," he yelled, "or we'll be blown to pieces!"

"We've lost our two officers," said one of the troopers. "We need to make contact with—"

Mike interrupted him, "No, you don't. We need to break in now or we'll all be slaughtered out in the open."

The GIGN troops had been caught by surprise, but they should have already breached the front door. The whole operation was starting to be bogged down, and that wasn't good. They were losing too many men too fast. Somebody needed to take charge.

"Where's the shield?" Mike screamed over the noise of automatic fire. A few seconds later, one of the officers took up position with a type III ballistic shield. Though that type of shield was useless against armor-piercing automatic fire, it weighed only thirty-four pounds, making it easy to carry and a good option for their purposes.

"We can't wait any longer," Mike said, taking control. "I'm going in behind the shield. The rest of you, fall in behind me and we'll move through this building following regular house-clearing protocols. Any questions?"

There was none. By taking the lead, Mike had grabbed their attention, and they were now ready to follow him.

"Now!"

A trooper shot off the hinges with a Remington 870 shotgun and kicked the door open. Mike threw a flash-bang, waited until it exploded, and then followed the trooper in with the shield.

—

Inside the house, Bin Alavi had wet his pants. He had dreamt so often of this moment, the day when he would become a martyr. Of when he would finally emerge from the shadow of his brother, Mohammad Alavi.

But as he crouched in a corner, clutching his AK-47 in his sweaty hands, he was more afraid than he had ever been in his entire life. Why had his brother left him here with the others when he'd gone for food?

Bin Alavi had always known that he was the weakest link of the group. It was no secret that his performance at the terror camps had been less than satisfactory. Even though he had tried to convince himself many times that Mohammad had chosen him for this mission for his valor, he knew now that he'd been fooling himself. The most important task his brother had assigned him during this whole mission had been to destroy a paper trail. A boy's job!

He had always thought that his brother would keep him out of harm's way if the mission took a turn for the worse, so he was shocked when Ali Ghassan had told him to take up his position. "Just shoot anyone that comes through that front door."

Then the bullets had started flying, and that was when Bin Alavi had wet himself. He was glad that his brother, the great freedom fighter and explosives genius Mohammad Alavi, had not been there to see him. If he had, he would probably have shot his younger brother himself just to save face.

When the infidels came crashing through the front door, Bin Alavi froze. The last thought that went through his head before he was stunned by a French flash grenade was *Shit. The paper trail.*

—

When Mike Walton rushed through the front door, he was surprised to see a blubbering insurgent cradling an AK-47 in his arms like a baby. The terrorist, incapacitated by the thundering flash grenade that had just exploded, had no time to react as Mike raised his weapon and shot him through his left eye.

Mike ordered the men to clear the first floor, which they did quickly. He could hear firing in the street, where several of the GIGN troopers had stayed behind to cover their entrance. Suddenly, the firing stopped. "We've downed three out here," came a voice through his headset. "One from the roof and one from a third-story window."

"Understood," Mike replied. "We're clearing the first floor, but I don't know how to access the upper levels."

"There must be a staircase around back that connects them all," came the voice through his earpiece.

"Roger that," said Mike. "Send two guys around the back of the building to secure the exit. We'll try to access the stairwell." He didn't want anyone escaping.

—

Karim Irfan was so concentrated on his task that he didn't notice the arrival of Ghassan coming to ask him if he was done yet. Irfan jumped at the unexpected voice behind him but recuperated quickly.

"It's taking longer than I thought," he said, his fingers still working rapidly. "I need another three or four minutes."

"We don't have three minutes!" shouted Ghassan. "The rest of the brothers are dead. I'll buy you as much time as I can. Just make sure the bomb is ready!"

Irfan nodded. Without taking his eyes from his work, he put on his ear protection to block out any further distractions.

—

Mike burst into the back room with four GIGN troopers. Just as he had expected, he was met by a closed door that, once kicked in, allowed access to a staircase that led to the upper floors.

"No hesitation," he said, feeling the adrenaline pumping in his veins. "Don't stop for anyone until the whole building is clear. Follow me!"

Leading the GIGN operators up the staircase, Mike was met by a locked door on the second-floor landing. Unsure of what to expect, he stepped aside so that the second in line could shoot out the hinges of the door with the shotgun. Mike kicked in the door and lobbed in a flash-bang. Two seconds later the grenade exploded, and the man holding the type III ballistic shield rushed into the room. Mike was right behind him, his MR73 5.25-inch revolver poised in his hands.

—

As Ghassan heard the GIGN troopers storming up the back staircase, he took cover behind the floor-to-ceiling brick pillar that Alavi had made them build for precisely that contingency. As Ghassan silently thanked his absent comrade for his foresight, he prayed that Allah would give him the courage he needed to sacrifice himself with dignity and to go down fighting. He stole a look at Irfan, who was working furiously in front of the Mac computer, lost in his own world of thought.

"Here they come!" Ghassad yelled, more for his own benefit than Irfan's. He hoped Irfan needed only a few more seconds to enter the codes into the computer that was linked to the bomb. Once entered, the chain of numbers would initiate an irreversible countdown that would lead to the detonation of the small tactical nuclear device twenty seconds later.

Hurry up, Irfan. I won't be able to hold them off for long...

Ghassad placed his hands over his ears to protect them from the flash grenade he knew would be coming. Then he closed his eyes and opened his mouth to attenuate the impact of the blast.

Ghassad opened fire when he saw the first GIGN officer appear. Then, aware that the trooper was holding his ballistic shield a fraction too high, Ghassad aimed his second round lower, shattering the attacker's right tibia.

—

The weight of the ballistic shield caused the shattered right leg of the trooper in front of Mike to collapse, sending him reeling back head-first down the staircase. Nearly knocked down the stairs himself, Mike never paused but climbed over the downed man, firing his MR73 in the general direction where he thought the threat was coming from.

As Mike peeled left, the man directly behind him peeled right to secure his corner. That's when Mike first saw that their target was using a homemade brick wall as fire cover thirty feet away. From behind the pillar, the terrorist opened fire on the GIGN trooper who had peeled right and hit him twice in the groin just beneath his body armor before hiding back behind his man-made cover. As Mike looked for a shot, he saw the GIGN trooper slide slowly down to the ground, his severed arteries leaving a trail of blood down the wall as he collapsed.

As the final two troopers entering the room attracted the terrorist's fire, Mike pointed his weapon at his now half-exposed target and pulled the trigger twice. His two rounds entered the right side of the insurgent's neck just as the troopers were hit in their trauma plate by the insurgent's last salvo. Exactly six seconds after they had breached the door leading to the staircase, Mike Walton shot at point-blank range one more round into the terrorist's forehead.

One of the troopers who had been hit in the body armor was finally able to catch his breath. "What's that in the corner?" he asked, raising his weapon in the direction of a light source in the farthest corner of the massive room.

Mike realized that the light was coming from a computer screen and that a person was hunched over a laptop concealed under a dark blanket. *What the...?* he wondered as he fired the final round of his revolver into the man's back.

The computer screen gave just enough light for Mike to see the figure slump and then topple lifelessly to the ground.

—

Less than ten minutes had passed since LeBreton notified Bleriot that his team's position on Cours Massena had been compromised. Once the firefight was over, Mike had sent one of the troopers to get LeBreton. He quickly made his way to Mike's location on the second floor of the safe house.

"What the hell...What is this?" LeBreton muttered, commenting on an object beyond the dead body of a terrorist. "It looks like a wired stainless steel garbage can."

"That, my friend, is a small nuclear device," Mike answered calmly.

The DCRI agent looked at him in pure disbelief. "You sure?"

Mike checked his Geiger counter again. "Yeah, I'm sure," he said before pointing toward a red USB cable. "This computer and the device are connected by this wire. My guess is these assholes were trying to slow us down to give themselves enough time to blow us all up."

"I can't believe this is happening in France," said LeBreton. "I don't—"

"Can I make a suggestion?" asked Mike, but he didn't wait for an answer. "You should order your team to evacuate the neighborhood. This bomb is still hot and dangerous."

LeBreton was about to turn around when Mike added, "In the meantime, I'll stay behind with two other volunteers from GIGN. We'll be looking for intel."

"Shouldn't you leave as well? You just said this thing could blow up anytime."

"I'll be right behind you," replied Mike.

CHAPTER 30

IMSI Headquarters
New York

Director, you better come to the control room. We have alarming news from Mike Walton," Anna Caprini said.

Mapother stood up from behind his desk and strode into the "bubble," where he found Caprini perched over a bunch of documents.

"Was the raid successful? "

"Mike indicated the operation was a success in that they neutralized all of the hostile targets, but that it came at a very high price."

"How high?" Mapother asked.

"He estimated the DCRI lost one man during the mission and that the GIGN lost at least eight."

"My God," exclaimed Mapother, shaking his head. "GIGN is renowned for executing raids like that."

"Nobody seems to know what went wrong," Caprini replied. "For whatever reason, they were rushed into the operation, and they weren't fully prepared."

"My guess is that the bad guys, whoever they were, were somehow expecting them," said the IMSI director. "I mean, you just don't take out eight GIGN troopers like that." He snapped his fingers for emphasis. "They're as tough as they get."

Mapother's mind was racing through the gears. He knew that somewhere in France, somebody's head was going to roll following the thorough investigation that would surely follow this fuckup.

"And that's not the worst of it, sir," said Caprini. "Mike discovered a small tactical nuke in the house."

Mapother was astonished.

"Fortunately for everyone, the device was not armed yet," she added.

Mapother let go of a breath. "If the targets had advance notice that GIGN was coming, don't you think they would have tried to detonate that damned nuclear device before they arrived?"

"Maybe they did try, and it failed for some reason," Caprini suggested.

Mapother considered this. Suddenly, he returned his attention to his assistant. "You said they neutralized all of the *hostile* targets. Did Mike and the rest of the GIGN capture anyone alive?"

"Negative, sir. The number of terrorists killed is uncertain at this time. But Mike reported that one person exited the house before the raid began and hasn't been accounted for since. He also said some correspondence was seized from the house, but nothing's in the system yet. I'll let you know when I receive any updates."

"Has this gone public yet?" Mapother asked, pacing the length of the room.

"No, sir. The French have been able to keep a lid on it, for now at least."

"They'll try to keep it quiet for as long as they can—especially now that the threat is nuclear."

"I don't see any reason for them to go public with that information until they can clearly pinpoint how the device got into their country. It would only cause pandemonium," Caprini conceded.

"And, Lord knows, the world can't handle much more of that," added Mapother gravely. "Please forward this new information to Jonathan Sanchez. He'll need every bit of support we can give him."

Anna nodded. "What about Mike?"

"His job is done. I want him out of there," Mapother replied.

"I'll advise Support Six to provide assistance, but he told me he had one more lead to follow."

"Damn it. He should know better than that. Did he explain?"

"No. I have no idea what he's doing."

CHAPTER 31

Gendarmerie Nationale Headquarters
XVI District, Paris

Zima Bernbaum, aka Marise Martin, was sitting in the director general's office taking notes. She couldn't believe what was happening today. In the back of her mind, she wondered if the mayhem had anything to do with General Claudel's mysterious visitor. She had finally received news from Ottawa confirming the validity of their doubts regarding General Claudel. The drives she had pocketed from his residence had been analyzed. They showed correspondence between the general and a man named Abdullah Ahmad Ghazi, an accountant with known links to the Sheik. The name Peter Georges was also mentioned, but no one seemed to know who that guy was. Zima asked herself how CSIS would communicate the newfound information they'd learned about General Claudel. Would he be arrested? If so, when? Maybe they were already too late.

General Mathias Deniaud slammed the handset of the phone into its cradle.

"*Merde*," he said.

The general was at the end of his rope, and she couldn't blame him. He'd held the office of the highest position in the French gendarmerie for less than a month, and today not only had a minister from an allied country been assassinated, but word of new disasters on an unprecedented scale were rolling into the office hourly.

Deniaud was competent enough, administratively speaking, but he was also known for his tendency to become overwhelmed by anything related to operations in the field. How he'd managed to climb the ladder within the gendarmerie was a mystery. Rumors indicated that he had called in a few favors—namely, his awareness of a previous security leak within the French National Assembly that he'd kept quiet until such time as he could be compensated with a hefty promotion. This time had arrived last month.

"Marise, if you're not terribly busy, would you mind putting on some coffee?" General Deniaud asked. "I have a feeling that this long day is going to turn into a long night."

Zima sent him her most disarming smile. "Of course, General," she responded, pouting her lips slightly.

"And please contact my deputy, General Claudel, and inform him that I require his presence immediately. He's probably still at his office. If not, send somebody to pick him up at his residence."

"Anything else, sir?"

"Advise my driver to remain on stand by. I'll be going to see the minister within the next two hours."

"Consider it done, General," said Zima.

"Thank you, Marise. You can go home whenever that's finished. It's been a long day for everyone."

"Very considerate of you, General. Thank you." She got up and walked out of Deniaud's office. She would have liked to stay; whatever Deniaud wanted to talk about with Claudel could be important. As she ruffled her hair and reapplied her lipstick, Zima wondered how she could listen in. She should find out what was discussed between the two men.

A few minutes later, she returned to the director general's door and knocked softly

"Come in," she heard her boss say through the door.

"Your coffee, sir," said Zima.

"Thank you, Marise," replied the general. He was behind his huge desk reading documents.

As Zima set down the tray on the far corner of the general's enormous desk, she placed a small but powerful listening device under the lip of the desktop. Her expert hands performed the task in less than two seconds, and she was out of the director general's office in less than ten

Once back at her desk, she contacted General Claudel's office and Deniaud's driver, just as she'd said she would. Then Zima turned off her computer screen, put on a light jacket, and exited the French gendarmerie headquarters.

When she was safely in her vehicle, she reached inside her purse for her personal cell phone. She dialed a local number. "Good evening."

"Good evening, Xavier. This is Marise."

"Ah, *Marise*. What can I do for you?"

"I had a stressful day at the office," Zima said. Aware that they were on an unsecured line, she chose her words carefully. "I was wondering if you and Étienne would be available for a night out. My treat."

"That's sounds wonderful. Should we meet at your place first?"

"That would be nice. See you then."

CHAPTER 32

Paris, France

As Zima Bernbaum got out of her car and stepped into the chilly evening air, her thoughts flew ahead to the discussion she would have with her two colleagues, Xavier Leblanc and Étienne Perrin.

She knew they were playing a dangerous game, but agents from the CSIS were trained to be fearless. Agents caught in Syria, Iran, Yemen, or similar countries could expect to be executed. That was the nature of the work, and they more or less accepted it as an occupational hazard. But her country's standing would be damaged if they were to get caught spying on friendly nations—particularly if they were caught spying on their federal police services.

These thoughts were running through Zima's mind as she crossed to the side of the street where her apartment building was located. She had chosen the one-bedroom apartment on Avenue Victor Hugo mostly because it was within a ten-minute walk from her office at the French gendarmerie headquarters on Rue Saint-Didier in Paris's sixteenth district.

That the apartment was located only a short distance from Place du Trocadero, where one could enjoy the best view of the Eiffel Tower and the Champ de Mars, had factored into her decision to take it. She had also grown quite fond of a small bakery a few steps down the street.

She picked up some pastries and three café lattes on her way up to her second-floor walk-up. Ten minutes later, she, Leblanc, and Perrin were seated in her modest but comfortable living room full of funky second-hand furniture and framed theater posters. To any outside observer, Marise Martin looked the part of a promising woman in her thirties who had just landed her first serious job.

For twenty minutes, the three secret operatives ate flaky chocolate croissants and listened to the director general of the French gendarmerie make a few phone calls. The sound coming out of the listening device was of particularly good quality.

After a call to his wife, they heard someone knocking on the general's office door.

"This might be it," Zima said. Leblanc and Perrin both took one last drag of their cigarettes before stubbing them out in the ashtray.

"Sir, you wanted to see me?"

Zima nodded to the others to confirm that she recognized the voice. General Claudel, she mouthed to them.

"Yes, Richard. Please have a seat. Would you like to join me for a drink?" asked General Deniaud. They could hear a faint pouring of liquid into a glass.

"No, sir. I need to keep my head clear to deal with this crisis," Claudel said curtly.

"Yes, of course. You're right, my friend. I should do the same," said General Deniaud.

There was some clinking of glassware. Zima looked between Leblanc and Perrin and rolled her eyes.

"Well," started General Deniaud, "we have a hell of a mess on our hands."

"Agreed. Eight of our best men dead is definitely what I'd consider a mess."

"But you have to acknowledge that the decision to send in the GIGN was the right one. I was surprised when you didn't support me in that assessment," continued Deniaud. "I am well aware that I don't have your experience when it comes to field operations, but I couldn't see any alternative."

"Waiting until we had proper backup and air support would have been a good alternative," argued General Claudel. "This operation has already blown up in our faces, and you know it!"

"I disagree, Richard. My guess is that if we'd waited any longer, a nuclear device might have been detonated on French soil."

"I highly doubt it, sir."

"We'll know for sure in a few days. I had a conversation with a GIGN officer, and he confirmed that his men found a number of curious documents inside the house."

"Really? Do we know what kind of information these documents contained?" asked General Claudel.

"We're not sure yet, but he thought they looked like official papers from the Ministry of the Interior. The *French* Ministry of the Interior," Deniaud added.

In a small two-story walk-up four blocks away, the three Canadian agents raised their eyebrows at one another.

"Oh?"

"He said he wanted to meet me in person to discuss his findings because some of the names associated with these documents were troublesome," said Deniaud.

"What did you tell him?" asked Claudel, sounding clearly uncomfortable.

"I ordered him to send the originals to our forensics team and copies to our counterterrorism group and my office."

"And when did you ask him to do that?"

"About an hour ago."

"Shit!" exploded General Claudel with fire in his voice. "Couldn't you just stay put and listen to me? Was that too much to ask of a goddamn fool like you?"

The three CSIS agents looked at one another, suddenly aware that the situation in Deniaud's office was spinning off its axis.

Damn it, what's happening? wondered Zima Bernbaum as a long silence ensued.

Then came some shuffling, followed by the unmistakable sound of a pistol's slide behind racked.

"What's with the gun, Richard?" came the eerily calm voice of Director General Deniaud.

Zima knew that Deniaud kept his own firearm in a locked cabinet on the other side of the room. Unreachable.

"You ungrateful son of a bitch," hissed Claudel. "I put you in this job, even though you're a colossal fuckup. I thought you'd at least follow my recommendations. Now you've screwed everything up."

Zima Bernbaum couldn't believe what she was hearing. She had no doubt anymore. General Claudel, the deputy director of the gendarmerie, was a traitor and working with or for the Sheik.

"For God's sake, Richard, what are you doing?"

Claudel ignored him and continued. "Now that I think of it, are you the one who sent agents to my house to retrieve my flash drives? Who did you give them to?"

"I don't know what you're talking about, Richard."

"And you never will," said Claudel a second later.

The Canadian agents jumped in their seats as two gunshots came over their speakers. After a short pause, they could hear the distinct tones of numbers being punched into a cell phone.

"This is the end of the road for me," said Claudel. "Alavi and his associates didn't destroy the correspondence."

Pause.

"Of course. He's already dead, and I'll erase the memory of my phone and its SD card."

Another pause.

"It might take a few days, but it will all lead them to me. You're still safe."

This time the pause was longer and the reply came from a man begging for something. "Please don't do this. I'll do it. Just…just don't hurt him okay? It was my fault. Not his."

The three agents could now hear someone knocking on the general's office door, asking if everything was okay. But before anyone could come in, they heard one final gunshot and then the clatter of someone crashing on the floor.

—

CSIS field agents did not have the same financial and technological means as their American and British counterparts, but they compensated for their lack of resources by using creativity in the field. The fact that they generally didn't have to check in with their superiors before making every little decision didn't hurt, either.

"We need to get out of France," said the agent known as Étienne Perrin after they'd heard the sole gunshot come over the speakers. His real name was Scott Bailey, and he was the senior CSIS agent in France.

"What about the listening device? Shouldn't we try to retrieve it?" asked Zima.

"No. That's the reason why we need to get out. The French will find it soon enough, and they'll trace it back to you in no time," replied Bailey. He looked between the two agents, then continued. "Use your secondary exit protocols. That is an official order. I'll meet you at our rendezvous in Athens in three days at sunset. Make sure you don't leave anything behind."

CHAPTER 33

Antibes, France

Mohammad Alavi was still alive, and that disappointed him. It meant that his brothers in arms had failed to detonate the nuclear device. Had they been successful, the building where he was presently hiding would have been decimated, along with the rest of the town.

His organization had spent a considerable fortune to prepare this mission. He wasn't even sure if the Sheik had the financial resources to make another attempt. They'd had to pay a lot of money to convince General Claudel to act as a conduit for the plutonium they had purchased from corrupt elements within the Ministry of Energy. Plus, the Sheik had paid a fortune for the services of three Russian scientists tasked with putting all the components together. The fact that Omar Al-Nashwan, the Sheik's right-hand man, had been sent to kill the Russians involved and retrieve the money wasn't lost on him either. His organization was in dire need of cash.

Once Alavi killed the DCRI agent, he had been afraid that his description might be sent out to all the French bus and train stations as well as the airports. So instead of trying to run the risk of being captured, he had decided to seek refuge in an apartment building that his men had chosen in case of emergency. It was located on Cours Massena, and Alavi had thought it would be the perfect spot to spend his final minutes on earth in quiet prayer to Allah.

The building was directly across the street from where he had killed the DCRI agent on Rue de la Tourraque. He'd made his way to a second-floor apartment and put his ear to the first door leading onto the staircase. From what he was able to hear, he guessed that the two elderly people living there were home. Not a problem. He would kill them.

He knocked, and an older gentleman cracked the door open a few inches. That was all the space Mohammad Alavi needed. Placing his foot in the door, Alavi shoved hard with his right shoulder. The force was enough to break the door's ancient security chain. The old man, who was probably in his late eighties, was thrown to the floor. The look on his face was one of naked surprise.

Moving inside rapidly, Alavi fell on top of the old man in a rush. Using the weight of his body to pin his victim to the floor, Alavi stifled his elderly victim's cries for help with his left hand. His right hand smoothly retrieved a fixed blade from a gray sheath at the small of his back. Before the old man understood his peril, Alavi's four-inch blade penetrated his wobbly neck just under the jawbone. With one strong twist and pull, Alavi severed the man's jugular.

The terrorist slowly rose to his feet, making sure not to step in the growing pool of blood, and replaced the knife in its sheath. He sensed that someone else was inside the apartment. He took the MAS G1 pistol from his jacket pocket and began to carefully search the small rooms. Holding his firearm close to his chest, he gently pushed the bedroom door open with a squeak.

"Jean?" a weak elderly woman's voice questioned.

He stepped inside the small bedroom, finding that the open door provided the only light into the room. The queen-size bed was less than two strides away. The room smelled of cheap shampoo and night creams.

Calmly, Alavi walked up to the confused woman and stabbed her directly in the heart. Then he cut her throat for good measure.

Satisfied that the apartment was now clear of any threats, Alavi walked back to the kitchen, where the old man's blood was already congealing in a big sticky pool. He couldn't pray to Allah amid this filth. Instead, he fixed himself a turkey sandwich, then took in his surroundings for the first time. *Not a bad place to die*, he decided.

—

Mike was about to pull the plug. He checked his wristwatch and groaned. For close to ten hours he'd been keeping his eyes on the front door of the building across the street. It had been a long day, and he had promised Anna Caprini he was going to call back. He had told her he'd found a lead inside the terrorists' safe house but hadn't revealed what it was. He was afraid Mapother would have insisted on Support Six's presence to cover him. Mike didn't want that. Since the takedown, enough police were swarming around the neighborhood, and he was not about to draw unwanted attention to himself. The folder he had found contained only one page of white paper on which an address had been written. With no phone number, no apartment number, no e-mail address, and no other information that could lead to who actually owned the place, Mike had been tempted to turn over the sheet to the gendarmerie if not for the French words *Location en cas d'urgence*, meaning *Emergency location* that had been written down in red on the folder. Using his smartphone to search the address, Mike found out the location was only a few blocks away from the terrorists' safe house.

Knowing one of the terrorists had escaped, Mike had decided to roll the dice and parked his BMW on a street perpendicular to Cours Massena. The darkened windows of the BMW allowed him to keep his eyes on the door while remaining inconspicuous. Looking at his watch for the fifth time in as many minutes, Mike was ready to acknowledge defeat when he spotted an Arab male exiting the apartment building. Adrenaline filled his veins when he recognized the man he had made eye contact with earlier in the day. He had not the slightest trace of doubt. It was Mohammad Alavi.

—

Eleven hours after the nuclear device had failed to detonate, Alavi knew he had to think of an escape plan. Maybe he should travel along the coast to Spain? He certainly couldn't remain in the little apartment in Antibes. First of all, he didn't want to risk the chance of having the elderly couple's relatives inquiring about their whereabouts. And second, their bodies were starting to smell.

He looked out the windows to see what was going on outside but failed to notice any type of surveillance. If anyone other than the policeman he had killed knew he'd gotten away, they were probably thinking he was far away. The main problem he had was that the borders would be hard to cross now. Alavi wondered what he was going to do. He needed help. Luckily, he knew exactly whom to call

—

Mike's first impulse was to shoot Mohammad Alavi on sight. It would be good riddance, and nobody would blame him for taking the life of a wanted terrorist. But as good as Alavi was at building bombs and creating havoc, Mike suspected he hadn't planned all this by himself.

He hadn't been the brain behind the attacks. Somebody was telling him what to do and when to do it. Taking Alavi out would only create a temporary setback for the network that had orchestrated the hits, and it would kill any chance he might have to gain more information about his father. He had to choose the harder option. He would follow Alavi to his leader and capture them. All of them.

It was time to call IMSI back. He would need their support after all.

CHAPTER 34

Cannes, France

The French authorities still had not reopened the Nice airport, so the Gulfstream landed at Cannes-Mandelieu Airport, located just west of Cannes. A member of the Directorate-General of Customs and Indirect Taxes, or DGCIT, quickly boarded the private jet and stamped Jonathan Sanchez's passport. The DGCIT was the French version of the US Immigration and Customs Enforcement, the US Customs and Border Protection, combined with the US Coast Guard. It was charged with preventing smuggling, surveying borders, and investigating counterfeit money, among other things.

Nice-Mandelieu was the second largest airport on the French Riviera, mostly used by chartered private jet companies and celebrities visiting the area. The hills surrounding Cannes made it next to impossible for larger carriers to land, and that had allowed the airport to remain attractive for a certain clientele that wanted more privacy. Its customer service was renowned for its excellence, so it was no surprise when the Gulfstream was rapidly refueled and rolled into a discreet hangar not far from the main terminal.

A silver Mercedes sedan transported Sanchez to the main terminal. He made his way to the VIP lounge, where Jasmine Carson was waiting for him.

Holy cow! A tall brunette with a ponytail. Why can't IMSI hire ugly women so I can focus on my job?

Carson was seated in a modern green armchair sipping a cup of coffee she had bought on her way to the airport. She got up when she saw her colleague.

"Dr. Jonathan Reznik, I presume?" asked Carson, using Sanchez's cover name, even though she knew the answer.

Beautiful voice, too.

"Yes, that's correct. I'm from the American Medical Life Insurance Company. I was told I would be met by a State Department official," answered Sanchez, for the benefit of anyone who might be listening.

"Glad to meet you, Dr. Reznik," said IMSI's Support Five team leader. "I'm Jasmine Carson from the American embassy. I'll help you get access to your patient, but we'll have to hurry. I assume you have no luggage?"

"No luggage, and the plane is ready to take off at ten minutes' notice," explained Sanchez.

"Great. In that case, please follow me."

With an ass like yours, it will be my pleasure.

Once outside the busy VIP lounge, Jasmine Carson took one last gulp of her coffee, then threw the extra-large plastic cup into a white garbage can. Sanchez followed her outside the terminal, where a black late-model BMW 7 series was waiting for them. Jasmine opened the back door for Sanchez and said, "Sandwiches and coffee are in the basket behind the driver's seat."

Sanchez nodded his thanks as he cautiously climbed into the luxurious backseat of the BMW. The long flight hadn't been kind to his left leg. He stretched it methodically and felt the benefits right away.

"What's wrong with your leg?" Carson asked as she sat at the back of the BMW with him.

"A 7.62 in the left knee," he replied positioning his cane in between him and Carson.

"Ouch! You're lucky to walk."

"Yeah, that's what I tell myself every morning when I wake up."

"Nice woodwork," she said examining the cane, her hand gliding over it. "Where did you get it?"

"I made it," Sanchez replied. "I crafted it myself while I was in rehab."

"You have capable hands—" Carson said before stopping herself. But it was too late.

"Like you wouldn't believe, Mrs. Carson."

"It's Miss Carson actually," she replied amused.

Sanchez grinned. *Is this what they call love at first sight?*

"Anyway, this is James Cooper," Carson said, pointing to the driver. "He's with IMSI as well."

"Nice to meet you, James."

"James is part of Support Five. He's the one who retrieved our asset's pistol and other items."

"Good job," Sanchez said, doing his best to concentrate on the task at hand. "I know that Charles was very pleased with what you did yesterday."

Why is my heart beating so fast?

"We still need to evacuate Lisa, or we'll risk the whole investigation into the bomb being traced back to IMSI," Carson said.

"That's why I'm here, *Miss Carson*. By the way, Lisa's alias for this mission is Rebecca Pyke. Headquarters provided me with a passport to prove it," Sanchez said, handing Carson a well-used American passport.

Carson scrutinized it for a minute. "That will do," she said giving it back to Sanchez.

"Have you been told what my mission is?"

"Yes. I also took it upon myself to share the information I received from New York with James. I figured that we might need a set of wheels ready to go in case we need to get out of Dodge quickly."

"Good thinking," Sanchez answered.

"Here," said Carson, reaching behind her to hand Sanchez what seemed to be an ID card on a necklace. "Wear this around your neck. It bears your cover name and identifies you as a medical representative of AMLIC."

Sanchez saw that his picture had been digitalized onto the card, giving it a look of authenticity. Carson had put a similar ID badge around her own neck.

"Mine identifies me as a State Department agent," said Carson. "If the French decide to investigate us, we have it covered. While you were on your way here, IMSI headquarters set us up with a solid cover that should withstand any type of light- to medium-depth inquiries. However, if they dig too deep, we'll get a call from Control to let us know that our story is getting thin."

"All right. Seems like a plan to me."

"We leased a private ambulance and two paramedics for the day."

Sanchez raised his eyebrows. "Why two paramedics? Isn't Lisa in stable condition?"

"We had no choice," replied Carson. "It was either take the two paramedics with the ambulance or take no ambulance at all. I could have probably pushed harder or paid the paramedics off, but I didn't want anyone to get suspicious."

"I see your point," Sanchez conceded.

"Besides," Carson continued, "I don't think it should cause any problems. After all, everything we're doing is legitimate. This type of medical intervention happens every week. Private medical insurance companies frequently send charter jets to bring back their patients."

"Maybe, but usually their patients are not involved in a failed terrorist attempt," remarked Sanchez.

The BMW was making good time on Pierre Mathis Highway. For a few minutes Sanchez lost himself in the splendid views that scrolled in front of his eyes. Beautiful buildings with astonishing architecture not seen outside the Riviera were lined up on each side of the highway. In the distance, he could see Mont Boron.

"I love this place," Carson said.

"Would be nice to be here simply to visit the sights and to relax for a few days," Sanchez replied. *Especially with a gorgeous woman like you by my side.*

Carson looked at him, her eyes questioning his intentions. But she was smiling, too. "Yes, it would."

They were now approaching the hospital. Carson gave her final instructions to Cooper: "Drive around and make sure to stay close. We might need you. If all goes according to plan, follow us on our way back to the airport, and try to see if we're tailed."

"Will do."

The BMW stopped in front of St. Roch Hospital on Rue de l'Hotel des Postes. Carson and Sanchez got out, and the BMW quickly accelerated away. The beige-colored main building was four stories high and had remained mostly unchanged since the time it was built in 1859. Its majestic elegance conveyed a proud history of service and healing.

After they climbed the steps leading to the main door, they identified themselves to the clerk sitting behind the reception desk. From there, Carson and Sanchez had no problem finding out where Lisa's room was. The clerk even told them that a uniformed member of the Nice municipal police department was guarding the door for extra security for the American heroine. They thanked her for her assistance and proceeded to the third floor of the east wing, where Lisa was located.

The clerk had been right. A young uniformed officer was stationed in front of Lisa's door, but he wasn't paying attention. He had his nose deep in the *Nice-Matin*, the daily regional newspaper, and only noticed the two IMSI agents when they were standing directly in front of him.

So much for security, thought Sanchez.

"*Oui, je peux vous aider?*" asked the officer, looking up from his newspaper.

"My name is Dr. Reznik," said Sanchez in French, showing his identification to the officer. "I would like to see my patient."

The police officer was confused. "But I thought that Dr. Lebrun was the doctor in charge of this patient. I've been ordered not to let anyone in without his authorization."

"Do you speak English, mister?" asked Carson briskly in English.

"Of course," replied the officer defensively.

"Then listen to me carefully," continued the Support Five team leader. She showed him her credentials identifying her as a special agent of the Bureau of Diplomatic Security of the US State Department. "This woman is a citizen of the United States, and my government believes that it would be in the best interest of Mrs. Pyke if she were to return home."

The inexperienced police officer was stunned by her tone of voice. After a few seconds, he looked at Sanchez sheepishly and said, "I understand your position, but I'll have to contact my supervisor and request further instructions."

"That's a great idea, Officer...?" asked Sanchez with a smile.

"Duvallon. Frederick Duvallon."

"Well, Officer Duvallon, why don't you contact your supervisor while we check in on our patient?"

Duvallon hesitated. For a moment Sanchez thought that he wouldn't let them through. So he added, "Why don't you come in with us? This way you'll be able to keep an eye on us and on the patient. How does that sound?"

"Okay," the officer finally said.

Just as they were about to enter, they heard a voice behind them. "Hey! What are you doing?"

Sanchez turned around to see a handsome man in his mid-fifties walking purposefully toward them. He was wearing a white lab coat over a blue shirt and a red tie. He was carrying a clipboard in his left hand and had a stethoscope around his neck.

"You must be Dr. Lebrun," Sanchez said with enthusiasm.

"That's right. And you are?"

"I am Dr. Jonathan Reznik from the American Medical Life Insurance Company." He showed him her credentials before continuing, "And this is Special Agent Jasmine Carson from the Diplomatic Security Service."

Carson nodded toward Dr. Lebrun and quickly flashed her DSS badge. Seeing the two Americans speaking with Dr. Lebrun, Frederick Duvallon retreated to his chair and promptly reached for his newspaper.

"May I assume that you are here for the American woman?" the French doctor asked.

"Her name is Rebecca Pyke," Sanchez answered. "My company sent me to bring Mrs. Pyke back to the US."

"Were you expecting trouble?" inquired Lebrun, looking pointedly at Carson.

"As I am sure you are aware, Doctor, the US State Department takes the security of Americans living abroad very seriously. Because of Mrs. Pyke's involvement in yesterday's tragedy and the fear that terrorists might want to exact revenge, it was decided at the highest level of our government that a layer of security should be added," lied Carson.

"I see," responded the doctor. He didn't seem convinced.

"For the same reason, I hope you yourself are taking additional precautions," added Carson for shock value.

This last sentiment had hit its desired target. Lebrun straightened his shoulders nervously. "I know that some gendarmerie officials wanted to speak with Mrs. Pyke regarding yesterday's events. I'm supposed to call them once I deem her fit enough to be interviewed. On the other hand, I understand that there might be an aggravated risk to the hospital if she were to remain here for a prolonged time."

Sanchez and Carson nodded in agreement. *He's gonna go for it*, realized Sanchez.

"Are you equipped to see to Mrs. Pyke's needs?" asked Dr. Lebrun.

Sanchez replied, "Of course. An ambulance is waiting for us across the street, and our airplane is supplied with all the medical equipment necessary to ensure her safe transfer back to the US."

"In that case, I see no reason why I should keep you from your duties. Mrs. Pyke is now in stable condition and should be fine to travel. Here's her chart and the rest of her file." He handed Sanchez several pages of medical notes and radiographies that had been attached to his clipboard.

Sanchez flipped through the papers.

Lebrun continued, "Mrs. Pyke was very fortunate. The police report indicated that her assailant stabbed her twice with a knife that had a three-and-a-half-inch blade. Fortunately, the first wound only went about two inches deep and missed her right kidney by less than an inch. The terrorist's second attempt was deflected off Mrs. Pyke's shoulder blade, so it didn't hit any vital organs. She's stitched up now and on light painkillers."

"Thank you for everything you have done, Dr. Lebrun," said Sanchez, and he meant it.

"Don't mention it. Now, if you'll excuse me, with all the atrocities that happened yesterday, I have many more patients to attend to. I'll only take down your names so that I can advise the authorities who took over the patient."

Sanchez and Carson were happy to oblige. They even left an address and a phone number, all of it set up by IMSI. Loud enough for the young officer to hear, they promised they would make sure that Rebecca Pyke was available if the gendarmerie wanted to talk with her once she was back in the US.

Dr. Lebrun shook hands with the Americans—first with Carson and then with Sanchez. He held his hand a little longer than necessary, looking directly into his eyes. From his frank and bemused expression, Sanchez had the feeling that he was telling him that he knew something was amiss but that he had more important things to do than play political games. He smiled at him and walked briskly down the hall.

"He's a good man," Sanchez said once the French doctor had left.

The two IMSI operatives entered Lisa's private room. She was lying on her belly with her head turned so she could keep an eye on the door. Her facial expression betrayed her absolute surprise at seeing Sanchez.

"Mrs. Pyke, I am Jasmine Carson from the American embassy," Carson said, acting out her role.

"Hello, Jasmine," Lisa replied, her eyes still fixed on Sanchez.

"I'm Dr. Jonathan Reznik from AMLIC's New York field office," Sanchez said, breaking the ice. "Your insurance company has decided that you are entitled to the best medical care available. We have an ambulance waiting outside to transport us to the Cannes-Mandelieu Airport, where a plane is waiting. We'll fly directly to Teterboro."

"Well, I'm glad you're here," Lisa said. "If a French insurance company started asking me questions about my coverage, it could have become complicated."

"Then I suggest that we get moving," Carson said. She looked at Sanchez and added, "I'll contact the paramedics and ask them to join us with a stretcher."

"Okay, do that. In the meantime, I'll let the pilots know that we would like to be wheels-up within the hour," Sanchez answered, already reaching for his cell phone.

CHAPTER 35

Southeast France

So far Zima had been following her planned exit strategy to a tee. She had used credit cards belonging to Marise Martin to purchase numerous train tickets to different destinations in the hope that the French authorities, if any were on her tail, would waste time figuring out which train she had taken. In reality, she took none of them.

She rented a car under the name of Lise Bourgeois, another of her aliases. She drove the white Peugeot 206 to the small seaside village of Cerbère, located along the French-Spanish border. From there she used the last of her aliases to purchase a return ticket to Barcelona the next morning.

Zima Bernbaum had always considered herself a city girl. She enjoyed shopping, eating in nice restaurants, and being surrounded by people. Nevertheless, she found the quaint village of Cerbère and its amazing view of the Mediterranean truly beautiful. For her overnight stay, she picked the Hotel La Dorade on Rue Maréchal Joffre, which was, as its name suggested, right in front of the sea.

The owner of the little family hotel, a tall, dark, handsome Frenchman, was manning the front desk and politely asked to see Zima's documents. She handed over a Canadian passport bearing the name Joanne Rochette.

"You're from the province of Quebec?" asked the charming owner in French.

"Yes," replied Zima in the same language. She smiled widely.

"And you can only stay for one night?" the innkeeper inquired.

"Unfortunately, yes," replied Zima. *Why do I think my answer disappointed him?*

"Oh, that's too bad," said the owner, "because I've got you in one of our nicest rooms." He handed over a room key to Zima—a real brass key, not a plastic key card. Zima smiled at the old world touch.

"Thank you so much for your hospitality."

"You're most welcome. Enjoy your stay with us, and make sure to try our restaurant for dinner. It's the best in town."

"I'll make sure to do that."

Zima carried her small bag up the narrow wooden staircase and entered the room she'd been assigned. The owner was right—the room was perfect, and it had a spectacular view. Zima went into the old-fashioned but retrofitted bathroom and turned on the ventilation fan. She took out all of her fake documents and burned them one by one in the bathroom sink. Next, she used scissors to cut the credit cards into tiny pieces, then rolled them in tissue and flushed them down the toilet. Tomorrow, if all went according to her plan, she would fly to London from Barcelona, and she didn't want to get caught with an arsenal of fake passports and credit cards bearing different names.

She changed into a pair of jeans and a loose-fitting black blouse. She had built up an appetite and decided to follow the hotel owner's recommendation to try out the hotel's bistro. She placed her cell phone in her jeans pocket and affixed her black custom-molded knife sheath around her ankle. *Should I bring my pistol instead?* she wondered, then dismissed the idea. *It's not like I would shoot a French police officer if I was caught.*

After making a mental note of the exact positioning of all her personal effects in the room, Zima stepped out into the hallway and closed the door behind her. As she walked through the small lobby, she saw the owner seated on a barstool enjoying the company of two gorgeous young ladies. Their eyes met when Zima walked past them, and he raised his drink to salute her. As she continued toward the terrace, she could feel his eyes burning on her back.

Yeah, thought Zima. *I've still got it.*

—

The hostess asked her if she wanted to enjoy the outside terrace or if she would prefer a more private setting inside. As the evening was warm and the wind light, Zima decided that dining outside would be just what she needed to release some of the tension that had been building in her shoulders ever since she'd heard General Deniaud get shot the evening before.

She was offered one of the small round tables on the tiny but well-appointed terrace and settled into a cane chair. Zima was impressed with the vitality of that small village. Young families were walking along the sidewalk, smiling and laughing; elderly couples were strolling hand in hand.

Maybe one day it will be my turn to walk aimlessly in the street, pushing a stroller with two little ones inside. Now, why am I thinking about the hotel's owner? Because he's sexy as hell, Zima. Your female cerebral cortex is letting you know he'd be a good suitor to raise a family with. That's why. That's crazy!

Her mother had talked to her about the internal clock all women had. So busy with her work, she'd never put too much thought into it. But now she wondered, *Is it time for me to settle down? Find someone to love and buy a house? Not yet. Maybe in a few years. But what if I meet someone special?*

Suddenly, Zima froze. Her body reacted before her brain could process what her eyes were seeing. Was it someone she knew? At a table one patio over, a tall, well-built man in his late thirties was sitting alone. He was dressed in white sneakers, blue jeans, and a white long-sleeve shirt. He had skin the color of milky coffee, black hair, and a somewhat unruly black beard. He was wearing a pair of mirrored aviator sunglasses even though the sun was getting low.

Zima's brain was working double time trying to figure out where she had seen this man. Under which of her aliases would he know her? A fraction of a second too late she became conscious that she was still staring and averted her eyes. *Shit. Rookie mistake*, she reprimanded herself. She didn't think he had noticed, but it was hard to tell with the sunglasses he was wearing.

Her mind finally clicked, and her body reacted as if it had been hit by lighting. She reached into her pocket for her cell phone and dialed the number of someone who would know what to do.

"Yes?" Scott Bailey answered.

"This is Joanne. Can you talk?"

"Absolutely. I was just enjoying a nice cup of coffee. What can I do for you? I hope all is well with your trip?"

"So far everything is going according to schedule," said Zima, sucking in her breath as she watched the Arab male get up from his table and throw a bill down beside his half-empty glass. He walked away in the direction of the train station.

She got up from her chair and apologized to the waiter, who was headed her way to take her order.

"I think I saw someone who's on the list," she continued cautiously.

The voice on the other end of the line suddenly sounded much more alert. "Are we talking about the same list, Joanne?"

They were both referring to the list that the CIA, CSIS, Mossad, and MI-6 kept at their headquarters with the names of the most sought after terrorists. Every agent had to know the names and the physical descriptions of these high-value targets.

"Yes." Zima lowered her voice. "I believe I saw Mohammad Alavi. The same guy General Richard Claudel mentioned in his phone call before killing himself."

"Listen to me carefully. What I want you to do is follow him while I contact Ottawa for more precise directives," the voice continued. "But don't get too close, because if this really is who you say, he's extremely dangerous."

"I know. I'll be careful."

—

There was no way Mike could have followed Mohammad Alavi from Antibes to Cerbère all by himself. There were just too many variables to guarantee success. Based on the briefing Mike had given Mapother after his sighting of Alavi, the IMSI director had given his asset the go-ahead to conduct surveillance on Alavi and confirmed Support Six availability.

Support Six had determined where Alavi was headed. Using a parabolic microphone, they'd been able to capture Alavi's request to purchase a bus ticket to Cerbère, a small village close to the Spanish's border. Mike had followed with the BMW while Support Six used their modified Mercedes Sprinter van. A few kilometers before reaching Cerbère, Mike passed the Mercedes van in order to arrive first at his destination. Once in town, all the people in the streets had allowed him to track Alavi without much difficulty.

Mike noticed Alavi looking at his watch one more time. *Is he waiting for someone? That would make sense. Cerbère is probably a transition point for him. Someone will give him his next instructions. If I'm right about this, I should probably back off a little because somebody's likely to conduct surveillance on him.*

"Mike from Support Six."

"Go ahead."

"For your information, we're deployed about three hundred meters southeast of your location on Rue Francois Arago."

"Got it."

"If you decide to snatch him, we're ready."

Mike had thought about grabbing Alavi but had come to the conclusion they were better off waiting for him to make contact.

"If I decide to choose this option, I'll give you as much notice as I can, but it won't be our primary solution," replied Mike. "Target just stopped walking. He's looking at a restaurant's menu."

Mike, who was following Alavi from the other side of the street, stopped walking as well. He counted to twenty before glancing over. The terrorist was now walking to a table accompanied by a server.

"He stopped at a restaurant. I can't stay immobile forever," said Mike. "I'm walking back north and will try to find a vantage point where I can keep an eye on him."

"There's another restaurant just north of you called *Le café de la plage*," offered Support Six. "You should have a visual on the target from there."

The restaurant in question had a huge terrace with blue parasols. He walked to it and selected a table offering him great views of his target. Mike didn't know how long he was going to stay, so he only ordered coffee and a newspaper. He hadn't the chance to get much sleep in the last two days, and he was physically and emotionally exhausted. He was missing Lisa dearly. Mapother had told him he had sent a team to conduct an exfiltration. Mike shook his head, still not believing what Lisa had done at the Nice airport. Why didn't she wait for him? These kinds of takedowns have a better chance of success when conducted by two people. She knew that! She not only risked her life, she risked a lot of bystander's lives.

Stop thinking like that, Mike, he ordered himself. *You know damn well why she did this. And you would have done the same if you'd been in her shoes. Just be grateful she's still alive.*

Massaging his temples, Mike hoped the coffee would do him some good.

Mike sighed as Alavi got up from his table and walked away from the restaurant. Mike left a few euros to cover the cost of the coffee he wouldn't drink and advised Support Six of the new development.

"Alavi's on the move. Southbound on Maréchal Joffre. He's walking faster."

Shit. That's a great move. Countersurveillance 101. Mike had practiced the same technique with his wife more than once. To work properly, this stop-and-go method needed at least two operatives. The objective was to get the rabbit—the person being followed—in a position where the people conducting surveillance couldn't miss him. The trick was to stay put long enough to force the surveillance team to readjust their position so they wouldn't remain conspicuous. The operative conducting countersurveillance would then position himself to watch the area surrounding the rabbit. The next time the rabbit moved, he would do so faster than before, usually resulting in confusion among the surveillance team.

Mike fought the urge to pick up the pace and swore at the fact that he didn't have a bigger team. *Damn it! I'm going to lose him!* Mike's eyes were moving fast behind his sunglasses. He was convinced someone was looking after Alavi's back.

"Support Six, you might have to set up a safety net," said Mike. "I'm about to lose him."

"Copy. Where do you want us?"

Mike was about to reply when he saw Zima Bernbaum getting up from a table. *Are you fucking kidding me? What is she doing here? It can't be a coincidence. Oh, my God, she's after Alavi.*

"Mike, where do you want us?"

"Sorry, Support Six, stay in position. I say again, stay in position."

"Copy."

If Zima was following Alavi, he could follow Zima. Was she by herself, or did an entire team of agents surround her? He doubted Zima was by herself, but he didn't think the team was huge either. He was going to give her lots of room to maneuver.

"Support Six, there's another team in play. An ex-colleague of mine just popped up."

"Canadian?"

"Unless she changed allegiance," replied Mike. "Contact headquarters and let them know Zima Bernbaum is in Cerbère."

What are you up to, Zima?

CHAPTER 36

Mohammad Alavi's heartbeat was pounding in his ears—a sensation he didn't usually experience. He thought he had covered his tracks well enough to smuggle himself out of France unseen. Apparently he hadn't.

Back in Antibes, before he'd left the elderly couple's apartment, Alavi had concluded that his best course of action was to contact Omar Al-Nashwan. He would know what he should do. After all, Al-Nashwan was, among many other things, the Sheik's eyes and ears in the field.

Their phone conversation had passed without Al-Nashwan condemning Alavi's failed mission. Perhaps he planned to deliver the Sheik's wrath later, in person. Either way, Al-Nashwan had suggested that Alavi exit France through Cerbère.

Alavi still wasn't sure if he was being lured to his death, but one way or the other, he would accept his fate with dignity. He couldn't run away from the Sheik's hangman.

But now he wasn't so sure that he would see the end of the day. The woman on the next terrace over had looked at him longer than she should have, then had taken out her cell phone and made a call. Not attractive enough to draw the attention of ladies, Alavi knew right away that she was watching him for another reason. Instinct told him to start moving. Had she seen his handgun? No, it was well concealed. Was she with the French police? That was a possibility, but he doubted it. If the French already knew where he was, they wouldn't hesitate to take him down.

The more he thought about it, the more convinced he became that the lady was an emissary of Al-Nashwan. His instructions had been clear. He was to go to the Cerbère train station and buy a one-way ticket to Barcelona. He would be met on the train while en route to his destination.

Maybe the woman is only reporting my arrival, thought Alavi. He was hoping that was the case. But if that was so, then why was she now following him? There was only one way to find out.

He would try to shake her off. It wouldn't be easy—the village was small, with no subway system or supermarkets in which he could easily disappear. *No*, he decided, *if she has any kind of training, I won't be able to lose her*. If he was going to learn what she wanted from him, he would have to confront her.

The thought brought a smile to his face.

—

Zima Bernbaum was now convinced that her prey was whom she had originally thought—Mohammad Alavi, a terrorist involved in a series of attacks that had caused mayhem around the world. He was believed to be a key player in the Sheik's terror organization, and Zima was sure he had played a role in the assassination of the energy minister. Capturing him alive would represent a major victory for CSIS, its allies at the CIA, and for her. She clenched her teeth as she thought about her two friends, Lisa and Mike, whose family was slaughtered by fanatics just like Alavi.

I won't rest until these bastards are all dead or captured. The house and husband will wait.

As ruthless as these types of terrorists were, they were no match for trained interrogators who had the chance to spend some time with them.

Once she was sure that Alavi wouldn't double back toward her, Zima complied with Bailey's orders and began to follow the man responsible for so many murders. She knew how perilous her task was, and she wished for that handgun. Trailing Mohammad Alavi by fifty meters, she made sure that she kept a visual shield between them. A young couple in their mid-twenties was unknowingly giving the Canadian operative some cover. Other pedestrians were also in her line of sight but were walking at a different pace and moving in and out of her buffer zone.

Instead of continuing on Rue Maréchal Joffre, Alavi took a slight left and walked about seventy-five meters before making another left on Rue des Douaniers. Unfortunately, the lovely young couple who was providing Zima cover continued toward Rue du Riberal, and she then realized that she would have to give Alavi a lot more room to maneuver.

Trailing a target alone was never easy. Police and intelligence services around the world usually employed half a dozen agents to follow a single target. More often than not, the target had to be abandoned in order to avoid tipping him off. However, in this case, Zima wasn't so sure. She didn't think losing such a target would be a good idea. Looking at her watch, she saw that it was time to call her contact back for directives on what needed to be done.

It was answered on the first ring. "Zima?"

"Yes, it's me. Were you able to contact Ottawa?"

"Yes. We have to take him."

"How?" was all she asked.

"If we can bring him in alive, we do it. If we can't, he dies in the street."

"Understood."

"Some helpers are on the way, but they won't reach you for another three hours. You're on your own, Zima. Tell me your location at this very moment." Bailey's voice on the other end of the line was reassuring.

"He's still walking westbound on Rue des Douaniers. He's a hundred feet in front of me, but the pedestrian traffic is light on this street." She tensed as her target deftly fished something from his jacket pocket, then relaxed when she realized that it was only a cell phone. "He's making a call now. He's dressed in a pair of blue jeans, a white long-sleeve shirt, white sneakers, and he's wearing aviator sunglasses. He's about six feet tall, with a dark complexion, black hair, and a beard."

"All right, Zima," came the calm voice. "I know exactly—"

"He just made a right," Zima interrupted. She tried to read the street sign thirty meters away, but the sun had already settled behind the horizon. "Damn it! I can't see the name of the street. I have to go. Stay close to your phone."

She returned her phone to her pocket and quickened her pace to catch up to Alavi. She couldn't lose him. She forced herself to think of a plan to take him down. She would play the nice tourist asking for directions before subduing him. The best way would be to confront him head on. As soon as she regained visual contact with her target, she'd run on a parallel street to pass him before positioning herself in front of him.

She could feel the adrenaline pumping through her veins. It helped her focus on her objective. She visualized how the operation would go down. Her mind's eye saw her successfully neutralizing Alavi, then stealing a car to make her escape to a safe house in Spain, where she would wait for her backup team to arrive.

She was so confident in how it would all go down that Zima forgot the number one rule of all espionage operations: expect the unexpected. As she turned onto Rue Mozart, she sensed rather than saw the movement directly to her right.

She had broken simple surveillance tradecraft by making her turn too close to the residential building instead of giving herself the chance to visually clear the way. Her right arm automatically went up in an attempt to block the blow that was about to land at the juncture of her neck and clavicle. Her hand-to-hand combat training paid off, as she successfully deflected Alavi's blow. Her reflexes, honed through hundreds of hours of extreme conditioning, propelled her left hand straight toward Alavi's abdomen.

She knew she was fighting for her life.

—

To Alavi's surprise, the woman had blocked his strike, which was not intended to kill her, rather to leave her unconscious. But she wasn't cooperating. Her left-handed punch to his solar plexus came as a shock, and he would have been knocked over by the powerful right-handed uppercut she followed up with if he hadn't partially blocked it with his left forearm.

Out of breath from the painful hit he had received, Alavi tried to reach for his pistol at the small of his back, but the female operative didn't leave him enough time. She was on him, armed with a blade. Where had the knife come from? He hadn't seen her draw it, and from the way she handled it, she knew how to use it. He didn't know of any women who were trained that well in his organization. Clearly, his friend Al-Nashwan had told him the truth on the phone when he said that he hadn't sent her.

He easily blocked her first slash but understood a quarter of a second too late that it was only a feint as her opposite leg swept at his ankles. He fell hard on his side, unable to stop her kick that landed directly in his face, breaking his nose and sending tears to his eyes. He heard himself yelp in pain.

—

As Alavi went down and Zima heard his bones break under the force of her kick, she saw a man from her past clearing the corner, making his way toward them with his firearm drawn.

Mike Powell. That's not possible, Zima thought, momentarily losing her focus in her surprise. For a trained fighter like Alavi, the pause was enough. Using all his remaining force, he pushed her off him and leaped to his feet. He was reaching for his gun when she heard the shot.

—

Mike had heard the scream and ran toward the sound right up until he had to clear his corner. With his gun leveled at the high ready, he walked the last five meters. There was still enough light out for him to see that Zima had gained the upper hand against Alavi. The terrorist was now on his belly and was about to be disarmed. She had both his arms pinned behind his back as she squatted on top of him, effectively blocking any movement of his arms with her own thighs. Then she saw him.

—

The call he'd received from Mohammad Alavi a few minutes ago was unexpected. Alavi had been forbidden to establish contact prior to the agreed upon time the next morning. But Alavi's voice, usually calm, was distraught. He explained that he believed he was being followed but was quite sure that the operative represented the French authorities. He had wondered aloud if the Sheik had decided to eliminate him and said that if that was the case, he was ready to accept his punishment—but that he didn't want to play his game.

Al-Nashwan had replied angrily that nobody from the Sheik's organization wanted Alavi dead, and that he would take care of the problem. Like Mike, Omar Al-Nashwan had also elected to conduct countersurveillance. Admittedly, he'd only begun his operation upon Alavi's arrival to Cerbère, but he hadn't noticed anything suspicious. Either the team they were playing against was extremely good, or they'd just started following Alavi.

After his colleague's phone call, Al-Nashwan picked up the brown-haired broad tailing Alavi. He instructed Alavi to bring her to a specific location and take her down in an alley. Al-Nashwan, doubting that the female was operating alone, had cleverly positioned himself so he could eliminate any backups she would have coming to her rescue once Alavi subdued her.

He'd been lucky that a parking space had been available for the small Peugeot he had stolen earlier in the day in Perpignan. The terrorist wasn't surprised when he saw a man pulling a pistol out of a shoulder holster. He watched as the backup approached Rue Mozart with his weapon drawn. The man's tradecraft was particularly good, noticed Al-Nashwan. And Alavi had been correct—even though he could see only the man's back, this was no French agent.

Al-Nashwan exited the car, making sure not to close the door of the vehicle behind him. He briskly walked toward where he knew the action would be, the rubber soles of his shoes ensuring his stealthy approach. Once he cleared the corner, he took in the sight before him in less than a second.

The man he had observed was moving in a position to cover his female partner, who had surprisingly incapacitated Alavi. Al-Nashwan instantly leveled his .22 caliber pistol and fired a round at his target's skull.

—

Keeping his firearm pointed in the general direction of the threat, Mike was about to position himself to properly cover her when he saw movement in his peripheral vision. Sensing danger, he turned to face the new threat just as the subsonic round that Omar Al-Nashwan fired from his suppressed pistol flew past the exact same place his head had been a quarter of a second earlier. Mike returned fire five times, but the man who'd shot at him was fast and had already sought cover behind the stone wall of the building. Dropping to his knees, he pivoted toward Alavi, who was now on his feet armed with a pistol. Zima, meanwhile, was running away toward Rue des Douaniers. Mike pulled the trigger instinctively before rolling to his right. His round hit Alavi's firearm, knocking it out of his hands.

Two bullets passing mere inches from his head forced Mike to reengage the other terrorist even though he could see from the corner of his eye that Alavi was escaping. Mike fired six times to cover his retreat, then sprinted out of the danger zone. He heard the whizzing sound of another round passing inches from his ear, followed a nanosecond later by a metallic chime as the bullet impacted one of the cars parked in the street. Reaching safety on Rue des Douaniers, he peeked right and saw Alavi already more than fifty meters away, running for his life. For a second, he was tempted to go after him but changed his mind and headed after Zima instead.

—

Seconds after turning the corner, Zima glanced behind her but didn't see anyone pursuing her. Though she felt guilty about leaving Mike by himself against two armed men, she kept running anyhow. What could she do? She was unarmed.

Damn it! It wasn't like her to run away. She stopped and was about to hurry back into the firefight when she saw Mike sprinting in her direction.

—

On Rue Mozart, Alavi had run a loop around the block. His nose was still bleeding profusely, and Al-Nashwan could see that his ego had been damaged as well. A woman had dropped him, and he wanted revenge.

"Let me go after her," Alavi said in Arabic, picking up his damaged MAS G1.

"Look at you, Mohammad," said Al-Nashwan. "Would it be wise?"

Alavi grunted in response. He knew Al-Nashwan was right.

"But she saw your face," Alavi insisted.

"Yes, she did, but she doesn't know who I am. My face isn't in any of their databases. Follow me. We're leaving."

Alavi, holding a tissue to his nose, followed Al-Nashwan to his car and sat himself in the passenger seat. Moments later they were on their way to Spain.

—

"Follow me, Zima," Mike said, running past her. "We have a pickup point two hundred meters north of here."

Without turning to look, Mike could hear Zima's footsteps behind him.

"Support Six, Support Six, are you in position?" Mike asked.

"Support Six is in position and ready to receive," he heard back.

Mike saw the Mercedes van a few seconds later and continued to sprint toward it. The side door opened when he was less than five meters away. He jumped in, followed closely by Zima. As soon as they were inside, the door closed, and the Mercedes accelerated away.

"Hello, Zima," Mike said, out of breath.

"What the fuck?" Zima replied, panting as well.

A Support Six member put his finger to his lips, silencing them. The next twenty minutes were spent in silence as Support Six listened for any alerts that might have been given about Mike or Zima. Once convinced they were in the clear, at least for the moment, the same man who had asked them to be quiet walked toward them. "Where to, boss?" he asked, handing each of them a water bottle.

"Barcelona," replied Mike between two gulps of water. "She needs to get out of here as soon as possible."

The man looked at his watch. "Barcelona is about one hundred and seventy kilometers away. We should be there within three hours."

When the man had retreated behind his laptop, Mike looked at Zima.

"It's a long story," he said.

"We have three hours," Zima pointed out reasonably.

"It's complicated, and to be blunt, I'm not sure I'm allowed to tell you anything. You being here is already a huge break in protocol."

Zima smiled at him and touched his cheek with her hand. "I'm glad to see you, Mike. The surgeons did a great job, but I would recognize you anywhere. I thought you were dead," she said. "And, for what it's worth, I'm happy you got involved. You saved my life back there."

Mike cracked a smile as well. "Me too, Zima. It's nice to see you. I'm sorry if I sound like a cold-hearted son of a bitch. The people I work for are very secretive."

Zima nodded. "Is Lisa alive?"

Mike thought about his answer and what exactly he could reveal. But Zima insisted. "Is my friend alive, Mike?"

He didn't have the courage to lie to her. And for what, really? She was one of the good guys too. "Yes, she is," Mike answered. "And I know she'd love to see you."

Zima was clearly relieved, and Mike could see she was fighting back tears. Then suddenly she jumped on him and hugged him. "How is she? I read that newspaper article, you know?"

"She's okay, I guess," Mike replied. *This ain't the time to get into specifics*, he decided.

"Give her my best, will you?"

"Of course," said Mike.

Mike pondered his next words carefully. He didn't want to look like he was being aggressive, but he needed to make his point. "Listen to me carefully, Zima," he said, grabbing both of her hands. "You can't tell anyone you saw me. Not a word about me or my team."

He could see Zima thinking about it. In a certain way, he trusted her. Whatever she was going to reply, he knew she would do it.

"Sure. I'll keep my mouth shut," she said, looking around. "Anyway, it looks like we're on the same team."

"You want to share notes, then?"

Zima hesitated, but Mike added, "I'll start."

"Fine. I'm listening."

Without compromising IMSI, Mike explained in as many details as he could what led to his confrontation with Mohammad Alavi. When he was done, Zima was shaking her head.

"That's unreal," she said. "I think you'll like what I've got." Zima started with the reasons behind her covert assignment. Mike listened carefully and took notes on a pad he had borrowed from one of the Support Six personnel. When Zima mentioned the break-in inside General Claudel's residence, Mike asked if she had the drives with her.

"Yeah. I left most of my stuff and the hotel room back in Cerbère, but I've got the drives right here in my pocket," she said, tapping her leg.

"You know my next question, right?"

She retrieved the drives and handed them to Mike.

"I want them back."

"Of course," replied Mike. "Thanks for doing that, Zima. We'll copy them and hand them back to you before we reach Barcelona."

"You know the RCMP and CSIS will be investigating this thing, right?" asked Zima.

Mike nodded.

"I'm not sure they'll keep me in the loop, though, you know what I mean?" she continued.

"Not to worry, Zima," said Mike, understanding too well what she was asking in return. He gave her his notepad and the pen. "Why don't you tell me how to contact you? I'll make sure to share what we find with you."

Zima wrote down her private e-mail address. "Send me a message at this address. Once we make contact, we'll set up a secure way of communicating."

"Who knows, maybe one of these drives will tell us why the minister was killed," said Mike.

"I have two different theories," ventured Zima. "Care to hear them?"

"Go ahead," replied Mike, finishing the last of his water.

"Based on what we've discussed earlier, I believe the minister might have been killed to protect the identity of General Claudel."

"The guy's dead, Zima," said Mike. "Why would they try to safeguard his identity?"

"Think about it, Mike," pressed Zima. "Claudel wasn't supposed to die. If Alavi and the rest of his cell were successful at detonating their bomb, the general wouldn't have been exposed and could have remained a powerful conduit for the Sheik's network."

Mike thought about what Zima had said for a moment. "Having the number two man of the gendarmerie on your side is a powerful tool for a terror organization," he agreed. "I understand why the Sheik would go to great lengths to protect his asset. Then again, do you really believe Claudel suspected the minister of having doubts about his integrity? Seems far-fetched to me."

"I agree it's a long shot, but it's a possibility."

"What's your second scenario?" asked Mike.

"The minister was killed because of the project he was working on."

Mike shrugged. "I'm not privy to what he was working on, Zima."

"Sorry. He was working on an oil pipeline project with the White House. It was supposed to be kept under wraps, but journalists with close ties to a radical environment group found out about it. They published an article, and all of a sudden, everybody knew about it. The president admitted the United States was looking to reduce its dependency on foreign oil, especially from unstable Middle Eastern countries."

Mike had read at length on this subject. The Persian Gulf represented about twenty-one percent of the Unites States' total oil imports. While the percentage was a lot less than what most Americans believed, it was still dangerous to send large sums of money to countries neither democratic nor allied with the United States.

"That makes sense," said Mike.

"With the Canadian energy minister dead, everything will be at a standstill for the foreseeable future," Zima concluded. "He was the link between the current White House's administration, the Canadian Parliament, and private interest groups. Without his influence, the pipeline project won't pass."

"Interesting theory," said Mike.

"Sir, for your information, we'll be in Barcelona in two hours," said a man in the front passenger seat.

Consulting his watch, Mike said, "Excellent, we're making great time."

"You'll drop me in Barcelona?" asked Zima.

"I'll be flying home later today," replied Mike. "You should do the same."

"I have to. I'll deliver the flash drives to the analysts." She gave him a wink. "With some luck, we'll find something."

CHAPTER 37

L'Estartit, Spain

The trip south to L'Estartit took them slightly more than one and a half hours. They didn't talk much. Alavi didn't know if he should be nervous about the prolonged silence or not. Al-Nashwan was deep in thought, and he knew better than to disturb him.

In his head, he kept replaying the events of the last few hours. He couldn't pinpoint where he'd gone wrong. He had come very close to being knocked out by a woman and, truth be told, he had been beaten fair and square. His nose would take a while to heal and would probably be permanently crooked. What he didn't understand was how he had been spotted in the first place.

"It was luck," said Omar Al-Nashwan quietly.

Alavi emerged from his reverie. "What?"

"I presume you're thinking about how you were sighted."

"I was."

"You're a great fighter, Mohammad. Throughout the last decade, you've proven yourself many times over—not only in combat, but also in the desert as you trained our young recruits. Don't forget, the Sheik handpicked you personally for that task."

Mohammad Alavi nodded. He wasn't sure where this discussion would lead, so he wanted to tread carefully.

"However," continued Al-Nashwan.

Here it comes, thought Alavi. An acrid taste entered his mouth.

"You were crushed by that woman," Al-Nashwan went on. "She recognized you, followed you, and put you down. She was an operative of some sort, but she wasn't from France—of that I'm sure. If she had been, more than one agent would have covered her."

Alavi looked over at Al-Nashwan questioningly.

"Let's be honest here, Mohammad. If not for me, you would either be dead or captured."

"I would have martyred myself before—" began Alavi, but Al-Nashwan gave him a disgusted look.

"Don't interrupt me again, Mohammad," Al-Nashwan said with a voice so calm that it sent chills down Alavi's spine. "Don't fool yourself into thinking that whatever organization was behind that grab operation isn't thorough. By now you would probably be in a safe house somewhere in Spain awaiting an extraction team that would smuggle you out of Europe."

Mohammad Alavi didn't reply. Al-Nashwan was right. Western intelligence agencies might not have Al-Nashwan's bio and photos on file, but they did have his.

Looking out the Peugeot's window, Alavi saw that they were entering the small town of L'Estartit. Wedged between the Montgri Massif and the Mediterranean Sea, the town had been flooded since the mid-1960s with a large influx of European visitors during the summer months. Its uncontrolled growth of hotels and restaurants had caused the town to lose the very charm that had made visitors come in the first place.

Slowly the car threaded its way through the streets and entered the well-protected port. A lot of people were strolling along the docks and picnicking on the promenade that ran parallel to a large beach just west of a marina.

Al-Nashwan parked the Peugeot and used his cell phone to make a call. "We've arrived," he said. "Before you join us, please take care of the car. I'll leave the key on the passenger-side front tire."

He closed his cell phone and looked at Alavi. "Follow me, Mohammad. We're going for a boat ride."

Alavi exited the car without much enthusiasm. He was still worried about what would happen to him. He followed Al-Nashwan down one of the finger docks. He noted that the docks were in good repair and that many different types of boats were moored in the marina. Some were small express cruisers operated by rental companies, while others were small- and medium-size sailboats and fishing vessels that probably belonged to L'Estartit residents. Several of the big fishing trawlers were most likely used by the professional fishermen who sold their catches to local and regional restaurants.

Alavi was surprised when they stopped at a small inflatable dinghy powered by a thirty-horsepower outboard engine. Al-Nashwan climbed down a small ladder and settled himself within the rubber craft. He yanked on the pull cord to start the engine. It caught on the first try. Al-Nashwan motioned for Alavi to get into the boat while he untied the lines.

The inflatable dinghy was equipped with a central helm and a small captain's seat but had no other places to sit. Alavi sat on the hard plywood bottom, more anxious than ever. If he were to get shot in the middle of the Mediterranean, so be it. He wouldn't resist. But he couldn't help but wonder why Al-Nashwan was going to so much trouble if that was his intention.

Al-Nashwan expertly maneuvered the boat out of its small slip and exited the marina. As soon as they were out of the no-wake zone, he pushed the throttle forward, and the inflatable vessel rapidly gained speed.

The wind was blowing from the north, and the waves were about two feet high, which wasn't dangerous for most boats. But in the dark and with nowhere to hold onto, Alavi was sure he was about to die. He could feel the boat's rough vibrations through his injured nose.

He glanced in Al-Nashwan's direction and saw for the first time that the other man had a pair of night-vision goggles on. He suddenly felt the boat change course while it gradually reduced its speed. He looked around in the darkness but couldn't see anything.

This is it, he thought, surprisingly calm. *I'll be shot in the head and fed to the fish.*

Al-Nashwan reached for something under the center console. Alavi's worst fears were confirmed when the moonlight reflected off the barrel of a black pistol pointed directly at him.

"Close your eyes, Mohammad," ordered Omar Al-Nashwan.

"No," answered Alavi bravely. "I prefer to keep them open. I don't want to enter paradise with my eyes closed."

He heard Al-Nashwan chuckle. "As you wish, Mohammad. As you wish."

Alavi was blinded by two quick flashes of light coming from the pistol's muzzle but was surprised that his body didn't register any pain. He felt himself fall from his seated position and land on his back anyhow.

Lying on his back facing the stars, Alavi sensed that the small boat was again moving. After a few seconds, Al-Nashwan's voice penetrated the darkness: "What are you doing, Mohammad? Get up and grab the line that Raphael will throw at us."

Confused, Alavi opened his eyes. They were moving toward a large boat that was illuminated only by the moon and what seemed to be blue underwater lights.

Al-Nashwan hadn't tried to kill him—he had simply used a flashlight to signal their arrival. Alavi shook his head and allowed himself to smile.

As they came within range, Raphael, one of the Sheik's assistants, was standing on the large cruiser's swim platform and threw a line at them. Alavi caught the rope and, following the instructions that the man yelled to him, attached it to their inflatable. Al-Nashwan cut the engine, and the only noise they heard was the water lapping at the hull of the big yacht.

The two terrorists ascended a short ladder to the cruiser's deck. Raphael shook Al-Nashwan's hand, then told them that they were expected in the salon and that he would take care of scuttling the inflatable.

Even though it was dark out, Alavi noticed that the boat was quite spacious. They climbed four steps onto a large upper deck, where a seating area was richly furnished with a dining table and an L-shaped lounge seat. Al-Nashwan gently knocked on the deeply tinted triple patio door before sliding it open.

The interior of the boat was spectacular. Alavi had never seen anything so luxurious in his life. The dimmed pot lights gave the interior an even more glamorous look. A lavish dining table was set up on the port side, and a settee big enough for six adults was on the starboard. A little farther and one step up, four leather helm seats were side by side, facing a huge windshield. Seated in one of the chairs with his two elbows firmly planted on the dining table was an Arabic man in his mid-sixties. *The Sheik.* He was casually dressed in a blue polo shirt and a pair of white linen pants. He got up and warmly embraced Al-Nashwan before looking at Alavi.

"Omar told me great things about you," said the Sheik. "We've been watching you closely, Mohammad." He was slightly taller than Alavi, and his build had remained muscular. His hair was getting thin on top of his head, but his eyes were penetrating.

Alavi felt his throat tighten. He'd met the Sheik in person just once before. His uncle had been one of his close advisers, but the only time Alavi had been in the physical presence of the Sheik was during the briefing of Ambassador Powell's abduction.

"Please, sit with me at my table," the Sheik offered, then went back to his seat and sat facing Al-Nashwan and Alavi.

"So tell me, Omar," the Sheik began, "everything went according to plan?"

"Yes, it did. The Russians are dead," replied Al-Nashwan simply.

"Great work, Omar. Once again, I'm very pleased with your services. The next few months will tell us if we have been successful."

"Indeed, Sheik Al-Assad. They will."

CHAPTER 38

Ottawa, Canada

I can assure you, Director, she's safe. I've made a few calls, and she's now on her way here."

"How did this happen? How the fuck did we manage to lose Mohammad Alavi?" asked Simon Corey, the director of the Canadian Security Intelligence Service. He was seated in his leather chair behind his heavy mahogany desk. He wanted answers, but the three men standing in front of him didn't have any to give.

"We're not sure yet," answered John Aschner, the deputy director of operations. Standing next to him was the assistant director of collection, Kevin Loewe, and his deputy, Joachim Persky.

"Well, what *do* we know?"

"Very little, I'm afraid," started Persky. "Our three agents were carrying out their exit protocols following the murder of General Mathias Deniaud, the French gendarmerie—"

"I am well aware of who General Deniaud was," Corey cut in, exasperated.

"Of c-course, Director. I'm sorry," Persky stuttered, trying to salvage the situation. "Zima Bernbaum successfully wiretapped a very strange conversation between General Deniaud and his deputy, General Claudel."

"Strange in what way?" Corey asked curtly.

"Well, it ended with Claudel shooting Deniaud before committing suicide."

The director showed more interest. "Do we have the tape in our possession?"

"Not yet, sir. But we'll get our hands on it very soon. As I said, Agent Bernbaum will join us shortly."

"Okay, Joachim. Please stick to what *did* happen," the director ordered.

"Yes, sir. As I was saying, our agents were following their exit protocols when Zima spotted Mohammad Alavi. She called Agent Bailey. Bailey then called us for instructions on how to proceed with Alavi. Their instructions were to grab him alive if they could, or to kill him if he didn't cooperate."

"And now Alavi is nowhere to be found!" exclaimed Corey. He slammed his palm onto his desk. "That's unacceptable!"

The three other men kept quiet as the director scrutinized them one by one. He took a few deep breaths to clear his mind. "Do we have any leads on where he is?"

"No, sir," Aschner replied. "But our contacts within the gendarmerie will keep us in the loop as the investigation unfolds. I should receive the first report within the hour."

The director sighed. He suddenly looked older than his sixty-seven years. When he slowly got up from his chair, he seemed to carry the weight of the whole world on his shoulders. "I'll have to go brief the prime minister. A political storm is brewing, and I see no way to hide the fact that we had an agent inside the French gendarmerie's headquarters."

"We could make her a cover story," Loewe suggested. "We've done it before."

The director shook his head. "I don't see how we can get out of this mess without political retaliation from the French—or, as a matter of fact, without political retaliation from the rest of the European Union. Once the word gets out that CSIS had a spy posing as a French citizen within General Deniaud's inner circle, we won't see the end of the ramifications for months. We could have dealt with a failed operation on French soil. At least in that scenario we'd have a chance to keep things under the rug; it would have cost us some political favors, but nothing more. But spying on an ally at the highest level? That won't fly."

"Sir," Loewe replied. "I believe there is a way out of this mess."

The director looked at him with curiosity. "I'm listening," he said, still standing behind his desk.

"I'm not exactly sure what's on the tape that Agent Bernbaum will bring back. However, if we are to believe what she told us before boarding her flight home, she has successfully recorded an admission of treason on the part of the second highest-ranking officer of the gendarmerie. We don't know why General Claudel killed Deniaud yet, but

I'm sure the French would like to keep the recording of their chief's murder a secret."

"You want to use this recording to blackmail the French into keeping quiet about our activities inside their headquarters?" Aschner asked incredulously.

"Absolutely," Loewe responded. "It might not work, but even if we fail, we won't be in a worse position than we are now." Beaming, he looked over at Director Corey.

"I like your idea, Kevin. But for it to work, we need to take the lead and contact them *now*, before they have a chance to spin the story into something they won't be able to undo." He looked at his deputy director. "This is your department, Aschner. I'll let you take the lead on this. Keep me apprised of your progress."

Aschner looked less than convinced. "Yes, sir."

CHAPTER 39

The Mediterranean Sea

Omar has done quite well," the Sheik said into his secure satellite phone. He was sitting behind his desk in the master cabin of the Azimut yacht.

"I knew years ago it would be with you that my son would contribute the most to our cause," answered his interlocutor.

"He saved the life of one of our cell commanders. I can commend him on his leadership and initiative."

"He's always been the best at what he does. Did you know that he finished first in his class at West Point?"

"He never mentioned that to me."

"Well, I'm not surprised. Alexander has always been discreet about his accomplishments."

"I believe that is one of his strengths," Sheik Al-Assad added. "It must run in the family."

"It's a shame that the final fireworks didn't turn out as we expected," returned the man, changing the subject. "That would have ended it, at least for the European portion of the plan."

"We did all we could, my friend. I still believe we had a good run. Now it's time to regroup and prepare for the final attacks. As you said, we're getting close to our ultimate objective. The European economy is already on the verge of collapsing. I believe that one more wave of attacks will bring it to the abyss."

"Let's hope so," replied the man. "I've shorted all my positions a week ago and made good money so far. But we need to see an even bigger downturn soon, before the economy has a chance to recover."

"It will be soon, but these operations take time. You know this," the Sheik said.

"I know, Qasim. But I'd hate the market to improve and have to cover my positions," the man said before changing subject. "And how are you doing financially?"

"We still have our agreement with the Africans, and that's enough to finance our operations," Sheik Al-Assad replied. He hesitated, then cleared his throat.

"But?" the man prodded.

"I feel that this African arrangement is our weakest link," he admitted. "We've been using them for a few years now, and I'm starting to sense that we might encounter some problems in the future."

"Go on."

"Your son thinks—and I agree with him—that Major Taylor is getting a little too comfortable with his standing within our organization. He's arrogant, and he's using drugs frequently. I'm not sure he'll keep his mouth shut. Also, some irregularities were noticed in many of the major's financial transactions."

"I see. Are you sure about these, er...irregularities?"

"I am. Our accountants double checked. It seems that Major Taylor might have been in business with another organization for a few months now."

"That's goes against our agreement," the man said angrily. "Did you confront him about it?"

"I'm not sure that's wise. E-mails, bank statements—the proof is there. Why give him a chance to lie to us?"

A long pause ensued, and Sheik Al-Assad wondered if his friend in the United States was still there. Finally, the man spoke again:

"Didn't you tell me that Taylor is afraid of Alexander?"

"He used to be. But as I said, he has become overly confident. He truly believes that he's irreplaceable."

"Can you scare him back to his place?"

"It might work for a short period of time, but in the end, I think it could backfire on us if he decides to talk to somebody he shouldn't. If he's caught and put under pressure, he'll talk. I can guarantee it. He knows too much about our final operation. In my opinion, he needs to go. "

"I see. Would you like me to leak some info on Jackson to the president's national security adviser? Hell, I could even speak to Muller myself and tell him I heard rumors about an African planning an Ebola outbreak in the US. That would take care of your problem, Qasim."

"Don't do that. If they don't kill him, he might talk. Then we'll have real trouble. I'll take care of him myself. This way, it will send a strong message not to cross us."

"Of course, you're right. I just hate it when people play behind my back."

"If we could use part of the money we stole in Iraq, it could finance our operations for the next twelve to sixteen months. That way I could deal with Jackson Taylor and sever all links we have with the Africans before it gets more complicated."

"What about the training? Didn't you say yourself that we needed him to train our new recruits?"

"I can think of many other places where young jihadis could receive training," replied the Sheik.

"I understand what you're saying, Qasim. But you must realize that using even part of that seventy million could be dangerous. I'm not saying it can't be done, but I'll have to think about it. Give me a few days."

"Fair enough. I'll call you once we reach Benalmádena."

"Very well, Qasim. There is just one more thing you need to know before I let you go."

"What's that?"

"Our main contact within the French gendarmerie is dead. He called me after shooting General Deniaud dead and before swallowing his own gun. He said that all evidence left by the Antibes team would lead to him and no one else."

"Let's hope he was right," said Sheik Al-Assad. "I'm surprised he committed suicide. I've never imagined him capable of doing that. I always thought I would have to send Omar to take care of it once we were done with him."

The Sheik heard his friend chuckle. "Let's just say that I mentioned that he shouldn't leave *any* loose ends if he didn't want his boyfriend to endure a lot of pain."

"I see. It's a shame we lost him so soon, though. He was greedy but a great asset."

"He was. I'll call you back in a few days with my decision regarding the funds," said the American. "Tell Alex I miss him, won't you?"

"Of course," replied the Sheik.

Al-Assad replaced his satellite phone in a special drawer under his bed. He could have pushed his friend a little more, but he wanted him to come to his own conclusion. Major Jackson Taylor needed to go. Insubordination couldn't be tolerated. He had already served his purpose. Their business arrangement with the Africans had been fruitful, but now it was time to pass on to better and brighter things.

He knew his American friend was worried about using the money they had stolen from the CIA just after the invasion of Iraq. That money was presently sitting in a vault in Switzerland, and Sheik Al-Assad thought that it was now time to put the funds to good use. He was aware that the US government could have put a trace on it, but he doubted it. That had been one of the first large shipments of money the CIA had sent to Iraq prior to the invasion in March 2003, and he was betting that the money had come from one of the spy agency's black projects—thus ensuring that the CIA would have erased all possible tracing mechanisms itself.

The Sheik poured himself a scotch from a crystal decanter on the sideboard, then sat in his favorite armchair, made from reclaimed leather. Allah would allow him this small indulgence. He and his friend went back a long way, and he respected the older man's judgment. They might not agree on everything, but the bond between them transcended any differences of opinion they had. In many ways, their bond was stronger than blood.

—

Forty years ago, Steve Shamrock had married the Sheik's sister while serving as an oil executive in the United Arab Emirates. Because he spoke fluent Arabic, Shamrock had been asked by the company's board of directors to act as their official negotiator regarding drilling rights on the land of the Sheik's father, Sheik Zafad Al-Assad. Most of the meetings between the parties had taken place inside Al-Assad's palace. Once an accord had been reached, Shamrock and the other senior company representatives had been invited to a gala at the palace. It was during this dinner that Steve Shamrock's life changed forever. Ghayda Al-Assad was an Arab beauty like Shamrock had never seen before. Her piercing brown eyes melted his heart quicker than ice under the sun. With the consent of Sheik Zafad Al-Assad, they were married five months later.

Less than a year after the wedding, Shamrock was promoted to vice president of public affairs and transferred back to the United States. His wife, who was then pregnant with their first child, was accepted as an intern at the Mayo Clinic. She gave birth to their baby boy, Alexander, at their private residence in Scottsdale. Baby Alexander, known to the Al-Assad family as Omar Al-Nashwan, attended the best schools Arizona had to offer. Like his father, he kept his faith to himself, knowing that it would set him apart from the other kids in his classes. In the states, he excelled in sports and academics, but it was during the many summers he spent in the Emirates with his Uncle Qasim that Omar felt most alive.

All was well for the Al-Assad family until, while on vacation in Damascus with his wife and daughter, Sheik Zafad Al-Assad was mistakenly assassinated by a CIA Special Activities Division team that had wrongly believed he was a wanted terrorist. The firefight between the Sheik's bodyguards and the SAD officers didn't last long. The Americans' fire had been accurate and deadly. None of their rounds had missed their mark, but the same couldn't be said for Al-Assad's bodyguards. Once the dust had settled, the three bodyguards were lying lifeless on the ground next to the sheik. His wife and daughter, caught in the crossfire, had both been mortally wounded and died during their transport to the hospital.

Even though five of the six Americans miraculously evaded capture, one of them was caught by the Syrian secret police less than a mile from the Lebanese border. They thought briefly about a prisoner exchange but wisely elected not to go with this option. Sheik Zafad Al-Assad had been a man with great influence in the UAE, and the Syrians concluded that transparency might be the best choice of action. When Qasim Al-Assad received the bad news from Syria, he immediately contacted Steve Shamrock. They were in Damascus less than twenty-four hours after the shooting.

The CIA agent resisted for a long time but finally caved in after hours of torture at the hands of the Syrian secret police. Qasim Al-Assad and Shamrock witnessed the confession given by the captured man, who, while in agony, admitted working for the CIA and that he was the one who had actually shot the old man.

In the dirty basement of that Syrian prison, the man who would become known as the Sheik and a future CEO of an important oil and gas company from the United States of America agreed to dedicate their lives to getting revenge. They would use Islam to recruit naive souls. They would use Allah's words to induce them into fighting for them. To die for them. Religion would be the stick used to motivate their own jihadis to attack the Americans where it would hurt them the most—their wallets.

—

The Sheik couldn't wait to take care of Major Jackson. As soon as he was removed, the network would concentrate its resources on one thing: the economic collapse of America.

CHAPTER 40

Brooklyn, New York

The debriefing lasted much longer than he had anticipated. He was drained, hungry, and eager to get home to his wife. They had talked on the phone on his way back, but her voice couldn't replace the warmth of her arms around him. Her voice had sounded happy and relaxed, almost welcoming, as if what had happened in France was nothing out of the ordinary.

If that was really the case—and Mike would know soon enough—it would confirm that his wife was made for this line of work. Was *he* ready for this?

The fact that she nearly died on her first mission didn't help either. As her husband, he felt the need to protect her, to shield her from any danger. But he knew he couldn't do that. Not if he wanted to stay married. Not after what she had endured.

He had come to the conclusion that Lisa was the only other human being he knew that could truly understand him now. Together, they had lived through an immeasurable loss and, somehow, they were surviving.

On our terms.

This last trip to France made him appreciate how much he needed her, not only psychologically but also physically. He was craving her company.

Badly.

Entering his building's underground garage, Mike parked his black Ford Explorer next to his wife's Cayenne. Walking toward the elevators, he remembered the breakdown he had experienced right there only two months ago. Mike wondered for a few moments where his relationship with his wife would be if he hadn't decided to run after her. He shivered at the thought.

Inside the elevator, he used his keycard to access his floor. There were only two penthouses in the building, and only the owners were allowed access. Mike liked the extra security it provided even though it wasn't foolproof. Opening the door of his apartment, Mike tried not to make any noise in order not to wake Lisa. But she must have known he was coming because as soon as he closed the door and turned around, there she was, wearing only a long white bathrobe and holding two glasses of red wine in her hands.

"Welcome home, baby," she said, handing him a glass.

My God is she beautiful.

He accepted the wine glass and swirled its red liquid before taking in its bouquet.

Red fruits, mocha, somewhat smoky...

"Pinot Noir?"

Lisa smiled. Her eyes were bright and playful. "Oh my, you're no fun," she said, her bathrobe falling to the floor, her body proudly showing the sutures of her wounds. She took a long sip of her wine and left the empty glass on the table next to her.

"Are you sure about this?" Mike asked. "The wounds are still fresh."

"Just be careful, Mike," softly replied Lisa. "If they don't bother you, they don't bother me."

Mike, convinced he'd never seen a more gorgeous woman in his life, placed his glass next to Lisa's and swept his wife up in his arms before carrying her to their bedroom.

—

"You could have guessed wrong, you know?" Lisa said, out of breath. "It would have ended the same way."

Mike chuckled. "I guess so, but I was in a hurry," he said, holding his wife tight against him, his heart still racing.

"You remember the last time we played this game?" she asked tenderly in his ear before she nicked it with her teeth.

Mike gasped, surprised.

"I was coming back from Los Angeles, wasn't I?" he answered moments later.

"Hmm, hmm. Not bad. You *do* remember."

Mike grinned. He remembered it very well. Lisa had challenged him with a red wine from Austria. "It was a 2005 Sattler Zweigelt, that tasted horrible, I might add."

"You had plenty of chances to guess it right, my dear. You were wearing a suit and tie while I had only my nightgown."

"You tricked me into thinking it was a cheap Portuguese wine!" They were both laughing now, remembering how Mike had lost all his clothes while Lisa had remained immobile in front of him.

"You didn't even guess the right country!" replied Lisa, her hand playing with Mike's hair.

"But it had a long finish," Mike said, turning toward his wife. He brushed his lips against hers.

Lisa smiled at him. "Yes, it lasted for quite a while." She hugged her husband and murmured, "I missed you so much, Mike. I couldn't wait for you to get back."

"I missed you too, my love."

"Charles told me about the raid you lead and the nuclear bomb you discovered," said Lisa, her voice cracking.

"That was a close call. But I'm here now, Lisa," said Mike, his right hand caressing the skin around her wounds.

Feeling her warm tears on his chest, Mike held her against him, careful not to hug her too hard, his own tears prickling in his eyes. Suddenly, the images and the sounds of the Antibes firefight played in his head. For a moment, he was paralyzed by fear and his breathing became shallow.

"Mike? Mike? You're okay?"

The concerned voice of his wife brought him back. "Yes, I'm sorry."

"You're shaking, baby. What happened?"

Mike gently kissed his wife on the forehead, taking his time inhaling the scent of her hair. "It's nothing. I'm all right," Mike lied.

What was that?

PART 4

CHAPTER 41

Brooklyn, New York

For the last few days Mike had been arriving at IMSI headquarters at nine. On his way, he stopped by a Starbucks to get the three warm coffees he was now carrying. He briefly wondered how Sanchez's teeth managed to stay white while he drank up to six cups of coffee a day.

Reaching Sanchez's office, Mike used his left foot to gently kick the door and waited for the electronic noise that would indicate the door had been unlocked. He then used his weight to push the door open and walked into Sanchez's workspace. Like Mapother's, his office had no window. His desk was neatly arranged, with not one sheet of paper out of place. The flat screen on the wall was tuned to CNN. Mike sat down in one of the two chairs in front of his friend's desk.

"Good morning, Mike," he said, raising his eyes from his computer screen. "Slept in?"

"Hey, I'm listening to my doctor's advice," he replied, handing him a coffee.

He thanked him and smelled his coffee's aroma before carefully taking a sip

"Toasted walnuts?" he asked.

Mike laughed and raised his hands in surrender. "You're too good, brother."

"Thank you very much. Try again tomorrow," Sanchez replied. "By the way, Charles wants to see you."

"Do you know what it's about?" Mike asked.

"Didn't say a word to me. But I have a feeling that he'll ask you if you think you're ready to deploy."

Mike exhaled loudly. "Have you seen Lisa this morning?" he asked. "She was already gone when I woke up this morning."

"I didn't see her coming in this morning."

"All right, I'll see you later then," Mike said, getting up.

—

Mapother was waiting for him. He shook Mike's hand and looked genuinely pleased to see him. "How are you this morning?"

"I feel pretty good," Mike said. He proffered the cup. "Do you want a cold coffee? I couldn't find Lisa this morning."

"I think I'll pass," said Mapother. He gestured for Mike to sit in one of the chairs facing his desk.

"We've received some news regarding the situation in France," started Mapother.

"Which situation are we talking about?"

"The death of General Deniaud."

Mike nodded. He had briefed Mapother on all the details of his recent mission, including his impromptu meeting with Zima Bernbaum. "His death has been officially declared a suicide, but we both know this isn't the case. That brings us to this," said Mapother, pointing to a binder on his desk.

"What is it?"

"This is all the intelligence IMSI was able to collect regarding the terrorism acts perpetrated in France," replied Mapother, pushing the binder toward Mike. "I want you to read it carefully, but I'll tell you right now what piqued our curiosity."

Mike was intrigued. "I'm listening."

"Thanks to the flash drives Agent Bernbaum found in General Claudel's residence, we have evidence of collusion among three people."

"Do we know who they are?"

"General Claudel, an accountant by the name of Abdullah Ahmad Ghazi and a man named Peter Georges."

"Do we have any intel on Ghazi and Georges?" asked Mike, opening the file.

"His name surfaced a few times through some NSA reports associated with the Sheik's terror network. We also know that close to two million dollars went through his account two months before all hell broke loose in France."

"Any pictures?"

"None. The man is a ghost, and he's covering his tracks well."

"So, we don't have anything concrete proving this man is in bed with the Sheik," said Mike, pointing out the obvious.

"Not yet," admitted Mapother. "But I hope you'll be in a position to shed some light on Mr. Georges."

Mike raised his eyebrows. "What do you mean?"

"I want you to join forces with Lisa in Sierra Leone."

"What? Lisa is in Africa?" Mike asked confused. "When did she leave?"

"She left early this morning to set up the operation," said Mapother. "I think she tried to call you."

Mike dug into his pocket to retrieve his smartphone.

Damn! Two missed calls.

"She did," Mike confirmed. "My phone was on vibrate, and I didn't feel it buzzing."

"Make sure you pick up if we call you, Mike," warned Mapother.

"So what's so important in Sierra Leone?"

"You see, Mr. Georges has been traveling to Sierra Leone frequently during the last few months. That's where he's heading next. I want you and Lisa to track him down. I want to see what he's up to so we can either confirm his link with the Sheik or move to another lead."

"When do I leave?"

CHAPTER 42

Freetown, Sierra Leone

His time spent in Benalmadena had been a true blessing from Allah. He had met many of Sheik Qasim Al-Assad's advisers, and they had all seemed genuinely pleased to meet him. Upon the yacht's arrival at the high-end marina, Alavi had been escorted to a nicely appointed room in a gated villa. He didn't know, and didn't ask, who the owner of the villa was; he was just grateful to be given a few days to rest. The last few months had taken their toll, and his body needed time to heal.

Finally, after two days spent relaxing by the villa's pool, sleeping late, and eating lavish meals prepared by servants, Alavi received a visit from Dr. Javed Arastoo, who introduced himself warmly. Alavi found him vaguely familiar but wasn't able to correctly identify him until Arastoo informed him that he had been a good friend of Alavi's late uncle, Dr. Ahmed Khaled.

Alavi knew his uncle had been very close to the Sheik, but he had never been told what had happened to him. Dr. Arastoo obliged him and went on to tell how his good friend had rejoined Allah. Alavi had always thought their enemies had finally caught his uncle and killed him after days of torture. The truth was much simpler, Dr. Arastoo assured him. While conducting a highly sensitive mission on behalf on the Sheik, Khaled had died in his sleep in a hotel in Zurich. The Sheik had been suspicious about the death, but following an autopsy performed by Dr. Arastoo himself, it was confirmed that Ahmed Khaled had died from a nocturnal heart attack following a heavier-than-normal meal enjoyed at one of Zurich's finest dining establishments. In Alavi's mind, Arastoo's version of events made perfect sense.

After exchanging a few pleasantries, Dr. Arastoo broached the real reason for his presence—changing Alavi's appearance. Nothing too complicated, but enough so that he could move freely across borders at airports and train stations. They spent the rest of the day practicing how to change Alavi's look in less than thirty minutes, using mostly theater paraphernalia.

On the fourth day, Al-Nashwan came to the villa to check on him. He told Alavi that he would have visited earlier, but the Sheik had kept him busy preparing for their next trip. When Alavi inquired what it would be, Al-Nashwan had replied that Sierra Leone would be their destination and they would leave as soon as Alavi was ready.

Two days later, Alavi boarded a plane from Brussels without a problem, using a fake passport provided by Al-Nashwan. The airport security was good, but Alavi's new identity and facial changes kept him from being detected. As his flight began its final descent toward Freetown-Lungi International Airport, Alavi once again went over the meticulous plan that Al-Nashwan had crafted.

Alavi exited the airport and headed for the water taxis that would take him across the Sierra Leone River to the capital city of Freetown. Even though the ride across the bay was bumpy, Alavi enjoyed it a lot more than renting a car for the four hours it would have taken to travel by road, he thought.

Threading his way through the throng of fish vendors who had set up shop along the shores of the river, Alavi wondered if Jackson Taylor had aged well since Alavi had last set foot in Sierra Leone. He doubted it.

Alavi took a cab and, twenty minutes later, checked in at the Country Lodge Hotel. His room on the first floor had a great view of the kidney-shaped pool and the ocean a few kilometers beyond it. The hotel was supposedly the best in the city, but it wouldn't have earned more than two stars by international standards.

Al-Nashwan had chosen this hotel for several reasons. First, he suspected that Taylor wouldn't agree to meet Alavi within the heart of the city for fear that some overzealous government official might recognize him. Even though he had been officially granted a pardon, Taylor was supposed to stay away from downtown Freetown. Second, the hotel was difficult to access. Only one road led up to it, and Alavi had a bird's-eye view of that access route from his room.

If he played his cards perfectly, Jackson Taylor wouldn't know what hit him.

—

Alavi spent three full days scouting the area around his hotel and reviewing all the possible escape routes. He also became very familiar with the route that Taylor's motorcade would use to drive up to the Country Lodge Hotel. He spent long hours walking along the dirt road, running his feet over the caked mud surface, and eyeing its soft sandy shoulders.

When Alavi was training terror recruits in Afghanistan, his specialty had been the assembly of improvised explosive devices. He taught his students how to appropriate the things they would need to fabricate the explosives, and he showed them how to build them from scratch in an old school gymnasium.

Depending on the location, it could be either moderately easy or damn near impossible to acquire the components necessary to build one. In some countries, buying the needed components could raise serious questions from the authorities. Luckily for Alavi, in a city like Freetown, cash could guarantee pretty much anything. On the fourth and fifth days following his arrival in Sierra Leone, Alavi went to numerous mechanical and electronic shops to purchase the tools and paraphernalia he needed to build a couple of devices that would be powerful enough to obliterate his intended targets.

Al-Nashwan, who had developed the security protocol for Taylor's bodyguards, had told him the major didn't travel in an armored car. The Range Rovers he usually used for travel were great for cross-country trips but were definitely not made to withstand the blast of IEDs.

Alavi spent the next two days assembling two improvised explosive devices. He didn't leave his room once and had room service leave his meals outside his door. He hung the *Do Not Disturb* sign on his door and focused all his concentration on ensuring that his devices would not detonate in his face. To disable the Rovers, Alavi opted for two cell phone-activated platter charges, smaller versions of the ones favored in Iraq and Afghanistan to fight against the invading American troops and their allies.

The platter-charge concept was based on the idea that if a sheet of explosives was backed against a steel plate, the detonation would project the blast wave away from the plate. If another plate of lighter weight was placed on the opposite face of the explosive charge, that plate would be projected like a missile in the opposite direction at a speed of close to six thousand feet per second.

Once his two IEDs were completed, Alavi decided that a Claymore type of explosive device would be perfect for finishing the job. The concept behind this device was pretty much the same but at a smaller scale. It still required an explosive charge, a detonator, and an initiation system, but instead of another lighter-weight steel plate, metal pellets were used as projectiles.

Building the backup explosive wasn't part of Al-Nashwan's original plan, but Alavi wanted to make sure that his mission was successful. He still burned with shame every time he recalled how the last one had failed. He rued the fact that he couldn't test his devices, but he had no choice. He'd have to trust that they would work.

The following night, Alavi went to his ambush site and planted the devices. By the time he was done, he knew that only someone who was trained in what to look for could spot them.

The hardest part of the plan was about to begin. He had to contact Taylor and convince him to come to the hotel. He knew very well that Taylor didn't like to come to Freetown, but he also knew that the man would be too greedy to refuse his invitation. Taylor had always been ready to take considerable risks if he believed that the reward was handsome enough.

Alavi punched Taylor's direct number into a disposable cell phone that he had purchased at an electronics shop in Freetown. It rang twice before someone answered. Alavi was somewhat surprised to hear Taylor's growling voice on the other end.

"Major Taylor! This is Mohammad Alavi."

"Mohammad! I see that you're calling from a Freetown number. I wasn't told you were in town."

Taylor had paid informants installed at the major ports and airports across Sierra Leone. Most of them were government officials hooked on the extra twenty dollars a month that Taylor paid them to keep him apprised of any interesting developments.

"Let's just say I am a little harder to recognize now."

"Ah. What can I do for you?"

"Actually, Major, I'm here on behalf of our mutual friend," answered Alavi, conscious that he was calling on an unprotected line. "He would consider it a personal favor if you would meet me face-to-face. I believe we have a great offer to present to you."

"Where are you, Mohammad?"

"I'm at the Country Lodge Hotel in Freetown."

The greed that filled Taylor's voice vanished. "You know I don't like Freetown. Corrupt cops and government officials would like nothing better than to arrest me on false charges."

"Hence the reason why I made sure that the hotel was not downtown. Your security is always our priority, Major. I'm sure you know that."

"Why don't you come to my headquarters? I can provide you with transportation if you wish," offered Taylor.

"Thank you for your offer, Major, but unfortunately, this is not an option. But I can give you my personal assurance that we'll make your trip worthwhile. Just off the top of my head, I can think of about half a million good reasons."

The lure of filthy lucre did the trick. "Is that so?"

"Besides, there is someone who would like to meet you," added Alavi, playing on the Major's need for praise from the highest ranks.

"Are you talking about our mutual friend?" inquired Taylor.

"Let's just say that you'll be quite happy that you made the trip."

Craftiness slipped back into his response. "My schedule is pretty full. Even if I could make it, it wouldn't be for a few days."

"We understand that your time is very valuable, Major. Especially as we are here unannounced."

Taylor sighed into the other end of the phone line. "I'll see what I can do, Mohammad. I'll call you in a few days to let you know when I'll have time to meet you."

"I'll be waiting for your call. I know you have the number."

Alavi heard Major Taylor hang up. Al-Nashwan and the Sheik were right in thinking that this man's arrogance had reached new heights. Then again, Alavi knew that it was only a charade. He was sure that the major was already ordering his security detail to make the necessary preparations for a road trip to Freetown. In Alavi's estimation, he would be in Freetown within thirty-six hours.

Although the trip was only four hundred kilometers, the roads in Sierra Leone were so bad that it would take Taylor's Range Rovers a great deal of time to travel the distance. Alavi didn't mind, though. He had a few finishing touches to complete.

CHAPTER 43

Freetown, Sierra Leone

There was no direct flight from New York to Freetown, so Mike Walton had to stop at Heathrow before continuing on to Sierra Leone. Eighteen hours after boarding his first flight at JFK, Mike emerged from Freetown's airport terminal with his duffel bag. Even though he'd slept in the plane, nightmares had kept him stirring left and right in his seat. Images of Commandant Bleriot, the GIGN leader who fell in Antibes, and other deceased GIGN troopers had haunted him. Mike was tired, irritated, and eager to take a shower.

Jonathan Sanchez had given him the address for the house IMSI had rented. It had been leased for six months at double the asking price through one of IMSI's shell companies. Mike didn't know what to expect, but he was hoping that running water was one of the luxuries included in the price.

The water taxi was on time, and Mike managed to find a taxi at the ferry terminal and gave the driver an address. It took over an hour and a half to travel ten kilometers. Without air conditioning, the car was like a microwave, and Mike's sweaty shirt clung to his body. As the taxi reached its destination, Mike gave the driver a ten-euro bill and exited the car as soon as it stopped. He swung his duffel bag over his shoulder and walked the short distance between the road and the beautiful white sandy beach.

The small house was located close to the traffic circle linking Lumley Beach Road with the Peninsular Highway. It didn't look like much from the exterior, but Mike had stayed in worse dwellings in Kosovo. As long as it was secure, he could deal without the niceties of daily life.

I'm wondering if I can say the same thing for Lisa...I'll know soon enough.

Just as he was going to knock on the door, it opened, unlocked from its electronic latch by the small device Lisa was holding in her hand. Mike stepped in, closed the door behind him, and looked around. The room had a dining table with four chairs stuck in a corner. Two cots had been placed next to it. One had been slept in while the other one had clean sheets neatly folded on its end. A faint aroma of coffee came from the minuscule kitchen on his left, and the door of the only bathroom was slightly ajar.

"Welcome to *mi casa*!" greeted Lisa.

"Thanks, honey," replied Mike, genuinely pleased to see her. "I've missed you."

"Same here," Lisa said, getting up. She walked to him and was about to kiss him when she stopped suddenly. "Good Lord! You smell!"

Mike laughed out loud. "Yeah, you're right." He stripped off his sweat-soaked shirt. "It's been a long freaking day. Is there a shower with running water in this shack?"

"Right in there," Lisa said, pointing. "Heater doesn't work, but you'll be fine. Just don't drink the water."

Mike dumped his duffel bag on his cot before heading into the shower. His wife was right. The water heater didn't work, and the water was somewhat cool. Still, in the heat it wasn't so bad. He was out in less than five minutes and dried himself with one of the dishrags that passed for towels in this rental.

By the time Mike exited the bathroom, Lisa had closed her laptop and placed an M9 pistol on top of Mike's duffel bag. Mike grabbed it, removed the loaded magazine, and racked the action open. He then carefully inspected the pistol before closing the action and reinserting a fifteen-round magazine.

"So what's up?" Mike asked, peeking at Lisa's computer screen.

"We've received our mission protocol from HQ," Lisa replied. "Looks like the techies at the office managed to get a picture of Peter Georges for us."

"Where did they get it from?"

"Don't know; they didn't say. My bet is that it was taken from the airport. They must have hacked into the security system and manually checked all the entries. Care to see our target?"

Lisa turned the laptop toward Mike and pressed a button, allowing the picture to expand to the full screen.

"I've seen this guy before!" exclaimed Mike.

"Where?"

Mike closed his eyes and processed the facial features.

"Got it," Mike finally said. "His name is Alexander Shamrock, and he's in the Army Special Forces. Last time I heard about him, he was somewhere in Africa."

Lisa looked at him with wide eyes. "How do you know that?"

"Prior to joining the Special Forces, he was an officer with the 75th Ranger Battalion. I spent three months embedded with them prior to my deployment in Kosovo."

"Oh yeah, Kosovo," Lisa challenged. "That's where you went while you were supposed to be training in Germany. Jonathan told me all about it."

Mike sighed. "I'm sorry, Lisa. I couldn't say anything."

"I know. Forget I said anything," Lisa said. "Let's concentrate on Shamrock instead."

"Thanks," Mike said, relieved. "Shamrock and I crossed paths several times."

"And you remember his name, why?"

Mike's face darkened. "Yeah, let's just say that one night we got into an argument in the officers' mess."

"Anything I should know about?"

Mike considered the question a moment before answering. "Truth is, I don't remember why. We were both drunk, I guess."

"Do you want to call it in, Mike?" Lisa asked after a short pause.

"Yeah, I'll call Mapother and see what he can find out on Alexander Shamrock."

—

IMSI didn't waste any time. Charles Mapother headed the research for information himself, and what he had found was a surprise.

"Are you sure Captain Alexander Shamrock was the man you saw in the picture?" asked Mapother, his voice loud and clear from the speaker of the secured sat phone.

"I'm positive, Charles. He's definitely older, but it's the same man I've spent time with in the Rangers battalion," replied Mike. He waited through a pause at the other end. "You're there, Charles?"

"I'm thinking, Mike. You see, Alexander Shamrock was KIA in Iraq years ago."

"Maybe it's another guy with the same name," Lisa proposed.

"Was his father an oil executive, Mike? Do you remember?" asked Mapother.

Mike searched his memory for a minute before replying. "Yes, you're right. Now that you mention it, I remember him talking about his dad being in the oil business."

"Then it's the same guy. There can be no doubt about it. I'm looking at the archives of a local Arizona newspaper, and there's an article about the death of Steve Shamrock's son, a captain with the United States Army Special Forces."

Mike had to mentally shake himself. "What's going on, then?"

"I don't know. I'll try to dig up some intel on this," said Mapother. "In the meantime, I want you to track him. Alexander Shamrock or not, this man might be a link to the Sheik."

And to my father.

"Mike and I will split up. That way we'll cover more ground," Lisa said. "What kind of support can we expect from IMSI?"

"Except for the equipment already in-country, not much, I'm afraid," replied Mapother. "As you know, for logistical reasons, your support team won't be able to reach you in Sierra Leone. HQ will try to access the phone lines in Freetown that are monitored by the NSA, but apart from that and hacking into the databases of the few hotels that have a computer system, you guys will be on your own."

"We understand," Mike said. "What do we do if we catch Peter Georges?"

"I would love to speak with him," answered Mapother. "I'm curious about all this, and he might end up being quite resourceful."

"Understood, sir," Mike said. "We'll keep you apprised of our—"

"Holy shit!" Mapother interrupted. "That was fast."

"What's going on?" asked Mike, surprised at his boss's outburst.

"I think we got lucky. Jonathan has a hit on a Peter Georges who recently checked in at the Country Lodge Hotel in Freetown."

Mike and Lisa were impressed. "How did he manage that?" Lisa asked.

This time it was Sanchez who answered over the speaker. "The Country Lodge is considered the best hotel in Freetown. It's not luxurious in any way, but they have Wi-Fi and it's not even password protected."

"We'll check that out, then," said Mike. "We'll contact you once we're at the location."

After hanging up, he said to his wife, "All right, partner. Pack up some gear and we'll be on our way."

CHAPTER 44

lavi walked to one of the windows that had a clear view of the ambush site. As he had guessed, Major Jackson Taylor called back to let him know he was on his way. Alavi mentally calculated the time remaining before his target arrived. Probably another seven or eight hours, he estimated. He replayed his exit strategies in his head, glad that he had spent so much time reconnoitering the surrounding neighborhoods in the car he'd rented for that purpose and was keeping in the underground parking garage.

He hadn't really considered what he would do if his IEDs didn't explode. He reminded himself that none of the hundreds of bombs he had built had ever malfunctioned.

Alavi was daydreaming about future strikes he would lead against infidels when the cell phone he used to call Major Taylor started vibrating. He hesitated before answering. Nobody except for the major had that number. Alavi didn't even know it himself. It must be Taylor calling back.

Alavi answered the phone.

"Mohammad?" asked Major Taylor.

Alavi breathed a sigh of relief. "Yes, Major."

"We'll be there in about two hours."

"Perfect. Everything will be ready. Are you traveling with your usual vehicles?" asked Alavi as nonchalantly as possible.

"Of course," snapped Major Taylor. Then, before Alavi could end the conversation, he added, "Why would you ask?"

Alavi winced. He hoped he hadn't compromised his opportunity for success by asking one question too many. Yet, he'd only made two bombs, plus the little backup.

"We want to make sure the hotel's employees treat you with the respect you deserve during your arrival. I'll let them know to expect a VIP."

"Good idea, Mohammad."

"See you in a couple of hours," said Alavi, hanging up.

The three cell phones he would use to activate the IEDs were already placed next to a pair of binoculars by the window he would use to spot his targets. The numbers he needed to dial to activate the IEDs were programmed into the cell phones; Alavi needed only to press one button to get the fireworks going.

He looked at his watch and decided he still had enough time to do a quick walk to the ambush site and make sure that his IEDs were still perfectly hidden. Heading outside to walk along the unpaved road, he was happy to see that the dirt around the IEDs was undisturbed. The Claymore-type IED was also still in position.

Back in his hotel room, after stopping at the front desk to return the soaked umbrella he'd borrowed before heading out, Alavi began packing his luggage. Major Taylor would arrive within the next hour, and he wanted to be ready to flee the area the moment Taylor had been taken out. He had already scouted the large metal trash bin where he would leave his luggage and where it would surely be stolen within a matter of minutes.

Once packed, Alavi set his mind to clearing the hotel room. Sierra Leone's police force wasn't known for being efficient, but Alavi took precautions anyway. He put on a pair of surgical gloves to reduce the risk of leaving fingerprints and wiped his entire room clean with a towel. As a final precaution, he tucked the coffee cup he'd been using into his luggage and took the cutlery off his room-service tray. He slipped the fork, tongs up, into his pants pocket, and slipped the steak knife into his waistband. He doubted that Freetown's police department would be advanced enough to trace DNA through saliva, but he refused to take any chances.

Satisfied that everything was in order, Alavi grabbed his binoculars and positioned himself in a way that allowed him to clearly observe the ambush site. The final countdown had started; Alavi wouldn't leave his post until his task was complete.

—

Omar Al-Nashwan was pleased to see that Alavi had taken all the steps necessary to ensure a successful mission. It was now Al-Nashwan's turn to do his part.

He unzipped the bag that had been given to him by the Sheik's contact in Freetown. From inside the reinforced duffel bag, Al-Nashwan took out two Chinese weapons, a QSZ-92 pistol and a QBU-88 sniper rifle. The People's Liberation Army currently used both types of weapons, and Al-Nashwan had received advanced training on them while he had attended the US Special Forces Q Course in Fort Bragg many years ago. He had also used them extensively, especially the sniper rifle, during his time in Africa, a decade ago, serving the Sheik while still a member of the US Special Forces.

Al-Nashwan had already cleaned the weapons twice and had lightly applied a small quantity of oil on some of the moving pieces to guarantee proper operation. With an effective range of up to eight hundred meters and firing 5.8 x 42mm ammunition, the gas-operated QBU-88 had more than enough power for the task at hand. Al-Nashwan adjusted his telescope sight to three hundred meters and attached the bipod that would allow him even more accuracy.

Stretching his arms over his head, Al-Nashwan got up off the bed and dead-bolted his hotel-room door. He then locked it again from the inside using the security chain. He dragged a heavy four-drawer chest in front of the door to delay any intruder. Of course, he knew full well that these precautions would also slow him down if he wanted to leave in a hurry, but it was a small price to pay to know that his back was covered.

He laid the pistol next to the two extra ten-round magazines he had put within a hand's reach of the rifle. If everything went well and if Alavi's IEDs did their job, he wouldn't need to fire a single shot. But just in case there were any members of Major Taylor's envoy who survived the blast, he would ensure their timely demise. With nothing else to do, Al-Nashwan comfortably positioned himself behind his rifle and adjusted his sight on the ambush location.

CHAPTER 45

Mike was driving the 4x4 they'd rented while Lisa was studying a map of Freetown.

"We're less than three hundred meters southwest of the hotel, Mike. We should find a place to park the truck and walk to the hotel from here."

Mike looked out the window. The clouds were about to burst but were still holding for now. *Good thing we're wearing Gore-Tex boots. The weather might get ugly soon.*

Mike parked the truck between two old colonial houses. The roads were absolutely dreadful, and without an SUV, Mike wasn't sure they would have managed them. They both were wearing dark clothing under military-style green ponchos and carried their firearms in a fanny pack. Lisa had also brought two pair of binoculars. The plan they had laid out in the truck was simple enough. They would approach the hotel on foot, trying not to be seen. Lisa had suggested they stay away from the road and make their advance using the partially wooded area west of the Country Lodge. *I would have made the same recommendation*, thought Mike. *Good for her.*

Because she had studied the map, she also took the lead. They had gone less than a hundred meters when she signaled her husband to stop. Mike immediately put a knee down, listening and watching for any threats. Lisa slowly pointed to her left and gestured that someone was walking on the road seventy meters to his left. Mike gently brought his binoculars to eye level. What he saw surprised him.

"Unbelievable," whispered Mike. "I think it's Mohammad Alavi."

Through her binocs, Lisa was watching a man walking with an umbrella. "You sure? It doesn't look like him."

"C'mon, Lisa, it's him. He's been on the list for a long time. Trust me."

Mike could see his wife considering what he'd just said. "It makes sense, especially if Peter Georges—aka Alexander Shamrock—is here," Lisa finally agreed. "What do you want to do?"

"We need to find out in which room he's staying," said Mike. "And I want him alive. If he's with the Sheik, he might know where my father is."

Lisa nodded her consent.

"I'll follow while you stay behind." He was already up and ready to go when his wife warned him to stay down. "Don't move! Sniper! Shooter is on the second-floor window, third from the left. Seen?"

"Damn it. Seen," replied Mike, hoping he hadn't been made.

"What the hell is going on here?" wondered Lisa aloud. "Do you think Alavi's the target?"

"Don't know."

The sniper was well concealed, and Mike was grateful his wife had spotted him. Only the glinting barrel could be seen. *I knew she was a natural.*

"I don't think the sniper is here to take out Alavi," Mike said. "If he was, he would have taken the shot already."

"Agreed," Lisa replied, who was now scanning the other windows and balconies of the hotel. "He's a backup of some sort."

"Why set up here, though?" Mike asked, looking around him. "There's nothing of value around here."

"Why don't we ask him?" Lisa suggested. "I'm sure I could gain access to his room easily."

Didn't Nice teach her anything?

"Bad idea, honey," said Mike. "We don't know what we're facing here. We better take it slow and make sure we know what we're getting into."

Lisa took a few seconds to answer. "All right," she finally said. "I'll position myself so I can see the front entrance."

Mike gave her his blessing. "Give me a sitrep once you're there."

While his wife angled toward the other side of the hotel, Mike tried to get a visual of the sniper. He and Lisa had definitely stumbled upon something. The question was what?

"Mike, I'm in position," Lisa said, breaking into Mike's thoughts.

"What do you see?"

"The main entrance has a small porch, but nobody's out. There doesn't seem to be any kind of valet or bellman either. Two other single doors are also visible on this side of the hotel."

"Okay. Thanks, hon. Now let's stay put for a while. I have the impression something will be going down."

CHAPTER 46

Concentration was everything. One second of inattention could ruin weeks of planning. Fortunately, Alavi was quite good at these types of operations, and his focus never wavered. He remained calm when the two Range Rovers appeared in his binoculars. Even though the vehicles' side windows were tinted, Alavi was able to look past the man in the passenger seat and identify Major Taylor. He was surprised that Taylor himself was driving the lead vehicle, but that didn't change anything in terms of his plan. Furthermore, the major would himself absorb most of the blast created by the explosions. And if that didn't kill him, the Claymore would do it.

Alavi smiled. He was ready.

As Taylor's motorcade reached the kill zone, Alavi calmly pressed the preprogrammed buttons on the cell phones. Nothing happened. Alarmed, Alavi pushed the buttons a second time, knowing that his chances of success were evaporating.

Nothing! He cursed loudly in Arabic. *This can't be happening!*

He couldn't believe it. What had gone wrong? He had checked and rechecked everything. It was now too late to even use the Claymore, as the two vehicles were already well past its range.

What now?

A sick feeling filled his stomach and traveled up his throat.

He used his binoculars to follow the motorcade for the last three hundred meters leading up to the hotel. That's when he saw the two antennas on top of each Range Rover.

—

The moment Omar Al-Nashwan spotted the two Rovers in his scope he knew they were in trouble. He recognized the antennas the instant he saw them. Adding to his frustration, he didn't have a shot at Taylor because he was partially hidden by the man seated in the passenger seat. An impossible shot. He cursed himself. This was all his fault.

He'd been the one who had recommended that Major Taylor add cell phone jamming devices to his motorcade. However, two years ago, Taylor hadn't been interested, stating that they were difficult to use and that he didn't want to attract the attention of would-be assassins to his otherwise unmarked vehicles.

Al-Nashwan slammed his fist into the hotel bed. *Fuck me!*

Taylor must have installed the jammers himself. Al-Nashwan took another look through his scope and groaned. Whoever Taylor had commissioned had made sure to get the most powerful jammers on the market.

The way the jammers operated was actually quite simple. The jammer transmitted a signal on the same frequency and at the same power as a cell phone. The result was that the signals canceled each other out. Some higher-end cell phones were designed to add power if they experienced low-level interference, so jammers were built to recognize this and match the power increase. Plus, cell phones usually used two frequencies, one for speaking and one for listening. Depending on the jammer, it could block either one or both of these frequencies.

Al-Nashwan didn't waste any time. He would have to follow plan B. While disassembling his rifle, he dialed Alavi's cell phone. The call didn't go through. Al-Nashwan rolled his eyes at his own stupidity and stuffed his phone back in his pocket. Within twenty seconds, the rifle was slipped back in the gym bag and the pistol was stowed in a holster hidden under a blue short-sleeve shirt. He had to hurry and speak with Alavi. He pushed the four-drawer chest out of the way, then exited his room and ran down the hall.

—

Lisa had just advised him that there was nothing new to report, when Mike said, "I have two black Range Rovers approaching from the west. Traveling speed is under thirty kilometers an hour. Follow-up truck is in defensive position."

His wife didn't reply.

Mike switched his binoculars back to the sniper's position. *Sniper's barrel isn't moving. That means he's not looking for new targets; he knows what his target looks like.* "You should have visual on the motorcade in twenty seconds." *Why the hell isn't she acknowledging?*

Mike wondered if the trucks weren't the targets. He half-expected to hear the rifle go off, but the small convoy rolled by without incident. His PDA suddenly vibrated in his pocket. Lisa had sent him a text message.

We're being jammed. Motorcade now in position in front of lobby.
10-4, Mike texted back.

Mike scanned the area for other vehicles and didn't see any. He then focused on the sniper's position, only to realize he couldn't see the barrel anymore.

I can't see the sniper anymore. He either relocated or he hauled ass.

I think we should go in, Mike.

Not yet, Lisa. We need to let headquarters know what's going on. Stand by while I contact them.

Mike was no fool. He knew Lisa was itching to go in. Her failure to neutralize the suicide bomber at the Nice airport all by herself had surely left her wanting another shot. Mike appreciated how tactically sound Lisa had become. *Seeing the sniper before me being the case in point.* The challenge was to keep her leashed until the time came to set her loose.

Knowing his Skype account didn't work on the same band, Mike rapidly launched his application and used its Internet connection to link with IMSI. "Anna, this is Mike," he said seconds later.

"What's your status, Mike?"

"Lisa and I are standing by at the Country Lodge. We think Mohammad Alavi is on location as well."

"Wait a sec, Mike," said Anna. "I'll patch the director in."

Seconds later, Mike heard Charles Mapother's voice. "Are you sure it's Alavi?"

"Ninety percent certainty, sir."

Mike let Mapother weigh the different options available to them.

All of a sudden, Lisa came on the air. "For some reason, they aren't jamming the frequencies anymore. Men are pouring out of the Range Rovers."

Mike advised Mapother to stay on the line as Lisa was communicating with him.

"I see seven men," Lisa continued. "All are dressed in dark blue suits over white shirts with the exception of one who's sporting a black suit. They're clearly packing."

"What type of weapons?" Mike asked.

"My guess is they're carrying pistols. I don't see any other kind of weapons. No one is carrying any bags either. Two of them have now assumed protective duties around the man wearing the black suit while two others entered the hotel. They look like they know what they're doing."

Mike relayed the new information to Mapother.

"You're the man on the ground, Mike, but if you believe you can take down Alavi and Peter Georges, you have the go-ahead."

The opportunity was too good to pass up. If they could confirm that both Alavi and Alexander Shamrock were there, he and Lisa had to kill them.

But not before I have a good chat with them. Either one could be the key to finding my father.

"Lisa, headquarters gave us the green light."

"Excellent."

"But we kill only in self-defense, okay? I'd love to know what they know about my father's whereabouts."

"Of course, Mike. Don't worry, we'll grab one of them."

I wish.

"You said earlier there were two other doors leading to the hotel. Do you think we could breach them without being seen?"

"Easy enough. Should take less than a minute," Lisa confirmed. "By the way, except for the two drivers, the whole party is now inside the hotel."

"Good. I'll approach the doors while you keep an eye on the bad guys."

"Sounds like a plan," Lisa answered, excitement filling her voice.

—

Alavi's confusion didn't last long. He had pretty much come to the same conclusion as Al-Nashwan. He wondered briefly why Allah hadn't allowed his plan to succeed. *Maybe he wants me to prove my worthiness in some other way.*

His options were limited. Without a firearm, there was no way he could take out the major's security detail without being killed. He was outnumbered, and he had lost the advantage of surprise. His only hope was that Taylor's goons would be the same he had helped to train and, out of familiarity toward him, would let their guard down. He tried to place himself in their situation. What would he do? They probably believed that any threat to the major would come from the outside and not from the man whom their boss had traveled so far to see. Their instructions would probably be to pay more attention to the employees and other guests in the hotel than to him. He would just have to play it by ear and hope that a suitable opportunity would arise.

Alavi took a deep breath. He'd have to go down to the lobby to greet his VIPs, or else the setup might look suspicious. After unlocking the dead bolt and cracking the door, he removed the surgical gloves he was still wearing. When he looked up, he was in no way prepared for what he saw in the doorway.

—

With Lisa covering him from twenty-five meters away, Mike sprinted to one of the metal doors. He had no idea where the door would lead, but it was the only way to enter covertly. He had just reached the door when it burst open. His reflexes allowed him to place his arm in between his head and the opening door, but Mike was pushed away. A man wearing the white uniform of a cook and holding a cigarette in his hand walked out. He was surprised to see Mike and asked him what he was doing there.

Without thinking, Mike punched the man in the solar plexus and followed with an elbow strike to the head. The man crumbled to the ground, unconscious. Mike looked at Lisa and signaled her to come over.

"What the hell?" Lisa said, looking at the cook lying in the dirt.

"He came out of nowhere! Couldn't take any chances," Mike replied, already using his bootlaces to bind the wrists and ankles of the man he had knocked out. "Let's put him in the bushes over there."

They grabbed the man by his feet and shoulders and carried him to the spot Mike indicated.

"Let's go," Mike said, once the man was hidden.

They ran back to the door that Lisa had kept open with a rock jammed in the doorframe, then entered an empty kitchen where a pot of water was boiling. Mike turned off the gas.

"This door leads directly to the lobby," advised Lisa, peeking through the door's small window. "Our friends are there."

"All of them?" asked Mike, approaching the window.

"I think so," his wife replied, leaving her spot. "Take a look."

The four bodyguards had positioned themselves around the man wearing the black suit. Mike could see the leader was annoyed. His demeanor was one of impatience and irritation. He was a man clearly used to being in charge, and he didn't like to wait on anyone.

"Who are these guys?" Mike whispered.

"No clue. But they are carrying heat, and they look like they mean business."

"We need to find out if they have anything to do with Alavi and Shamrock."

"If they leave the lobby, I can have a chat with one of the drivers," Lisa suggested. "He'll tell me what we need to know."

"It might come to that," Mike replied. "But we would have to do it together. There are two of them."

Lisa placed her hand on Mike's shoulder. "Then we wouldn't know where they're going in the hotel. You need to follow these guys. I can take care of the drivers myself, Mike. Trust me."

—

Omar Al-Nashwan had just arrived in front of Alavi's door when it suddenly opened. Al-Nashwan didn't hesitate. He jabbed Alavi in the stomach before pushing the stunned bomb maker back into his room and closing the door behind them. He wasn't sure if Alavi recognized him or not, but he didn't want to risk a confrontation.

"It's me, Mohammad," Al-Nashwan said. "Omar."

—

Hunched over from the blow, Alavi looked up at the familiar voice and immediately saw through his mentor's disguise. He got up slowly with the help of Al-Nashwan's outstretched hand.

"What are you doing here?" asked Alavi, still breathless from the preemptive strike he'd absorbed.

"Listen to me carefully, my friend. We don't have much time."

The master terrorist spent the next minute rapidly explaining his plan.

That could work, thought Alavi.

CHAPTER 47

Major Jackson Taylor was dressed in a loose-fitting black jacket over an open-collared white shirt. He had gained a few pounds since Alavi had last seen him, but he remained fit enough. His security guards were all wearing dark blue suits, also with open-collared white shirts. They were carrying their weapons concealed in leather holsters.

As soon as Taylor climbed out of his black Range Rover, the guard who had been riding shotgun got out and took his boss's place behind the wheel. He shut down the jamming system so he could communicate with his boss if necessary. The other driver stayed in the second Rover as the other bodyguards climbed out of the vehicle. One of them took up position in front of Taylor and another behind him. Two others went inside to screen the lobby. A few moments later, they reappeared in the hotel doorway and signaled that it was safe to enter.

Upon entering the lobby, Major Taylor was surprised that nobody was waiting to receive him. He had expected Alavi to be standing with the hotel manager and had even hoped that the Sheik himself would greet him.

Hadn't he done enough for this raghead's organization to warrant such basic respect? Alavi had told him to expect VIP treatment, but all he saw was a couple of guests sitting on one of the lobby's sofas. A front desk employee was standing behind his counter at an old IBM computer. He looked in Taylor's direction but avoided eye contact. Frustrated, Taylor was about to return to his vehicle when he saw a vaguely familiar figure walking toward him.

"Mohammad?" asked Taylor as his bodyguards moved their hands toward their holsters and placed themselves between their boss and the approaching stranger.

"It's me, Major. I changed my appearance somewhat," Alavi answered.

"He's fine, boys," Taylor barked at his bodyguards. "Don't you recognize your old friend?"

The bodyguards let Alavi pass, and two of them greeted him.

"Major, it's good to see you again," said Alavi, embracing the man he was supposed to kill.

While Taylor was patting him on the back, Alavi surreptitiously observed the bodyguards. He had been right: only one of them was even looking in his direction, while two others had already retreated outside. The last bodyguard was standing a dozen feet away, keeping an eye on the hotel guests and the one employee in sight.

"I've traveled far to see you, old friend."

"Thank you, Major. Someone important wanted to thank you personally for everything you've contributed to our efforts over the last few years."

"I was well compensated," said Taylor.

"Indeed you were. But we believe that our relationship with our greatest African ally should grow even more," said Alavi, carefully selecting his words. "Why don't we go up to my room to discuss this privately? I have some refreshments that I'm sure you'll enjoy."

"Excellent idea," answered Taylor.

Alavi was glad to see that all four bodyguards were now forming a loose square around him and the major. If they remembered Al-Nashwan's training, two would check out Alavi's room before allowing their boss inside, and the other two would stay outside the door after their boss had entered.

The hotel's marble hallways were narrow, and some parts were slippery from puddles of water, presumably from guests returning to their rooms still wet from the earlier rain shower or their swim in the pool. Alavi made a mental note to be careful once he and Al-Nashwan sprang into action, for a fall would definitely break their momentum.

—

The man with the black suit looked like he was about to leave when someone Mike recognized as Mohammad Alavi appeared.

"Wait," Mike said to Lisa, who was on her way to have a "chat" with the drivers. "Mohammad Alavi just walked into the lobby."

His wife approached him and watched what was going on through the small window. "They seem to know each other. They wouldn't embrace each other like that if they didn't," she observed. "Even two of the bodyguards shook his hand."

Mike's brain was working in overdrive to find a solution that would allow them to learn where Alavi's room was located while remaining unseen.

"They're leaving the lobby," Lisa announced.

"As soon as they're gone, I'll enter the lobby," explained Mike, looking at a map of the hotel he had found attached to the wall next to him. "There's an elevator down this way." Mike pointed out the area to Lisa before continuing. "There's also an emergency staircase at the end of the same corridor."

"Yeah, I see it," Lisa confirmed. "If you can tell me which floor they're headed to, I can take the stairs and wait for you there."

"All right. Stay here until I can call the floor. Then we'll have to move fast."

Lisa nodded and Mike exited the kitchen. There was only one employee present in the lobby, and he didn't make an effort to look at Mike. The lobby wasn't big, so Mike crossed it in no time. He was about to enter the corridor leading to the elevator when he saw something that stopped him dead in his tracks.

He quickly turned around, confident no one had seen his hesitation.

"Lisa, I believe Alavi's room is right next to the lobby. Two of the bodyguards went in, and two others stayed behind with the VIP," Mike whispered through their communication system.

"You want me to join you?"

"Negative. The VIP just went in the room, and now three bodyguards are stationed outside there."

"I'm looking at the map of the hotel, Mike," Lisa said moments later. "I suggest I go back outside to see if I can observe what's going on inside the room."

"Do it, Lisa," Mike replied. "Check on the guy I put down earlier as well. I don't want him to cause any fuss."

"Will do."

Using a sports magazine he'd found on one of the lobby coffee tables, Mike positioned himself in such a manner that he could keep a watch on Alavi's hotel door. Soon enough, the door opened and someone handed water bottles to the guards.

They're holding a meeting in this room. We know Alavi is present. There is at least one other member engaged in providing security if we take into consideration the sniper. What else? Who's this guy with the bodyguards? How can we take them down?

His thoughts were interrupted by Lisa's voice in his ear. "The man is still out cold, but I can't see inside the room. The angle isn't right."

"Roger that. Stay put—holy fuck!" shouted Mike inadvertently as two of the three bodyguards went down in a pool of blood. "Someone's attacking the guards," continued Mike, reaching for his gun. "Shit. It's Alexander Shamrock."

—

As the party reached Alavi's room, two bodyguards went in first, just as Alavi had predicted. A few seconds later, they received the all-clear signal, and Alavi led his guest into the room. Only one guard remained inside with them, and the other three took up posts in the hallway.

"Would you like juice or soda? Or maybe something stronger?" asked Alavi.

"What do you have on hand?"

"Would a rum and coke be satisfactory?"

"Ha! I see that you remember my tastes, Mohammad."

Alavi remembered well. Major Taylor's version of rum and coke was like no other. Back when Alavi was still Taylor's adjutant, he had many occasions to witness the major pouring rum over a gram or two of cocaine.

"But let's conduct our business first," added Taylor. "Then we party, yes?"

"Bottled water, then?" asked Alavi. Part of Al-Nashwan's plan was to get something into all the bodyguards' hands.

Taylor nodded. "When will I meet the Sheik?"

Alavi smiled. "I knew you would understand."

"So, when will he be here?" Major Taylor repeated.

"He'll arrive shortly. He had to take an unscheduled phone call. It has to do with what we will discuss with you."

That excuse seemed to satisfy Major Taylor. He walked toward the balcony as Alavi threw a bottle of water to one of the bodyguards.

"You have a beautiful view from here, Mohammad."

"Yes. I was quite pleased with it myself," said Alavi. He loaded his hands with three more bottles of water, then casually passed them to the bodyguard to distribute to the guards outside the room.

"You know, Mohammad, I've been thinking about a few things recently," began Taylor.

"Oh?" returned Alavi, looking at his watch. *Any moment now...*

"With the price of gold reaching new heights, I think we should expand our current activities—"

Major Taylor was interrupted by the sound of two shots going off in the hallway. Inside the room, Taylor's bodyguard reacted immediately, pulling his gun out of its holster and pointing it toward the door. Suddenly, the door burst open, and a bloody Omar Al-Nashwan entered with his pistol drawn.

CHAPTER 48

Al-Nashwan had rapidly explained his plan to Alavi. His protégé had asked a few questions but agreed with him that it was the best they could do in so little time. Yet the plan required perfect execution from both of them.

Once Major Taylor and his security detail were out of the lobby, Al-Nashwan exited his room and used the emergency staircase to go down to the first floor, where a utility door was located. He deposited Alavi's duffel bag into the kitchen's large metallic trash bin, then attached a silencer to his QSZ-92 pistol. Al-Nashwan felt the adrenaline rush throughout his body. It didn't matter how many times he had done these kinds of things before; being close to death had always given him chills.

Just a bullet away.

The light drizzle had now become a violent rainfall, and within a few seconds, Al-Nashwan felt his shirt clinging to his upper body. He didn't care about that, though; he knew the rain would help him during the first phase of his plan.

Without a way to holster his pistol with the silencer attached, he kept his weapon close to his leg as he walked toward the corner of the building, where he was hoping to get a good look at where the Rovers were parked. From his semiconcealed position behind the trash containers, Al-Nashwan was able to see the two black SUVs parked one behind the other. The drivers had kept the engines running, but most likely that was only so that they could enjoy the vehicle's air conditioning as they relaxed after a long journey. Al-Nashwan knew from experience that once the boss was out of sight, they would let their guard down.

The heavy rain would make it difficult for the drivers inside the vehicles to see what was going on around them. After checking that his weapon had a round in the chamber, Al-Nashwan ran from his cover to the rear bumper of the first Range Rover fifteen meters away. He nearly slipped as his combat boots lost their grip on the muddy road but was miraculously able to regain his balance.

Crouching down, Al-Nashwan rested his back on the rear bumper and thought about how the next minute or so would unfold. Once he'd visualized it a few times, he was ready to make his move. He stayed low, remaining out of view from both drivers, and slithered to the front passenger door of the first Rover. He guessed that the SUV's door would be locked and was prepared to fire through the window, but he tried the handle first anyway. He was only half-surprised to find that the lazy driver had failed to lock the door. *Stupid mistake, buddy. You deserve to die.*

The driver instinctively turned toward the opening door but was shot twice in the head before he had the chance to identify the sound. Al-Nashwan opened the rear passenger door and dragged the dead driver's body into the backseat, where it would be harder to see from outside.

Looking down, Al-Nashwan saw that spatters of blood from his victim's wound had found their way onto his shirt, but he had no time to do anything about it now. His entry into the hotel would be a bit trickier, but he'd be prepared. He closed the Range Rover's passenger doors and proceeded toward the second SUV.

This driver, while no more attentive than the first, had at least locked the doors. Unfortunately for him, he was playing a video game on a smartphone instead of watching what was happening around him. Omar Al-Nashwan fired three rounds just inches from the passenger side window. The first bullet shattered the glass and hit the driver in his right shoulder. The second and third bullets mushroomed into his brain.

After hastily removing what was left of the window, Al-Nashwan opened the side door and quickly stashed the second driver in the trunk of the first SUV. He inserted a new magazine into his pistol and kept the half-spent one in his left pocket.

Knowing that he and Alavi would need a swift getaway, he left the SUV's engine running. Keeping his pistol close to his right leg, Al-Nashwan went back inside the hotel, using the same utility door he had used before.

So far, so good. Yet the next minute would be crucial.

He reentered the emergency staircase area and cautiously opened the door leading to the hallway. He chanced a quick peek into the corridor. What he saw pleased him.

Of the four remaining bodyguards, three were outside Alavi's room, chatting. Each was holding a bottle of water, which would considerably slow their reaction time. He still didn't know what to expect inside Alavi's room, but he trusted Alavi to do his part—or at least to get out of the way.

He turned the corner into the corridor and, with his weapon extended in front of him and his eyes steady on the front sight of the pistol, Al-Nashwan got two shots off before any of the bodyguards realized that an intruder was attacking them.

The first bodyguard didn't stand a chance. After taking Al-Nashwan's first two shots in the chest, he fell hard. The second dropped his bottle of water and managed to get his right hand to his holster before Al-Nashwan's third round pierced his heart.

The fourth time Al-Nashwan pulled the trigger, nothing happened. Jammed![6]

—

Al-Nashwan automatically tapped the magazine and racked the pistol's action. That process was called an immediate action, and it was enough to clear a jammed pistol ninety percent of the time. Al-Nashwan could see that this particular one was due to a bad round that hadn't exploded.

Although Al-Nashwan cleared his malfunction in less than three-quarters of a second, it provided the third bodyguard with precious time. He drew his pistol and fired a booming round in the general direction of the assailant before Al-Nashwan's fifth round hit him in the middle of the forehead.

Al-Nashwan swore under his breath. The bodyguard's bullet had flown less than an inch from his head, and that was too close. Worse, the surprise element was now gone; the advantage had slipped to the other side as soon as the single loud shot had rung out.

Now they would be waiting for him on the other side of the door. Knowing that any hesitation on his part would mean certain death, Al-Nashwan kicked the door open and was about to enter when some one yelled his name.

—

As Alexander Shamrock turned to face him, Mike fired his weapon. His target was slammed against the doorframe of Alavi's room by the force of the impact. But before he could fire again, Al-Nashwan slipped inside the room and closed the door behind him.

"What's going on, Mike? I'm running back to you," Lisa said, her breathing heavy.

"He's here. I just shot Shamrock," Mike explained. "I don't know how bad he's hit, but he's now inside the room."

The next few seconds were filled by the sound of gunfire coming from Alavi's room. Mike didn't think anyone would be left alive.

"I'm coming in through the front door," Lisa said. "Shit! Someone shot up both drivers."

"We'll deal with that later, Lisa. Just get in here."

His wife burst down the hallway, sweeping her weapon left and right in search of targets. Kneeling next to Mike, she asked, "What do you want to do?"

"It's been twenty seconds since the last gunshot," Mike explained. "We'll give it another minute, then we'll approach the room. If we don't hear anything, we're going in. Anyone with a weapon is to be considered hostile."

"What if someone decides to exit while we wait?"

"We take them out."

And say goodbye to any chances I have left to see my father alive.

CHAPTER 49

The round deflected off his bulletproof vest but knocked the wind out of him. Fortunately, his instincts kicked in right away, and he pushed inside the room, out of the gunman's line of fire. *Who the hell was that? Someone who knew me as Alexander Shamrock?*

He closed the door with his foot, and the first thing he saw was Taylor's fourth bodyguard, confused to see the Sheik's right-hand man. They fired at the same time, and Al-Nashwan felt the bullet cut through his thigh, followed by an immense pain that nearly paralyzed him. His target was still standing, but Alavi jumped on him before he could fire a second time. The two men rolled on the hotel-room floor, preventing Al-Nashwan from firing.

Taylor was nowhere in sight. Al-Nashwan, fighting through the pain, had a pretty good idea where he was as he cleared the room's entrance foyer and moved into the main bedroom area, keeping himself low to present the smallest target possible. But Major Taylor was ready and fired at Al-Nashwan as soon as he rounded the corner. The 9mm bullet fired by the British Army-issued Browning missed the vest and hit high on his left shoulder.

FUCK!

The impact brought him down, but his life was saved when Taylor's second and third rounds went high. Using the last of his energy, Al-Nashwan pumped the rest of his magazine into Major Taylor's body.

—

Alavi was still wrestling with Taylor's bodyguard. The man had been hit in the stomach by Al-Nashwan's bullet, but he wouldn't give up. Both struggling men were using most of their strength to keep the end of the barrel away from them. For a few seconds, Alavi was pinned down by the weight of the other man. Seeing Al-Nashwan's body lying in a growing pool of blood and clutching his injured shoulder, Alavi knew he was on his own.

Without taking his hand off the bodyguard's pistol, Alavi tried to knee his opponent in the groin. He heard a grunt and felt the man's grip on the firearm waver. He twisted hard and punched the body-guard in the face with such force that he broke his own wrist. But with the strength of that strike, his foe became unfocused. With his good hand, Alavi went for the steak knife he'd tucked into his belt earlier. The bodyguard hadn't yet recuperated from the devastating blow to his face when Alavi plunged the knife past the bone and into the heart.

Leaving his knife where it stuck, Alavi looked over at Al-Nashwan. His mentor was quickly losing blood from two bullet wounds and was in urgent need of medical assistance. He grabbed Al-Nashwan's pistol and checked how many rounds were left in the magazine. Seeing that there were none, he cursed fiercely and discarded it.

They had to move now or else face the police.

"Mohammad, we have to get out of here," Al-Nashwan said weakly. "We can't use the door. Someone is waiting for us on the other side."

"What? Who?" Alavi didn't understand. Did Major Taylor bring more men than they had thought?

"It doesn't matter," Al-Nashwan said, gasping. "We need to get out of here."

"Can you walk?"

"I think one of the bullets hit an artery. Help me to my feet," answered Al-Nashwan, looking down at his pants.

He winced in pain, but with the help of Alavi, he was able to get up.

"I left a Range Rover with the engine running just outside the kitchen," said Al-Nashwan.

"Let's go. We'll use the sliding glass door."

They were able to cross the patio before Al-Nashwan's legs col-lapsed under him. There was nothing Alavi could do to support him, and Al-Nashwan's unconscious body fell to the pavement. Alavi picked him up in a fireman's hold, fighting the excruciating pain in his wrist, and then fled for his life.

—

The two IMSI operatives had positioned themselves to cover three hundred and sixty degrees. Even though the firefight had come from Alavi's room, they couldn't take the chance of being surprised from behind. So far nobody had entered the lobby, and the sole employee Mike had seen earlier had ducked behind his desk, out of sight.

"I don't know if an alarm has been raised or not, Lisa, but we have to move. We can't get caught here. The local police is probably the most corrupt institution in the country."

"I'm ready when you are."

Mike took the lead, his pistol extended in front of him. Lisa, following closely, peeked behind him a few times to ensure no threats were coming from the rear.

"Checking for survivors," said Mike once they had reached the bodyguards.

"Covering," replied Lisa, placing her back to the wall and scanning left and right.

Mike released the dead men from their weapons and confirmed they had no pulse.

"They're gone," he said. He checked their clothes for any IDs and pocketed their wallets before taking a stance opposite his partner.

"I don't hear anything," Lisa said.

"Me neither. You're ready?"

His wife smiled. *She's actually enjoying this. That's just crazy!*

Mike fired five shots at the door-lock mechanism and kicked the door open. He entered the room and immediately saw the body of the fourth bodyguard lying on the hotel-room floor, a steak knife protruding from his chest. Clearing the corner of the room with Lisa right behind him, Mike couldn't miss the wide-open patio door. Traces of smeared blood were visible on the terrace. Mike exited the room through the patio door, his weapon at the high ready. He looked left and right. Nobody. He swore under his breath. *We've waited too long.*

"This guy's still breathing," his wife called from inside the room. Mike went back in, frustrated.

The body of the VIP was slumped against the opposite wall. He had been shot multiple times, but by some miracle, he was still breathing.

Mike kneeled down next to him. The man looked at him with a dazed, hopeless expression. He had only minutes to live. "Alavi and Shamrock are gone. They can't be far," Mike said.

"I'm going after them," Lisa replied.

"Keep the communications open. I want to know what's going on."

"Sure thing."

With Lisa gone, he focused his attention on the dying man.

"What's your name?"

The man tried to spit but couldn't.

"That wasn't smart. Listen, there's no way around it; you're dying. You're in a lot of pain, yes?"

The man closed his eyes and nodded.

"You have a sucking wound. I can make it easier for you if you speak to me. Would you like me to do that for you?"

"Yes," murmured the man.

Mike placed the man in a more comfortable position and grabbed a plastic glass from the work desk. With his knife, he cut open the man's white shirt and placed the small plastic glass on the wound. The objective was to prevent the air from entering the lung by the hole the bullet had created.

"Better now?"

The man's eyes filled with tears. "How long?"

"A few minutes in relative comfort if you help me, but it could also become agonizing if you don't."

The man didn't say anything, but Mike knew he would cooperate. "What's your name?"

"Jackson Taylor."

"What are you doing here?"

"I...I was supposed to meet with the Sheik."

Mike couldn't believe it. "You know him?"

The man was now shaking uncontrollably, but he still managed to smile. "He fucked me over. He sent Alavi and his henchman to kill me," he said, blood pouring out of his mouth. Mike was aware that Taylor's lungs were filling up quickly. He had a minute left at the most. The man coughed, splattering Mike's face with his blood.

"Who was the guy with Alavi?" said Mike, wiping his face.

"Omar Al-Nashwan. He's the henchman. A sick fuck."

Yeah, and a damn traitor, too.

"Jackson, do you know where the Sheik keeps Ambassador Ray Powell hidden?"

Taylor gave him a puzzled look. "Who?" he asked weakly.

"Don't play games with me, asshole!" Mike yelled, his frustration taking over. He removed the plastic glass, and Taylor's breathing became erratic.

One, two, three, four, five, six, seven, eight, nine, ten.

At the count of ten, Mike replaced the glass and repeated his question. "Where does the Sheik keep Ambassador Powell?"

Tears were now streaming down Jackson's cheeks. "Don't...know."

Shit! He really doesn't know.

All of a sudden, Lisa's voice and the sound of gunshots came in through Mike's earpiece. "I've got them. They're climbing aboard one of the Range Rovers. They're in front of the hotel."

Mike could hear his wife firing her weapon while speaking. "They're getting away, and they punctured the tires of the other Range Rover. We need to get back to our truck and chase them."

"All right, Lisa. Calm down and come back here. We'll leave together."

Focusing on Jackson Taylor, Mike asked him another question. "Where's the Sheik?"

Taylor slowly rolled his head from left to right. "I...don't...know. He has a...a yacht he uses as headquarters. Always...moving. In...my...truck...suitcase...suitcase—"

"What's in the suitcase, Jackson?" Mike asked. But the man's head had rolled to one side.

Lisa ran into the room. "Let's go, Mike. We need to get moving. Now."

"We need to get back to one of the Range Rovers."

His wife looked at him skeptically. "Why?"

"This guy said there's a suitcase in one of the Rovers," Mike explained, pointing toward Jackson Taylor. "I don't know what it contains, but the intel might be useful."

"Whatever you say. I just hope the other guys didn't leave with the wrong truck."

CHAPTER 50

Alavi dreaded that someone would try to stop them. With no weapons, they had no way to fight anybody. Alavi's heart was racing as he lumbered across the lawn of the Country Lodge under his heavy load.

Alavi spotted the parked Range Rover as soon as he rounded the rear of the building. He reached for the rear door handle but lost his balance on the slippery road. He fell hard and couldn't help but drop Al-Nashwan's body. He heard a crack and correctly guessed that his mentor had just broken a bone. Although Al-Nashwan was still unconscious, Alavi heard him grunt—a good sign. He slowly got up and opened the SUV door. He carefully positioned Al-Nashwan in the backseat. Using the truck's doorframe as a step, he reached for the jammer antennas on top of the vehicle and yanked them off, tossing them to the ground.

Alavi had to take a few deep breaths. The shrieking pain in his wrist was causing spots to twinkle before his eyes. When the dizzy spell had somewhat cleared, he stepped down and closed the rear passenger door. He climbed into the driver's seat and carefully engaged the transmission.

A bullet hit the rear window, shattering it. Knowing Jackson Taylor always carried a handgun in the glove compartment, Alavi lunged for it as the second and third rounds hit his side mirror. He wasn't sure where the shooter was, but he fired at the other Range Rover's tires and accelerated away.

Following the road past his failed IEDs, he drove until he reached the first junction, where he turned left onto a paved road. Al-Nashwan needed immediate medical assistance, but Alavi didn't know where he could get it. With no other choice, he placed a call to the number he'd committed to memory—the number he was supposed to call only in a situation of extreme urgency.

"Yes?"

"Do you know who I am?" asked Alavi.

"I don't need to know who you are," said the voice, speaking with a strong British accent. "I know who you represent, and that's enough."

"We had complications, and we need to ditch a car. Also, one of us needs immediate medical assistance."

The voice became crisper. "Gunshot wounds?"

"Yes. At least two," answered Alavi.

"What type of car?"

"A black Range Rover," replied Alavi, hoping he hadn't just signed their death warrants by providing this information.

"Can I call you back at this number in five minutes?"

Mohammad Alavi looked behind him at Al-Nashwan, who was still slumped in the backseat. His breathing was quick and shallow and not getting any better.

"Yes, but hurry up. My friend has lost a lot of blood."

"Five minutes," repeated the man before hanging up.

CHAPTER 51

Kobani, Syria

Ray Powell ate his stale bowl of stew and drank his tea in silence. His body, stricken and weak, needed the calories. His will to live, unwavering only months ago, had shattered with the news that his whole family had died.

He'd hoped it was another one of the Sheik's hoaxes, but deep down, he knew better. They'd taken pictures of him crying over the death of his son, no doubt to harass his government by sending them to all known news outlets. He didn't care. He was a broken man.

But I have one fight left in me.

Since his kidnapping, the Sheik had moved him often, but when Powell looked around him, there was a certain finality about this cell—no windows, a thin mattress to sleep on that didn't do much of a job to stop the damp cold from entering his spine, and a bucket to do whatever a human body needed to do.

If I don't get out of here soon, I'll catch a disease and die much more painfully than with a bullet to the head.

Even though Powell doubted that the man with the British accent who brought him his meals and emptied his bucket was the only one guarding him, he had never seen anyone else since his transfer to this location. *I guess I'll know for sure how many there are once I get out of here.*

Being unafraid of dying was a new sensation for Powell. Now that he had lost everything, he didn't care what happened to him. His only objective was to let the world know who the Sheik's mole within the US government was.

The proof may have been destroyed, but my word has to count for something.

By all accounts, the president of the United States was a good man, and Powell was ready to give him the benefit of the doubt that he wasn't aware of Steve Shamrock's treacherous activities. Still, he'd get exposed, and news that one of his college buddies was financing the Sheik's terror network would see him impeached.

But first I need to get out of this hellhole.

CHAPTER 52

Freetown, Sierra Leone

Alavi didn't know if anyone was looking for them. At least one person back at the hotel had seen them leave with the black SUV. He wasn't sure what type of police response would be sent to the hotel—he hadn't seen any sign of police activity—but he wanted to be as far away as possible in case anyone provided them with a description of the vehicle.

He kept driving until he found a small alley between two decrepit buildings. He backed the SUV in and turned off the ignition. Outside, the weather had not improved at all. The noise, created by raindrops drumming on the aluminum panels of the Range Rover, made Alavi afraid that he wouldn't hear his cell phone if it rang. Unable to find the vibrate function, he pressed the volume button a few times before cramming the phone back into his jacket pocket.

He extricated himself from the driver's seat and crawled over the center console. He had learned first aid in the training camp, and his hands worked fast and efficiently. He applied pressure and placed bandages on Al-Nashwan's wounds, using the emergency kit he had found jammed beneath the front seat. Once he had done everything he could, he nervously checked his watch.

It's been seven minutes! I'll give him another three before I call back.

Then he remembered that he had left his passport at the hotel. Did Al-Nashwan leave his as well? He must have, as all guests were required to hand over their passports to the hotel upon check-in. That was one loose end he didn't want. Although the name on the passport was fake, it still carried a picture of his new appearance. He couldn't believe his bad luck. His last terrorist operation had been a failure, and now this!

Al-Nashwan's breathing had become shallow, and Alavi wondered what punishment the Sheik would bestow upon him if the organization's master assassin were to die because of him. Without Al-Nashwan's assistance, not only would his mission have been a complete fiasco, but he would probably be dead by now.

When his cell phone rang, Alavi jumped.

"Yes?"

"What's your current location?"

Alavi looked through the window but couldn't see a thing. It was raining too hard.

"I'm not sure, but hang on."

Protecting the phone from the rain in his pocket, Alavi opened the door of the SUV. He climbed out of the vehicle and jogged to the nearest intersection, searching for the street names.

"We are close to the intersection of Davies and Oxley!" yelled Alavi into the phone.

"Fine. Someone with a white Toyota pickup truck will meet you there in fifteen minutes. When he asks you if you had lunch today, you'll tell him that you had an apple. Understood?"

"Yes. What about my injured brother and our SUV?"

"Everything will be taken care of."

CHAPTER 53

Kobani, Syria

Usually the man with the British accent gave him five minutes to eat and drink. On a good day, he might have a minute more, but it had never happened before that twenty minutes had elapsed between the time the tray was given to him until it was taken away.

Damn! What's going on?

If it had happened the day before, Powell couldn't have cared less. But today? The break in routine was unexpected. And unwanted. Today was the day he had decided to make his move.

Either it's brave or dumb. I don't know yet. We'll see if I'm still breathing at the end of the day...

As the minutes passed, Powell's resolve began to wane. *Maybe I should wait for a better time? Something is going on. It's taking too long.*

Powell shook his head. *No! Focus! Think about what these cowards did to your family. Stop thinking about yourself.*

The door of his cell opened abruptly. Powell hadn't heard the footsteps leading to the lock being disengaged. He must have been staring at the man who had just entered because the man started shouting at him. "What are you looking at!"

Powell diverted his eyes. "Thank you, sir," he replied. That seemed to surprise the man with the British accent.

"For what?" he asked, pushing Powell against the dirty wall of his cell. "You're thanking me for what?"

"The stew was delicious."

The man cocked his head to one side, looking perplexed. That's when Powell kicked him between the legs with all his might. As the man's head came down, Powell delivered a bone-crashing knee strike to the man's face. Powell felt the man's knees go limp, and he let him fall head-first to the ground. Powell searched the man and retrieved a cell phone from a pocket of his slacks. Powell looked at the display to confirm it was charged but immediately saw there was no signal. *I'm probably in a basement of some sort.* Powell pocketed the cell phone and continued to go through the man's clothes. *Nothing! No IDs, nothing!*

"Ben," Powell heard from the hallway outside his cell. "Is every-thing all right?"

Shit! There's more than one after all. Powell ran to the wall close to the cell's door and flattened himself against it.

"Ben? Where are you?" The accent was once again British, and Powell could hear footsteps approaching. Then he recognized the sound of a pistol coming out of a leather holster. *He probably realized that the cell's door is open. If he's well trained, he'll come in with his pistol up, notice his partner on the ground, and will automatically turn right to clear his corner. That's when I'll strike.*

Powell's mouth was so dry that his throat hurt. His heart rate had skyrocketed, and pearls of sweat were quickly forming on his forehead and on the small of his back. *I'm too old for this shit!* His hands were shaking. Powell willed himself to focus.

The man was not only well trained. He was a pro. When he came in through the door, his pistol was indeed up, but he kept it close to his chest. To Powell's disbelief, the man didn't lose a fraction of a sec-ond on his downed partner. Instead, as soon as he cleared the space in front of him, he pivoted to his right. Powell was on him in an instant, his hands going for the man's pistol. But, the other man was too quick, too young. With a quick flex of his wrist, he brought the barrel of his pistol down on Powell's head. The next second, Powell felt a powerful kick connect with his solar plexus, expulsing all the air out of his lungs. After another flick of the man's wrists, the butt of the pistol crashed on Powell's skull. On his knees, Powell tried to catch his breath, but the other man, still holding his pistol in a two-handed grip, elbowed him in his jaw. This time Powell collapsed on the ground, next to two of the three teeth the last strike had sent flying. He opened his eyes just long enough to see the man kick him in the head.

CHAPTER 54

Freetown, Sierra Leone

Gathering all the equipment they could find in Alavi's room, Mike and Lisa hurried back outside the hotel, where the last Range Rover was. While his wife covered him, Mike opened the door of the SUV and searched for Jackson's suitcase. They were in luck.

"I got it," Mike said.

"Let's get out of here," Lisa replied. "I hear sirens."

Mike paused to listen. The strident sirens of the Freetown Metropolitan Police cars were fast approaching.

"We can't use the road," Lisa calculated. "There's no way we'll make it to our truck without being intercepted. We need to go back the same way we came in."

Mike agreed. As they were moving west amid the bushes they'd used as concealment on their earlier approach to the hotel, several vehicles of the Operational Support Division of the Sierra Leone police roared up the road leading to the Country Lodge. Men wearing paramilitary uniforms and carrying assault weapons were being dropped off along the road.

"If they dropped soldiers farther back down the road, we might come in contact with a patrol," Mike whispered. They both kneeled down behind a tree. The rain had started again, and they were soaked to the bone. "If we're caught, we won't see the light of day for years."

"What are you saying, Mike?"

"We need to get this material to headquarters," said Mike, holding the suitcase. "It might provide a way inside the Sheik's network. That's the priority."

Lisa verified the ammunition for her pistol and inserted a new clip. Mike did the same. "Let's go," he said.

They were only a few hundred meters from the road, but they moved cautiously. As one of them advanced ten meters, the other covered. They leaped-frogged like this until they were less than twenty-five meters from the road. Mike raised his fist and signaled Lisa to join him. Mike gestured that he had seen one man standing watch on the road. He pointed in the direction of the lone soldier. Lisa nodded. Mike motioned that he wanted the man taken care of. That didn't necessarily mean to kill him. He was merely giving his wife the authority to do what she thought was needed to stop the man from engaging them.

Lisa stealthily approached the police officer from behind. Mike watched her with some kind of detached admiration. Lisa was like a tigress stalking her prey. Her movements were gracious, precise, and deadly. She stopped about five feet from her target and paused, studying her surroundings and her tactical advantage. A second later, her left arm slid under the soldier's collar, while she used her right foot to kick the back of the soldier's right knee to make him lose his balance. Using her weight, Lisa propelled the FMP officer over him. The officer landed on his belly with Lisa still locking him in a choke hold.

Ten seconds later, with the unconscious soldier at her feet, Lisa signaled Mike that all was clear. Not wasting time hiding the body in the bushes, they ran to their SUV and were long gone before the Sierra Leone police realized they were missing a man.

CHAPTER 55

IMSI Headquarters
New York

Within minutes of receiving Mike Walton's report, Anna Caprini and the rest of the available analysts were running Major Jackson Taylor's name through all their search engines. Before long, hits started to appear on their screens. An hour later, Mapother was reading the preliminary report his staff had prepared regarding Jackson Taylor.

So, the account we played with belonged to Taylor after all, thought Mapother. *The Sheik didn't appreciate Taylor's supposed disloyalty and sent Peter Georges—aka Alexander Shamrock—to kill him.*

Mapother was about to call Anna to request everything they had on Alexander Shamrock when someone knocked on the door. He pressed the button unlocking the door, and Jonathan Sanchez entered his office.

"I thought you would like to read the info we have on Shamrock," said Sanchez, handing him a three-page report.

"You read my mind, Jonathan," said Mapother. "Did you write it?"

"I did. Did you know his father, Steve Shamrock, is the CEO of Denatek?"

"The oil and gas company?"

"Yep," Sanchez replied. "And that he was married to a woman named Ghayda Al-Assad?"

Mapother raised an eyebrow. "No, I can't say I did."

"She was the daughter of Sheik Zefad Al-Assad, once a powerful figure in the UAE."

"What do you mean?"

"Sheik Zefad Al-Assad's family owned land on which an important oil field was discovered. An American oil company—for whom

Alexander Shamrock's father was working—negotiated a deal allowing them to drill. However, even though Al-Assad respected all the clauses in the contract, he was killed by the CIA a few years later."

"Are you sure about this?" asked Mapother, who had stopped reading. Sanchez had his full attention.

"Yes. It's not clear-cut, but if you read through the lines, you'll come to the same conclusion. The CIA erroneously believed he was a known terrorist and sent a team to kill him."

"That's terrible."

"Even more so for Steve Shamrock. His wife, Ghayda, was also killed in the raid."

"Oh shit!"

"My thoughts exactly, Charles. After the massacre, the only Al-Assad family member left was Qasim, Zetad's son. Within two years of his father's death, he sold all his family's territories to the Chinese and swore never to do business with the Americans again."

Mapother was shaking his head. "So you're telling me that the son of one of the most powerful men in the oil and gas industry in the United States is a terrorist?"

"The facts are there," Sanchez said. "And we have to think that Alexander's father is involved as well."

God! Jonathan's right.

Anna Caprini knocking on the door interrupted them.

"What do you have?" asked Mapother.

"What Mike and Lisa sent from Sierra Leone is like a gold mine. We're only starting to put all the pieces together, but one fact jumped right out."

Mapother signaled Anna to sit down. "What is it?"

"Major Jackson Taylor was definitely a close ally of the Sheik. We believe he's the guy who trained most of the Sheik's men prior to them deploying overseas to wreak havoc."

"It's too bad he's dead," Sanchez said. "It would have been nice to hear what he had to say, especially after he learned the Sheik had sent someone to kill him."

"I agree. Anything else?" Mapother asked.

"Does the name Abdullah Ahmad Ghazi ring a bell?"

"I can't say it does," Sanchez replied.

"Me neither," said Mapother. "Why?"

"As I said earlier," explained Anna, "we're not quite sure yet, but this Ghazi guy might be the financial link between the Sheik's organization and Jackson Taylor's. Years ago, the FBI put Ghazi on a soft watch alert. They believed he was facilitating money transfers between Muslim charity organizations and the Taliban in Afghanistan."

"Were they successful?" Sanchez asked.

"Not really. Mr. Ghazi disappeared, and the FBI never thought about investigating him further."

"They have a lot on their plate," said Mapother. "Should we try to find this guy ourselves?"

Anna shrugged. "We may need to, Charles."

"Explain."

"We'll know more in a few hours, but there's a high probability the Sheik is about to launch another offensive against us or one of our allies."

Mapother and Sanchez remained silent, waiting for her to give more details.

"In Major Taylor's computer we've found schematics and maps of installations similar to oil pipelines. I can't imagine why he had these plans if not for training purposes."

"These guys never train for fun," said Mapother. "When they put a plan to paper, it usually means they expect to carry it out."

"But there's one more thing I should add," said Anna. "The diary date for the scenarios was last week."

The IMSI director rose from behind his desk to study the map of the world hanging on the wall. "That means the Sheik's operatives could already be on their way to their targets. Wherever they are."

"That's right, sir."

"In this case, I concur with your previous assessment. We need to find Abdullah Ahmad Ghazi or Alexander Shamrock before it's too late. And we need to figure out what the targets are."

—

For the next few hours, all IMSI personnel worked tirelessly through the intelligence they gathered from Taylor's laptop. They checked every piece of information and tried to connect them to something they already know. They consulted all the federal databases they had access to, hoping to find something solid enough to justify sending assets to investigate. Ultimately, Jonathan Sanchez found the link—one that would once again send his friend and his wife in harm's way.

PART 5

CHAPTER 56

Lisbon, Portugal

By using the keywords *Alexander Shamrock* in the FBI main server, Sanchez detected a money trail linked to seventy million dollars that the CIA had lost during the initial days of the second Iraqi war. A Special Forces team had been dispatched to escort the money sent by helicopter to the head generals of the peshmerga forces, who were fighting alongside the US forces.

The helicopter never reached its destination, however, so nobody had ever learned what happened to that Special Forces team led by a certain Captain Alexander Shamrock. After a few weeks of searching, it was assumed that enemy forces had shot down the chopper and that the money had evaporated. What the CIA had not told the Army was that the money had been marked.

Agents had spent days entering the numbers of more than twenty thousand one-hundred-dollar bills into the system, hoping to learn how the Kurds were going to use the money and to what advantage. The CIA knew that the chances of some of that money eventually showing up in a foreign-held European bank account were high, and they wanted to know whose pockets the American taxpayers were padding.

Two days before, the Portuguese law enforcement agency responsible for policing the country's large urban area had a takedown in one of Lisbon's best-known bordellos. Twelve prostitutes and eight patrons were arrested and sent to jail for the night. An amount totaling almost seven thousand Euros was seized.

Hours later, a Portuguese officer ran the numbers of all the seized American bills into his system, and one came back positive. The officer sent a message to Interpol explaining that he had a seized American hundred-dollar bill that had been marked. His message trickled up the

Interpol ranks slowly until it was sent to the FBI. IMSI analysts immediately forwarded the information to Mapother.

Mapother instantly made the connection to what Sanchez had found earlier in the day. *No wonder the CIA wanted to keep a low profile on this one. There would be hell to pay if it became public knowledge that seventy million dollars had disappeared without a trace.* He could understand if a helicopter carrying a couple million had been shot down, but one carrying *seventy* million? The authorization for that kind of money to travel in a single helicopter was a strategic mistake on the part of somebody very high up the CIA food chain.

Mapother walked by Anna's office and asked her the whereabouts of Mike and Lisa.

"They're both still in Sierra Leone, sir."

"Could you please contact them and arrange a secure link?" asked Mapother.

In less than three minutes, Mapother had his two operatives on the line.

"What can we do to help?" Mike asked.

"Good job, guys. The intel we got from that computer is priceless. It also means, I'm afraid, that you'll be traveling to Portugal."

"What's in Portugal?" asked Mike.

"The scoop is that we might have found a link leading to about seventy million dollars of missing CIA money. And guess who was in charge of protecting that money? Alexander Shamrock," Mapother supplied. "I'm sending everything we've got to your server. Once you get the details, work out a plan and let me know if you need anything."

"Will Support Five be available?"

"Yes, they will."

"Anything else, sir?" asked Lisa.

"Keep me in the loop and good luck."

—

True to his word, Mapother sent his agents the mission's protocols forty-five minutes later. They read the file in silence, then decided that because Lisa was fluent in Portuguese, she would meet with the Portuguese officer, who had written the message to Interpol. They arranged their own separate transportation, and both operatives were out of Sierra Leone the next day.

Once in Portugal, Lisa easily tracked down Officer Geraldo Barros of the commercial crime section of the Polícia de Segurança Pública.

When Lisa called the PSP's general inquiry line, she was transferred directly to Officer Barros.

Meanwhile, Mike checked in at the hotel where Support Five had rented a room for him and contacted them once again to arrange for FBI identification. They met him at a busy café a few hours later, and Jasmine Carson handed over two FBI special agent credentials.

Lisa met Barros at his office in central Lisbon and introduced herself as Special Agent Maria Vincelli of the Federal Bureau of Investigation. Officer Barros didn't hide his surprise at seeing a Portuguese-speaking female FBI agent in his office. He was nevertheless professional, and after verifying Vincelli's credentials, he shared everything he had, including which brothel they'd raided and where the money had been found.

When he asked Lisa why a single hundred-dollar bill justified a trip overseas to interview the officer who had uncovered it, Lisa used all her charm in answering. "I made the mistake of letting my office know where I was spending my vacation."

Upon his departure, Lisa hailed a taxi and asked to be driven to Avenue de Liberdade in the historic district. She gave the taxi driver a few extra euros as a tip, then, as a security precaution, climbed out to walk the last half mile to her final destination.

As she walked toward the restaurant where her husband was waiting for her, she noticed that the sidewalk was made of beautiful marble stones hand placed in abstract patterns. This part of Lisbon was gorgeous, and Lisa briefly wondered how much it would cost to live on this street. As she strolled past shops such as Armani, Prada, and Burberry, she couldn't help but remember her past life, where she would have probably spent a small fortune on children's and babies' clothes. She then passed an enormous stone monument dedicated to the fifty thousand Portuguese soldiers who had fought in World War I, seven thousand of whom were lost.

She reached the rendezvous a few minutes later and sat down with her husband, who was a nursing a bottle of mineral water. Mike had chosen a table on the patio far away from any other patrons.

"How did it go?" asked Mike.

"The guy was friendly, and he gave me everything we need."

"Such as?"

"The location of the bordello and the name of the only patron they seized who paid in American dollars."

"What do you want to do?"

"You should pay the bordello a visit," answered Lisa.

"Most brothels have a hidden CCTV to protect the staff," said Mike. "Did the policeman mention anything regarding a CCTV system?"

"He didn't, but I didn't ask either."

"I'm sure they do have one, and I wouldn't be surprised if it's still there. I don't think the police would have seized it."

"Why would they?" Lisa replied. "In Portugal, prostitution isn't illegal—it's only illegal for a third party to profit from it, and that law is difficult to enforce. The PSP probably only raided the bordello to satisfy some angry neighbors. Am I right?"

"You are, honey," Mike replied, "and I think I know where you're going with this."

"Finish my thought, then," said Lisa, downing the last of her mineral water.

"The PSP knows that a CCTV system protects the bordello's staff against violent clients. If they were to remove or seize the system or even just seize the tapes, they would put the staff in danger."

"They could end up with a dead sex worker and a probable lawsuit on their hands," concluded Lisa.

"Okay then, I guess we'll have to visit this place after all," said Mike, signaling a waiter that they were ready to order. "Let's have lunch and think of a plan for how to gain access to what the brothel has to give up to us."

CHAPTER 57

Mike entered the small lobby of an Internet café. As Lisa had detailed, instead of continuing toward the pay-per-minute Internet cubicles, Mike opened a red door located on his right that led to a staircase. He went up the flight of stairs and gently knocked on the door. He was glad to see a CCTV camera perched above the doorframe. He looked directly into the lens and saw the reflection of his tiny, distorted image. He was dressed in a pair of blue jeans and a golf shirt. He was also sporting a false beard that he'd applied in the washroom of the restaurant and had added a pair of blue-tinted contact lenses for good measure.

Mike was about to knock a second time when he heard the electric lock buzz. He pushed the door gently and entered the brothel. Unlike his partner, he'd never been in a bordello before, so he wasn't sure what to expect. But he never thought that it would look like this. Dirty, cheap, soiled—those were adjectives that he associated with brothels. Instead, the light aroma of white tea and essential oils filled his nostrils. The soft, subtle fragrance was a perfect match for the elaborate décor surrounding him. Leather furniture that looked brand-new was impeccably arranged on a rich Persian rug that warmed up the room. Stunning prints and original art works were hung on red walls. It all reminded Mike of a gentleman's club he had visited in London. The room had no windows, but the ambient light had been adjusted to correspond with the rest of the space. Mike counted two more CCTV cameras in the reception area alone.

"Welcome to Sylvia's," said a feminine voice behind him in English.

Mike turned to find an elegantly dressed woman about his age. She was an attractive lady with long brown hair that reached the middle of her back. Her white dress was like what any other professional woman would wear to work. What set her apart was the small riding whip she held in her hand. There was no mistake that she was in charge.

"I'm Sylvia, the madam of this establishment," she continued. "We take cash, Visa, and American Express."

"You don't mess around, do you?" joked Mike.

"We always try to clear the unpleasantness of the transaction process early on in our guests' visits," she replied, returning his smile.

Mike had hoped that the brothel would be more low-end. Then he could simply bribe the madam to access the video feed. He wasn't at all sure a bribe would work in this case. He had a feeling that the madam was quite protective of her clients. He would have to change tactics.

"Do I have to pay now?" he asked.

"Yes. There is a flat fee of two hundred and fifty euros. That will buy you seventy minutes with any girl or boy you choose. You can do whatever you want, but violence or gagging is not allowed. For your convenience, if you wish to use a credit card, the billing will appear as though a gift shop had charged you."

"Very thoughtful of you," said Mike. "But I prefer to pay cash."

"Cash is always our preferred method of payment as well."

Mike reached inside his pocket for the roll of American dollars that Support Five had provided him. He was counting out four hundred-dollar bills when the madam interrupted him.

"I'm deeply sorry, sir. I can only accept euros," she said.

"Oh," exclaimed Mike, surprised. "My friend told me that US dollars were fine."

"Unfortunately, we can't get a good exchange rate around here. I'm afraid that the mighty US dollar isn't worth what it once was."

Mike replaced the dollars and pulled out a small fold of euros from his other pocket. He peeled off six fifty-euro notes, hoping that the extra would help lubricate his mission. He handed them over.

"Have a seat and relax," she told him. "Your selections will be out shortly."

"Thank you," he replied. He took a seat on one of the leather sofas facing a replica of a Picasso painting.

"Would you like anything to drink? A scotch maybe?" the madam asked, letting her right hand brush against his shoulders.

"No, thank you. But may I ask you a question?"

"Especially if it's a naughty one," she murmured softly in his ear.

"Do these cameras work, or are they just deterrents?"

His question took her by surprise and broke the sensual aura. She took a step away from him.

"Why do you ask?" she asked defensively.

"Curiosity. Let's just say that I'm camera shy."

"Is that so? You don't look like the shy type to me."

"All right," admitted Mike, laughing. "You're too good. Here's the truth. My friend came here about a month ago while on a business trip. He had marital problems and decided to blow off some steam by using your services."

He saw that the madam understood where he was going with this. She resorted to being a gracious hostess.

"You know, that wouldn't be the first time a married man decided to come here," she said, glancing down at Mike's left ring finger.

"I'm sure you're right. But the twist here is that my friend is now back with his wife and he's suffering from remorse. He saw the CCTV cameras, and he's wondering if his visit here won't end up on the Internet. He's quite worried, to be honest. The fact that he was with a man isn't helping either, if you know what I mean."

"You can reassure your friend that we only monitor this reception area and the stairs that you used to come up. Also, everything is automatically erased after six weeks."

"Listen," said Mike, "I don't doubt for a second that what you're saying is the truth. I could tell right away that you're working hard to keep this place safe, and that confidentiality is an important business practice for you."

The madam smiled warmly in acknowledgment.

"But there's a small problem," Mike went on. "My friend is a well-known figure in the United States, and I promised him I would take care of the problem. He hasn't slept for the last few days thinking about what might happen if his infidelities were to become public knowledge."

"I don't know how I could be of service to you," she said, trying politely to close the subject.

Mike forged on. "I have an idea. One that might be of great benefit to both my friend and you. Would you care to hear it?"

She shrugged, feigning indifference. But Mike could see that she was interested.

"I know that the PSP were here recently and seized some money from you," he said.

"How do you know that?" she demanded angrily.

"That's of no concern to you. What I'm proposing is for you to keep the three hundred euros I already gave you, plus I'll give you a one-thousand-dollar bonus if you help me find my friend on your videotapes and answer a few questions. Do we have a deal?"

"Ten thousand dollars," she replied after a few moments.

"Three thousand," he said, knowing he had her.

"Six thousand is my last offer," she said, crossing her arms.

"I only have five thousand dollars on me, but it's yours. Do we have a deal?"

"I'll take five thousand and that nice watch."

Mike looked down at his wrist. The Tag Heuer watch was the only item he cared about. Lisa had given it to him during their first year of dating. Nonetheless, he removed it and placed it on the table next to him. *She'll be pissed.* He took out the wad of American dollars and gave it to the madam, who smiled in return.

"I'll put this in a safe place, and I'll be back to help you out in your search," she said, grabbing the watch off the table as she passed.

She left the room using a door that Mike guessed led to the suites. Once alone, he focused his thoughts on how to hone in on the client who had slipped the hundred-dollar bill to the madam, who supposedly only accepted euros. The whole mission now resided on the madam's ability to remember who it was.

The door the madam had exited through suddenly swung open. Two goons dressed in tuxedos walked purposefully toward Mike. He shook his head, resigned. He'd hoped to achieve his objective without any bloodshed. It didn't look like this would be the case after all. Both men were taller than Mike, and both looked menacing. One of them had a shaved head, while the other had a long black ponytail. Standing up, Mike relaxed only slightly when he saw that they had no weapons.

"The madam would like for you to leave now," said the bald man.

"I am afraid you're mistaken," replied Mike, already coiled for action. "I have a special arrangement with her. I'm sure she'll confirm this with you if you take the time to ask her."

The two thugs looked at each other as if in pure disbelief that he was talking back to them. Without another word, they approached him from each side.

Mike knew they wouldn't take a swing at him until they had at least pretended to try to bring him out peacefully. He made his move when the ponytailed man attempted to push him toward the exit by placing both his hands on his back. Mike let his body move forward but pivoted on his right foot while using his right arm to deflect the goon's hands. Making an abrupt about-face toward his opponent, Mike delivered a devastating left hook that landed squarely on the other man's jaw. The goon stumbled backward but didn't go down. Mike, not letting him recuperate, delivered a powerful right jab to the nose followed by another left hook that uplifted the thug's chin. This time the man's legs collapsed under him.

Mike felt the second goon approaching fast and sent a high kick back toward the threat. His heel met the man's solar plexus, but the bald thug was beefy and the force only stopped his momentum. Mike used the advantage to throw a series of lightning-fast punches that his opponent had difficulty blocking. After a few good hits, the goon became unfocused. Seizing his opportunity, Mike grabbed him behind the head and pulled down hard, using his body weight against his opponent's height. At the same time, he raised his left leg and delivered a crushing knee strike directly into the man's face. The impact sent the recipient crashing backward into a mirrored wall, which shattered into a thousand pieces.

Knowing that the madam was watching everything through her CCTV, Mike hurriedly crossed the reception area and entered the door the goons had just come through. It led to a carpeted hallway that had eight doors on the right and three on the left.

Like any hotel hallway, the doors each had a number—except for one. Mike decided that it was the door to the madam's office. He tried the doorknob, but It was locked. He took a step back, and, using all his strength, he rammed the door with his shoulder. The simple lock gave way, and the door swung open. The medium-size room was sparsely furnished but had a small kitchenette next to an old Ikea-type dining table.

Just as Mike had anticipated, the madam had been monitoring his progress via three small flat screen televisions mounted on the wall. They were connected to a large black computer located on a desk close to the kitchenette. Two of the screens were displaying images of the lobby, while the other one was showing the staircase leading up to the brothel.

The madam had retreated to the corner farthest from the door. She had deposited the whip and was holding a police baton in her steady hands. She didn't wait for Mike to advance. Showing no fear toward the intruder, she moved toward him holding the baton like a baseball bat. When she was within range, she swung the baton hard, trying for his temple.

Mike ducked the first blow and grabbed her wrists as she was bringing the baton down for another try. He then moved his hands onto the weapon, placing one just above her hands and the other toward the baton's end. He gave it a good clockwise twist, and the baton slipped out of her grasp. Looking defiantly into his eyes, she reached for her riding whip. But Mike, who'd had enough of this bullshit, took hold of her shoulders and swung her around, sweeping his right arm around her neck in a choke hold. He applied just enough pressure for her to feel the pain and the dizziness of having less blood moving to her brain.

"Enough," Mike said quietly. "Or I'll break your neck here and now."

He wanted to show her who was in charge. He'd tried to play nice, but that had gotten him nowhere.

He felt that she was trying to speak, so he released the pressure by a fraction.

"O-okay...I'll help you."

"No more games. If I feel you're not being honest..."

The madam shook her head vigorously.

"Are you the only one who collects the fees from the clients?"

"Yes," she murmured.

"If I release you, will you do anything stupid?" he asked.

"I won't," she said softly.

Mike knew that tone of voice well. He had heard it many times in the past while interrogating suspects who had lost their will to fight. He let her go.

She turned fully around and looked at him. She didn't say anything, but Mike could see that she was grateful for her life. She had played a dangerous game and lost.

Wasting no more time, Mike got to the point. "A couple days ago, someone gave you an American hundred-dollar bill. I want to know who that person was."

"The story about your friend in the US was false?"

"I didn't say that. Just answer the question," barked Mike, feeling his temper rising.

"Of course I remember. Our patrons are mostly locals who pay in euros, so I remember when someone wants to pay with US dollars. Before today, the only US bill I've seen in the last few weeks came from a foreigner. The funny thing is that he paid his fee in euros, then decided to leave me a hundred-dollar tip on his way out."

"Is that transaction on camera?"

"Um, yes, it should be. I was in the lounge when he came to me and slipped that bill into my bra," she said.

"Show it to me," ordered Mike. "Do it fast and I'll let you keep my money."

As the madam busied herself on the large black computer, Mike's mind shifted to other impending problems. He had to get the information and get out of this place fast. He wasn't sure how long the two goons would remain unconscious, but it wouldn't be much longer. He assessed the two monitors showing the lobby to see if they had started to regain their senses. Not yet.

"Here! Look! I found him," Sylvia said triumphantly.

Mike looked over her shoulder at the computer screen. The video quality was surprisingly sharp, and the CCTV had taken a few good shots of the man slipping a bill to the madam. Mike didn't recognize the Arabic face but remained confident he had just found a picture of Abdullah Ahmad Ghazi.

"Make a digital copy of that video for me," he commanded.

Sylvia pressed a few buttons on her keyboard and inserted a flash drive into one of the computer's USB ports. A few seconds later, she took it out and handed it to Mike.

Not caring if he blew his cover story, he asked, "Do you know what his name is?"

She thought about it for a few seconds. "He was with Olivier. I...I can't remember his name, I swear," she insisted.

"Never mind. Just delete today's recordings. And don't try to fool me—I know how these things work," he lied.

After a few seconds, he saw a pop-up window appearing on the computer screen asking if the administrator really wanted to permanently delete all the recordings from the last twenty-four hours. The madam looked at him to make sure he was watching what she was doing. She brought the cursor to the *yes* icon and clicked on it. A new pop up window appeared to confirm that all of the day's recordings had been erased.

"All right, here's the new deal," Mike said.

"You told me you were going to leave," she answered with fear in her voice.

"I will. But there is one more thing you need to do to earn the money I gave you."

Mike could tell that she expected the worst.

He wrote down a number on a piece of paper and gave it to her. "If this man ever comes back here, you will leave a message at this number as soon as he's with one of your prostitutes."

Relieved, she nodded her head vigorously.

"You will not tell him or anyone else that I came to ask you questions regarding this man."

She continued nodding her head.

"If you do as you're asked, you will be left alone. If you don't, your business will be torched, and you and all your employees will be hunted down and killed," he warned her.

She swallowed hard.

"Is that understood?"

She was too terrified to speak, but he knew he had made himself clear. Of course, he would never dream of doing anything like that, but he needed her to obey.

"One more thing," he added. "I want my watch back."

"Ricardo took it," she replied, looking down at the floor.

"One of those creeps?" he asked, pointing at the heap of limbs on the lobby monitor.

"Yes, the one with the long hair."

Taking one more look at the monitors, he saw that the bald security guard was starting to move. It was time to leave. As he passed through the hallway, a few of the suite's doors swiftly closed. Mike realized that parts of his discussion with the madam might have been overheard, but that didn't change anything. He had accomplished his mission.

Keeping his back to the two cameras in the lobby, Mike approached the two men on the ground. "Don't even think about it," he warned the bald guard who was trying to get up. The barely conscious goon obeyed, watching as Mike retrieved the Tag Heuer from his comrade's wrist. He let the limp arm drop loudly to the floor.

"Buy your own, asshole."

CHAPTER 58

Mike exited the building without a backward glance by the same entrance he had used twenty-five minutes before. Once on the sidewalk, he placed his right hand in his pocket and scratched his nose with his left index finger. That prearranged signal indicated to Lisa that all was well and that he would meet her later as scheduled.

Mike turned at the next intersection and walked until he was able to hail a taxi driving in the opposite direction.

"The Decorative Arts Museum," Mike told the cab driver.

Lisbon had a wealth of exceptional museums, from the world-class Calouste Gulbenkian to the outstanding Ancient Art Museum. Mike had always enjoyed exploring museums, but this time he was visiting one for a different reason. They were easy places for someone trying to evade potential surveillance to disappear.

After the taxicab dropped him in front of the red seventeenth-century palace, Mike walked into the lobby to pay the four-euro admission fee. A group of twenty elderly tourists was waiting close to the entrance, next to a single security guard wearing a white shirt and a black tie that was too short. Seeing that Mike was by himself, the clerk pointed toward the group of tourists and inquired if he wanted to join the guided tour that was about to start for an additional five euros. Mike paid the clerk and got his hand stamped as proof of his additional payment.

"Where is the men's room?" he asked with his charming smile.

"Make a left after the elevator," replied the clerk, pointing behind Mike. "And don't forget that the tour starts in a couple of minutes."

Mike found the bathroom and entered, locking the door behind him. After confirming that he was alone, he found a garbage can under the sink. He removed the green garbage bag, which contained mostly used paper towels, and lifted out another bag that had been hidden underneath by Support Five a few hours before. He confirmed that the bag was holding the right things, then unlocked the door of the bathroom.

He chose the cleanest looking stall and closed the door behind him, then set the manual lock. He removed his beard and contact lenses, then spent five seconds scratching his face to get rid of the horrible feeling that the false beard had given him. He changed into the clothes that had been left and stashed his old ones in the bag.

He walked out of the bathroom and caught up with the group of tourists at the first exhibit. He stayed with the group for ten minutes before they passed the employee entrance en route to another room containing fifteenth-century French furniture. He exited via a small back alleyway and turned left toward Rua São Tomé, where he knew a yellow electric tram passed every fifteen minutes. Mike didn't have to wait long before he climbed aboard. He got out a few stops later and hailed a taxi to bring him back to his hotel.

Nodding his thanks to the doorman, he took the elevator to the sixth floor, where his room was located. The *Do Not Disturb* card was still inserted in the electronic keypad. That meant that no hotel employee should have entered his room. Still, he'd left a postage stamp-sized infrared interruption counter that would let him know if anyone had entered the room in his absence. Mike had linked it to a nanny cam that had a direct view of the hotel-room door and would activate itself if the infrared counter was triggered.

Once he verified that no one had entered the room, he opened the minibar and poured himself a cold Sagres. The bitter taste of the pale lager felt good. He finished his beer rapidly and poured himself another one. He sat at the end of the queen-size bed and turned on the television. BBC World was talking about another bad day for the vast majority of European stock markets and the repercussion it would have on the Dow Jones.

The telephone rang, interrupting Mike's thoughts. He looked at his watch before answering.

"Mike, this is Lisa. All is good?"

"Absolutely," answered Mike. Any other answer was code that he was under duress.

"Glad to hear it. I'll be up in a few minutes."

Soon after came five gentle knocks on the door. He let his wife in and offered her the last Sagres from the minibar. She declined and grabbed a small bottle of local white wine from the minibar instead. She took a seat in a red armchair next to the balcony door.

As Lisa turned on her laptop and inserted the flash drive Mike had given her into the USB port, Mike called IMSI headquarters. After the second ring, two beeps and then silence came across the line.

"Walton on a secure line. ID number four-nine-two-three-four."

A few seconds later, a female voice came on the line. "Hello, Mike."

"Nice to talk to you, Anna."

"I'll be sending a video of the man we believe gave the flagged bill to the prostitute. He's Arab, so there's a possibility he's Abdullah Ahmad Ghazi."

"Stay put until we review the tape," said Mapother, who was also on the line. "Chances are that we won't be able to come up with anything actionable, but we'll see where this leads."

"Yes, sir."

"Anna or I will call you within the next two hours," said Mapother. "Isn't it dinnertime in Lisbon anyway?"

"Yes, sir."

"Once you've sent us the data, go have something to eat. But make sure to stay available."

"That goes without saying," said Mike, hanging up.

"Hey, honey, you hungry?"

—

After they returned from dinner at a local Portuguese restaurant, Mike dialed IMSI headquarters on his secure satellite phone.

Anna Caprini came on the line.

"Mike, the director's expecting your call. One moment please."

"Mike," greeted Mapother moments later.

"Sir, I have Lisa with me."

"And I'm with Jonathan."

"Hey, Joe," said Mike. "How are you?"

"Can't complain."

"I'll let Jonathan talk you through what we've found out," said Mapother.

"Let me first congratulate both of you on a job well done," started Sanchez. "The video allowed us to identify the man in possession of the bill with ninety-nine percent accuracy. It's Abdullah Ahmad Ghazi, an accountant with lowlife contacts, including ties to the Taliban in Afghanistan. In light of all the intelligence we reviewed, I'm confident to say he's the Sheik's moneyman. You find him, you find the Sheik."

"Does the CIA knows this?" asked Mike.

"The CIA's theory is that he's some sort of courier. The thing is, nobody's ever spent too much time on this guy. They wrongly thought he was too low on the totem pole."

"That just changed, didn't it?" asked Mike.

"Not really," chimed in Mapother. "As far as the US intelligence apparatus is concerned, he's not even on the radar. But we've been ordered to detain Mr. Ghazi and to bring him in for interrogation."

Mike and Lisa looked at each other with quizzical expressions. As far as they knew, the IMSI answered to nobody but the president. It wasn't even supposed to exist.

"Ordered, sir?" asked Mike finally.

"I'll spare you the details other than that this came directly from the very top. You understand?"

"Yes, sir," the two operatives in Lisbon answered at the same time.

—

The details were actually quite simple. Word had quickly spread through the upper echelon of the CIA that a very interesting marked bill had surfaced—a bill possibly belonging to the seventy-million-dollar parcel the agency had lost in the opening days of Operation Iraqi Freedom. The CIA had already written off the funds and closed their file on the matter. Now, because the new discovery might indicate their findings had been wrong, they didn't want to hear anything about some missing marked bill showing up somewhere in Europe.

Donald Poole, the director of the CIA, was furious when he learned that somehow a closed CIA file had been left open on the Interpol network. He became livid less than ten minutes later when Richard Phillips, the director of National Intelligence—also known as the DNI—told him the FBI had launched a formal complaint over the CIA's use of the FBI network. The DNI smoothed some of Poole's feathers when he promised that the FBI wasn't going to investigate anything or anyone regarding this issue—as long as the CIA didn't try to make matters worse by sending their own people over to Europe.

Following his conversation with the CIA director, the director of National Intelligence called Mapother's direct line.

"Charles, Dick Phillips here."

"Isn't it a bit late, even for you, Dick?" asked Mapother, taking a look at his Rolex.

"I could say the same for you, old friend," replied the DNI. Phillips was the only politician other than the president who knew about IMSI's existence. He continued to be a source of support for Mapother and IMSI.

"What can I do for you, Dick?"

"Listen, Charles, I know you have carte blanche to do pretty much anything you want, but I have a favor to ask you."

"I'm listening," said Mapother, who already knew what his friend wanted.

"I have a small problem," Phillips began. "Many years ago, the CIA lost about seventy million dollars in Iraq."

"I heard about that somewhere."

"How do you know anything about that?" asked Phillips, surprised. "Scratch that," he said two seconds later. "I don't want to know. Where was I?"

"Seventy million," supplied Mapother.

"That's right. The CIA, after a somewhat hasty investigation, concluded that enemy forces had shot down the helicopter that was carrying the money and the Special Forces squad tasked with protecting it. It was written off as having been lost in action."

"And now some of that money has popped up in a Portuguese whorehouse."

It took the DNI a few seconds to reply. "I won't ask you how you know that, but essentially that's correct."

"You want me to look into it?"

"I was hoping you could see where it could lead us. On a strictly unofficial basis, of course."

"I'm already on it," said Mapother. "The guy's name is Abdullah Ahmad Ghazi. He's an accountant with ties to the Taliban. We're pretty sure he's the Sheik's moneyman."

"Good God!"

"What do you want me to do with him?"

"Wouldn't you agree that it would be nice to know where he got that bill? And why money that was supposed to have been lost in Iraq ended up in the hands of someone with connections to the Taliban?"

"I'll see if I can arrange for someone to speak with him."

"Thanks, Charles. I appreciate it. One last thing."

"Shoot."

"Can you act quickly? I convinced Poole to keep the CIA standing still on this one by promising him the FBI wouldn't be investigating the missing seventy million. I don't know how long those promises will last, though."

"I understand. I'll call you as soon as I have anything."

"Thanks again, Charles. I'll owe you one."

CHAPTER 59

Ottawa, Canada

Simon Corey was intrigued by the unexpected call he received from the CIA director, Donald Poole. As the director of the Canadian Security Intelligence Service, Corey had a lot of latitude in terms of what he could do. Most of the time, he asked for the consent of the prime minister only after an operation had started, and he didn't answer to anyone else. Corey knew that his arrogance never ceased to annoy the prime minister, but nobody could deny that the head of the CSIS had an outstanding track record.

However, since the blunder in Paris fifteen days ago, Corey had been walking on eggshells. Donald Poole wanted Corey to use CSIS personnel to help him find out what was going on in his own backyard, behind some important backs. And Corey was hesitant about sticking his nose in places it didn't belong.

Poole was playing a dangerous game, but he had successfully backed Corey into a corner. If Corey said no to the CIA director's request, Poole could make his life miserable by more or less stopping the flow of information that the CIA provided CSIS. If he said yes, he would have to act behind the back of his own prime minister.

Damn it! He was in a tight spot. He would have to keep the operation low-key. He dialed Kevin Loewe's extension and waited for him to pick up.

"Yes, Director?" answered the assistant director of collection.

"When you have a minute, would you be so kind as to come and see me?"

"I'll be right there, sir."

Loewe entered Corey's office less than five minutes later. He brought with him the three most important files he was working on.

Corey was seated behind his desk and gestured for Loewe to have a seat in one of the armchairs. "I need an agent who speaks English and Portuguese," he said.

"For an operation in Portugal?"

"Yes. A covert operation approved directly by the office of the director."

Loewe cleared his throat. "I understand."

Yes, you do. And you don't like it one bit. But it's my neck on the chopping block, not yours.

"The danger level for this mission is low. I just need a trained field agent who will be able to take surveillance photographs and do a little digging for our American friends."

Loewe offered the obvious choice. "Zima Bernbaum?"

"She just got back from a difficult mission. Is she ready?"

"She's the best available agent we have right now. She's done with her debrief, and our psychologist cleared her for operational duty."

"All right. Send her to my office. I'll brief her personally on what I want her to do in Portugal."

CHAPTER 60

Lisbon, Portugal

Despite spending many hours on Google Earth and studying the map of the city, Mike was still not a hundred percent at ease with his real-life surroundings. He wished he could have spent more time on the ground before being tasked with capturing Abdullah Ahmad Ghazi. However, his training had taught him how to improvise and get the job done with a minimum of preparation.[7]

The Chiado neighborhood, where Mike had been discreetly tailing his target for the past half hour, was an elegant and sophisticated district full of theaters, bookshops, and cafés. As his target ordered an espresso at an outdoor coffee bar, Mike concealed himself behind a pillar. He was pretty sure that Ghazi didn't have a clue he was being followed. His mannerisms were genuine, and he made no attempts to change direction unnaturally.

They had picked up Abdullah Ahmad Ghazi's trail when he exited the Hotel do Chiado, where he'd been staying for the last three days. Finding the accountant had been easier than they'd expected. Thanks to the flash drives Zima Bernbaum had seized in Paris, IMSI analysts and Support Five were able to comb through Ghazi's credit card statements and discovered that the accountant was staying at a hotel in Lisbon. Mike and Lisa had originally feared that he would be long gone, but it seemed that Lisbon was his place of residence.

Why was he staying at hotels, then? The IMSI agents had come to the conclusion that Ghazi was meeting frequently with people he didn't wish to be associated with—like terrorists. They were hoping that Ghazi would lead them to bigger players, but after twenty-four hours of surveillance, there was nothing to report. Ghazi had spent most of his time shopping around the neighborhood.

Mapother had approved an additional six hours of observation and had even ordered Support Five leader Jasmine Carson to help Mike and Lisa during the surveillance phase of the operation. But at the end of the six hours, they would have to grab Ghazi before someone at the CIA decided to make a move of their own.

They got their break shortly after lunch. To an untrained eye, their opening could easily have been missed, but Mike didn't fail to notice a stealthy exchange between Ghazi and another man less than fifty feet away.

"Brush pass with a man wearing a pair of blue jeans and brown T-shirt at the corner of Crucifixo and Conceicao," said Mike into his lapel microphone.

"Got it," Lisa replied. "I'm eighty feet behind you and will take chase on number two. Carson, stay with Mike."

"Understood," answered Carson, who was walking a parallel street one block south. "You're solo with number two."

"Number one seems to be heading for his hotel," said Mike. "I'll give him some slack in case he doubles back."

For the next two minutes, the three IMSI agents were silent as they followed their subjects. Mike had guessed right. Ghazi entered his hotel lobby by the front entrance. There was a slight possibility that Mike would miss a second contact between Ghazi and another person waiting for him in the lobby, but he doubted it. More likely, his sole contact was the man whom Lisa was trailing now.

"Number two is taking evasive actions," Mike heard Lisa say through his earpiece.

"I'll give you a hand. Ghazi's back at the hotel," said Carson. "What's your location?"

"Easthound on Commercio approaching Ouro," Lisa replied.

"I'm one block north, approaching Ouro," Carson said.

"Shit! He got into a cab on Ouro," Lisa exclaimed seconds later.

"You want me to intercept?" asked Carson.

"Negative. Let him go," Lisa ordered. "He was probably a gofer. Mike, can you confirm that Ghazi is back in his room?"

"Stand by," Mike replied as he unlocked his PDA.

Last evening, as his wife had taken over watching Ghazi eating out, Mike had broken into the accountant's room and installed two hidden microphones and a video camera. The microphones—one in the bathroom, the other near the queen-size bed—were easy to conceal. Although no bigger than a dime, they had the ability to transmit live via any secure smartphone that was equipped with the correct application and authorization code. The bugs were linked to the small video camera, which was hidden in plain sight as an eight-outlet power bar.

"Ghazi's in his room," said Mike, moments later. He was looking at a clear video feed of Ghazi removing his shoes.

"Let's meet in Mike's room, arriving at seven- and ten-minute intervals," Lisa said.

Twenty-five minutes later, the three IMSI agents were watching Ghazi on Mike's computer. Ghazi was nervously pacing the length of his room.

"He keeps looking at his watch," Carson mentioned.

"He's probably waiting for someone," Mike said.

"Or a phone call," Lisa offered.

"Whatever happens," Mike continued, "we're taking him down tonight."

CHAPTER 61

Zima Bernbaum, traveling under the alias of Sophia Mendes, checked in at the Hotel do Chiado just as the three IMSI operatives were finishing their third review of their operational plan to capture the Sheik's accountant, Abdullah Ahmad Ghazi.

Zima had made a stop at the residence of an ex-CSIS field operation officer who provided her with a Walther PPK with two magazines of ammunition, as well as a syringe filled with a powerful sedative capable of incapacitating a 200-pound man for up to thirty minutes.

Even if it meant cancelling a date with a nice guy she had met at the Laundromat, Zima was glad she'd been given the opportunity to continue working on the case. The director had briefed her personally and had explained she was the reason they knew so much about Ghazi. The pictures her colleague Xavier Leblanc had taken in Paris had confirmed the identity of the accountant.

Her blue-carpeted room had two twin beds that had been put side by side to form one king-size bed. The two armchairs facing the ten-year-old television were in good repair but had lost their original brightness some time ago. Zima closed the door behind her and locked it with the small dead bolt. She sat in one of the armchairs and turned on her laptop, which would allow a secure connection with Ottawa. Her virtual mailbox had a new message containing the latest updates on her mission. As she read, she realized that her assignment had changed since her departure from Canada. CSIS had been told that Ghazi had knowledge of a threat that might be directed toward Canada. An extraction team was already en route to her location, with an estimated time of arrival of less than twelve hours. In the meantime, she was to secure the accountant in his room and wait for the team, which would proceed with the extraction.

Zima's heart rate began accelerating. She didn't know what had happened during the last twenty-four hours to warrant such a drastic change in her mission, but she would carry out the job.

The first thing to do was to find out which room was Ghazi's. She unzipped the top pocket of her carry-on and grabbed a brand-new copy of a Lisbon travel guide. Placing it in a hotel envelope, which she sealed using a dampened face cloth, she then wrote the accountant's name on it. She verified that her ankle holster was still properly attached and that her Walther PPK was in working order. Then she went into the bathroom and put her hair up in a net and donned a thin ski mask that she rolled all the way up. She concealed the net and ski mask with a dark-colored baseball cap and then looked at her reflection in the mirror to make sure the mask didn't show.

"Here we go again," she said to herself before heading out.

CHAPTER 62

Abdullah Ahmad Ghazi was more nervous than he ever remembered. The last few days had been nerve-racking, and he was starting to regret his affiliation with the Sheik. With his lover Richard Claudel dead, he didn't know where to turn. He and Claudel had been greedy and stupid—and now that he was alone, he wanted out. For God's sake, the Sheik had also sent Omar Al-Nashwan to kill Major Jackson Taylor, one of his closest allies! If Taylor and Richard could be killed, so could he. But he couldn't understand why all this was happening. He had received instructions requesting that he be at a certain place at a certain time; all he had to do was wait until he was contacted. The fact that a man other than the Sheik had contacted him caused him to wonder if the next meeting wouldn't be his last one on this earth.

A week ago, the Sheik had requested that he transfer money from one account to another. The sum hadn't been that impressive: a million dollars. What was unusual was the method used to transfer the funds. His instructions had been to visit a Lisbon branch of the Millennium BCP, a privately owned Portuguese bank. The branch manager, who had escorted him to the vault and given him a black duffel bag weighing approximately eleven kilograms, had told him that it contained ten thousand hundred-dollar bills.

His job had been to transport the money to another privately owned bank in Malaga, Spain, that was managed by some British investors. Driving the seven hundred kilometers to Malaga had taken nearly eight hours. After parking his car as close as possible to the main entrance, he had asked to speak with the manager. A tall British man had welcomed him to Malaga and led him to the bank vault, where he closed the heavy door behind them.

"Congratulations on your successful journey," the manager said while he opened the duffel bag. He counted two hundred one-hundred-dollar bills and placed them in a blue backpack. "Here's your fee for a job well done. You're now free to go."

Ghazi hadn't wasted any time on his way back to Lisbon. Out of the twenty thousand dollars, he deposited nineteen in his checking account and kept the remaining thousand dollars in cash. He splurged on a nice dinner in one of the best restaurants in town and bought two bottles of expensive Dom Perignon. He gave the last hundred-dollar bill to the lady who owned the brothel he had gone to for dessert.

He had never seen the man who had carefully placed the message in his hand and presumed he wouldn't see him again. The Sheik's organization was well compartmentalized, and that was what was making him so anxious. He disliked dealing with people he didn't know.

The message had been straightforward. He was to repeat the same operation he'd done a week ago. This time, however, he would have to transfer two duffel bags instead of one. He briefly wondered if he should ask for an increase of his fee but quickly dismissed the idea. He was not suicidal.

The telephone made him jump. Who could that be? Nobody knew he was there.

"Yes?" he answered.

"Mr. Ghazi?"

"Speaking."

"This is the concierge calling. There is a package for you at the front desk."

"From whom?"

"I couldn't say."

"I see. Could you please bring it to my room?"

"Right away, sir."

Ghazi hung up the phone, wondering if the package contained more precise instructions. He would know soon enough. In the meantime, he turned on the television and poured himself a glass of water from the faucet. The taste was dreadful, and he spat the water back into the sink. Shaking his head in disgust, he walked to his minibar, where he grabbed a bottle of purified water. A small sign attached to the neck of the bottle notified him that he would be charged five euros for its consumption. Five euros? He could buy the same bottle at the market across the street for less than one euro.

He was still considering his beverage options when a sharp knock sounded. When he opened his hotel room door, he found the concierge carrying a fat envelope in his white-gloved hands.

"Did you know that the bottle of water in my room cost five euros?" Ghazi asked the concierge.

"Pardon me, sir?"

"Never mind. Thank you," said Ghazi, taking the package and shutting the door curtly.

Ghazi sat down at the small round table next to his bed and opened the envelope. He was surprised to find a guidebook and nothing else. He opened the book's cover, but there was nothing written inside. He shook the book while shuffling through the pages, hoping that something would fall out but quickly came to the conclusion that the guidebook was really what it seemed: a guidebook, and nothing more.

Weird.

He wasn't surprised when he heard another knock. Perhaps the concierge had forgotten to attach an explanatory note card that went along with the package?

He opened the door huffily, expecting to see the sorry face of a bellhop. Instead, he found himself face-to-face with someone wearing a ski mask and a baseball cap.

CHAPTER 63

Zima Bernbaum's plan had worked perfectly. She had dropped the package at the front desk without anyone noticing her and had seated herself on a comfortable sofa in the lobby. She had waited patiently for the concierge to contact Ghazi and then headed toward the elevators, knowing that the concierge would be right behind her. She had pressed the *up* button and within moments was stepping into an elevator. The concierge had quickened his pace through the foyer to make it inside the same elevator before the doors closed.

He pressed the button for the eighth floor and asked her where she was going. "Eight as well," she replied with a smile. When the doors opened on the eighth floor, the concierge rushed out into the hall as Zima pretended to search her purse for something. She followed at a distance as the concierge knocked on Ghazi's door. Having completed his delivery, the concierge was just turning to leave as Zima passed him in the hall. *Room eight-one-six*, she noted to herself as she passed by.

Zima walked to the end of the long hall, then casually turned back toward the accountant's room while keeping an eye out for any witnesses. If she saw anyone in the hallway, she would continue to the elevator and try again later. Luckily, no one came along. She stopped a few feet from Ghazi's door and put on a pair of tight black leather gloves. She rolled down her ski mask and knocked.

Ghazi opened the door, then opened his mouth to say something, but no sound came out. He was holding the guidebook Zima had placed in the envelope.

"Mr. Ghazi, how are you?" asked the CSIS agent.

Ghazi sputtered at her without replying. Then, without any notice, she kicked him hard between his legs. Ghazi went down like a bag of potatoes. She stepped inside the room, closed the door behind herself, and pulled her Walther PPK from her ankle holster. She searched the small room, and once she was sure that nobody else was present, she turned to Ghazi. He'd been winded by the force of Zima's blow and couldn't speak. He looked at her, his eyes pleading.

"Get on your belly, and turn your head to the left," ordered Zima.

The accountant didn't follow orders fast enough for Zima's liking. In an instant she rolled him onto his stomach and pulled his two arms behind his back. Before he had time to process what was happening, she secured his hands and feet with a pair of double-flex cuffs.

"That's one strike," said Zima. "Once you reach three strikes, you die."

Ghazi swallowed hard. She could tell he was afraid. Men were easy to read when you knew what to look for; the Adam's apple was often a dead giveaway.

"Get up."

Ghazi slowly got up using only his legs.

"Go sit on the chair."

Because his feet were tied together with a flex cuff, the accountant made small hops toward the chair. As Zima watched his slow progress, she couldn't help but feel that something wasn't right. She knew she wasn't in imminent danger, but something was bothering her.

She couldn't pinpoint what it was, but she had the feeling that someone was watching her.

—

Lisa and Mike Walton, and Jasmine Carson were shocked. Via the hidden video camera Mike had planted, they watched an unknown woman gain entry into Ghazi's room and nearly knock him out with a powerful kick to the crotch. She then professionally cleared the room with what seemed to be a small pistol.

"A Walther PPK," offered Carson.

She cuffed Ghazi's hands and feet with the help of two flex cuffs, then tied him to a chair with a generous amount of duct tape.

"Who *is* he?" asked Lisa.

"I think it's a *she*," replied Carson. "The voice certainly didn't sound like any man I know."

"The only thing we can be sure of is that she isn't with us," Mike replied, snapping his mobile phone shut. "I just spoke with Anna Caprini. We're the only three operatives in the region."

"What are our orders?" Lisa asked.

"Nothing has changed. We're still a go, but we're speeding the timetable up."

"What about her?" Lisa wondered out loud.

"We'll try to find out who she is, but our primary objective remains Ghazi," Mike replied. "Take him down, then get him to Montijo Air Base, where we can securely question him—and then get the hell out of here if we need to."

"What is she doing?" Lisa asked, looking at the video feed.

"Maybe she's looking for us," Mike said.

—

Once Zima was finished tying Ghazi to the chair, she carefully rechecked his room. On the bathroom counter, near the sink, she discovered a piece of paper folded in eight. She opened it and read the message:

> *Same routine. You will have two bags to carry. Fee will be the same, paid on delivery. Be at your destination within the next seventy-two hours.*

Zima walked back to the bedroom and saw that Ghazi was trying to free himself. An impossible task. However, he was making a commotion, bouncing his chair on the floor every time he made an effort. That wasn't good. She gave him a hard stare, and he stopped immediately. She took the syringe out of its box and showed it to her prisoner.

"This will help you relax," she told him.

Ghazi started to struggle in his chair with renewed fervor.

"Believe me, if I wanted you dead, you'd be dead already," said Zima. "And, if you don't stop moving, I'll kill you right now." After he had calmed down, she poked the needle into his arm. Within seconds, the accountant relaxed considerably.

She placed Ghazi's message flat on the bed and took a picture of it with her smartphone. She sent it immediately to CSIS headquarters with a code indicating that the mission was going according to plan.

As she continued searching the room, the uneasiness she felt earlier resurged. She checked for a glint that would betray any sign of a camera but spotted none. It was strange, she thought, to have her sixth sense tingling like that.

—

Earlier in the day, Carson had brought a blue suitcase containing all the equipment they would need for the operation. Carson and Lisa each opted for a Sig Sauer P226 Tactical with six magazines of fifteen rounds each. Though the Tactical version of the P226 was five inches longer than the original, it allowed the barrel to accept suppressors. Both IMSI operatives made sure to put a silencer in their pockets, as the pistol wouldn't fit in their holsters with the suppressors on. Mike chose a subcompact Glock 26 with tritium night sights, then added a Taser gun to his arsenal.

By now they had figured out that the well-trained female who'd captured Ghazi was waiting for backup before moving the accountant somewhere else. Because of the ski mask she was wearing, identification wasn't possible with the camera angle they had. They didn't know how long it would be before her reinforcement arrived, so the three IMSI operatives decided to make their move right away. They couldn't risk waiting for nightfall as their original plan dictated. Mapother had cleared them, and Carson guaranteed that the rest of the Support Five team would be there shortly to wipe their rooms clean and take care of the equipment left behind.

Their hotel was across the street from Ghazi's, and they reached his room in no time. They took separate routes to the eighth floor, then met in the vicinity of Ghazi's door. Nobody else was in the hallway.

The plan was for Mike to go in first with the nonlethal Taser. Lisa would follow a second later, as Carson—who didn't have the same level of training—would monitor the situation outside the room. Once the room was secured, Carson would get the vehicle and wait for the others outside the main entrance.

"She's looking out the window," Lisa said, watching the video feed on her smartphone, "and she has a cell phone in her hands. Ghazi is still unconscious and tied to a chair. He's out of the way. We're good to go."

"Remember, we want to keep her alive long enough to question her," Mike said. "We need all the information about Ghazi's associates that we can get." He took one last look around the hallway before nodding to Lisa, who responded with a smile. She mouthed "I love you" before taking up a position in front of the door. Two seconds later, she fired three rounds at the lock. Mike kicked the door open and went in, his Taser extended in front of him.

He saw the woman's silhouette against the background of the window and pressed the trigger of his Taser just as the silhouette was able to pull a shot from the hip with her own silenced weapon. Mike felt the bullet fly past him and heard Lisa grunt in pain.

No!

The woman was shoved hard against the glass by the impact of the electric shock and collapsed to the floor.

"Jasmine, get in here," Mike ordered. "Lisa's hit! Secure the hostiles while I check on her." Carson, who had already moved into the room when she had heard the suppressed pistol go off, closed the door behind her and proceeded to secure Ghazi and the woman. Mike's heart was beating faster than ever as he approached his wife.

Lisa was on her knees at the foot of the bed, trying to catch her breath. Mike carefully moved her to her back and saw that she had been hit square in the chest by the woman's round. He opened Lisa's shirt for a closer inspection.

"She's been hit, but the vest took it. No penetration. She'll be fine," announced Mike fighting to keep his voice under control. *Thank God!* "Honey, are you okay?"

Lisa was in agony. She moaned quietly. "Lisa, we need to get out of here. Do you understand?" Mike asked.

"Yeah," she managed to say. "I feel like I've been hit by a train."

"It's your first time getting shot, baby," Mike said, helping his wife to sit. He hugged her and kissed her neck. "Let's go," he added, getting up.

Mike walked to the woman who had shot at his wife. Carson had tied her up with a plastic cuff. Mike checked her pulse before removing the ski mask and the net that was holding her hair together.

Holy shit! Zima!

"Lisa, it's Zima. Zima's here!"

Lisa joined him, her body language betraying how much pain she was in. "I can't believe this. What is she doing here?" she asked.

"Who's Zima?" asked Carson.

"She's a Canadian agent—and a damned good one at that," Mike said. "She's a good friend too."

"What do you want to do?" Carson asked.

"We need to get out of here right now," Lisa said. She winced.

"You okay, baby?" Mike asked, looking over at her.

"It hurts like hell, but I'm fine."

"Good. Jasmine, why don't you get the car as Lisa and I clean things up a bit?"

"Roger that," responded Carson. "I'll be in front in ten minutes."

After Carson closed the door behind her, Lisa went around the room removing the listening devices and the hidden video camera. Mike searched Zima for anything that would help them learn why she was there.

"Hey Lisa, look at this," said Mike, holding up Zima's smartphone. "It was in her pocket."

Lisa took it from Mike. "We're in luck!" she exclaimed. "She must have been using it just before we got in because it isn't locked."

"You're kidding me."

Lisa shook her head. She went into the contact list, but it was empty. There had been a few phone calls made recently, however. Lisa called IMSI headquarters and, after giving them a quick situation report, asked them to trace the numbers used by Zima.

"Nothing out of the ordinary," came the voice of Jonathan Sanchez from New York. "Two of the numbers are Canadian."

"What about the others?"

"All Lisbon area."

"Thanks," she said before ending the call. Lisa looked over at Mike, who was finishing a search of the room for any other clues.

"Anything?"

"Just this," Mike replied, showing her a piece of paper he'd found on the bed. "I think it might very well be the message Ghazi received in the brush pass."

Lisa read it and agreed with Mike. "This is definitely it. I'll send it to headquarters right away," she said, reaching for her smartphone.

From the chair where she was tied near the window, Zima coughed a few times and moaned in pain. Mike approached her just as she opened her eyes.

"Zima? Wake up, Zima," he said. "It's me, Mike."

Zima looked at him, unsure. "Mike?" she asked weakly.

"That's right, Zima. I need to know what you're doing here. And I need the answer now."

"You know who I work for, Mike," she said, exasperated. "What do you think I'm doing here?" Mike could see she was pissed at being tied to a chair.

"Hey, Zima," Lisa jumped in.

"Lisa!" exclaimed Zima, a big smile appearing on her face. "Oh my God! I just shot at you."

Lisa showed her where the round had hit the vest. "Good thing I was wearing this."

"Holy shit!"

"C'mon, Mike," Lisa said. "Untie her, will you?"

Mike cut through the plastic cuff with his knife.

"Look in my mailbox," Zima said to Lisa, who was still holding her smartphone. "The last message is from the assistant director of foreign collection."

Lisa read the message. "It looks genuine," she said to Mike. "Her orders are to capture Ghazi and wait until the arrival of an extraction team."

"Ghazi is the guy who entered Claudel's house while I was breaking in. I told you about him. We didn't know at the time that he was the Sheik's accountant, but we figured it out. Happy now?" she asked, her eyes grilling into Mike's.

"Of course. I'm sorry about all this. We didn't know who you were."

"We should go," Zima replied.

"She's coming with us," said Mike. "I'll brief Charles as we go, but we need to get out of here."

"What are you doing, Mike? I'm not going anywhere with you," said Zima.

Mike looked her in the eye. "You want a shot at taking down the Sheik and the man who shot at you in Antibes?"

She nodded eagerly.

"This man," continued Mike, pointing to Ghazi, "is the closest link to the Sheik and Alexander Shamrock we know of."

"That's the name of the guy who shot at me?"

"Yes, he's a former Special Forces officer and the son of a very rich man."

Mike could see Zima was thinking about her options.

"Who are you with, Mike?" she finally asked. "I need to know who you're working for."

"That never changed, Zima. Lisa and I are with the good guys."

CHAPTER 64

The accountant was starting to regain consciousness. "We need to move before he becomes agitated," Lisa said. "Help me out."

Mike and Lisa each took one of Ghazi's arms and helped him to his feet while Zima grabbed his suitcase and other personal items. The drug was losing its effect rapidly. Within minutes, Ghazi would regain his faculties, and that would make transporting him anywhere much more difficult.

The two IMSI operatives and Zima Bernbaum left the room and closed the door. Luckily, they didn't encounter anyone in the elevator. The hotel lobby was busy enough, but nobody took a second look at them, with the exception of a lone couple enjoying a late-afternoon drink at the bar. They smiled at Mike knowingly. *He had too much to drink, and his buddies are taking him home.*

As promised, Carson was waiting in front of the hotel with the rental car, a black late-model Audi A6. Mike and his wife sat in the back of the sedan with Ghazi trapped in between them while Zima took the passenger's seat. If Carson had questions about Zima's presence, she kept them to herself. She engaged the manual transmission, and the doors locked automatically.

"Montijo Air Base?" asked Carson.

"You got it," replied Mike. "Primary route is fine."

He consulted his watch. "The plane should be there by now. As soon as we arrive at the airport, I'll call headquarters to let them know about the latest developments."

A few moments later, Ghazi opened his eyes. To his credit, he didn't panic. He simply looked at Lisa and Mike and asked in English, "Who are you?"

"The only thing you need to know right now is that you're coming with us."

"I really hope you're Americans."

"Why is that?" inquired Mike.

"Because if you can prove to me that you're Americans, I'll cooperate fully with you."

"Interesting. But why?" Mike asked again.

"Because I don't trust anyone anymore. My partner is dead, and I fear that I know too much. The Sheik isn't someone to let loose ends go."

"Your partner?" asked Zima from the front seat.

"Yes, my partner," answered Ghazi, no shame in his voice. "Richard Claudel. He was a general in the French gendarmerie. He's dead. The media are saying he died during the attack in Nice, but I know this isn't true. The Sheik killed him. And I'm next."

"Why would the Sheik want to kill you?" asked Mike. "You've served him well, haven't you?"

"I told you—I know too much. I'm the moneyman. I'm the one who delivers payments. I don't know any of the operational details of the next wave of attacks, but I know where the cells are located."

If that's true, he needs to be debriefed as soon as possible, thought Mike. He motioned him to continue.

"I'm not asking for money, but I want protection. Will you protect me?" Ghazi pleaded.

"We can if the information is worth it."

"It's worth it, all right," Ghazi replied. "I think I know where the Sheik is."

—

The traffic on the way to Montijo Air Base was light, probably because of the rain. They were stopped at the gate by two military policemen armed with automatic rifles. The police officers checked Lisa's documents to confirm her identity as an FBI agent, and the Audi was quickly cleared through the gate. The hangar where IMSI's plane was parked was a short drive away. The doors of the hangar were open, and the Audi drove right in, stopping next to a Gulfstream IV whose nose was facing toward the exit.

Lisa and Carson helped Ghazi out of the Audi while Mike opened the passenger door and said to Zima, "You stay in the car. I need to consult with my boss about what to do with you."

Zima shrugged. "Do what you must," she replied and closed the door herself.

"He says he needs the bathroom," called Lisa, halfway between the car and the airplane.

"That's fine. Go in the plane. Stay with him, and once he's done, give him something to drink."

"Will do," Lisa replied, already pulling Ghazi toward the awaiting jet. "The way this night is going, I might need something to drink myself."

—

As Ghazi exited the lavatory, Lisa searched him one more time to make sure that the accountant hadn't gotten his hands on a weapon. Satisfied, Lisa walked Ghazi to a seat facing Mike. They let him drink some water and offered him a bowl of fresh fruit. They wanted Ghazi to feel safe with them. Safe enough to spill his guts.

Once Ghazi's drink was refilled, Mike took the lead.

"What can you tell us about your employer?"

The accountant swallowed hard, then began to talk. For the next half hour he told the IMSI agents everything he knew about the Sheik, Omar Al-Nashwan, and what they'd asked him to do for them. He answered all of Mike's questions in detail, and before long Mike reached the conclusion that time wasn't on their side. The Sheik was about to launch an unprecedented series of attacks that would put the Nice bombings to shame.

Mike asked Jasmine Carson to stay with Ghazi while he went outside the plane to consult with his wife.

"Do you believe him?" Lisa asked.

"Seems legit to me," Mike replied. "But you never quite know with these guys. He might believe he's telling us the truth when he's in fact been fed misinformation."

"Could the Sheik really be in Spain?"

"Why not? He doesn't need to be close to the actual attacks. Where was Bin Laden on September Eleventh? Certainly not in New York."

Mike weighed his options. "Ghazi told us the attacks would take place within the next two or three days. He also said the cells never initiate a strike on their own; they wait for the Sheik's signal. If we find him before he gives the green light, we might be able to prevent the next wave."

"Agreed."

"I'll call headquarters and let them know what we've found."

Lisa nodded. "What do you want to do with Zima?"

Shit! I forgot all about her. She's still in the car. She must be fuming. "I'll talk to Mapother. Because Ghazi mentioned that many cells were located in Canada, we should brief her on what we've learned. She might be in a position to help us find the actual targets."

"If she still wants to, Mike," Lisa said. "You left her in the car!"

CHAPTER 65

Lisbon, Portugal // Malaga, Spain

Following Mike's call, IMSI sprang into action. Instead of flying Ghazi to New York to perform a more in-depth interrogation, it had devised a plan that they hoped would bring them closer to the Sheik's mobile headquarters. Mapother had agreed that if Mike was confident enough to use Zima's services, the decision came with the understanding Zima could never return to CSIS.

To Mike's surprise, Zima refused to quit. Mike declining to tell her for which organization she'd be working probably played a role in her decision. She had nonetheless agreed to help them out but insisted on being briefed completely. Mike had agreed and told her everything.

When Zima learned that three cells were in Canada, she had Mike promise to keep her apprised of any new intelligence regarding potential attacks on her country. Then she requested to be taken to the closest international airport to fly home.

—

In exchange for protection, Ghazi promised to help them achieve their objective. That meant they would allow Ghazi to deliver the money as ordered.

Mike and Lisa spent hours explaining and rehearsing with him the role he would have to play. It was imperative that the bank official in Malaga felt that nothing was out of the ordinary. Ghazi would bring the two duffel bags from Lisbon to Malaga then plant at least one sticky camera and one listening device inside the vault. Nobody had any doubts about what would happen if Ghazi was caught. The operation would be blown, and Ghazi would be slaughtered without mercy.

While Ghazi was being coached on his part in the operation, Support Five secured an apartment in Malaga with a view of the bank where Ghazi was to bring the money.

They didn't have a lot of time. The note indicated that the money was expected in Malaga within forty-eight hours of receiving the message. They'd already used up more than twenty-four of those hours preparing for the mission.

Support Five remained in Malaga while Mike and Lisa provided discreet cover for Ghazi with the help of Jasmine Carson. The pickup of the two duffel bags had gone well, and Ghazi was now driving toward Malaga in his private vehicle, which Mike had tagged with a locator device.

"He's slowing down," announced Mike into his hands-free cell phone as the screen on the dashboard monitored Ghazi's progress. "He's about six hundred meters behind you now."

Lisa was driving the lead surveillance vehicle, staying ahead of the accountant's car to scan the route for a possible ambush. Mike was driving a second vehicle, trailing the accountant to make sure he didn't try anything funny.

"He probably needs gas and a bathroom break," Lisa replied. "I passed a gas station about a minute ago."

"Copy that, Lisa. He's making a right into the gas station," Mike said. "I'm about five hundred meters behind."

"Okay, Mike. I'll pull over. Let me know when he's on the road again."

"Will do."

Mike pulled into the gas station himself and parked off to the side. Ghazi climbed out of his car and prepaid his gas with his credit card. Nothing seemed suspicious, and within a few minutes, they were back on the road progressing toward Malaga, which was located less than a hundred kilometers away.

Ghazi followed the exact same routine he had the previous week. He parked his vehicle in the visitors' lot of the bank. Next, he removed the two black duffel bags from his trunk and walked into the bank.

"He's in," said Jasmine Carson, stationed in the rental apartment on the other side of the street. On the table next to her was the video feed coming out of the hidden camera affixed to Ghazi's jacket.

—

In spite of the air conditioning, Ghazi couldn't stop sweating. He couldn't remember a time when he had been this nervous, and he wondered if he was going to see another sunrise.

After he entered the lobby of the bank, he walked to the customer service desk and asked for the manager. The clerk told him to have a seat. As Ghazi waited in one of the orange armchairs, he worried about all the things that could go wrong. He didn't see the man approach him from behind and jumped when he was squeezed on the shoulder.

The bank manager chuckled. "Nice to see you again, Mr. Ghazi."

Ghazi got to his feet and shook the manager's extended hand. His heart was beating faster than it ever had.

"Same here," replied Ghazi.

"Please, follow me to the vault," requested the manager.

As he'd done the previous time, the manager ordered Ghazi to place the duffel bags on the table in the middle of the vault. He opened one of the bags and counted out twenty thousand American dollars in hundred-dollar bills.

That was when Ghazi made his move.

Shaking, he carefully reached inside his pants pocket to retrieve the listening device that the Americans wanted him to plant in the vault. The miniature device was already activated and would start transmitting immediately. It was fixed with an adhesive substance that would allow it to stick to any nonliquid surface. Ghazi had practiced placing the device many times in Lisbon but nearly dropped it anyway. In any case, the bank manager was so concentrated on counting the money that he missed Ghazi's clumsiness as he affixed the microphone to the underside of the table.

However, it had taken more time than anticipated, so he didn't feel that he could safely place the sticky camera, too. The Americans would be upset, he knew, but they were the ones who had told him that not being caught trumped every other consideration.

The manager placed the money in a black pouch, then handed it to Ghazi and thanked him once again for a successful trip. Ghazi exited the bank and walked to his car, relieved that the worst was now behind him.

—

"What will we do with him now?" Lisa asked as Ghazi walked to his car.

"Nothing for now," answered Mike, who had joined Carson in the apartment across the street.

"*For now?*" Lisa repeated.

"I asked Support Five to bug his apartment and his car. We'll know if he goes anywhere. Either way, we can't attempt to do anything here. It's too risky," said Mike.

"And once he's back in Lisbon?" Lisa asked.

She wants to kill him!

Mike kept his voice even. "I know what you want to do, Lisa, but we might still need him if this doesn't work. And I'm sure our director would love to have a chat with him. But if Mapother decides we're through with him and he gives the order, he's all yours."

His wife nodded, satisfied. Carson didn't say anything but looked away.

The punishment was harsh, especially because Ghazi had collaborated with them. However, they all knew that very soon someone from the other side of the board would come to Ghazi asking questions—especially once their financing method was blown out of the water. The accountant had seen them, and they couldn't afford to have him give a complete description of them to his terrorist connections.

But Mike wasn't sure how to react to Lisa's wish. She had proven herself a capable operator, but wanting to actually kill someone to keep them quiet was something different. *I'll have to keep an eye on her.*

CHAPTER 66

IMSI Headquarters
Brooklyn, New York

Jonathan Sanchez, like the other analysts, was poring through all the intelligence Mike and Lisa had sent their way. The amount of information wasn't overwhelming but needed to be corroborated with prior intel received from different sources, including the flash drives Zima Bernbaum had provided. He hadn't seen Charles Mapother lately but knew he was occupied briefing his contacts within the federal government. With clear indications an attack was imminent, Jonathan presumed all the major police forces and intelligence agencies would be put on high alert.

Sending out warnings was good, but Sanchez was very much aware that wasn't enough. They needed specifics. Abdullah Ahmad Ghazi had mentioned Canada. Really? What was so important in Canada? It didn't make sense to attack Canada when a direct wave of attacks could push the US economy down the drain. Didn't the Sheik already create havoc when he tried to destroy the Irving Oil Refinery? If not for Mike and others who stopped it from happening, the destruction of the refinery would have caused severe economic problems for the eastern parts of Canada and the United States. It didn't make sense. Unless...

Oh, my God! Could it be that simple?

Sanchez's fingers were drumming his keyboard in anticipation. He needed to check a few things out before calling Charles Mapother. He pulled the report they'd obtained from CSIS and read it for the third time. It said the Canadian energy minister, prior to his assassination, had reason to believe that General Richard Claudel from the French gendarmerie had tried on numerous occasions to acquire specific information regarding the Irving Oil Refinery in New Brunswick. Next, Sanchez lifted his coffee cup and reached for the document underneath.

It contained the complete report on the material gained from Jackson Taylor's laptop. He found what he was looking for on page nine: oil pipeline schematics. Precise oil pipeline schematics.

He called Mapother.

"Charles," he said, "we always believed the Sheik was running multiple small- to medium-size operations. Am I right?"

"It seemed so," answered Mapother.

"We thought his actions were a little scattershot, wouldn't you agree?" continued Sanchez. "God knows, members of our team suffered and are still suffering greatly from the consequences of his attacks, but if I take the long view of his operations, I can't stop thinking there's something beneath the surface."

"What are you talking about, Jonathan? His attacks were all over the place. The Ottawa bombings, the—"

Sanchez interrupted him, frustrated. "I know, I know, but hear me out. What if some of these strikes were only to keep pressure on us?"

"What do you mean?"

"I think his first objective was to destroy the oil refinery in New Brunswick. He failed to do that. As saddened as I am about it," continued Sanchez, "I think the bombing at the train station was designed to send the investigator false signals. The Sheik wanted to thin the investigators by creating more than one terror scene."

"Like a painting hidden in another?"

"Yes, something like that," replied Sanchez, swallowing the rest of his cold coffee. "What I'm saying is that if we look at all the clues we have access to, I think I know what the Sheik's plan is."

"I'll be in your office in a minute."

CHAPTER 67

Edmonton, Alberta, Canada

They were all waiting anxiously for the e-mail that would initiate the final phase of their operation. Abdelkarim Kashmiri was seated at the kitchen table facing his laptop. He and his four men had been in Canada for ten days. They all knew it was their final mission and felt blessed the Sheik had selected them. The assignment was straightforward and had not required any further preparation beyond what they had already mapped out in Sierra Leone.

Before training for this mission, Kashmiri didn't even know Alberta existed. Bordered by the US state of Montana to the south and British Columbia to the west, Alberta was the richest province of Canada, thanks to its oil reserves. The province had the third-largest proven global crude reserves in the world after Saudi Arabia and Venezuela. More important, Alberta was helping the United States to wean itself from its dependency on Middle Eastern oil.

His men had all arrived in Canada on different flights. They had rented separate hotel rooms and never talked to each other until yesterday. They wanted to minimize the chance of being caught. But now that the final day had arrived, they had all converged at Kashmiri's apartment.

"Have you received it?" asked one of his men, who was watching television across the room.

"Not yet, brother. Soon. Why don't you get the others and prepare yourself?"

Kashmiri watched the man get up from the couch and talk to the other members of his cell. He was proud of his men. They weren't afraid to die; they only feared failure. So did he. He didn't doubt the Sheik would send Omar Al-Nashwan after them if they didn't complete their task. He preferred dying by serving jihad than at the murderous hands of Al-Nashwan.

An hour later, his men were clean-shaven and had completed their ablutions. They prayed together before reviewing their plan one last time.

"Remember, the Enbridge pipeline is responsible for supplying more than thirteen percent of the great Satan's daily oil imports. Our target is the Edmonton Terminal," explained Kashmiri, pointing his finger to the map he had spread on the dining table. "It's the starting point of the mainline system, the world's longest and most complex crude oil pipeline. It can export up to two and a half million barrels a day."

Kashmiri could tell by his men's faces that he was boring them. They had already learned all this and were anxious for him to get to the point. He spent the next hour challenging them on what they needed to accomplish. When he was all done, he asked if they had any final questions. There were none. They were ready.

—

"That makes sense, Jonathan," said Mapother thoughtfully. "Thank you."

Sanchez had showed him all the documents and had explained the reasoning behind his conclusion. First was the attempt on the oil refinery, then the assassination of the Canadian energy minister. Next came the information they had gained from the flash drives Zima Bernbaum had seized from General Claudel's residence. Supplemented with the pipeline schematics Mike had sent from Sierra Leone and the intelligence the Sheik's accountant had provided them, all the collected leads added up to one destination: the Enbridge Terminal in Edmonton. It was the only location with strategic importance vital to the US that could link all the pieces of evidence together.

"I'll call DNI Phillips with this and strongly suggest he contact the Canadian authorities right away," said Mapother. "I hope it's not too late."

"Should we bring back Mike and Lisa?" Sanchez asked, "Maybe they could help the Canadians figure out what's going on in their backyard."

Mapother had reached the door but turned to face Sanchez. "No. It wouldn't do us any good. Plus, the government has enough operatives to take care of the problem."

"As long as they didn't receive the green light to proceed."

"That's exactly why I want our two assets to remain in Spain. They're our last chance to catch the Sheik before it's too late."

CHAPTER 68

Spain

Following the successful transfer of the funds, Mike and Lisa spent the next couple of hours watching the entrance of the bank and listening to the conversations occurring in the vault. Only one person was needed to do this, so Mike instituted a three-hours-on, six-hours-off schedule that allowed each of them enough downtime to remain vigilant when it was someone's turn to monitor the situation.

Mike was about to wake Carson, who was sleeping in the bedroom before her turn at watch duty, when Lisa announced that a black Mercedes GL550 had just pulled up outside the main entrance of the bank.

"Three guys. One is still behind the wheel with the engine running. The windows are darkened; I can't see his face. The two others are entering the bank as we speak. They look the part, Mike," Lisa said.

Mike felt a familiar rush of adrenaline. Now, they'd see some excitement. "I'll go wake up Carson. Give me a second."

Less than a minute later, Carson and Mike entered the living room.

"Anything?" asked Carson.

"Not yet. Nobody has entered the vault," Lisa said. "But these guys look like mercenaries."

"Okay," said Mike. "Lisa, jump in one of our cars and make sure that you're in position to tail the Mercedes if it comes to that. Jasmine, take her place at the scope."

Lisa nodded and, after grabbing his equipment, kissed her husband and ran out of the apartment.

"I have something," exclaimed Carson a few minutes later. She put the conversation she was hearing in her earphones on speaker. "This is coming from the vault."

The voices sounded distant, but Mike could easily make out their words:

"Everything went well?"

"As far as I know, though the courier seemed more nervous than last time."

"You counted the money?"

"It's all there, minus our fees."

They heard a rustling of paper and the sound of a zipper.

"Very well. Now that we have these, we'll be on our way."

"Let me accompany you out."

The sound of a heavy door being slammed informed the IMSI agents that their targets were on the move.

"Honey, they just picked up the duffel bags," said Mike into his radio.

"Copy that."

Mike turned toward Jasmine. "Try to take a few shots of them, then join us in your car."

"No problem," replied Carson, who already had her camera ready and its telephoto lens directed out the window.

Mike exited the apartment and hurried down the staircase. He used the back entrance of the building. The rented gray sedans provided by Support Five were only a few feet away.

"I got a few good face shots," Mike heard Carson say through his earpiece. "I'm sending them to James Cooper and Support Five along with the license plate number of the Mercedes."

"Excellent," said Mike.

"They're on the move," Lisa announced.

With two cars at their disposal to trail the Mercedes SUV, Mike and Lisa didn't have much difficulty following it through the city of Malaga. By the time they reached the A-7, Carson had caught up to them.

"Still traveling at a hundred kilometers an hour on A-7 west," Lisa said.

"Copy that. I'm about fifteen cars behind you," Mike replied.

"My team just got back to me regarding the pictures I sent them," came Carson's voice. "Their names are Raphael Dupont and Louis Toutant. They both served in the French Foreign Legion for a while before disappearing in 2002 during a mission in Africa."

"And the Mercedes?"

"It's registered through a numbered company based in the Emirates. Support Five sent the info to headquarters for further research."

"They're taking the exit toward Torremolinos," came Mike's voice suddenly.

"Roger that."

"Damn it!" exclaimed Mike. "All my buffers continued on A-7, and I'm stuck between them. Jasmine, you'll need to take the lead. I'll be burned if I make the next turn with them."

"No problem," replied Carson as she pressed the gas pedal. "Lisa, stay on the highway in case they're doing a stop and go."

"Will do. I'll take the next exit if they're serious about Torremolinos."

"Same here," Mike said.

Confirmation that the Mercedes SUV wasn't going to return to the A-7 came rapidly. "We're taking N-340 west, boys," came Carson's voice.

"That makes no sense," Lisa said. "The driver could have taken the N-340 all the way from Malaga. It would have been a lot faster."

"It makes sense if they're conducting countersurveillance," replied Mike. "They must have at least one guy watching their rear."

"Right," said Carson. "I'll lay off, then. You guys rejoin them, but keep a fair distance. Lisa, what's your location?" she asked.

"I should be able to link with the N-340 east in a few minutes."

"Good. Let me know once you've reached it."

By the time Lisa informed them that she was traveling eastbound on the N-340, the Mercedes had made a left on Calle de Goya.

"That will be my last turn with them," announced Carson. "Lisa, you better hurry up."

"I'm two minutes out," she replied.

"Calle de Goya leads right into a traffic circle," Mike intervened, looking at his GPS. "There will be a Riu Hotel just before you reach the circle."

"What else?"

"There's a big marina, a shopping center, a few other hotels, and residential buildings in the area."

"Is this a destination or a detour?" wondered Carson over her hands-free device.

"If he's making a detour through this neighborhood, he'll either take Avenue del Puerto, Calle el Mar, or backtrack to Calle de Valazquez," Mike responded.

"I think they're heading toward the marina," came Carson's voice.

"Are you sure?" asked Mike.

"Positive," she replied after a moment. "They just parked the SUV in the marina parking lot."

"Okay, I'll be there shortly," informed Mike.

"You want me in there as well?" came Lisa's voice.

"No. Stay in reserve."

Carson lost sight of the Mercedes SUV for a few minutes while she parked her car on a side street and walked back toward the marina. The place was beautiful. Its architecture gave way to a stream of restaurants, shops, and small cafès. With palm trees on either side of the boardwalk, it was exactly what tourists loved about the Costa del Sol.

Carson found the Mercedes SUV in no time. Its three occupants were climbing out, and the rear hatch opened automatically to reveal the two black duffel bags. Carson entered a café patio and sat at a table where she had a great view of the marina.

"I'm at a café close to the marina entrance," she said into her concealed microphone.

"I see you, Jasmine," Mike replied. "I also have a visual on our three friends. Some kind of security guard is talking to them."

"He's probably screening who has access to the yachts," Lisa said.

Just at this moment, one of the men turned around, and Mike saw his face. His heart stopped a beat. *Bingo!* It was Mohammad Alavi.

"I have an ID for the third member of our group," he said.

"Say again," Lisa said.

"Mohammad Alavi is the third passenger of the Mercedes SUV. I repeat, it's Mohammad Alavi."

"I confirm," Carson replied, who was using her camera to zoom in on Alavi.

"They're through," Mike said after a moment. "They must have a boat somewhere in the marina."

"Or else they're visiting someone who has one," added Carson.

CHAPTER 69

Ottawa, Canada

Zima Bernbaum was beat. Following her flight back to Ottawa, she'd spent the entire day filing reports regarding the events in Portugal. Simon Corey, the director of CSIS, and the deputy director of operations, John Aschner, had conducted the verbal debriefing themselves.

Zima had told them exactly what happened in Lisbon but kept Mike and Lisa Walton out of her story. It wouldn't serve any purpose. She'd told her superiors she believed that Israeli assets had intervened. She was looking forward to going home, having a glass of red wine, and enjoying a long hot bath. *And I need a massage. Maybe I should call the laundry boy...*

Her phone rang, and her pleasant chain of thought was broken.

"Bernbaum."

"Zima, this is DDO Aschner."

What now? "Yes, sir?"

"Please come to the director's office immediately," said Aschner, hanging up without leaving her the time to reply.

She sighed. She would have loved a few hours of sleep. She was tired and emotionally exhausted. She wondered what the director wanted. She'd given them everything, and she'd hoped the info would be enough to start sending agents in the field poking their informants for more intelligence. She was slowly getting up out of her chair when her phone vibrated, indicating a new text message. She glanced at her phone display.

It's from Mike! The text was short but to the point.

We got a breakthrough. I believe all the intel has been sent to your boss. Good luck and stay safe. M.

She closed her phone and ran to the director's office, all signs of fatigue gone.

All their hard work was paying off.

CHAPTER 70

Benalmadena, Spain

"I'll try to find a favorable vantage point," Mike said, walking along the boardwalk parallel to Alavi and the two ex–French legionnaires. Luckily, the dock on which his targets were walking was one of the closer ones to land.

They finally stopped next to a large red-and white boat Mike recognized as an Azimut. He couldn't be sure what model it was, but he knew it was expensive—in the four- to six-million-dollar range. Not the type of toy two ex-soldiers could afford.

He sat on a park bench and took his binoculars out of his backpack. Playing the part of a boat enthusiast, Mike started examining the vessel through his binoculars.

"Support Five from Mike."

"Go ahead."

"Please check the registration number of an Azimut yacht through all available databases."

"Go ahead with the number."

Mike gave it to them.

"We'll get back to you as soon as we have something."

Mike wished the sun could stay up a little longer, but it was retreating below the horizon quickly. Another thirty minutes and it would be dark. He didn't want anyone to become suspicious of him, but at the same time, he wanted to verify how many people were on the boat. He informed the rest of his team of his intention to stay put until darkness fell, then he let his mind wander a bit as he watched the yacht and the docks. Mike couldn't help but remember when he was a young boy and his parents took him out on their sailboat. They had spent so many happy afternoons on the water. He felt a lump rise in his throat. *At least I have Lisa, and who knows, my dad might still be alive.*

Only about ten minutes of daylight were left when James Cooper from Support Five came on the air.

"Guys, we have something for you that you'll find quite interesting."

"Shoot," Mike said.

"We sent all we had on the Mercedes to headquarters and did the same thing for the Azimut."

"And?" inquired Lisa, who was still parked outside the neighborhood.

"There was absolutely nothing in the FBI or CIA databases, but Jonathan Sanchez came up with a little lead. It appears that the NSA intercepted a message sent via an e-mail address they had a lock on. An e-mail address they suspect belongs to someone who's part of the Sheik's network."

"What did the message say?" asked Mike.

"It didn't say anything. It only contained a bunch of numbers, but nobody was able to figure out what they meant."

"And you did?"

"Not me. It was Sanchez who put it together."

Thumbs up, my friend. "And?"

"The numbers in the message were actually the name of the company that owns the Mercedes SUV you followed from Malaga to Benalmadena."

The IMSI operatives remained silent as they assessed what that meant.

"There's more," continued Cooper. "We just received a message confirming the Azimut is owned by the same company."

Holy shit! Mike thought. *This was it! They'd found the Sheik. Jackson Taylor had said so before dying. The Sheik's mobile headquarters was a boat. I can't fucking believe this. The man responsible for my daughters' deaths is a mere two hundred meters away.* Anger and rage mixed together in a torrent. He jumped up from the bench. He wanted to simply run to the boat and gun down everyone inside, but Lisa said, "I know you, Mike. I can't see you right now, but I know what you're thinking. Don't. Let's do this *to-ge-ther.* We're a team, honey. You've told me so yourself not too long ago."

She's right. I'll probably get shot before I set foot on the yacht. And what if my father is there?

"Lisa," Mike said, "if this is indeed the Sheik's boat, there's a slim chance that my father could be there."

"It's a possibility, honey. We need to do this the right way, even if it's a long shot."

"I know," replied Mike. He considered possible options but then said, "Meet me with Jasmine at the café. We'll figure something out."

—

Mohammad Alavi checked his watch. *Not long now*, he thought. He let the two ex-legionnaires plot the course the yacht would take to reach Tangier. Since the events in Sierra Leone, Al-Nashwan and the Sheik had been very nice to him and had even offered him his own quarters, albeit the ones next to the kitchen, aboard the big yacht. Because of Al-Nashwan's severe injuries, the Sheik had been relying heavily on him, and Alavi had come to appreciate the responsibilities of serving Sheik Al-Assad.

Now that the final countdown had started and nothing could stop the destruction of the Edmonton oil pipeline terminal, they were moving to Tangier for the recruiting phase of the next operation. Alavi was looking forward to this; he'd had enough of living among the infidels in Spain. With ninety-nine percent of Morocco's population being of the Muslim faith, Alavi was sure he would feel right at home.

Walking toward Omar Al-Nashwan's cabin, Alavi felt ecstatic. He could hardly believe he'd reached the top of the pyramid. Never in a million years did he think he would become an important part of the Sheik's inner circle. *Allah is great!*

He knocked on Al-Nashwan's door and waited to be invited in. Al-Nashwan was seated at a small desk in front of a portable computer. He'd recuperated well from his injuries, but he would not be strong enough to go out for a few more days.

"Yes, Mohammad?" Because a sling and swath bandage had been used to immobilize his injured shoulder, Al-Nashwan had to turn his whole body to look at Alavi, who was standing in the door.

"Did he call?"

"There's time left, Mohammad. You know how the Sheik operates; everything will be done according to the time frame all the cells agreed upon. It's important to respect the timing that has been established."

"Of course."

Al-Nashwan smiled at his protégé. "Don't worry, Mohammad. Go back to your room. As you can see, I'm all hooked up and ready to send the go-ahead as soon as I receive his word to do so. I'll let you know once we're ready. I'll let you type the message if you wish."

Alavi beamed, pleased he was the one who would precipitate the fall of the Great Satan.

—

Mike's phone conversation with the IMSI director was brief. Mapother's instructions were clear. Whoever was on that boat needed to be taken down.

Because IMSI had no means of tracking the Azimut if it headed out to sea, Mike and Lisa were ordered to board the vessel to try and capture all the men aboard. If they couldn't be captured, Mapother had authorized deadly force. Once they had seized control of the vessel and its occupants, they were to bring the Azimut to Naval Station Rota, near the Strait of Gibraltar, where US officials would meet them and the captives would be questioned. The IMSI director also informed Mike he had passed along the info to the proper Canadian authority and that he was confident an operation was already under way. Mike knew that was true, as Zima had replied to him earlier in the day to let him know she was being deployed in an attempt to intercept the terrorist cells.

After leaving Carson at the café to keep an eye on the target, Mike and Lisa sat in one of their rented sedans to devise a plan. Their first challenge would be to approach the dock without raising suspicion. Mike, who earlier had seen a boat brokerage office on a nearby street, suggested that one of them should act as a broker. Support Five was given the task of fabricating proper documentation.

While Support Five was busy creating Lisa's profile, the two IMSI assets used the Azimut's corporate website to review the vessel's technical characteristics and layout. The eighty-six-foot yacht had a nineteen-foot beam. A fully equipped galley was located at the aft lower deck, where the crew's cabin and one of the heads were also located. Still on the lower deck but toward the bow were four luxurious cabins and the three remaining heads.

Looking at how the yacht was designed, Mike immediately identified a serious problem. They could not access the cabins from the kitchen. If they were to come in through the galley, the most logical point of entry, the IMSI operatives would have to climb up to the main deck and then take the other flight of stairs to clean the cabin area. If they encountered any type of resistance in the kitchen, they might very well lose the advantage of surprise—the only advantage they'd likely have.

With only two fully trained operatives and Jasmine Carson conducting the assault, their options were limited. They would have to act fast and aggressively to prevent a firefight in a place they weren't familiar with. But, Mike and Lisa agreed, the risk was worth the attempt—to avenge their family.

—

A knock on his cabin's door jolted Alavi from a surprisingly deep sleep. The first thing he did was look at his watch. Had he missed the count-down? How could he have fallen asleep at a time like this?

"You're ready, Mohammad? It's time," said Al-Nashwan, his head appearing in the cabin. "Follow me."

Thank you, Allah, for letting me serve you.

Alavi followed Al-Nashwan to his room and was startled when his mentor handed him a satellite phone.

"Yes?" said Alavi into the receiver.

"It's me, Mohammad. Omar told me you've earned the right to send the message, and I agree. It is time. See to it." And with that, the Sheik hung up.

Al-Nashwan was looking at him, smiling. "I've already logged in to our account. Our message will be received instantly by our brothers in Edmonton."

Alavi swallowed hard and sat behind the computer. He started typing.

CHAPTER 71

Edmonton, Alberta

The plane had landed at the Canadian Forces Base in Edmonton less than thirty minutes before. Zima and her team were already racing toward the address attached to the first bank account linked to the Sheik's network. During her meeting with the CSIS director and the DDO, she had learned CSIS had received reliable intelligence that three terrorist cells were about to attack Enbridge's oil terminal in Edmonton. The security at the terminal had been advised, but they were ill-equipped to face any real menace.

The Canadian prime minister had ordered three RCMP ERT teams usually attached to INSET to make themselves available to CSIS. Zima had been put in charge of one team, and they had flown together to Edmonton aboard a plane CSIS had chartered from Air Canada.

"How long before we reach the apartment?" asked Zima. She was seated between two huge ERT guys in the backseat of the lead Suburban.

"Less than ten minutes," the driver replied.

"As soon as we get within two kilometers of the apartment, I want all lights and sirens off."

"Understood."

Zima hoped to arrive before the cell was activated—otherwise things could get messy in a hurry.

"Do we still have eyes on the apartment?"

"We do," answered the man next to her. "I spoke with someone from Special O—the surveillance unit—and they told me there's no movement."

All right. We're still good, thought Zima. The objective was to hit the three cells at the same time, making sure none of them could warn the others when attacked.

"Damn it! Engage! Engage! They can't get away, and we're still two minutes out," said the ERT team leader into his radio.

"What's going on?" asked Zima.

The team leader, seated in the front passenger seat, made eye contact with her using the rearview mirror. "The surveillance unit at our address spotted five men exiting the apartment."

Shit! We were so close. "What about the other teams?"

"Nothing yet, but if you agree with me, I'll order them to move in now."

Zima didn't hesitate. "Do it."

"Team Two and Team Three, we've been compromised. I say again, we've been compromised. Move in when you're ready," said the team leader.

"Thirty seconds!" yelled the driver.

"Sir," said the trooper next to Zima. "Special O has two men down. They're engaging five tangos armed with automatic rifles."

The team leader rolled down his black ski mask and turned around to face his men. "Get ready. We're coming in hot. Check your muzzle when you exit the vehicle, and get out of the *X*."

Zima found her mouth was dry with apprehension. The memory of exchanged gunfire in that seaside French village came back to her with perfect clarity. She could feel all her senses become sharper. Even though the engine of the Suburban was revving high, she could hear the clatter of automatic weapons in the background.

Yet preparations were not enough. Without warning, bullets started piercing the windshield, and she saw the team leader's head snap backward as a round hit him in the face.

CHAPTER 72

Benalmadena, Spain

Lisa had just picked up her boat broker's credentials from a nearby garbage can, where a member of Support Five had dropped it. If anyone were to check, they would find that Suzy Newton had been a licensed boat broker for the last ten years.

"They started their engines!" announced Jasmine Carson, who had just finished memorizing the plan she had received from Mike via her PDA.

"Damn it!" exclaimed Mike. "All right, guys. Check your weapons, and let's proceed to our rendezvous point. We can only hope they'll wait for us a little longer."

They met in front of the marina's security gate. Mike and Carson, walking hand in hand as a couple, arrived first and were challenged by the security guard manning the entrance.

"Sorry about that, mate. I didn't know we needed an escort to enter the docks," explained Mike, smiling.

The security guard was neither impressed nor particularly at ease with the English language.

"Can we go see it?" continued Mike, undeterred. "We'll only be a few minutes."

"*Solo los corredores certificados pueden entrar sin escolta,*" replied the guard, pointing at his own identification badge to elucidate his point.

"Mr. and Mrs. Graham?" Lisa asked, walking rapidly toward them. "I'm Suzy Newton from the brokerage agency."

The three of them shook hands like it was the first time they'd met. Lisa showed her broker's credentials to the security guard and told him in Spanish, "They're with me. We have an appointment to view a boat."

"You're not from the area," the guard said.

"You're right. I'm new to Benalmadena." Lisa smiled, extending her hand to the guard.

The guard looked down at her hand without shaking it but had a change of heart when he saw that Lisa was palming a few euros. The guard shook hands vigorously and pocketed the cash.

"Next time," said the guard, "you'll have to call in advance, and the boat's owner will need to leave a message with your name, authorizing the visit."

"Understood. Can we go ahead, then?"

"Just after I check with your office," the guard replied. He called the number that was on Newton's business card. Unknown to him, his call was bounced around the world a few times before he was finally connected with someone at IMSI headquarters in New York. An analyst answered in Spanish and confirmed that Suzy Newton was a new member of the Marina Marbella Brokerage Group. After he hung up the phone, the guard gave Sanchez the access code for the gate before returning to his paperback novel.

Mike and Carson followed behind Lisa on the docks, walking as fast as they dared. The Azimut's big diesel engines had been running for over ten minutes, and Mike knew that was about the time they required to reach operating temperature. They passed boats of all sizes, but the farther they got from the security gate, the bigger the boats became.

As they neared the Azimut, all three covertly screwed on their suppressors and double checked that they each had at least two spare magazines. The IMSI operatives were dressed in black slacks and dark windbreakers that made them difficult to see in the darkness. With the rubber soles of their boots silencing their approach, they were able to get within twenty meters of the target yacht before they saw that a crew member, who had been in the process of rolling back the lines prior to departure, had spotted them. By the moonlight and from the profile headquarters had sent over, Mike identified the man as Raphael Dupont.

In a flash, Dupont stood up and reached inside his jacket pocket. Mike, whose weapon was already drawn, fired two muffled shots.

For Melissa.

Dupont fell backward and toppled into the black water with a soft splash. Mike immediately scanned the area for more targets but didn't see any.

Lisa, who had a better view of the depth of the main deck, gestured to Mike and Carson that it was clear. While Carson stayed back to make sure that Dupont wouldn't surprise them, Mike stepped onto the swim platform and climbed the four steps leading to the above-deck living space. Lisa followed.

On the other side of the glass, a man they recognized as Louis Toutant was in the well-lit cabin concentrating on charts he had laid in front of him. As Mike fixed his barrel on Toutant's head through the glass, Lisa quietly slid open the patio door and stepped inside.

"Can we leave?" Toutant asked in French, most likely thinking that it was Dupont reentering. "I'm about done plotting our course."

Toutant turned his head, and his eyes widened when he saw the two IMSI operatives with pistols pointing at him.

"Where's Raphael?" he asked. The look on his face told Mike that he already knew the answer.

"How many are inside the cabin?" Mike asked.

Toutant spat and told him crudely, "*Va chier.*"

He turned around and was able to press the horn button twice before Mike and Lisa each shot him numerous times in the back. "Go, go, go!" Mike shouted, knowing that the loud honking noise had just cost them their biggest advantage. "Jasmine, up here. Fast!"

As they had planned, Mike took the lead, heading to the first set of stairs and went down to the kitchen area. Lisa was right behind him.

CHAPTER 73

Edmonton, Canada

Abdelkarim Kashmiri was furious. They had been so careful. His mind couldn't grasp the reasons why Allah would permit such a thing to happen. Failure! He had received the message from the Sheik and was walking toward the rental minivan with his men when he heard the first gunshot. He turned toward the sound and realized three men were shooting at them with pistols. The sight of one of his men clutching his stomach pushed him over the edge. Who were these people? They didn't wear uniforms, and two of them had long hair. They couldn't be the police.

Kashmiri, like the rest of his men, had trained under Major Jackson Taylor back in Sierra Leone. Their protocols kicked in almost immediately, and his men reacted the way they'd been drilled. They kneeled down and returned a suppressing fire. Within seconds, they were the only ones shooting, for the men with the pistols had retreated behind their vehicles. Kashmiri wasn't sure if they'd hit anyone, and he was about to order his men to advance toward the vehicles when he heard the engines of the Suburbans.

"They're coming!" he yelled to his men. "Take cover and be ready." When he looked back to the street, he saw a pair of black Suburbans speeding toward them. Kashmiri leveled his assault rifle and aimed it directly at the front Suburban's windshield. When the truck was seventy meters away, he pressed the trigger.

—

"Josh is hit! Josh is hit!" yelled the driver, looking at his team leader in horror. Two seconds later, he pressed the brakes hard. "Go, go, go!"

Zima followed the last instruction left by the team leader and burst free of the X-zone—the impact/hot zone. At a double-time trot she ran behind Shane, the ERT member who'd been seated to her right, while looking for a target to engage. The sounds of gunfire came from everywhere, and her ears were already ringing. She didn't know what the bad guys looked like, but she figured anyone shooting at her was hostile.

When the man in front of her dropped to the ground, she instinctively did the same. "Contact left," said Shane, aiming his MP5 toward a white van parked across the street. Zima looked in the direction of the van but couldn't see anything.

"Where?" she asked.

Suddenly, a head popped out from the edge of the van, and Steve fired a single shot. Zima saw a man fall from behind the white van. "Right there."

—

Kashmiri knew he'd lost two of his brothers-in-arms. The police had too many men for him to even contemplate surviving the encounter. He didn't know how long he had left on this earth, but he was going to take with him as many enemies of his faith as he could.

To his right, Marwan was hidden behind the tire of the white van they were using to conceal themselves. "Marwan!" shouted Kashmiri over the ear-splitting sounds of the firefight. "I'll attach a charge underneath the van."

Marwan nodded. "I'll cover you."

Kashmiri reached for the explosive charge in his backpack. It was a real shame his team wasn't going to be able to accomplish their mission. *At least*, he thought, looking at the plastic C-4 he had in his hands, *Allah has given me a chance to redeem myself*. He inserted the detonator and set the charge to two minutes. This was how long he had left to live. When he turned to inform Marwan that the explosives were ready, he saw his companion's body sprawled on the ground next to the van. Kashmiri clenched his teeth and moved his finger on the trigger of his weapon.

—

Zima had her MP5 sight trained on the terrorist Shane had shot. She wasn't convinced he was dead until she saw the hole in his forehead.

No shots had been fired for the last fifteen seconds, and the ERT members were trying to figure out how many targets they had taken out. They weren't sure if any of the terrorists were still alive. *Caution* was the key word.

"I give up, I give up," she heard from behind the van. She immediately dropped to her belly, her weapon trained on the terrorist she could see kneeling down from under the van.

"One man, on his knees. Behind the white van on your left," she told Shane.

Once the ERT member positioned himself to cover the terrorist with his weapon, Zima got up and joined him. She picked up the terrorist's assault rifle and placed it out of range. "What do you want to do with him?" Shane asked.

"Arrest him for the murder of an RCMP officer. I'm sure other terror charges will follow suit," Zima replied, aiming her weapon at the man's head.

The ERT officer cuffed the man before advising the others that he had the fifth terrorist in custody. He then asked him to stand up, but he refused. "What's your name?" Shane asked. The man smiled and said in perfect English, "My name is Abdelkarim Kashmiri."

"Well, Abdelkarim, I'm in no mood to argue with you, so you better stand up."

"Or what?" asked the terrorist.

The arrogance of this coward frustrated Zima, and she could see Shane had to hold back from punching him in the face. Yet a question entered her mind. Why had this one given up when all the others died fighting? Wasn't he supposed to martyr himself? She decided it didn't matter. *You failed. We won.*

Shane looked at her. "We just got word through our communication system that all the teams have been successful. No additional losses for us."

"That's good news," said Zima.

"They also say we should look for plastic explosives. It seemed they were all carrying some."

She looked around and spotted a blue backpack a few feet in front of the van. She reached it and looked inside. The bag was empty, but the smell still lingered. *Where's the C-4?*

She walked back to the man and kicked him hard between his legs. A guttural sound came out of his mouth, and he collapsed on his side. She needed to show him who was in charge.

Zima pressed her right knee against his neck, squeezing it against the road.

"Where are the explosives? And don't even try to tell me you don't know what I'm talking about."

She could hear the terrorist babbling something and released some of the pressure.

"Guarantee me immunity, I'll tell you where the C-4 is."

What the hell? This guy is more stupid than I thought. What game is he playing? "The only thing I can guarantee you right now is there won't be immunity for you, not after what you've done," she said.

"It is your choice, not mine," replied Kashmiri through his clenched teeth. "You should call your supervisor. Maybe you have at least enough authority to do that?"

Zima couldn't understand why he was trying to negotiate with her. The explosives couldn't be far away, as they'd hit the terrorists just minutes ago. *What would I have done if I were in his shoes? Oh, my God!*

"Get him out of here now!" she yelled to Steve. "He already planted the C-4."

"What?"

"Get him out of here!" she shouted.

She tried to open the door of the van, but it was locked. She kneeled down and looked under the van. Her heart sank.

I'm dead.

—

Abdelkarim Kashmiri's balls were burning with pain, but he didn't care. The dumb Western bitch was wasting precious time trying to intimidate him. How clueless was she? *Did she really think I would tell her anything because she kicked me in the genitals? So typical! Ignorant to the point of believing I would betray Allah's trust just to evade physical pain. Only thirty seconds left. Oh Allah! To you I surrender. Allahu Akbar!*

All of a sudden, Kashmiri started panicking. What was she doing? Why had she released the pressure on his neck? He heard her yell at her partner to get clear. That the C-4 had already been planted. He saw the bitch try to open the van's door. He wished he had put the timer at ninety seconds instead of two minutes.

She's too late anyway. Any second now. Allahu Akbar.

Then all went black as Kashmiri felt himself fall forward.

—

When Zima saw that there were only six seconds left on the timer, she turned toward Shane and screamed, "Move! The van's gonna blow in six seconds!"

She saw him use the butt of his rifle to strike Kashmiri in the back of the head. He ran toward her with the speed and agility of a lion. He grabbed her from under her arms and lifted her up before she had the time to jump on her feet. She started running and felt the man's hands on her back pushing faster. They hadn't gone ten meters when he jumped on her, covering her with his own body.

The explosion knocked the breath out of her lungs and pierced both her eardrums. The heat wave that passed over them was like an inferno. Pieces of flying glass from the van's windows cut through her exposed skin.

Zima wasn't capable of breathing properly. Her head was getting lighter and her eyelids heavier. She wasn't sure if she'd passed out or how long she stayed beneath Shane, but one thing was certain: his weight was crushing her, and she didn't have the strength to crawl out from under him.

At some hazy point, she felt someone turn her on her back and shine a flashlight in her eyes. She sensed being lifted onto a stretcher and rolled down to a waiting ambulance. She used all her remaining strength to glance to her right, where a paramedic was pushing an identical stretcher. A white sheet stained with blood was pulled over the head of a man wearing an ERT uniform.

Zima's eyes filled with tears as she realized that Shane was dead. She began to sob quietly, not understanding why a man she didn't even know had sacrificed his life to save her.

CHAPTER 74

Benalmedina, Spain

Mohammad Alavi was daydreaming about the mayhem the Sheik's plan would create when he heard the Azimut's horn honk twice. Alavi could feel that the diesel engines were rumbling. That was probably why Louis had honked twice—they were ready to leave port. That made him smile. He'd had a good day today, and he couldn't wait to hear the first reports regarding the attacks in Alberta. He got up off the bed, wanting to watch the Spanish skyline recede into the dark distance.

When two Caucasian intruders burst into the cabin, Alavi was taken by utter surprise. He dove for the pistol under his pillow, but both men fired at him. Unimaginable pain shrieked through both his legs as he crashed to the floor.

—

Mike fired his weapon twice and knew he had hit Alavi at least once. However, the wounded man wasn't surrendering. He kept crawling toward his bed, trying to reach for something—most certainly a firearm hidden under a pillow.

"Don't!" Mike yelled, striding toward Alavi. But the terrorist must have sensed that he wanted to take him alive because he never hesitated. Looking directly into Mike's eyes, he put the muzzle of his pistol in his mouth and pulled the trigger before Mike and Lisa could do anything to stop him.

—

Alexander Shamrock was alone in Sheik Al-Assad's master cabin when he heard the shot fired by Alavi.

"I think we have a problem," he told the Sheik urgently over the secured phone line.

"Was that a gunshot, Omar?" the Sheik asked.

"Yes," replied Al-Nashwan, reaching for the Desert Eagle pistol in the bedside table drawer. He expertly checked the magazine and made sure that he had a round in the chamber.

"How many are they?"

"I don't know, Sheik. I have to go. If I don't call you back within a few minutes, you'll know that I have fallen."

"Erase the data. Use the flash drive, Alexander," ordered Sheik Al-Assad. He only used Al-Nashwan's birth name when things were desperate. All the information regarding their next series of attacks in the Gulf of Mexico was stored on the laptop across the room.

"It will be done," replied Al-Nashwan, squeezing the secure satellite phone between his cheek and left shoulder. "Anything else?"

"*Inshallah*. Take care of yourself, Omar," said the Sheik.

"I will. Thank you for everything," replied Al-Nashwan while frantically searching for the flash drive programmed to wipe the Sheik's computer clean.

His fingers had just wrapped around the device when his peripheral vision caught movement coming through the master cabin's door.

—

After Alavi's shot echoed through the boat, Mike gave his wife the order to storm the forward area of the lower deck and informed her that he'd be right behind with Carson.

Lisa rushed down the stairs and reached the lower deck a few seconds later. She had already memorized the layout of the boat. She took a quick look around to see if any doors were open. All the cabins and heads still needed to be secured. Seeing that all the doors were closed, she started with the closest one. She opened the door slowly, and, after a short peek inside, confirmed that nobody was occupying the small guest cabin.

Mike and Carson reached the forward lower deck just as Lisa had finished clearing the first cabin. He gestured that the other three cabins still had not been secured. Carson nodded and indicated that she was going to take the aft master cabin. Mike, knowing this was the largest one, positioned himself behind her to provide cover in a regular two-man entry fashion. It was a shame they didn't have any flash-bangs, but they had to work with what they had.

Carson checked to see if the cabin door was locked. It wasn't. She motioned to Mike and silently counted to three. Then she flung the door open and rushed inside.

The loud double crack of a firearm going off surprised Mike, but he didn't flinch. The body of Jasmine Carson fell amid spatters of blood, her neck ripped open by a .50 round. Mike's brain continued on autopilot, even as he felt the second round graze his right cheek.

He fired numerous times in the general direction of the threat while retreating a few steps. His ears, ringing from the discharge of Al-Nashwan's Desert Eagle, had kept him from hearing the terrorist's grunt as he was hit in the shoulder.

—

Al-Nashwan used his left hand to grapple for the pistol he had dropped after Mike's first round shattered his already injured right shoulder blade. He fired a few stray rounds at the retreating assaulter to cover his effort to reach the computer where all the Sheik's projects had been saved. The pain in his shoulder was unbearable, causing him to move woodenly. The throbbing in his head indicated that he was about to lose consciousness as well. He knew the effects of shock and wondered how much time he had left before his body refused to obey his brain.

Having only one hand available, he set his pistol next to the computer and struggled to insert the flash drive into the laptop's USB port. Finally, the device slid into the computer, and Al-Nashwan exhaled with relief.

He had mere seconds before the intruders surged forward again, so he grabbed his Desert Eagle and placed himself in the best defensive position he could assume. His eyes flickered for a moment on the satellite phone that he had dropped in the first few seconds of the engagement, and he wondered if the Sheik was still on the line.

The Sheik's master cabin had only one access door. Al-Nashwan was confident that, even if he was only able to fire from his weak hand, he would be able to take down at least one other assailant before being overrun.

—

What Al-Nashwan hadn't considered was that Mike had positioned himself in the adjacent cabin with his weapon pointed at the wall where he thought the terrorist might be standing. Mike's plan was to fire through the wall in an attempt to cover the retrieval of Carson. With Lisa confirming that the target was still on the port side of the cabin, Mike pulled the trigger.

—

The rounds coming through the flimsy wall under the flat-screen television took Al-Nashwan by complete surprise. He had no time to react before Mike's bullets found their mark, hitting him twice in the chest. Meanwhile, he saw a woman pull the other woman he had just killed by her feet into the hallway, dragging her out of further danger.

Al-Nashwan's body slammed into the wall behind him and slid with agonizing slowness to the floor. He realized that his lungs were incapable of expanding. It was the most terrifying sensation he had ever felt, like drowning out of water.

Was this how it would finally end? *Maybe for me,* he thought, *but not for the mission.* He smiled at what the Sheik had in store for their enemies. But the feeling was short-lived as his vision settled on the front of the laptop. He suddenly realized that the computer had a hole through the keyboard. Was the data being wiped clean? He had to make sure. He couldn't allow the Sheik's enemies to gain access to their plans. When he saw the familiar pop-up window appear on the laptop's screen asking if the administrator wanted to proceed with the operation, Al-Nashwan knew he had only to press *yes* to wipe all the data clean.

Determination took over, and for an instant, Al-Nashwan didn't feel the pain of his wounds anymore. All he was aware of was the burning fury raging inside him.

I need to do this.

Wincing, he tried to get up, but someone violently shoved him back against the wall. In frustration, he raised his head to find a man and a woman dressed in dark clothes standing over him, their weapons drawn. Hatred filled their faces.

"Alexander Shamrock?"

Al-Nashwan tried to focus on his interlocutor, who seemed vaguely familiar.

"You fucking traitor," the man said disgustedly.

Then it came back to him.

"Mike Powell," said Shamrock weakly. "Aren't you supposed to be dead?"

"I could say the same. We thought you died bravely. They put your name on a monument, for Chrissake!"

Shamrock started laughing uncontrollably, blood pouring out of his wounds at an accelerated rate. "What's so funny?"

"Your father," Shamrock said, coughing blood and trying to buy time as he crawled slowly toward the laptop, now only two feet away.

"Where is he? Where's my father?" asked Mike, his voice low and guttural.

"Fuck you, Powell. And fuck your father, too!" Shamrock replied between two coughs of blood and mucus, his fingers only inches from the laptop.

Just as he was reaching the key that would wipe the data off the hard drive, Mike hurled him to the floor face-first and zip tied his wrists together so tight the plastic cut through his flesh. Using the last bit of strength he had left, Shamrock forced himself to his back so he could see his former colleague.

"That's what you were going for, asshole?" Mike asked him, holding the laptop in his hands. He removed the flash drive and pocketed it. "No need to answer, Alexander. Our techies will be all over this."

—

"Jasmine's gone," Lisa announced in a hollow voice, reentering the cabin. She was holding Al-Nashwan's Desert Eagle in her hands.

"We need to get out of here ASAP," Mike said, concentrating on the task at hand. "The port authorities have probably sent for the cops already, and that could get messy for headquarters."

"What do we do with him?" Lisa asked, pointing to Al-Nashwan, who was now violently coughing up blood.

"Keep an eye on him," Mike said, then considered it. "And stay on the lower deck. No need to risk having someone see you."

"Okay. I'll call Support Five while you try to get us out of here," his wife replied, already punching the numbers into her secure smartphone.

—

Mike hurried up the stairs and took the helm.

Ray isn't here. And I don't have time to interrogate Shamrock about it. With any luck, we'll find clues on the yacht once we reach a safe harbor.

Mike noticed that the yacht was now rubbing up against the neighboring vessel on its port side. They must have boarded the boat at the last possible moment, he realized, because there were no more lines holding the yacht in place. Mike said a silent thank-you to whatever power had kept the current in their favor and had prevented them from drifting into danger.

Mike, who had driven large boats on Lake Ontario, was at ease behind the helm. He gently pushed the electronic throttles forward and heard the yacht's transmission engage. The Azimut glided out of her slip while fireworks illuminated the sky behind them, sending short and brilliant flashes of light. A few minutes later, after they had cleared the marina, Mike fed more diesel to the two engines. The Azimut accelerated rapidly until it reached its cruising speed of thirty-five knots. Looking at the two fuel gauges, Mike validated that the tanks were full. A quick calculation confirmed that it would take them approximately five to six hours to reach Naval Station Rota, which was located close to the Spanish city of Cadiz.

They were half an hour into their trip when Lisa came up and sat next to Mike in one of the two captain's chairs.

"Shamrock's dead," she said simply.

Mike sighed. He had expected this much.

"Did he say anything?"

"No. I don't think he had the strength to do anything except moan. He simply bled out and died."

"He knew about my father, Lisa," Mike said, frustrated for coming so close to learning the truth about the whereabouts of his dad.

"We'll find him," his wife replied. "Together," she added with a smile.

Mike kissed his wife. "Thank you for being here."

"Happy to be here."

After a moment, Mike asked, "Did you take care of Jasmine?"

"I cleaned her up the best I could and wrapped her with bed sheets. We'll bring her back with us," Lisa replied.

Mike nodded. "Did you talk to Mapother?"

"I did. He said it's a damn shame for Jasmine. Those were his exact words."

"Fuck! She wasn't trained for that, Lisa. She shouldn't have been here with us. Damn it! This death is on us. No, it's on me. I should have been the first one to enter the room."

"We did our best, Mike," Lisa said. "Jasmine knew the risks. We all did."

A few minutes later, Mike finally asked, "Anything else?"

"Support Five will take care of the things we left behind in Spain. They also said that there was no call made to the police about gunshots at the port, possibly because of the fireworks."

"Makes sense. We were lucky then," said Mike, slightly adjusting the throttles.

They spent the next hour riding in silence, lost in their thoughts. As the adrenaline of combat drained from their systems, they were left exhausted.

Lisa had nearly dozed off when the sound of her smartphone ringing made her jump. "Yes?"

"You'll be met in Rota by a guy named Jack," came Mapother's voice from IMSI headquarters.

"We're bringing Jasmine's body with us," Lisa warned him.

"Of course you are," replied Mapother. "An IMSI plane will be waiting for you upon your arrival. Don't talk to anyone other than Jack, and don't hang around too long."

"Copy that."

"Two more things."

"What are they?"

"*Primo*, try to get as much intelligence as you can aboard the vessel. Once you get into Rota, IMSI won't have access to the boat anymore, and all the intelligence will have to be shared with the Spaniards. I don't think they need to know that Alexander Shamrock, former US Special Forces officer, was in fact a master terrorist close to the Sheik."

"I understand."

"*Secondo*, the Canadians successfully neutralized the three terrorist cells that were planning to blow a pipeline terminal in Alberta. Zima led one of the team but was wounded during the raid. She'll be fine."

"She's a strong girl."

"And could become a great asset for us," added Mapother.

"She didn't think so when Mike asked her back in Portugal."

"We'll see. Maybe in a few months, who knows? See you in New York. And Lisa?"

"Yeah?"

"Good job. I'm very proud of what you and Mike have accomplished. Please pass along my message to him."

"Will do, sir."

"I was right about you two," Mapother said before signing off.

Lisa replaced her smartphone in her pocket and told Mike what Mapother had said. She then spent the remainder of their trip getting as much intel as she could from the boat. She placed the laptop and all the documents she uncovered in two backpacks she had found in one of the boat's closets before asking Mike to gear down. Once her husband brought the boat to a rocking halt, they grabbed Shamrock's corpse and dragged it up the stairs onto the main deck and the swim platform before throwing it overboard. With all the blood seeping from his wounds, they knew the sharks wouldn't take long to arrive. She then used the freshwater hose to clean the deck and the swim platform from Shamrock's blood.

As they approached the naval station, they saw that two patrol boats, one Spanish and one American, were waiting for them. The American boat summoned the Azimut by radio. Mike was asked to follow the Spanish boat into port, while the American one stayed behind them.

After receiving his final instructions on where to dock the Azimut, Mike effortlessly parked it alongside a cement pier. On the wharf, they saw a dozen US Marines waiting for them. Their leader was a man of medium height dressed in a dark business suit. It was easy to see that he wasn't happy to be there.

Mike cut the engines and grabbed the backpack Lisa handed him. Once they had disembarked, the dark-suited man walked over to them but didn't offer his hand.

"I'm Jack, and I don't want to know who you are. I work for Dick Phillips."

"The DNI," said Mike.

"That's right. Follow me, and don't ask questions." Jack abruptly started walking toward a waiting Suburban.

"Jack?" called Mike.

The man stopped dead in his tracks and turned. "What did I just tell you?" he asked impatiently.

"This is important," insisted Mike.

"What is it?"

Mike explained that a colleague of theirs was still on the boat and that there was no way they would leave her behind.

"Why isn't she here then?" asked Jack, his voice seething with irritation.

"She's dead," Lisa replied, struggling to keep her temper in check.

"I see," replied Jack. He then yelled, "Sergeant Izsek, come over here, will you?"

A black man wearing a US Marine uniform jogged up to them and nodded to Mike and Lisa.

"Sergeant," Jack began, "you and another man of your choice will accompany these two back to the yacht."

"Aye aye, sir!" snapped Izsek.

"You'll then respectfully carry the remains of their colleague to the Suburban."

Izsek nodded and gave a crisp salute.

Mike and Lisa looked at each other. This wasn't how their mission was supposed to end.

—

The ride from the dock to the airport was a short one. The two IMSI operatives insisted on transporting the remains of their friend from the Suburban to the plane themselves. IMSI's pilots, William Talbot, and Martin St. Onge, had prepared multiple buckets of ice to keep the body cool.

As Mike climbed aboard the plane, he took his seat and closed his eyes, thinking about his daughter Melissa. What would he do, he asked himself wearily, to see her one last time? But he already knew the answer: anything.

CHAPTER 75

Kobani, Syria

Since his attempt to escape, Ray Powell's rations had been cut in half. To make matters worse, his jailors had removed his bucket. He was now forced to urinate and crap on the floor of his cell. At the beginning, the stench had been unbearable. Now, he didn't even smell it anymore. His body was becoming weaker by the day. At least the beatings had stopped.

He had not seen "Ben" since their fight, and Powell wondered if maybe he had killed him.

I certainly hope so.

The pain in his broken jaw had only subsided a little. Looking at his skinny body, Powell knew he didn't have enough energy to try another evasion. *That was probably their intention when they decided to starve me.*

Unexpectedly, the ground under his feet started to shake. For the last week or so, Powell had noticed small vibrations within his cell similar to the ones an earthquake would produce. But never one of this magnitude. This was different. Powell closed his eyes and tried to concentrate on any movements or sounds coming in from the outside. Once again, the ground vibrated even stronger this time—and dust came down from the ceiling.

An explosion! Powell was sure of it. An explosion had caused this. But it couldn't be a rescue attempt. Not after all these years. Maybe he was in a war zone? That would make sense. Powell glued his ear to his cell's door, trying to listen for any reaction from his jailors. He had not been in position for ten seconds before another violent shockwave made him lose his balance.

Dammit! That was close.

"Hey!" Powell yelled, thumping on his cell door with his forearms. "Can you hear me? Hey!"

Two flash-bang explosions, one after the other, made him jump. The sound of automatic weapons firing followed a second later. *What's going on?* Powell frantically looked around him to see if he could find anything he could use to defend himself. But he knew better. There was nothing.

Just grout, piss, and shit.

He could hear men yelling orders in Arabic. They were approaching his cell, their boots betraying their advance. Powell relaxed his muscles and took a few deep breaths.

Here they come. He was half-surprised when he heard a key being inserted in the lock and a voice speaking to him in English. "Ambassador Powell?"

No point in lying. "Who's asking?"

"I'm Major-General Fuad Younis, commanding officer of the Fifteenth Special Forces Division of the Syrian Army. We're here to rescue you."

The Syrian Army? I'm in Syria? What am I supposed to say?

"Okay," Powell replied shaking his head. "Please come in?"

As soon as the door opened, two soldiers dressed in combat gear entered and cleared the room. Moments later, a tall gentleman also dressed in combat gear approached Powell. If the stench of the cell bothered him, he didn't show it. "I'm General Younis, Syrian Army, Mr. Ambassador," the man said, pumping Powell's hand. His thick accent made it difficult for Powell to understand. "Can you walk?"

"Yes, of course I can walk," replied Powell. "Where are we?"

The general looked at him, confused. "You're in Syria. You didn't know this?"

"No," Powell said. "What's today's date?"

The general told him.

Oh, my God! I've been in custody for more than two years...

"What are you planning to do with me, General?" Powell asked.

"We're here to send you home, Mr. Ambassador."

CHAPTER 76

Dubai, United Arab Emirates

Sheik Al-Assad was shaken. First, the frantic call he'd received in the morning from his associate in Syria informing him that the compound was under attack. *Under attack? Didn't I pay the damn Syrians enough to protect it? Traitors!* When his calls to General Younis weren't returned, the Sheik knew the turncoat had been squeezed into collaborating with his government. His guess was that Powell would be sent back to Canada to gain some political points for the Syrian regime. They needed all the help they could get to help them in their fight against ISIS.

Now he had just overheard the final minutes of his most trusted helper's life. He had been having a lavish dinner with his American friend when Al-Nashwan called to discuss the final details of the recruiting plan he and Alavi had put together. The Sheik had excused himself from the table to listen to what his lieutenant had to say. He was once again impressed by their performance and was looking forward to the next wave of attacks, planned to start within the next few months.

The strike against his most trusted team members was hard to accept. It was a severe blow, though not a fatal one. Most of his international network was still intact. Yet one question kept returning to his mind in the minutes following the call. What was he to do with his longtime friend Steve Shamrock?

After the firefight had ended, Sheik Al-Assad had remained on the line and heard one of the assaulters calling Al-Nashwan by his birth name. How was that possible? The Sheik had promptly come to the conclusion that the assaulters must be Americans. Delta? DEVGRU? CIA Special Activities? That would explain why someone had recognized Alexander. Maybe they had served together while he was part of Special Forces.

Mike Powell.

Those had been the last words on Alexander's lips. Could it be possible that the son of Ambassador Ray Powell was alive? The Sheik dismissed the idea. Mike Powell had died at the Ottawa airport. Many newspapers had published a piece about his death. No, that wasn't possible. The man was dead. He would look into that and see what he could dig up.

But for now, he had a tough decision to make. No matter what American agency had conducted the raid, the US intelligence apparatus would shortly learn that Alexander Shamrock had been involved in the Sheik's terrorist network. The investigation would surely lead to his father. And then, who knew?

That raised a real problem. If he decided to part ways with his friend, he could forget about the rest of the seventy million. Would he be able to find other sources to fund his jihad against the United States and its allies? The Chinese and Russians would be more than happy to do business with him—as long as he kept his attacks directed toward the Americans. Would Steve Shamrock understand? They had started this journey together, to get revenge for the loss of their family—their beloved Ghayda, his beloved father.

After painful deliberation, he made his decision and walked back into the dining room, where Shamrock was seated at a table set for two.

"You have that peaceful look, my friend. You received good news? Is it about our operation in Edmonton?" Shamrock asked. He picked up a mouthful of braised lamb. "I didn't think we would get a report so soon."

"It's not about that, Steve. I had to make a hard decision."

"And that calmed you? I guess I need to make more tough decisions myself," Shamrock said, chuckling.

"It always brings me peace when I know I'm doing the right thing," replied the Sheik.

The CEO of Donatek nodded in understanding. "And what would that be in this instance?" he asked.

"That we need to part ways, old friend," replied the Sheik.

His hand rose, and he shot his best friend at point-blank range in the head.

Shamrock toppled backward in his chair, and the contents of his brain splattered across the expensive painting behind him.

Two of the Sheik's bodyguards appeared at his side seconds later.

"Clean that up, and take care of his driver," ordered Sheik Al-Assad. "And burn their bodies," he added before briskly walking out of the dining room.

All of this unpleasantness had ruined his appetite.

CHAPTER 77

Miami, Florida

Mapother had given them a few days off following their lengthy debriefing. The loss of Jasmine Carson had taken its toll on all of them, but mostly on Mike, who kept replaying the events leading to her death. He couldn't shake the feeling that he had let her down somehow.

After Jasmine's funeral, Mike and Lisa had flown commercial to Miami. They hoped the warmer weather, coupled with a few Coronas, would allow them to relax with each other. Sitting on the balcony of their corner suite, Mike looked over at his wife. She had her eyes closed, enjoying the breeze coming from the Atlantic Ocean. *She's at peace*, he thought. *Even though we didn't get the Sheik, she's happy.* He reached for her hand, and she gently squeezed his.

He was so proud of her. She had played a critical part in stopping the Sheik from annihilating the flow of oil into the United States. She had pulled herself together when she needed to and had proven to Mapother she could be depended upon. Because of her and the rest of the team, IMSI had averted an immense catastrophe that would have stopped dead in its tracks the fragile economic recovery the world needed so much.

What's next? wondered Mike, his gaze lost over the horizon. Authorities in Dubai had found the remains of Steve Shamrock and his driver. Their official conclusion was that criminals had attacked them before burning their bodies. Mike thought otherwise and suspected the Sheik had put an end to his longtime relationship with his US ally. The Sheik had disappeared for the time being, but Mapother had promised Mike that IMSI wouldn't rest until they had him in custody. The vital intelligence they had collected on the Sheik's yacht had allowed IMSI to gather enough of the puzzle's pieces to determine the locations of the next attacks and to recover close to sixty-five of the seventy million dollars stolen from the CIA. But no clues were found regarding his father's location.

IMSI had sent a detailed report to DNI Phillips that included a full analysis of the Sheik's network and options on how to stop him. Phillips had then disseminated the information to the proper agencies for follow-up action. Mike was confident he and Lisa would be called upon to go hunting for the Sheik in the near future. But for now, he would enjoy the sun and his wife's company.

He hadn't closed his eyes for more than a minute when five sharp knocks had him on his feet. Lisa looked at him, wondering who it could be. Mike approached the door with one hand on the butt of the pistol tucked inside his jeans. Looking through the peephole, he relaxed immediately.

"Hey, brother," said Sanchez as he entered the suite. They shook hands heartily. "Great room."

"Thanks, man."

"Nice to see you, Jonathan," said Lisa, stepping into the room from the glass door leading to the balcony.

Sanchez came forward and gave her a hug. "Nice to see you too, Lisa."

"You want a beer?" asked Mike.

"That's why I'm here, bro."

Mike opened the fridge door and grabbed three ice-cold Coronas before cutting three lime wedges. He then walked to the balcony, where Lisa and Sanchez were enjoying the view.

"So, what brings you here?" asked Mike once they each had a beer in hand. "Except for the beer, of course."

"Zima Bernbaum."

"How is she?" asked Lisa.

"Her eardrums should heal by themselves within a couple of months. Thanks to the ERT guy who covered her with his body, the rest of her injuries were superficial."

"Yeah," said Mike, remembering his time with ERT. "I knew Shane. He was one hell of an operator."

"So was Jasmine," Sanchez said, his voice breaking.

Shit! Did he fall under her spell? I'm so sorry, brother.

"To Shane and Jasmine then," said Mike, raising his Corona.

"To Shane and Jasmine," replied Sanchez and Lisa together before drinking a long pull of their beers.

Out at sea, boats of all sizes were cruising the calm ocean waters while children played in the heated pool just below them, their parents keeping an eye on them from the lounge chairs a few feet away. Close to the beach, swimmers were taking advantage of the serene surf to snorkel near tiny underwater reefs.

They were well into their third Corona when Sanchez said, "I think Zima will be joining us in New York."

"I thought she refused Mike's offer," said Lisa. "What changed her mind?"

"I don't know what changed her mind, Lisa," replied Sanchez. "All I know is that she sent me a text message three days ago wondering if our offer was still valid."

"What did you say?" asked Mike, finishing the last of his beer.

"I didn't reply yet. And I'm wondering who gave her my cell number," Sanchez replied. "Is she pretty?"

Mike and Lisa looked at each other and laughed. "You could say that, my friend," Mike replied once he had stopped laughing. "What did you say to her?"

"I wanted to talk to you about it before I even approached Mapother with this."

Mike and Sanchez followed Lisa to the kitchen, where she proceeded to open a bottle of Sauvignon Blanc. She poured three glasses and said, "I know Charles thinks she would be a formidable asset. He told me so."

"I agree she would be a great asset, but I'm worried about her commitment," said Mike.

"How can you say that after all she's been through?" asked Sanchez.

Mike swirled his wine and sniffed its aroma before answering. "Zima is a good agent, but I fear she might not be ready for what's coming next. I have a feeling that within a month or two, we'll be going hard after the Sheik, leaving a trail of bodies behind us. I doubt that's her cup of tea."

"You think she isn't strong enough mentally?" challenged Lisa. "Charles will put her through the same training we had. That should settle it if she passes."

"I agree," said Sanchez in support of his friend's wife. "That *would* settle it."

"You guys are really pushing for her," Mike observed.

"You said it yourself, Mike," said Sanchez. "The next few months will be busy, and we'll need good people who can be trusted."

Mike thought about it and wondered what had triggered the change in Zima's mind since he'd last seen her. What happened that was so decisive that she wanted to join an organization she knew so little about?

Another way to look at it was to ask himself: What had changed *his* mind? Why did *he* become a hunter? The answers were simple. *Melissa. Chloe. His parents. His in-laws.*

So, why did he care about Zima's reasons? They were hers and hers only.

"All right," Mike said, reaching in his pocket to retrieve his vibrating cell phone. "Let's bring her in."

Lisa and Sanchez smiled and toasted each other.

Looking at the display, Mike saw the call was from Mapother. "Don't tell me you already have a lead on the Sheik, Charles?" Mike asked.

"No, no lead on the Sheik, yet," came Mapother's reply. "But we do have one on your father."

Notes

[1] During an intense scene in which ambassador Ray Powell's armored SUV is ambushed, Eric, the ambassador's driver, tried to get out of the hot zone by performing a high-speed J-turn.

The J-turn is one of the techniques we employ to get out of a sticky situation when we feel the threat is in front of us. This technique allows us to disengage rapidly from a possible dangerous situation.

If there's a security vehicle (S2) attached to the armored vehicle, it is the duty of the bodyguard seated in the passenger seat of the armored vehicle to announce the potential danger via radio. Once the information has been transmitted, S2 will accelerate and position itself in front of the armored vehicle to engage the threat while the armored vehicle will perform a J-Turn (or any other techniques the situation dictates). Once the armored vehicle transporting the VIP is out of danger, S2 will disengage and retake its position behind the VIP's vehicle.

[2] What is the Canadian Security Intelligence Service? Is it like the CIA? Or the British MI-6? Yes and no. Let me explain.

An Act of Parliament created CSIS in 1984 after allegations that the Royal Canadian Mounted Police Security Service (RCMP SS) had been involved in illegal activities. Since then, CSIS is Canada's primary intelligence service. It is responsible for collecting and analyzing intelligence on threats to Canada's national security. To do this, CSIS conducts covert and overt operations in Canada and abroad.

Before September 11, 2001, CSIS's main mandate was to combat foreign intelligence agencies engaged in espionage operations within Canada. It was forbidden to directly seek overseas intelligence about Canadians or other threats. Following the 9/11 tragedies, CSIS's role evolved into investigating more of the threats posed by terrorism activities when it was given a legislated loophole:

> CSIS Act Section 12 allows agents to travel anywhere in order to collect intelligence pertaining to individuals or organizations suspected of engaging in activities that may threaten the security of Canada (espionage, sabotage, terrorism, and clandestine activities by foreign governments).

However, contrary to the American CIA and British MI-6, CSIS's mandate is to collect only "security intelligence." The distinction between "security intelligence" and "foreign intelligence" is clear. "Security intelligence" usually pertains to domestic threats, like espionage or terrorism, while "foreign intelligence" relates to the acquisition of political and economical information from a foreign state and military analysis of foreign powers.

A debate is actually raging in Ottawa. Following the attack on Parliament Hill in October 2014, many politicians are now demanding that CSIS's mandate be expanded to include the collection of foreign intelligence. Presently, Canada is the only G7 country without a dedicated foreign intelligence service. While some agree that expanding CSIS might be a good idea, some experts are totally against it. Such experts think that these two types of intelligence gathering require very different skill sets and oversight. That is why Great Britain has MI-5 (domestic) and MI-6 (foreign). The United States has the FBI and the CIA, while France, as I mentioned in *The Thin Black Line*, has the DCRI (domestic) and DGSE (foreign).

[3] In this chapter, I talk about how Major Jackson Taylor and the Sheik financed their activities. It is a well-known fact within the law enforcement and counterterrorism communities that terrorist organizations are using the trade of conflict diamonds (also known as blood diamonds) to finance their actions. For your information, conflict diamonds are diamonds used to fuel or finance violent conflicts. In *The Thin Black Line*, I chose Sierra Leone as the home of Major Jackson Taylor. I picked it because Sierra Leone is one of the countries that has been the most affected by the trade of blood diamonds because its diamond fields were controlled by the Revolutionary United Front. In the book, Major Jackson Taylor is part of the RUF. When I described the RUF as merciless, I didn't exaggerate. The RUF was responsible for many atrocities, including cutting off the arms and legs of civilians (including children) and the abduction of thousands of children who were then forced to fight for them.

In 1998, following the al-Qa'aida attacks on the US embassies in Kenya and Tanzania, the Clinton administration froze over 200 million dollars in assets belonging to the Taliban. Unaware that the United States had the legal authority to seize this money, the Taliban and al-Qa'aida were caught by surprise. After this debacle, al-Qa'aida leadership began a systematic withdrawal of their funds from the formal banking sector. They decided to put their money into something that wasn't as vulnerable or as traceable: diamonds. Unfortunately, the logistical infrastructure needed to acquire blood diamonds wasn't difficult to build or to maintain since they were available in countries (like Sierra Leone) that exercised little or no control over their territory.

Growing international pressure from NGOs played a crucial role in forcing the diamond industry to take action and to remove conflict diamonds from international trade. In 2003, the Kimberley Process Certification Scheme (KPCS) was established. Its goal was to ensure that conflict diamonds wouldn't make it to the international market. But even with this scheme, terrorist organizations had been able to finance themselves through the trade of conflict diamonds. In 2011, Global Witness, a London-based NGO and key member of the KPCS, abandoned the scheme, claiming it had failed to provide the assurance that conflict diamonds weren't entering the market.

[4] In chapter 21, CSIS agent Zima Bernbaum is tasked with an important mission. She must find evidence linking General Claudel to the Sheik's terror network. To do so, she'll need to gain access to his residence and search it while the general is away.

In real life, is an agent allowed to initiate this kind of operation on his or her own? Absolutely not. The decision to either open a clandestine investigation or not is the responsibility of the Target Approval and Review Committee (TARC). The Director of CSIS and senior CSIS officers as well as representatives from the Department of Justice chair the committee. The Solicitor General of Canada must also be consulted before a TARC certificate is issued.

There are three levels of investigation:

Level 1 allows agents to conduct a short-term investigation. It includes collecting information from open sources and communicating with foreign police or intelligence agencies in order to obtain additional information on a subject.

Level 2 is where agents receive the green light to conduct physical surveillance of the subject.

Level 3 means that agents are allowed to use intrusive measures to obtain the intelligence needed. In *The Thin Black Line*, Zima is given the equivalent of a level 3 authorization.

Every year, there is an annual audit of all CSIS investigative activities to make sure that it had reasonable grounds to suspect a threat to the security of Canada and that the level of intrusiveness of the investigation was appropriate.

[5] In chapter 26, my two main protagonists take on Abbud Rasshid, a suicide bomber. In my opinion, these men and women who are ready to sacrifice themselves for their cause are the most difficult terrorists to stop. It is so because the terrorist knows that his success depends on his willingness to die. Even if the terrorist is stopped before he reaches his intended target, he can still activate his bomb and injure or kill the first responders brave enough to take action.

When I was working with my organization's counterterrorism unit, I received extensive training on how to engage a suicide bomber. Fortunately, I never had to use this training in real life, but I've gone through dozens of training scenarios. A good friend of mine with whom I've worked counterterrorism for years is now an instructor. I asked him if they were still teaching how to handle suicide bombers during the initial phase of training. "Of course," he said. "We always will."

I consider suicide bombers to be precision weapons, as they are difficult to detect. I think terrorist organizations like using suicide bombers because of the simplicity of such an attack. There is no need for extraction or escape and nobody will be left standing to be interrogated. In *The Thin Black Line*, Abbud Raashid is using a pressure-release-type detonation device that he's holding in his hand. That means that the explosive payload will detonate as soon as the pressure is released and will explode even if the terrorist is killed. There are only two ways to defeat this scary situation, and both involve the use of deadly force. There's simply no way around it.

The first way is to be used only if the suicide bomber is far away from civilians. It also requires the intervening operator to be armed, as the technique is to shoot the bomber from a protected position from as far away as possible.

The second way is to do exactly as Lisa did in the book. However, this method is much more effective if there are two operators working together. The first operator's only focus should be to secure the trigger mechanism while the second operator is responsible for killing the terrorist. Once the terrorist is dead, the operator who secured the trigger will remain in position until the arrival of a bomb technician. Usually, the second operator will tape his colleague's hands together with the dead terrorist's hands to make sure there is no movement.

In conclusion, dealing with a suicide bomber is one of the toughest situations an operator can face. In mere seconds he must not only identify the threat and assess the situation, he must also act decisively. There will be no time to wait for orders or to exhibit self-doubt. As I am writing this, I have shivers just thinking about the intense scenarios I had to go through during training. I can only imagine the terror and stress a real situation would entail.

[6] In chapter 48, Omar Al-Nashwan tries to engage three different targets simultaneously. To do this, he's using a Chinese-made QSZ-92. Within seconds, two targets are down. The first one fell with two bullets in the chest while the second one got his heart pierced by Al-Nashwan's third round. When Al-Nashwan pulled the trigger for a fourth time, he heard what we call "the click of death."

Someone wiser than me once said, "There are two things you don't want to hear from a pistol. The first is a click when it was supposed to be a bang, and the second is a bang when you thought it would go *click*." During my career as an infantry officer and then as a federal agent, I fired thousands and thousands of live rounds, and I can count on two hands the number of times that happened. Luckily for me, it never went *bang* when I thought it would go *click*...

There are different categories of malfunctions, but this particular one is called a "failure to fire." This occurs when the trigger is pressed and the hammer is released. The firing pin then hits the cartridge but does not fire. That usually, but not always, means that the round was a dud or that the cartridge was not properly transferred from the magazine to the chamber. The best way to clear this malfunction is called the Tap-Rack-Fire drill.

Tap: With your support hand, give a good slam to the bottom of the magazine. It will ensure it is seated properly.

Rack: This means to cycle the slide of the pistol rearward. It will clear the misfired round and will chamber the next one.

Fire: This is when you'll press the trigger again to reengage your target.

This drill is something all police officers practice repeatedly, especially the ones who are part of a specialized unit. The Tap-Rack-Fire drill needs to become second nature. Of course, this drill doesn't clear all malfunctions, but it did work for Al-Nashwan.

[7] Mike, Lisa, and Jasmine Carson are conducting physical surveillance on the Sheik's moneyman, Abdullah Ahmad Ghazi. To write this chapter, I used my experience as a countersurveillance specialist. *Specialist* is a strong word and in this instance didn't mean I was the best or the more experienced officer either. Surveillance is an art that demands a special set

of skills that takes years to acquire and refine. I was a "specialist" because from 2012 to 2014, it was my assignment and I was doing surveillance and countersurveillance fifty hours a week.

When my agency reviewed my manuscript prior to publication, I had to remove a portion that they felt disclosed too much of our surveillance techniques. So I won't be able to go into too much detail, but I'll share a little more here than I did in the novel itself.

Effective surveillance requires teamwork. And, to be efficient, a team needs lots of training. In my former unit, twenty hours per month were spent on training. In *The Thin Black Line*, Mike, Lisa, and Jasmine Carson are conducting two different categories of surveillance. When they are either on foot or in their vehicles, it is called *mobile surveillance*. They also conduct *static surveillance* in chapter 66 when they use an apartment to get the "eye" on the bank Ghazi used to deposit the cash the Sheik requested.

As you all know, surveillance is the act of watching a person, usually one under suspicion, or a place suspected of being connected with a criminal/ terrorist organization. There are many reasons to conduct surveillance; intelligence gathering, evidence gathering, and identification of suspects are only a few of them. In law enforcement, there are two distinct attitudes toward physical surveillance. The first one is that everyone can do it and that it's an easy job. The other is that surveillance work demands the capabilities of officers who have been specially trained for that purpose. By experience, I can tell you it's not easy. Anyone who'll tell you otherwise wasn't doing his or her job properly.

To accomplish its goal, a surveillance operation must be done by professionals who understand that "watching" a subject simply won't do. Surveillance officers need to "observe" in order to be successful. The officer must be totally aware of what is going on around him or her at all times. In the book, Mike Walton identified a brush pass between Ghazi and another man. In real life, this type of exchange is easy to miss even for an experienced officer. The level of concentration needed to recognize what is happening is great. Experienced criminals/terrorists are fully cognizant of law enforcement tactics. That is why they will do everything to shake the surveillance team off their backs. They'll alternate between driving or walking slow and fast, they'll often stop to take in their surroundings, and they'll purposefully drive in circles or into dead end streets. The successful criminals/terrorists are the ones who are resourceful and skillful when it comes to eluding surveillance. This is why the person conducting surveillance must be alert and have a clear understanding of what is happening at all times.

Acknowledgments

It takes many hands to launch a publication. I'm very fortunate to have some of the best people in the business helping me out. Lou Aronica, my editor extraordinaire at The Story Plant, offered timeless advice that made the book so much better. His insights into the publishing industry kept me focused on what I needed to do to write the best book I could. I also thank Aaron Brown and the rest of the team at The Story Plant for all of their hard work on my behalf. Another thank-you goes to my friend and literary agent Eric Myers of The Spieler Agency. If all the literary agents were like you, the world would be a better place.

I am thankful for all the assistance I've received from the International Thriller Writers (ITW) organization. Special thanks to my friends: Kimberley Howe, David Morrell, Steve and Liz Berry, Jon Land, Steven James, James R. Hannibal, Barry Lancet, Lee Child, and many others behind the scenes. I'm also grateful to John Paine, Elizabeth Bond, my friend and photographer Esther Campeau, and my parents Céline and Raymond who were brutally honest with me when they read the first draft a few years back.

I want to save the best thank-you for last. I'm indebted to my wonderful and beautiful wife, Lisane, who believed in me before anyone else did. There would be no book if it wasn't for her continuous support and encouragement. And truth be told, *The Thin Black Line* wouldn't be half as good if it weren't for her honest feedback throughout its creation. Thank you for standing by me. You're my inspiration. I love you.

Un gros merci à Florence et Gabriel. Vos sourires me réchauffent le cœur. Papa vous aime.

About the Author

Simon Gervais is a former federal agent who was tasked with guarding foreign heads of state visiting Canada. Among many others, he served on the protection details of Queen Elizabeth II, US President Barack Obama, and Chinese President Hu Jianto. He has also protected the families of three different Canadian prime ministers. Prior to this, Simon spent five years in an anti-terrorism unit and was deployed in many European and Middle Eastern countries. He now writes full-time and is a member of the International Thriller Writers organization. He lives in Ottawa with his wife and two children. Find Simon online at SimonGervaisBooks.com, facebook.com/simongervaisbooks, and Twitter.com/GervaisBooks.

CPSIA information can be obtained at www.ICGtesting.com
Printed in the USA
LVOW10s1047130515

438331LV00002B/10/P